THE DEVIL'S BARGAIN

KIRA SINCLAIR

AFTER HOURS REDEMPTION

KIANNA ALEXANDER

MILLS & BOON

First Published in Great Britain 2020
by Mills & Boon, an imprint of HarperCollinsPublishers,
1 London Bridge Street, London, SE1 9GF

The Devil's Bargain © 2020 Kira Bazzel
After Hours Redemption © 2020 Eboni Manning

ISBN: 978-0-263-28006-7

1020

MIX
Paper from
responsible sources
FSC™ C007454

This book is produced from independently certified FSC™ paper to ensure responsible forest management.

For more information visit: www.harpercollins.co.uk/green

Printed and bound in Spain
by CPI, Barcelona

THE DEVIL'S BARGAIN

KIRA SINCLAIR

Family is everything.
Over the years, my daughters have given me
constant encouragement, purpose, unconditional
love and support. Angel and Sunshine, this one
is for you. I love you both! (And I'll ignore the fact
that the dirty dishes are still in the sink.) ♥

One

Three years. That's how long she'd successfully avoided Finn DeLuca. Apparently, the reprieve was over.

Genevieve Reilly stared at her attorney…waiting for him to laugh. Or tell her April fool. Or pinch her so she'd finally wake up.

"At least the judge recognized the validity of our argument against letting him take Noah overnight."

Oh, because that was the silver lining in this nightmare.

"How? How could this happen? You promised me he'd never be granted visitation. He's a convicted felon, for God's sake."

"No." Lance reached across the conference table and placed a soothing hand on her arm. "I told you it wasn't likely. But it appears Mr. DeLuca has not only influence of his own, but also friends in high places. Anderson Stone spoke on his behalf as a character witness."

"Another convicted felon."

"With billions of dollars and a media campaign touting him as a hero who saved the love of his life from a rapist."

"Whoop-dee-do. That has nothing to do with Finn. Finn isn't a hero. In fact, I'm pretty sure he's the devil's son."

Genevieve rubbed at the ache lodged right between her eyes. She'd regret the day she ever met Finn DeLuca... except that would mean she'd have to regret her son. And nothing could ever make that happen. Noah was the best thing in her life.

Having Noah had given her the strength to walk away from a life that was slowly poisoning her. Yes, the decision meant she and Noah had to fight for everything they had... but the fight was worth it. She'd do without if it meant raising her son in an environment that was healthy and happy.

Lance shrugged his shoulders. "Devil or not, he's Noah's father. And let's be honest, he has enough money that he could have fought us as long as he wanted."

That had sorta been her hope...and also what had kept her up at night. As long as they were in a court battle, then she didn't have to face him. But she didn't have access to unlimited bank accounts anymore so paying for all those legal bills would have been difficult. She'd have managed. Somehow.

They could appeal the judge's decision, but in the meantime Finn would get visitation. Which meant she'd have to see him. A reality she'd been both dreading...and dreaming about.

Waking up with her sex throbbing from memories of Finn was something she tried not to think about. She didn't really want him. Couldn't, wouldn't let herself.

Nope, she refused to admit that any part of her wanted to see Finn DeLuca again.

Her last memory of him had been less than happy. Blue-and-red lights reflecting off the forecourt of her grandfather's estate. The cool, remote expression on Finn's face as an officer placed a hand to the top of his head and guided him into the back seat of the cruiser.

She'd refused to attend his trial. There'd been no point. And, thank God, the prosecutor hadn't needed her to testify. Not when Finn had been caught red-handed with a fifteen-million-dollar diamond stuffed in his pocket.

Her diamond. Or, rather, her family's. Nearly losing the Star of Reilly to the charismatic, smooth-talking devil had almost gotten her disowned…a fate Genevieve had spent her entire life bending over backward to avoid. It was the threat her grandfather had used to keep her in line from the time she was very young.

After losing her parents at an early age, her grandfather had been the only family she'd ever known. He might have been the monster in her closet, but he was all she had. So she'd grown up desperate to please him. Desperate not to lose him, too.

Who knew a few months after Finn's arrest she'd be the one walking away? Life was funny…and not for the faint of heart.

And the thought of seeing Finn again had Genevieve's stomach flipping uncomfortably close to her throat. He was handsome, charismatic, dynamic and dangerous. He was temptation personified, and despite everything, Genevieve didn't exactly trust herself to hate him. Even if she should.

"Mr. DeLuca's attorney has requested you provide your preferred location for the visit. He expressed his client's desire for you to be comfortable."

Well, wasn't that just dandy? And not a thing like the Finn she knew. The man she remembered had been selfish and self-centered. Generous to a fault with those around him, but only because being charming was innate, not because he gave a damn about anyone else. Even now, she'd bet everything she owned that his generosity had nothing to do with Genevieve's comfort.

Finn DeLuca wanted something—something more than access to her son. She just hadn't figured out what. Yet.

At least she could guarantee he no longer wanted to use her for her access to the Reilly estate. He had to be aware of her change in circumstances. In fact, the tiny shreds of the check he'd sent, which were sitting on top of her dresser, were proof that he knew her grandfather didn't support her anymore.

Like Finn could buy his way back into her life. Or Noah's life. She didn't need his money and wouldn't have taken it even if she had. Noah might not have boarding school in his future, but she could afford to provide for her son without Finn's tainted offering.

"Genevieve?"

Hell, this was really happening. She'd spent the last couple months hoping this day wouldn't come. She'd refused to allow herself to contemplate the possibility that it might. So, she wasn't prepared.

"Tell him to come by my place Saturday morning. Ten o'clock. We'll figure out what to do from there. But he isn't taking my son anywhere without me. Not until I know for certain he's capable of caring for him and keeping him safe."

"I'm fairly certain Mr. DeLuca will agree to whatever you want."

That was a lie. Because if it were true, Finn would have respected her wishes and disappeared from her life for good.

Finn DeLuca stared at the file spread across the desk in front of him. His feet were kicked up onto the hard surface beside the eight-by-ten glossy of his son being pushed on one of those baby swings in the park.

He looked exactly like Finn's younger brother had at that age. Before everything went to hell.

Noah's pale blue eyes were alight with pure joy as wind ruffled his dirty-blond curls. His cheeks were chubby and pink and the perfect bow of his mouth was open on a peal of laughter.

This wasn't the first time Finn had seen the photograph. Or the first time he'd found himself staring at it, lost in a complex web of emotions he didn't have the experience to unravel.

He wasn't used to giving a damn about anything but himself.

But from the first time he'd seen a picture of his son— the one the hospital took when he'd been born—Finn had been lost.

No, that wasn't entirely true. He'd had a similar response the first time he'd laid eyes on Noah's mother. Genevieve… perplexed him. Enticed him in a way no one else ever had.

Unbidden, Finn's gaze traveled to the image of the woman standing behind Noah. Her arms were outstretched, waiting for the swing to return so she could push him again. Her flame-red hair had been pulled up into a tight knot at the top of her head, but the few strands that had fallen down were fluttering around her face.

He knew it was long…when she chose to let it down. Which was oh-so-rare. He could count on one hand the number of times he'd seen it in anything aside from a knot or a tail. And those few times had been because he'd asked her to leave it free.

He remembered running his fingers through the soft strands, reveling in the silky texture of it. Spreading it out across his pillow. The soft, blurred expression in her pale green eyes with the evergreen ring as his fingers played across her naked skin.

Dammit, he had to get control of himself. Sporting a half-hard erection at the mere thought of Genevieve's head on his pillow wasn't going to get him very far with her. In fact, it would have her building her walls even higher and faster.

And he needed her buy-in to have access to his son.

Shaking his head, Finn shuffled the photograph beneath the report he'd just been handed.

"Thanks, man. What do I owe you?"

Across the desk, Anderson Stone frowned at him, clearly perturbed at the question.

"Nothing. You know I'd do anything to help you. I'm just glad you're finally getting the chance to meet him. It's been a long six months."

It had been, but things were finally coming together. He might be reckless, but Finn had always understood the benefit of patience and laying the groundwork for success. Part of what he'd loved most about pulling off heists was the planning and anticipation.

Not to mention the adrenaline rush of triumph.

Running a finger over his lips, Finn sent his friend a chiding glance. "You know, the purpose of running a business is to make a profit."

"I'm aware," Stone drawled out.

"Apparently not, since I'm unaware of any other clients you're currently assisting. See, how it works is, when you provide services you request payment from those who benefit."

"Oh, is that how it works? Remind me, which one of us holds an MBA?"

Finn scoffed. "Just because I don't have an overpriced piece of paper with my name scrolled across it in fancy font doesn't mean I don't know what I'm talking about. Conversely, it doesn't make you an expert."

"I'm not hearing any complaints about the information you've been provided."

No, and he wouldn't complain. Finn was grateful for everything Stone and Gray, the other leg in their tripod, had done for him.

Who would have expected them to go into business together? Opening Stone Surveillance had seemed unexpected when his friends had first told him they were going to do it. But once he began thinking…it made sense. Both of them had this drive to help people, a need to right wrongs.

Maybe because they'd both been wronged.

Finn, on the other hand, had never felt the need to assist anyone in his life. People got what they deserved. If they were stupid, they deserved to be taken advantage of. Then they could learn. The way he looked at it, any time he stole something pretty and valuable, he was providing a service. Highlighting the flaws in their security so they could correct the problem and prevent more loss.

If in the process he managed to acquire something he wanted…more the better.

The challenge was what drove him. Woe be it to anyone touting security that no one could break.

"You know we're not letting you pay, Finn. Besides, if you'd come on board like we asked months ago, then you'd be a full partner, anyway."

"Nope, thanks. I have a job."

Stone scoffed. "That isn't a job. When's the last time you stepped foot inside DeLuca Industries?"

"Uh…" Finn glanced up at the ceiling, seriously considering Stone's question. "Probably seven years ago, give or take six or seven months." His lips quirked into a self-deprecating smile. "They obviously don't need me. You know I review the quarterly financial and management reports. See, the key to running a successful business is hiring competent people to take care of it for you."

Stone shook his head. This was an argument they'd had many times over the last few years. His friend couldn't understand Finn's perspective because he came from a family that was entirely wrapped up in the day-to-day minutia of running the family business. Sure, that business was a multibillion-dollar corporation with a worldwide reach, but that didn't really change anything.

Finn, on the other hand, had decided early on that he wanted nothing to do with the family business. And felt not a single speck of guilt when he inherited it and handed it straight over to others to run.

Success and money afforded him the opportunity to do exactly as he pleased.

"Stealing things isn't a job, either."

Finn let a full-blown smile pull at his lips. "I haven't stolen a single thing, officer. At least, not since I've been out."

Stone scoffed. "Uh-huh. Is that because you've been preoccupied with Noah? I know you, Finn DeLuca. You're going to get bored. All I'm asking is that when it happens, don't do something stupid. I promise, we'll find a way to use your skills in a way that's beneficial to all of us…and keeps your ass outta jail."

Finn leaned back farther in his chair, tipping it onto the back two legs. Folding his hands behind his head, he enjoyed the sensation of being balanced on the edge…just waiting for something to tip him one direction or the other.

The precipice was what called to him. The danger of walking on the brink. The potential of being caught was what made the rush so thrilling. Without it…

"Stone, I'm smart enough to keep myself out of jail. I've said it before, she's—" he gestured to the photograph beneath the pile of papers "—the only reason I got caught. I have no intention of ever letting that happen again."

Stone made a sound in the back of his throat that clearly stated his skepticism.

"I successfully pulled off more than two dozen jobs before her. I let myself get caught," Finn insisted.

"Uh-huh."

"I chose to go back. I put myself in that position."

Genevieve had distracted him. Made him sloppy. And he'd done something stupid. He had no intention of letting that happen again. What he needed right now was to win back Genevieve's trust so he could have access to his son. Period.

Stone's eyebrow rose, but he chose not to push him. Smart man. "Genevieve might be starting to make a splash on the jewelry scene, but her finances are precarious at best. What little money she got from her family is mostly tied up in inventory. Loose stones, precious metals."

His friend wasn't telling him anything Finn wasn't already aware of. He'd been going over Genevieve's financials just as closely as his own. He might ignore his company, but information was knowledge and he wouldn't let anyone take advantage of him.

What he didn't know was where Stone was going with this. "Your point?"

"She spent money she didn't have to hire a damn good lawyer to fight you."

Which was nothing less than what Finn had expected. And he hated to think of Genevieve putting herself and his son in that situation, but he'd remedy it as soon as possible.

"I tried to give her money. She hasn't cashed the check." Which also wasn't a surprise. But he had a plan to get her an influx of cash…one she couldn't afford to refuse. "Don't worry, man. I have everything under control."

Stone gave him a hard look. "I hope you know what you're doing."

Yeah, so did he.

Everything was riding on the next few weeks. One hiccup could cost him everything. But Finn was used to betting everything on a single well-planned adventure.

Genevieve paced through her living room, the heels of her shoes clicking against the hardwoods she'd refinished herself. Hands tucked beneath her crossed arms, she couldn't stop herself from looking out the open blinds to the street in front of her little house. Waiting.

Down the hall she could hear Maddie's happy, high-pitched voice as she read a book to Noah. She had no idea what she would have done over the last three years without her best friend. She'd been with Genevieve every step of the way…including being in the delivery room when Noah was born.

Maddie had also been there when Finn first slammed into Genevieve's life. There'd been something about him, something that drew Genevieve from the first moment they'd met, at a charity gala hosted by her grandfather.

Certainly, Finn was charismatic and handsome. Every female there that night had taken notice of him. But for Genevieve…it was more. She'd sensed the dangerous edge behind the polished exterior. And despite herself, she'd been tempted by it. For someone who'd been raised under a sheltered, strict upbringing that temptation had felt…deliciously forbidden. And so had he.

The sensual pull had only heightened when, without asking permission, he'd pulled her onto the dance floor. The warmth of his smooth palm caressed across her bare back. From that first encounter, she'd craved him.

Unfortunately, despite everything, there was a huge part of her that worried she still did.

Glancing at her watch, Genevieve felt her heart lurch into her throat. Five minutes.

What she couldn't understand was why Finn had fought so hard to meet Noah. The man she'd known had worked hard to avoid any semblance of responsibility to the point of outsourcing the management of his family's company. It wasn't likely he'd suddenly developed a burning desire to be a father.

Her biggest concern was the impact this was going to

have on Noah. She really didn't want her son falling in love with his daddy only to have Finn disappear. Or disappoint. Both highly likely.

A car door slammed. Genevieve glanced at her watch again. Exactly ten. The chime on her front door pealed. Swallowing down the butterflies storming her belly, she stalked across the room to yank it open.

And lost her breath.

Damn him for being exactly as she remembered. His feet were spread, encased in large black motorcycle boots planted on the pale boards of her front porch. Shoulders packed with muscle, nearly as wide as her doorway, blocked her view of the car undoubtedly sitting at her curb. A perverse part of her wondered if he still drove the sleek Maserati he'd delighted in racing through the city at top speed, practically taunting the local police to pull him over.

He'd been reckless and wild. So different than she was, which was undoubtedly what had attracted her in the first place. Finn DeLuca was a force. A storm, beautiful and raging. Uncaring what he destroyed in his path.

His hair was just as dark, almost jet-black, and untamed as the rest of him. A thick scruff covered his chin and cheeks, giving the impression he couldn't be bothered to shave rather than he was cultivating an actual beard.

But it was his eyes that got to her. Every damn time. So dark they almost appeared black. But she'd been close enough to know they were actually a deep, dark shade of coffee brown. What had gotten her more than the color, though, was the way he'd looked at her…like he'd actually seen her. All of her, especially the pieces she'd gotten very good at hiding from everyone, including herself.

He'd been the devil sitting on her shoulder, tempting her to sin. With him, she'd felt powerful, intelligent and beautiful. He'd convinced her she could be daring, too.

Finn DeLuca had the uncanny ability to make her feel like she had no secrets…and that she didn't need any. Turns out he'd been right. She hadn't had any secrets from him because he'd researched every damn aspect of her life. And used each piece of knowledge against her. To make her care for him. Love him.

Trust him.

All so he could steal what he wanted—the Star of Reilly—without regard to the damage he inflicted on her life.

"The neighbors might start talking if you leave me standing on the front porch all day, Genni."

"Don't call me that." Her response was automatic. So was the way she stepped back, doing exactly what he'd wanted her to.

He paused beside her as he moved into her home. For a second she thought he was going to touch her. Genevieve tensed, not certain how she'd react. But instead of reaching out, Finn slowly turned his head and flashed her that dangerous, mischievous grin. The one that always made her knees go weak. Because whatever nefarious thought was usually behind that grin had inevitably left her a naked, quaking, pleasure-infused mess.

Nope, that wasn't happening now.

Shoving the door closed, Genevieve purposely walked away from him. She stopped in the middle of her living room and swiveled, wrapping her arms around herself in a comforting hold.

"I don't know what you're hoping to gain here, Finn, but whatever it is, you can't have it."

"The only thing I want is the chance to get to know my son. You look real good, Genni."

She shook her head. "We both know that's not how you work, so cut the BS. I haven't figured out your play yet, but I will. And just in case you're not aware, although I'm sure you are, I no longer have access to the Reilly estate, including any of the jewels, the business or the art."

"Yep, I'm fully aware. Why do you think I wrote you that check?"

"Speaking of which, you can have the pieces back. And so we're clear, flattery won't get you anywhere with me. We both know you have the ability to spout pretty words with no substance. Don't waste your breath."

Finn's face drew tight. His mouth flattened into a sharp line, giving her an expression she'd never seen before. But that was probably because he'd only shown her what he wanted her to see.

"I meant what I said. And just so you know, I meant every word I've ever said to you. I might have done many things, but I never once lied to you."

Genevieve laughed, the sound of it very out of place. "Sure, except when you told me I could trust you and promised you'd never hurt me."

He took a single step toward her. Genevieve held up both hands.

"I'm sorry, Genevieve."

It was tempting to believe he actually meant the short declaration. She heard sincerity in the words. And there was a part of her that thought maybe he *was* sorry.

At least sorry he'd gotten caught.

"It doesn't matter anymore. I don't actually hate you, even though you deserve it. You gave me Noah. And even if it wasn't the way I would have preferred, you showed me I could have a life I didn't think possible. And gave me the confidence to fight for me and my son when I needed to. I'm happier now. But that doesn't mean I intend to forgive you or forget how you used and manipulated me."

It was Genevieve who closed the gap between them. She walked straight into his personal space, going toe-to-toe with him. She looked up into his dark, swarthy expression and said, "But I promise you this, I will never let you hurt or manipulate my son. So, for your sake, I hope you're telling me the truth. Because I'm not the naive, malleable girl you knew three years ago."

Two

Boy was she telling the truth.

Genevieve wasn't the innocent girl he'd known before. Back then he'd fought against the urge to protect and shelter her. To hurt her grandfather for the way he'd treated her. She'd been so meek. Beaten down by years of hearing she couldn't do anything right. Being constantly reminded of every mistake or flaw.

Even then Finn had known there was a fire deep inside her, banked and waiting for the right fuel to fan into something beautiful and mesmerizing.

He had been right.

The fierce expression in her gaze as she stared up at him made the blood whoosh faster in his veins. It made him want to grab her, yank her hard against him and devour that passion. And her soft, pink mouth.

But that would no doubt get him slapped.

And might cost him the opportunity to get to know his son.

Just the thought of that word had his stomach cramping. He had no idea what to do with a toddler.

He hadn't exactly had a wonderful role model in either of his parents. They'd been too wrapped up in their own worlds to even remember they had children for the most part. His mother and father had been more like Santa Claus or the Easter Bunny, dropping into his life once or twice a year, bringing lots of excitement and presents he didn't really want or need.

Because while they were stingy with their attention, they made damn certain their sons had every material thing they could possibly want.

Too bad those things hadn't made a damn bit of difference to Sawyer. Or Finn, for that matter.

He was not going to be that kind of parent. Refused. He might not know how to handle a baby, but he was going to damn well figure it out.

Genevieve stared at him and he realized he'd been silent a little too long. He needed to get his head in the game before he blew it.

"I don't expect you to forgive me, Genevieve. But I am sorry for what happened. And while you might not believe me—"

"Because you've given me no reason to, but every reason to distrust you."

Finn nodded his head, acknowledging she had a point. Not that he was going to let it stand between him and what he wanted.

"I wasn't stealing the Star that night."

"You were caught with the stone in your possession. And a fake was in its place."

"Genni, I'd had the stone for three days by that point. I came back that night to return it. The plan all along was to take it and disappear. But I couldn't go. For the first time ever, something—someone—was more important to me than the rush of success."

Genevieve stared up at him. A tangle of emotions flitted across her features. God, he loved her terrible poker face.

She was probably one of the most forthright people he'd ever met. And, given the world she'd lived in, that surprised him.

Anyone else might have become jaded or hard, but not Genevieve. She'd been a sweet breath of fresh air. Because he *was* jaded.

She was everything Finn wished he could be and just wasn't.

After several seconds, her tongue licked cautiously across pink lips. "What?"

"I was putting the stone back," he said again.

Getting the Star out had been easy. His plan executed flawlessly.

His conscience had been his downfall. Not to mention his inability to walk away from Genevieve.

He hadn't prepared a plan for returning the stone. Who would have thought that would turn out to be the harder task?

Genevieve frowned. "What's that supposed to change, Finn? You still stole it."

"True, but I couldn't keep it. You were more important."

"If that was true you wouldn't have taken it in the first place."

"If you knew anything about me, you'd realize just how far off that statement really is."

Her mouth flattened into a hard line. "You're right. I know nothing about you. But whose fault is that? I spent weeks thinking I was getting to know this amazing man I was falling in love with only to discover it was all a lie."

"Not all."

"So you've said. But the problem is, there's no way for me to untangle the lies from the truth to figure out what I might be able to trust. And I'm not willing to make the effort even if I could. The past is over, Finn. I'm letting you into my son's life because the court says I don't have a choice. But I fully expect this is a novelty for you. Something your incarceration has convinced you that you should do. In a couple months some other shiny new toy will catch your interest and you'll be gone."

Finn couldn't stop himself. He moved into her personal space, crowding Genevieve in a way that would have had the girl he knew shying away. Instead, she tipped her head back and glared at him.

Pride swelled through his chest, mixing with a healthy dose of amusement. Leaning down, he brought his mouth close enough to feel the heat of her skin caressing his lips and murmured, "Don't count on it. I'm not going anywhere, Genni."

She couldn't hide the shiver that rocked her body. With a huff, Genevieve stepped back, finally putting space between them.

Tilting his head, Finn said, "If we're done dealing with the past—" obviously, they weren't, but they'd at least made a start "—can I please meet Noah now?"

Her glare raked across his body, as if he was lower than the gunk on the bottom of her shoe. She might want to feel that way, but her reaction suggested she didn't really.

Finn simply waited her out, knowing his calm would irritate her. Now he was just being perverse, but he liked the snap of her temper. The way it made her eyes glitter and her skin glow.

Finally, she said, "He's in the back. I'll get him."

She turned to go, no doubt assuming he'd wait. It was the polite thing to do. But he'd never cared about being polite.

Following two steps behind her, he said, "No need. I'll come with you."

Genevieve paused halfway down the darkened hallway. She didn't turn and after several seconds began walking again. It didn't suck that he got a view of her jeans molded to her pert ass. His palm itched to reach out and smack it.

But he wasn't a complete idiot.

They passed by a couple rooms. One was clearly set up as an office. Not just for the boring details no doubt necessary for running her business. Finn also caught glimpses of the tools she used in her work. None of the expensive jewels she sometimes used in her pieces, but shiny bits of rock, mineral and twisted metal.

Another room was most likely a guest room. Genevieve paused in front of a doorway. It was closest to the shut door at the very end of the hallway. Probably her master.

She blocked Finn's view of what was inside, but it really didn't matter. The expression on her face told him everything he needed to know. Pure love and adoration filled her expression.

His own mother had never once looked at him with that kind of love. No one ever had.

No, that wasn't true.

Genevieve had. But she certainly didn't anymore.

She wasn't ready. For Finn or for what was about to happen.

How could she still react to him? After everything the man had done to her…

His betrayal had cut so deep. Starving for affection, approval, acceptance, she'd been ripe to fall for Finn DeLuca's lies. She'd wanted to believe him when he told her she was beautiful. Basked in his praise when he said she was amazingly talented and intelligent.

Considering she'd grown up beneath the harsh and disapproving glare of her grandfather, a man who routinely pointed out that she was useless and couldn't be trusted to do anything correctly, it probably wouldn't have taken much warmth and sunlight for her to flourish. But Finn had given her more than a small taste of what she'd always craved.

Stupid of her for believing him.

But to her credit, she'd been naive and sheltered before. She hadn't been aware of what was lacking in her life until Finn. Hadn't understood that she'd deserved better than the demeaning and degrading verbal and emotional abuse her grandfather had subjected her to.

Now, she was much more aware, and stronger.

Which begged the question, what the hell was wrong with her? Because her body had reacted the moment he walked through her front door. Her heart fluttered and her breath caught. Her palms went clammy and her panties were uncomfortably damp.

Sure, that was understandable considering the man was a walking advertisement for bad-boy perfection. But she *knew* his smile was a facade and every word out of his mouth was suspect.

Apparently, her body was stupid and her brain had a poor memory. At least her heart was less susceptible.

She hoped.

Either way, this visit had absolutely nothing to do with her and Finn. Noah was all that mattered.

Taking a deep, calming breath, Genevieve whispered, "Come meet your son."

Waving him over, she backed from the doorway to give him room. She wanted to train her gaze on Noah, to watch his reaction when he realized there was someone new in the house. But Genevieve couldn't stop her eyes from shifting from the blond-haired boy happily sitting in Maddie's lap to his father.

A tight band constricted her chest at the utter awe stamped across Finn's face. Something unexpected swam through his intent gaze. Something genuine and real. If she didn't know better, Genevieve would have called it long-ing and hope.

"He looks like my brother."

"He looks like you," Genevieve countered. Except for the blond hair and blue eyes, her son was the spitting image of his father.

Finn gave a quick shake of his head and she wondered if he really couldn't see it. When he was little, it was less obvious, but as Noah had grown, becoming more of a lit-tle boy instead of a baby, the resemblance was unavoid-able. The only things she'd given their son were his pert nose and bowed mouth. Everything else was pure Finn... including his mischievous, playful nature.

Because, God knew, he hadn't gotten that from Gene-vieve. But she loved the fact that her son had the opportu-nity to be a kid. Something she'd never gotten.

Finally sensing them hovering in the doorway, Noah's little head shot up. His expression lit up, as it always did when he saw her. Crossing to them, Genevieve pulled Noah into her arms as she said, "Thanks, Maddie."

"Anytime." Pushing up, Maddie paused on her way out to flash an angry, warning gaze at Finn. Several seconds later the front door reverberated shut, leaving the three of them alone.

Genevieve had the sudden and overwhelming urge to call Maddie back. She needed that buffer, any buffer.

Noah broke the moment, smacking his hands against Genevieve's face and forcing her to look at him. "Mama."

Bouncing him on her hip to resettle him, Genevieve moved closer to Finn. "Noah, this is your daddy. Finn, this is Noah."

Noah tilted his little head sideways, a move she'd seen Finn do not ten minutes before. His cherub lips pursed into a mew and his eyes narrowed. They all held a breath.

That apparently was unnecessary because after several

seconds, Noah held his arms out to Finn and demanded, "Up."

To her utter surprise, Finn did just that, scooping her son out of her arms and into his without hesitation. They went nose-to-nose, staring at each other. Noah blinked. And the most gorgeous smile spread across Finn's face.

Pointing to the bookshelf, her son issued a familiar demand. "Book."

Making himself at home, Finn obliged. Grabbing a book from the shelf, he settled into the rocking chair, plopping Noah into his lap like they'd done it a million times.

Genevieve watched for several seconds before quietly turning and leaving.

She couldn't stay. It hurt.

And she hated herself a little because it did.

Casing the place was second nature. Finn didn't even have to try to catalog the security weaknesses as he walked through the front doors at the trendy jewelry boutique in downtown Charleston. The kind of place that catered to wealthy customers even as it proclaimed itself bohemian and unusual.

Hypocritical as far as he was concerned. They wanted to make beaucoup money, but pretend they were in it for the art.

The security guy they'd hired stuck out like a sore thumb, even as he tried to blend in. First, his cheap suit was trying too hard to parade as expensive. Not to mention, the cut of it was terrible, the gun under his arm bulging out visibly when he moved.

Their technology sucked. The cameras were in obvious positions—watching the door, each of the counters and the hallway into the back room. They were at least ten years old and if he had to guess not even digital. No doubt there were blind spots everywhere and the quality of the recordings next to useless.

Sticking his hands in his pockets, Finn wandered slowly through the cramped store. He made a show of inspecting the merchandise, but was really memorizing the staff's movements.

They made it too damn easy.

Knocking over this place would be child's play. With little effort he could have a flawless plan in probably two hours. And most of that time would be replenishing equipment he no longer owned. Hell, he could probably pocket a couple of loose stones without even trying.

But that wasn't why he was here.

Not to mention, he was going straight…for now. Not only did he need to keep on the right side of his parole officer, but no doubt one whiff of theft and Genevieve would deny him access to Noah, court order or not.

"Sir, can I help you?"

Flipping up his wrist, Finn looked at the Piaget there before flicking his gaze up to the woman who'd finally greeted him. Eight minutes and thirteen seconds. Not great.

"Yes. I'd like to look at some pieces I understand you have on consignment."

The woman visibly perked up. Of course she did. First, he hadn't missed her attention to his watch and the dollar signs she'd finally started ringing up as her gaze swept over him. And all the consignment collections the boutique happened to be hosting were high dollar.

She was about to make a hefty commission.

"Wonderful. What collection were you interested in viewing? We have some wonderful pieces from Maximillian Broussard, a former designer with Harry Winston."

"No, I'm familiar with his work, but his pieces are too heavy for what I'm looking for."

The woman's mouth pursed. Broussard's pieces were no doubt going for more than Genevieve's. For now.

"You're looking for something more delicate and intricate?"

Finn nodded.

"I'm Denise and I have just the thing. Follow me." She spun and trotted off across the store toward what was no doubt a private showroom behind a heavy velvet curtain.

Finn's eyebrows rose as she pulled back the rich sapphire barrier and swept her hand, indicating he should precede her inside. As expected, the room was set up with an elegant table in the center covered in black velvet. There were three chairs and the space was flooded with bright lights. The kind that could catch even the worst cut angle of a gem and make it sparkle like the most flawless diamond.

He accepted a chair and waited. "We have several exclusive pieces from an up-and-coming designer. She's just beginning to make a name for herself, but she's been around gemstones her entire life. She's known for the intricate details of her work and the flawless way she displays stones, emphasizing their strengths and camouflaging their flaws. What kind of piece were you looking for?"

"I'm interested in buying something for a woman who's important to me."

"Necklace, bracelet, earrings…all three?"

He could practically hear the hope in Denise's voice. He was about to make her ever-loving day. "Possibly. If I find the right pieces. Why don't you show me what you have and we'll go from there?"

Denise nearly clapped her hands together with glee. "Absolutely. Let me pour you a drink while I go gather a few things to show you. Bourbon? Wine?"

"Bourbon would be lovely." He really didn't want it, but it always set people at ease when they left you something to do with your hands and mouth.

The minute Denise was gone, Finn abandoned the un-comfortable chair and began wandering the room. If he'd wanted to, he could have been into the back rooms, prob-ably cracked their shitty safe and had a pocket stuffed full of stones before she returned.

His palms itched and the enticing memory of adrenaline and triumph called to him. Stupid people practically begged to be taken advantage of. He had no respect for those who refused to protect what they valued. However, this place hardly presented a big enough challenge to honestly tempt him. It wasn't worth it.

Denise bustled back in and spread several trays out across the top of the table. Finn would have known the pieces were Genevieve's even if there hadn't been a dis-creet card with her name in a filigreed logo tucked into the corner of each.

They were so her. Light and gorgeous. Breathtaking and delicate. But with a core of strength emanating from the twisting, looping metal surrounding the beautiful stones. None of the pieces held diamonds, which didn't necessarily surprise him. That would have been too expected.

Besides, Genevieve liked color.

One grouping had the dark, deep red of Burmese ru-bies. Another with sapphires and water opals. They were all gorgeous. But the last set of emeralds called to him. Maybe because the varying shades of green reminded him of Genevieve's eyes. The paler green center with the ever-green ring at the edge.

Pulling the tray closer, Finn let his gaze travel across the matching set. The necklace was gorgeous, a single teardrop emerald with exquisite saturation and color. Finn itched to ask for a loupe, but didn't want to reveal the extent of his knowledge. The stone was small, but he'd guess almost inclusion free. No doubt it had cost Genevieve quite a bit.

The stones in the matching bracelet and earrings were

smaller and less impressive, but that wasn't surprising. The necklace was the showpiece. He could imagine it nestled right in the hollow of Genevieve's throat.

"I'll take them," he declared, pushing the tray away and sitting back. The spindly chair creaked ominously beneath him. Seriously, this place needed a full upgrade on everything.

"Wonderful. She's a lucky woman."

Finn fought back a laugh. That might be, but something told him if—no, when—Genevieve found out he'd purchased these pieces she was going to be less than pleased.

There was more than one way to get his money into her hands.

Three

"You sold the three emerald pieces."

Genevieve's belly clenched. She should be so happy. That sale alone would support her and Noah for the next several months. And if any of the other sets had sold she wouldn't be conflicted. But from the moment she'd held that teardrop emerald she'd felt a connection to it.

It wasn't the first time. And hopefully, it wouldn't be the last. She always felt a kinship with the stones she worked with. She routinely spent days or weeks studying them. Analyzing them from every angle to determine the best way to put them on display.

But there'd been something very special about that emerald.

However, she couldn't afford to keep a stone simply because she wanted to. She'd had almost fifty grand tied up in that emerald alone. That was one of the drawbacks of running her own design company. The materials she worked with were expensive. But they paid off when they sold.

She hadn't sold a piece in a few weeks so this really came at a great time. That's what she was going to focus on.

Maybe after the collection launch she'd think about planning a trip for Noah to Disney next year. For his birthday.

"Genevieve? Did you hear me?"

Shaking her head, she brought her focus back to Eric, the owner of one of the boutiques she'd consigned with. "Yes, I'm sorry. That's wonderful! Can you tell me who bought the pieces?"

She always liked to know something about the people who purchased her jewelry. It helped her complete the circle in her head. To imagine the look of excitement, or shock and surprise, on a woman's face when her husband presented her with one of her pieces. She liked to know if there was a story behind it. Was it to commemorate the birth of a child? Or fifty years together?

It gave her a sense of pride and happiness to know something she created could give those feelings to someone else.

"I don't know much. Denise didn't get a lot of details. A gentleman came in, but he wasn't certain what he wanted. He chose the emerald pieces as soon as she brought them out, though."

Well, that was something. Maybe the person who'd purchased them had connected to them as much as she had. That gave her a little bit of comfort.

"Can you send over the name and address?"

She liked to send her customers a personal note of thanks. It was something she'd done in the beginning and many of her customers had made repeat purchases, partly because they liked her style, but also because they appreciated the personal touch.

It was one of the few downsides to expanding her business. She wasn't certain how she would maintain that same connection.

The upcoming collection had the potential to make a huge splash. Her partnership with Mitchell Brothers Jewelry, a major chain within the southeast, was already receiving some amazing press. It was nice to have that kind of experience and marketing behind her collection.

In a matter of weeks, she would go from having her pieces displayed in a handful of boutiques to appearing in over fifty locations in twelve states across the South.

It would mean more security for Noah. She'd simply have to find a way to keep the personal touch she'd become known for.

"Absolutely," Eric said. "I'll email the information to you. And we'll send the direct deposit within the week."

"Thanks, Eric. I appreciate it."

Genevieve hung up and walked back into the studio where she designed. Noah was with Nicole, the woman Genevieve had hired to watch her son while she worked. Nicole was a college student, which was convenient for Genevieve, who often worked weird hours when she was in the middle of a design. She had at least another two hours before she needed to be home.

She stared at the stones spread across the table before her. They were gorgeous. A perfect example of alexandrite, a rare semiprecious stone known for color shifting based on the light. She'd been studying the seven stones for the past few days, trying to decide what they were destined to be.

The biggest was slightly over a carat. Three more were roughly three quarters each. The other three varied, but were all just below a half. It would make sense to set the largest stone in a necklace, two of the smaller as stud earrings and then a bracelet of some kind.

That would be logical. But that wasn't what her instincts were calling for her to do. The problem was, no alternative was coming to her, either.

She let her fingers sift across the stones, enjoying their cool surface and the way they rolled beneath her touch. She could feel the hard edges. See the brilliant fire trapped deep inside.

Scooping them into her palm, she rearranged them once more, hoping inspiration would hit.

Nothing.

She'd sunk a lot of money into these stones and really needed to finish it before the opening. Frustration tightened her shoulders until they pulled up close to her ears.

The ding of an email arriving on her phone cut through the unhappy silence of her studio.

Perfect. She needed a distraction.

Snatching up her phone, Genevieve unlocked the screen and pulled up the email from Eric.

A growl escaped when she read the information he'd forwarded.

She was going to kill Finn.

Finn was naked when the doorman buzzed up to let him know he had a visitor—a female—waiting for him downstairs. The only woman who had his address was Stone's girlfriend, Piper. And he couldn't think of a single reason she'd stop by. Especially without calling.

A half smile twisted his lips. That just left Genevieve.

The familiar edge of excitement shot through his veins. Whatever brought her to his doorstep at seven at night, it wasn't likely to be because she wanted to rip his clothes off.

Grabbing a pair of sweatpants, Finn slipped them on, but didn't bother with a shirt. Padding across his penthouse loft, he rubbed a towel across his wet hair as he went. Pulling open his front door, he left it wide-open and wandered back into his living room.

No doubt she'd find him.

It didn't take her long. He heard the sharp tap of her feet against his floor. She was wearing heels. He loved when he wore heels. They made her calves and thighs look amazing.

His front door slammed shut and her voice hissed behind him, "How many times do I have to say this? I don't want your money."

Finished with the towel, Finn tossed it onto the arm of the sofa before taking his time to turn. His gaze traveled slowly down her body. It wasn't intentional. He simply couldn't stop his response to her.

She was even more gorgeous when she was pissed.

Her green eyes spit fire and twin flags of color stained her cheeks. Her hands were balled into fists and set high and tight on her hips. Her entire body leaned toward him even as she maintained about ten feet of distance.

"You've made that clear."

"And yet, that didn't stop you from pulling a stunt."

"Stunt?" Finn decided to play dumb, although it probably wasn't going to get him anywhere. But he'd learned a long time ago not to admit guilt unless he knew for certain he was already caught. "What are you talking about?"

"Oh, don't feign stupid. We both know you're not. You're always five steps ahead of everyone around you."

"Thank you?" he asked, pretty certain she hadn't meant her words to be the compliment they were.

"Return the pieces."

Finn shrugged. "No."

"You don't want them or need them. And I refuse to take your guilt money. Noah and I don't need it."

He'd been in a perfectly jovial mood until that moment. Dropping the affable facade, Finn quickly closed the gap between them. Genevieve apparently realized her tactical error because she scrambled several steps backward. However, she'd miscalculated because that move brought her up hard against the exposed brick wall.

He heard her body hit with a thud, but he didn't stop until both his hands were spread on either side of her head. The rough brick edges scraped across his palms. His thigh brushed against hers. And he tried not to notice the way her breath stuttered in her lungs.

"Let's make one thing crystal clear, Genevieve. Guilt has nothing to do with anything I'm doing. You're raising my son and there's no reason for either you or he to go without."

"I'm perfectly capable of providing for *my* son, Finn."

"Yes, I'm aware. I've seen your tax returns for the last three years and have a detailed financial report for your business. I know exactly how much money you have tied up in materials and inventory. I know you're stretched thin preparing for this opening, but we both know you'll be fine once that happens because you're a brilliant designer. The world just doesn't know it yet."

Genevieve blinked. Her mouth thinned with irritation, but he didn't pause long enough to give her a chance to voice it.

"However, there's no need for you ever to be in a position to worry. I have enough money to support a third-world country."

"Then by all means, give *them* a check for a million dollars."

"I have."

She tilted her head sideways, a tell indicating he'd just surprised her. Which shouldn't surprise him, but it did. It also hurt a little. He wasn't a heartless monster, dammit.

"You wouldn't accept my help any other way, so I found a way you couldn't refuse."

"I won't let you purchase those pieces."

"Genevieve," he murmured, disappointment filling his voice. "We both know I'm already in possession of the emeralds."

"Then give them back."

"No. They're mine."

"What are you going to do with them?"

"None of your business."

Her teeth ground together, frustration and something more personal filling her gaze.

"I'll simply refuse the money from Eric."

Finn used his height advantage to crowd even farther into her personal space. Genevieve shifted, but there was nowhere for her to go so the gesture simply had her body brushing tantalizingly against his.

Every cell in his body lit up. The driving need to touch her, taste her, take her was a pounding tattoo deep in his blood. Instead, he gently cupped his hand beneath her jaw and brought her gaze to meet his.

"Don't do that," he said. His words might have been soft; however, the order beneath them was anything but.

"Or what?" she challenged, eyes flashing fire.

Her mouth was so close he could feel the heat of her breath against his skin. Her lips, parted in anger, practically begged him to touch.

A temptation Finn couldn't deny. His fingers slipped across the silky texture of her cheek. It had been so long since he'd touched her. Too long.

And this moment wasn't nearly enough. Not when memories of Genevieve, writhing beneath him in pleasure, filled his brain.

His grip on her tightened. Finn pulled her mouth to his, the driving need to steal a taste of her too much to ignore.

The moment his lips touched hers it was all over. Heat and need claimed him. The emptiness he'd been carrying around for so long began to ache. That throb only she'd ever been able to touch.

Any good intentions he might have been able to scrounge up burned to ash. And he simply began to take. Opening his mouth, Finn released a sigh of relief when she did the same, unconsciously letting him in. Her hands gripped his shoulders, not pulling him closer, but not pushing him away.

He took everything she was willing to give him. Darting his tongue deep inside her mouth, relishing the sweet, spicy taste of her suffusing his senses.

Nope, he needed to get a grip.

Pulling away, Finn dropped his forehead to hers. He simply froze, trying to find his equilibrium…and sense. His harsh breaths mingled with her stuttered pulls of air.

Eventually, he put a little space between them. Just enough to be able to look her straight in the eye and say, "I don't want to take anything from you, Genevieve. I promise. I just want to give. Please, let me."

Shit, shit, shit.

She was an idiot.

Because she wanted to believe him. But her brain was screaming at her that she shouldn't. She knew better. He'd fooled her once with his earnest expression and slick words.

But he also wasn't wrong.

She really needed the money from the sale of the emeralds. She'd been eyeing some black opals that would make an amazing choker, but she just didn't have the capital to invest in the stones right now.

There was a part of her that hated knowing Finn was going to be the one to own the emeralds, as well. And she refused to let herself contemplate him giving them to another woman. The expression of joy and surprise on that woman's face as he leaned close to clasp the necklace around her slim neck…

Nope, Genevieve wasn't going there.

Besides, her commission from the sale wasn't anywhere near what he'd tried to give her a couple months ago. That check had smelled of guilt and she wasn't ready to let him off the hook by accepting it.

This, however, was a business exchange. Nothing more and nothing less.

"Fine. Keep the emeralds. I'll take the commission. As long as you promise not to buy any more pieces."

Finn shrugged. "I promise not to buy any pieces for the sole purpose of giving you money, how about that?"

She couldn't contemplate any other reason for him to invest hundreds of thousands of dollars in jewelry right now, so... "Fine. Thank you. There are some black opals I've been coveting. I'll be able to buy them and finish the last two pieces for my collection."

"Mmm," he murmured. "Black opals?"

Genevieve felt the excitement bubbling up inside her and couldn't tamp it down. "They're gorgeous. The play-of-color is...unbelievable, and they're perfect for a choker I've designed but just haven't found the right stones for. The shades of blue and purple against the black background...and they all came from the same rough stone. They're just..."

She hadn't realized how gushy she sounded until she looked up to find Finn staring at her. Slowly, the excitement leaked out. Genevieve literally felt her entire body deflating.

"I'm sorry. You probably don't care."

"Don't," he said, stepping closer. "I enjoy seeing the fire in your eyes while you talk about stones. Your passion for what you do is one of the things I like most about you, Genevieve, and always have."

She shook her head, unsure how to handle what he'd said. What was she supposed to do with that?

Sure, she missed having someone to share her enthusiasm with. That was one of the things she missed most about working at Reilly. She'd been surrounded by people who understood her stupid obsession with hard bits of minerals and rock.

It was something she and Finn had shared before. For those few weeks he'd been a part of her life, she'd had a confidant who wanted to have a conversation about gemstones.

Of course, that was because he'd been trying to pull information from her so he could steal her family's most prized possession.

Shifting away from him, Genevieve waved her hand. "It doesn't matter. I hope whomever you bought the emeralds for enjoys them. Those pieces had a special place in my heart."

Finn tipped his head sideways and his gaze narrowed. "I'm hopeful their new owner will appreciate having them."

Something sharp pinched in the center of her chest. "No doubt."

Crap.

"Well… I should leave." Genevieve waved lamely toward the door she'd burst through only a few minutes ago. Where was the ball of anger that had fueled her then?

Incinerated by that kiss.

That stupid kiss that she was just going to pretend never happened.

Finn watched as she backed slowly toward the door. The way his gaze followed her, the corner of his lips tipped into a telling half smile, made her itchy and uncomfortable. He had the uncanny ability to make her feel unfettered and awkward at the same time. Like he saw something deep inside her that she wasn't sure really existed.

Pausing with her hand on the knob, Genevieve fought against the weird desire to lock the door and stay on this side instead of walking away. "Call me later in the week and you can stop by to see Noah again."

There was nothing suppressed about the smile that brightened Finn's face. "I'd like that."

A few days ago, she'd been worried about Finn's ability to be a dad. But after watching him with her son yesterday, she was no longer concerned. Finn was a natural with Noah, possibly because in many ways Finn still acted like a child himself.

Although that didn't precisely assuage all of her concerns. In fact, it only added a couple more.

Closing the door behind her, Genevieve found herself sagging against it, unable to walk away. Her knees were mushy and her legs next to useless.

And she was no longer confident in her ability to be in the same room with Finn DeLuca and not want him.

Four

Twenty-four hours later, Finn couldn't get that kiss out of his head. Passion had never been their issue. In fact, from the moment he laid eyes on Genevieve, he'd wanted her.

Which had ultimately been his downfall.

At first, he'd been drawn to her in the same way he'd fallen in love with a Rembrandt when he was a teenager or a glorious ruby the size of his fist ten years later. Incidentally, he'd eventually owned both.

He'd always had an affinity for beautiful things. And there was certainly something ethereal and wholesome about Genevieve. So different from the jaded world Finn had lived in for his entire life.

Early on, he'd convinced himself it was an act. It had to be. No one was that naive and trusting. Especially knowing her grandfather, Lackland Reilly, and his influence on her life. But Finn soon realized she *was* that trusting.

Or she used to be.

He'd ruined that about her, and right now he hated himself for stealing the clear innocence that had shone from her eyes. He might have replaced the Star, but he couldn't fix the other damage he'd caused.

Although watching her with their son...he might even be more attracted to her now than he'd been before.

Lackland had worked hard to keep Genevieve sheltered and unaware of how the world really worked. He'd home-schooled her, surrounded her with nothing but adults who did and said what he demanded. And he'd expected the same of Genevieve, to follow his commands without question. Treating her more like an employee than a family member. A commodity.

And that had pissed Finn off. It wasn't the first time he'd encountered that kind of dictatorial sense of entitlement in their world. And hell, he'd never given a damn about how anyone else was treated.

Until Genevieve.

He'd always sensed an inner strength, hidden deep. Like the roughest uncut diamond, just waiting for the skill and patience to bring out the sparkle and fire.

Why did it bother him that he hadn't been the catalyst that had brought her fire forth?

Although maybe he could take some of the credit. The way she'd stormed into his apartment yesterday, her eyes blazing, ready to go toe-to-toe with him... The Genevieve he'd known before wouldn't have had the backbone to do that.

Even now, Finn felt his sex stir at the memory. He'd been unable to control his reaction to her. His physical need to touch and taste, to capture that energy and make it his own.

But he couldn't give in to that need. Not without jeopardizing what he really wanted. Getting distracted by Genevieve had cost him before...he wasn't willing to make that mistake again. Their attraction was dangerous. It made him sloppy and stupid.

What really mattered was that she'd said he could visit

Noah again. A step in the right direction, but he wanted more. He wanted to be able to show his son the world.

Finn needed to move slowly with Genevieve. Convince her that he was different from the man who'd seduced her for his own purposes three years ago. Because he was.

Or he wanted to be. For his son. For the family he'd never thought he'd have again when Sawyer died.

The phone on the table in front of him buzzed, rattling against the wooden surface. Scooping it up, he punched the green button to answer.

"Stone."

"I've got the equipment you asked for. Please tell me you're not doing anything illegal with it. No, wait. On second thought, don't tell me a damn thing. Deniability is a beautiful thing."

Finn laughed. One good thing about Stone, he always managed to make Finn smile.

"I'm not doing anything illegal." Exactly... Although perhaps he was walking a fine line. Genevieve probably wouldn't agree to the surveillance equipment he was about to install outside her studio and home, but that was only because she didn't understand how vulnerable she really was.

He, on the other hand, knew exactly where her security weaknesses were hiding. And he intended to patch a few of the holes...until he could convince her to give him access inside to cover the rest. No way was he going to let something—someone—important to him remain needlessly vulnerable. He robbed idiots like that and he refused to be an idiot.

On this, he'd risk asking for forgiveness instead of permission. Genevieve and Noah were important to him. Her business and designs were important to her. So he was going to protect them.

"Uh-huh," Stone's skeptical voice ghosted down the line.

"You've got enough cameras, microphones and storage capacity here to make the Met envious."

"That's a nasty exaggeration."

"Fine, just tell me you're not going to do something stupid."

"I'm going to set up external surveillance at Genevieve's studio and home. Her security leaves a lot to be desired."

The silence that followed practically screamed Stone's disapproval. His friend was fully aware of the history between Finn and Genevieve. He was also privy to the six-month fight Finn had just engaged in to get access to his son.

No doubt Stone thought this was asking for trouble. And maybe he was right, but Finn was going to do it, anyway.

Finally, Stone said, "I'm going out on a limb here and guessing she has no idea her every move is about to be recorded?"

"Uh…" Finn really didn't want to answer that question.

"Jesus," Stone swore. "You're gonna end up back in jail, aren't you?"

"No." Finn had no intention of getting caught, either with this, or with anything else. "Can your team install everything? And set up the feed on my computer and phone?"

Stone sighed. "Yeah. I'll send someone over tomorrow. Let them know how you want it all set up. It should only take a couple hours."

"They'll be discreet?"

"You mean, they won't tip your baby mama off that she's being watched?"

Finn had to bite back a retort at Stone's words. He knew the man had used them on purpose, hoping to get a rise out of Finn.

"Yes," he ground out.

"They're skilled at being unseen when I need them to be."

Perfect.

* * *

Genevieve stared at the jewels sparkling on the table in front of her. They were gorgeous. Something about them made her chest tighten with joy and anticipation. Her blood thrummed faster in her veins, sort of like it did the minute Finn got close enough for her to smell his spicy, tempting scent. Whatever shampoo or soap he used, she wanted to have it banned in all fifty states…as a lethal weapon.

Nope, she wasn't going to think about him right now. She'd spent the last couple days trying to wipe out the memory of her tirade at his apartment…and the kiss that had sent her scurrying for safety.

Because she was a damn fool. And her body epitomized the definition of weakness.

Even knowing exactly the kind of man he was and the deception he was capable of…she'd wanted him. So much. Where had her libido been the last three years? Because it certainly had been MIA.

Even now, the damn man was messing with her life. She'd come into the studio to work. She really needed to get this piece finished…which was a problem since she couldn't even seem to get it started.

She'd been staring at the stones, moving them around on the table, as her mind ping-ponged ninety miles an hour on everything except her work. No, that wasn't true. She knew exactly what her mind had been focused on.

Flipping her cell phone over, she glanced at the screen and registered that it was close to midnight. She needed to head out and let Nicole go home. She didn't have class in the morning, but that didn't mean she wasn't looking forward to crawling into her own bed.

Frustrated that she'd wasted several hours and accomplished nothing, Genevieve gathered the stones and locked them back into the state-of-the art vault where she kept her loose stones and finished pieces.

That was one thing Nick, her only employee and head of security, had insisted on. He'd allowed her to scrimp in other areas in exchange for an expensive-as-hell vault. His rationale was that anyone just knocking over the place would be outclassed and leave empty-handed. She'd been around the business long enough to understand the value of protecting the investment she'd made in materials.

But at the end of the day, even if this was her livelihood, the gemstones were just things. Certainly, they were beautiful, but so was the sound of her son's laughter. At least to her.

Locking the back door, Genevieve took several steps outside when an unexpected shiver snaked down her spine. The hair on the back of her neck stood on end and she paused midstride. A burst of adrenaline shot into her system.

But she had no idea why.

Gaze darting around the empty parking lot, Genevieve attempted to find something out of place. But everything was quiet and still. Shadows shifted, but they were leaves from the grand oak trees at the back of the property rustling in the late-night breeze.

It was her imagination. She was being paranoid, that was all. Quickening her pace, Genevieve grasped her keys, unlocked the door to her SUV, slid inside and quickly locked it again.

Her heart was beating way too fast considering nothing had happened. Shaking her head, Genevieve cranked her car and headed home. She needed sleep, that was all.

She'd take another crack at the alexandrite tomorrow. Maybe during the day. A change of scenery might be what she needed. In the meantime, she was going to head home and spend some time with her sketch pad. Maybe brilliance would strike.

* * *

Finn stared at the computer screen open in front of him. His loft was pitch-black, the only light coming from the glow in front of him. His feet were kicked up onto the coffee table, a glass of red wine close to his elbow.

Anyone who walked in would probably assume he was completely relaxed, watching a movie or something.

In reality, he was desperately trying to control his temper.

It was his turn to want to race across town, barge into Genevieve's home and read her the riot act. What was she thinking, working alone that late at night? The neighborhood her studio was in was decent, but any place could be dangerous after midnight.

Especially when you added the temptation of pricey gemstones.

And from what he'd gathered, her late-night foray to the studio wasn't an anomaly. She hadn't even bothered to call in the yahoo she'd hired to handle her security.

Oh, you better believe he'd had the idiot checked. And while on the outside he appeared capable of handling the job, it was obvious he wasn't. Or Genevieve never would have been at the studio alone at midnight.

Clearly, he'd gotten the job because she'd known him from her time at Reilly. And, from watching the man for the last few days, Finn did not like the way his gaze followed Genevieve. Finn's gut told him more than loyalty had what's-his-name following Genni when she left the family business.

Finn sat up straighter in his chair when Genevieve's car appeared on the right half of the split screen. Maybe he needed to ask Stone to put a tracker on her car so he could monitor her on the way home. Although that was probably crossing a line, the dead space between her leaving the studio and arriving at her place made him nervous.

Genevieve parked in her driveway, pulling in beside the old sedan her babysitter drove. She disappeared inside only to reappear on the front stoop as the other woman left.

Nicole's hair was pulled up into a knot on the top of her head, but at some point it had gotten a little off-kilter. Her eyes were heavy-lidded and she moved sluggishly, as if she was half-asleep.

In contrast, Genevieve was wide-awake.

She gave the other woman a hug, asked her a question, which was answered with a definitive nod, and then watched as she drove away. Crossing her arms over her chest, Genevieve stood outside for several seconds before slipping back inside.

Finn watched the progression of lights as they went dark throughout her house. He had no doubt she stood at Noah's doorway for several seconds before disappearing into her own room. Not only because there was a pause before the hallway light was extinguished, but because that was the kind of mother she would be.

It took about fifteen minutes for all the lights in her home to flip off. He should follow suit and go to bed, as well, but he couldn't. Not merely because of his irritation at Genevieve's lack of self-preservation.

He wanted to be there with her, slipping into bed beside her. Yes, touching and tasting her, but also pulling her close and tucking her into the shelter of his body. Falling asleep to the quiet sound of her breathing. The heat of her skin sinking deep into his own.

Genevieve made him want things he shouldn't.

Nope, he wasn't going there.

Finn was about to close the lid of his laptop when something made him pause. His hand rested on the top of the lid as his gaze sharpened on the left side of his screen.

Right there. Again. A flicker.

His heart kicked inside his chest, ticking into a faster

rhythm, one that was comfortable and familiar. He lived for the heightened physical state, that hit adrenaline gave during high-stress situations.

Something wasn't right.

Pulling the feed at Genevieve's studio up full screen, Finn zoomed in tighter and waited.

It didn't take long for one of the many shadows to move against all the others, materializing into a dark figure skulking at the back door.

Shit.

Before he could react, Finn watched it open wide enough for whoever was there to slip inside.

Vaulting up from his position on the sofa, Finn juggled the computer in one hand while he snatched up his phone with the other. The first call he made was to the police. The second was to Stone.

The third was to Genevieve.

Genevieve tossed and turned for about twenty minutes, her brain simply refusing to settle. Finally, in that space right before falling asleep, her body had just begun to sink down into the bed when her cell phone rang out from the bedside table.

The noise startled her, jolting her upright. Her brain was sluggish enough that it took her a couple seconds before registering what the sound was. Snatching up the phone for fear the noise would wake Noah, she didn't recognize the number before hitting Accept. Telemarketers didn't call after midnight, so it really didn't matter. But if this was a wrong number she was going to get cranky.

"Hello," she whispered, resituating herself in bed so she could rest against the headboard.

"Genevieve?"

Her eyebrows beetled. "Finn?"

"Yeah, listen—"

She cut him off. "What the hell are you doing calling me this late? Whatever you have to say can wait until in the morning."

"Genevieve." Finn's voice was urgent and demanding, much different from the unconcerned billionaire she knew. "Someone broke into your studio. I've called the police and a friend, but you should get over here."

Blinking, she didn't even know how to respond to what he'd just said. "What?" was about all her brain would spit out.

"I'm so sorry to call this way," he responded, his voice going soft and apologetic.

Her grandfather's snide voice sounded in the back of her mind. *Use your head, girl. It isn't a coincidence this is happening just days after he's back in your life.*

She hadn't spoken to her grandfather in three years. She'd avoided any chance encounter by cutting ties with anyone in his life. And it pissed her off that even now his voice could invade her mind. Influence her thoughts.

But, dammit, he wasn't wrong.

"Is this your fault?"

"What? No. Why would you even ask that?"

Why wouldn't she? He was guilty of breaking into her grandfather's vault...and most likely a hundred more. Although she couldn't for the life of her figure out his angle for calling and telling her.

But that didn't mean he didn't have one.

"The police are on their way," he reiterated.

For some reason, that statement made her stomach dive straight to her toes. He was serious if he'd called the cops. She couldn't fathom Finn DeLuca voluntarily communicating with the authorities.

Dammit.

"I'll be there in ten minutes." Genevieve didn't bother waiting for Finn's response before hanging up.

Vaulting out of bed, she raced to Noah's room and gently scooped him up, blanket and all. He barely stirred when she strapped him into his car seat, mumbling a couple nonsense words before his half-opened eyelids closed again.

The streets were deserted as she raced across the city to her studio. Several stoplights caught her, red only to make her impatiently wait while terrible thoughts spun through her brain.

Her show was ruined. Every single one of her pieces was inside the safe in her studio. She was an idiot for leaving them all there, but considering she had nowhere else to secure them…it had been her only choice.

Turning the corner, Genevieve wanted to scream and cry when she saw the trio of police cars parked haphazardly in the street outside her studio. Blue-and-red lights flashed across the empty pavement, bouncing off the brick facade of the buildings surrounding them. The revolving lights made her dizzy.

She had no idea why she bothered to park inside the lines of the space in front of the sidewalk, other than habit.

Genevieve was half out of the car when a figure appeared inside her opened door. She yelped before realizing who was standing beside her.

Finn's hand cupped her elbow, supporting her as she stood. A zing of electricity shot up her arm and across her chest.

She couldn't deal with him right now.

Shaking him off, Genevieve maneuvered away, rounding the back of the car to the other side.

"I don't need this right now, Finn. Please go away."

Without waiting for his response, she opened the back door and ducked inside so she could gently extricate Noah, hoping the whole time that he might remain asleep. Although that probably wouldn't last long.

She had the buckle undone and the straps off his arms when she felt Finn's heat at her back.

Seriously, she just couldn't right now.

But before she could say anything, his hands were over hers, stopping her from finishing what she was doing.

Strong hands grasped her and hauled her backward out of the open doorway.

That's when he made a huge tactical error. Finn positioned himself between her and her son.

"What the hell are you doing?" she angrily whispered. "Get out of the way. This is not the time."

"No."

"Excuse me?"

"I won't let you wake him up. Noah should be home, asleep in his own bed right now."

"No joke, asshole. And the sooner you get out of my way, the sooner I can speak to the police, figure out what the hell is going on here, just how much damage has been done, so I can go home and put Noah back to bed."

"Why didn't you call Nicole back?"

Had he really just asked her that? "Because it's almost one o'clock in the morning."

"Maddie, then."

"Because that would make it better? I'm not calling anyone in the middle of the night to take care of my son. I'm perfectly capable. I'm not happy about his sleep being disturbed, but it's not an everyday occurrence. Shit happens, and as a single mother, I do the best I can to handle the obstacles." Her voice began to escalate, until it was loud enough to echo off the walls beside them. "I'm damn good at it, because I've been doing it for a long time. Noah and I can handle this. We don't need you here."

His entire face pulled tight, aristocratic features sharp and pinched. His dark coffee eyes flashed with an unexpected fire that had breath backing into her lungs.

"Tough. I'm here, anyway. I'm not judging your decisions as a mother, Genevieve. You're a damn good one and I didn't need the report sitting on my desk to tell me that. I never doubted you'd be anything but a good mother. You have an uncanny ability to put everyone else's needs before your own, a trait that motherhood has only enhanced. You need to go inside, speak to the police and tell them what's missing. I can't do that for you. What I can do is take our son home and put him back to bed. Because there's no reason he has to be here."

Genevieve stared at Finn for several seconds. A lump formed in her throat, but she refused to let it build into the emotional breakdown that threatened.

Was she an idiot for contemplating letting him take Noah?

Probably. Finn DeLuca was selfish, egotistical and too charming for his own good. But there wasn't a single part of her afraid he wouldn't take care of their son.

The man had fought too hard to get access to Noah to screw it up by doing something stupid.

"You don't know anything about taking care of a toddler."

"True, but I think I can handle unhooking the harness and getting him back into bed. Unless you expect he's going to wake up and want to throw a rave?"

Unexpected laughter burst out of her. She could totally see Finn throwing a toddler techno party, complete with funneling chocolate milk and popping fruit snacks like they were pills.

She was clearly exhausted and punch-drunk.

Her gaze drifted behind Finn to where Noah sat in his car seat. His little head was lolling against the headrest, completely oblivious to the blue-and-red lights flashing intermittently across his face.

She didn't want him here.

"Fine," she found herself saying before the decision had even fully formed. "The gold one is the key to the door from the garage." Grabbing his hand, she slapped her keys into Finn's palm.

Before she could pull away, his fingers closed around her wrist, trapping her in place. Digging something out of his pocket, he gently uncurled her fingers before placing a single car key in her palm. Instinctively, her hand closed around the hard plastic, still warm from his body heat.

"I parked by the back door. I'll text you when we get home and he's back in bed."

Nodding, Genevieve took a huge step back. "Thanks."

Her mind was a jumbled mess as she watched Finn fold his tall, muscular body into her small SUV and back away. She stared at his brake lights until they disappeared around the corner.

And only when an officer walked up beside her saying, "Ms. Reilly? I need to ask you a few questions," did she shake herself back into focus on what was going on around her.

Five

It didn't take Genevieve long to realize nothing had been stolen. Thank God whoever had broken in hadn't gotten to the vault. Probably because Finn had called in the cavalry.

It really sucked that she was annoyed and grateful at the same time, but the man had the uncanny ability to stir up a jumbled mess of emotions inside her.

A back window had been shattered. Tiny shards of glass twinkled in the bright lights someone had flipped on overhead. They reminded her of the jewels the thief had no doubt planned to snag.

Her design table had been knocked over, a spool of thin copper wire unraveling as it rolled across the floor. Papers from the desk were strewn across the room as if someone had gathered them up and just tossed them into the air. Invoices, design sketches, consignment contracts… everywhere.

But on the far wall, the vault stood, untouched.

Everything was a mess, but that could be remedied.

"I'm sorry." Nick, her head of security—her only security—walked up beside her. He shook his head as he surveyed the destruction littering the floor.

"For what? You didn't do this."

He hummed in the back of his throat. "It's my job to prevent stuff like this. We're just lucky someone saw what was happening and called it in."

Weren't they just. And as soon as she got home she was going to have a nice chat with the Good Samaritan to figure out just why the hell he'd been watching her studio late at night.

Not to mention how he'd known her babysitter's name and that Genevieve would be calling her *back*. Which implied he already knew she'd been there and left once tonight.

Maybe he was pissed someone had beaten him to breaking in. Because, really, the only reason she could think he'd be so aware of the activity at her studio would be for casing the place.

But she wasn't about to bring that up to Nick. Not yet, anyway.

"Luckily, none of the pieces were taken. It'll probably take me a couple days to clean up and organize, which will put me behind on the last two pieces. But I'll figure out how to make it work."

Assuming she ever figured out what she wanted to do with those damn stones. If she didn't…a break-in wasn't the only thing that could tank her career before it ever really got off the ground.

"I'll review the surveillance footage, see if I can find anything that might help us catch this guy. Identify any weaknesses we can shore up quickly and easily."

"And cheaply," Genevieve added with an unhappy twist of her lips.

Nick nodded, his own mouth pulling tight.

"I'm pretty sure this was just a smash and grab. The

back window was an easy target, which I already knew. I'll figure out why the glass break malfunctioned. We should have gotten an alert the minute that window shattered."

"Thanks, Nick," Genevieve said, exhaustion stealing through her body.

She'd already spent over an hour answering questions about her movements that evening, helping the police piece together a timeline. She couldn't even think about starting to tackle the mess, although at the very least the window needed to be taken care of.

On a sigh, she walked forward, ignoring the crunch of glass beneath her feet.

"If you'll wait for a few more minutes, I'll find a board to nail up over the window and drive you home."

"Thanks. I'm fine to drive home. But I'd really appreciate if you'd handle the window. I just don't have the energy. I was here late working and had just started to fall asleep when I got the call."

Nick didn't look happy but he didn't argue with her, which was a good thing because she couldn't have handled that right now. "Did you call in Nicole?"

"No."

Nick's eyes narrowed. "Then who's with Noah?"

She sighed. This wasn't going to go over well. Nick had been her friend when she worked at Reilly and was fully aware of the events surrounding her pregnancy…and the last six months as she'd fought to keep Finn out of her son's life.

"His dad."

Shock crossed Nick's face, quickly replaced with an anger that flushed his skin a mottled red. "What? How the hell did that happen?"

Not that she needed to explain herself to Nick, but she felt a responsibility to do it, anyway. He'd stuck by her side, following her even before she'd had enough money to offer him a job. He was a good friend, if a little overly protective at times. Although that was sorta his job.

"It's a long story. Let's just say he was in the right place at the right time when I needed him."

Nick's entire face twisted into a sneer. "Of course he was. Hell, he's probably responsible for the break-in in the first place. Did you think about that?"

"Yes. But it doesn't make sense. He bought the emeralds the other day. Because I refused to take his money for Noah and he was hell-bent on getting some funds in my hands. Why would he do that only to turn around and rob me?"

Nick shook his head. "You can be so naive. I have to admit it's one of the things I like best about you…normally. But not tonight. Who says his goal was stealing from you? Let me guess, he was the one who called the police."

"Yes."

"Playing the white knight is exactly the kind of con he'd set up simply to get in your good graces and earn your trust."

Nick wasn't wrong. Finn was definitely capable of orchestrating complex scenarios in order to accomplish whatever goal he wanted.

And he *had* made it clear he was hoping to become a part of her and Noah's life, whether she wanted him there or not.

"I'm not naive, Nick. I haven't been for three years."

Finn was responsible for that, and not entirely because he'd screwed her over. Even before stealing the Star… From almost their first encounter, Finn had challenged her, made her question the existence her grandfather had built around her. He'd made her realize just how sheltered—and messed up—her family dynamic was. There was nothing quite like viewing your life through someone else's eyes, especially when they thought your life was shit.

At least that was one thing he'd given her. An understanding that she didn't have to accept the way her grand-father treated her. And the strength to demand more when the time had come…and walk away when her grandfather refused.

But that didn't negate the negative things Finn had also done. "I'm fully aware he has his own agenda and I have no intention of letting it affect my own choices or path."

Nick watched her for several seconds, the hard weight of his stare making her uncomfortable. She was afraid he could see right through her. She wanted the words to be true, but…she wasn't entirely certain they were. Yet.

She let out a silent sigh when he finally said, "Good."

Closing the gap between them, Nick wrapped his arms around her. There was something comforting about his hold. Supportive and protective, something she'd needed over the last few years. Nick had become the big brother she'd never had but always wanted.

"Go home. Get some sleep. I'll fix the window and we can tackle the rest tomorrow."

Nodding against his shoulder, Genevieve blurted out, "Noah and I are lucky to have you. Thank you for all you've done for us over the past few years."

His arms tightened for a second before he was pushing her away. "Go home."

Throwing him a grateful look, Genevieve didn't hesi-tate. She was exhausted and wanted nothing better than to crawl into bed and collapse.

Although sinking down into the warm leather seat of Finn's car didn't exactly make her feel comfortable. In fact, it made her jittery. Like what she was headed for was going to be just as difficult to deal with as what she'd left behind.

Finn stood in the middle of Genevieve's living room and stared. Her place was…*adequate* was probably the best word to describe it. Nothing special, other than the personal touches she'd used to make it her own, always with an artistic eye.

The artwork on her walls might not be the masters that had hung in the drawing room at her grandfather's estate, but they were beautiful. Abstract strokes of color that made him think of calm, quiet mountains and peace.

The sofa was overstuffed and appeared pretty comfortable. A far cry from the leather monstrosity her grandfather had insisted on. Functional, not there for the appearance of a welcome with the reality of being so uninviting that whoever sat down never stayed.

He'd taken the opportunity to wander through her home. Her kitchen was spotless and the pantry well stocked with what he assumed were baby essentials. Her clothes were neat and perfectly arranged, even if her wardrobe barely filled up a quarter of the walk-in closet.

And yes, it potentially made him a pervert, but he'd opened her drawers and run his fingertips over the soft silk of her panties. At least he hadn't stolen a pair.

Really, what he'd been looking for was something he could do for her. A chore he could take off her plate since she'd no doubt have plenty to worry about in the next couple days.

But there was nothing, not even a load of laundry waiting in a hamper.

He should have known, though; Genevieve was all about the details. He'd watched her work, not only the intricate designs she was creating now, but the body of pieces she'd created for Reilly over the years. She designed with an intensity, focus and passion that was...awe-inspiring. Not to mention tempting as hell.

Noah had barely stirred when Finn lifted his son from his car seat, carried him inside and gently placed him in his crib. He'd watched Noah's little body burrow deep into the mattress, his tiny butt wiggling for several seconds until he'd found a comfortable position and dropped back to sleep.

Now what? Without anything else to keep him occupied, Finn stood in the middle of Genevieve's living room, a little at a loss.

Which wasn't comfortable at all.

He could imagine her here, curled up on her sofa, relaxed after a long day, with a glass of wine in her hand. Or in the kitchen, barefoot, a huge smile stretching her gorgeous lips as she stirred something delicious at the stove. The subtle scent of her surrounded him, making his blood whoosh faster in his veins.

This moment felt more intimate than he wanted it to be. Like he was invading her space…and she was invading his mind.

Walking over to the sofa, Finn sank down, grabbed the remote and turned the TV to some old Western rerun, hoping it would offer a distraction.

And was asleep when Genevieve walked in a little while later.

Genevieve had never felt so exhausted in her life. Not even in those first few months after bringing Noah home from the hospital, when she couldn't afford any help and had been trying to do it all herself.

God, those first months had been rough.

But tonight…she was just bone weary. Mentally, emotionally and physically exhausted.

She wasn't prepared to walk through her back door only to be stopped dead in her tracks by the sight of Finn stretched out on her couch, the video screen from the baby monitor hugged against his chest like their son was there instead.

His face was turned away from her, but even in profile

he appeared relaxed. Until that moment, she hadn't realized the complete change in him.

Before, Finn had always been relaxed. The man hadn't a care in the world. Only through hindsight had she realized nothing had been important enough to make him anxious or have him worry.

Now that the familiar expression had slackened his features, she realized Finn had been walking around carrying the serious weight of stress the handful of times she'd seen him since he'd returned.

Was it her? Noah? His time in prison? All of the above?

And did it really matter?

She didn't want it to, but maybe it did. *Crap.*

Kicking off her shoes and leaving them in a pile near the kitchen door, Genevieve padded across the room on quiet feet. Leaning over, she attempted to gently uncurl Finn's fingers from around the screen so she could take it to the bedroom with her.

Her plan was simply to leave him right where he was. It was damn late and only someone heartless would make him go home at this hour. Especially since he'd not only saved her studio, but taken care of her son so she could handle the fallout.

However, that plan didn't quite go as expected.

One second he was clearly asleep, the next his hand was wrapped around her wrist, and before she could blink, he'd pulled and had her tumbling across his hard body.

Genevieve let out a startled gasp. Her mouth landed against the warm curve of his throat, and before she could stop herself, her tongue darted out to steal a taste of his salty skin.

The soft angles of her body melted against his solid form. The hard band of his arm snaked around her waist, even as his fingers tightened their hold on her wrist.

His dark eyes glowed as he silently watched her, making heat spread through her entire body. Genevieve stared down at him, afraid to even breathe.

Slowly, he blinked. And just as quickly as she'd tumbled onto him, she found herself back on her feet. His fingers dragged against her skin, letting her go and taking several steps backward.

"I'm sorry, Genni. You startled me. Are you okay?"

Was she? Clearing her throat, she forced herself to say, "I'm fine. I didn't mean to startle *you*."

The warmth of his throaty chuckle washed across her senses. "I guess we both got a surprise."

That was one way to put it.

"Everything go okay with the police? They have any thoughts on who might have broken in?"

Genevieve's throat was bone-dry, but somehow she was able to answer, "I don't really want to talk about it right now. What I need is to go to bed. No doubt Noah will be up bright and early like always. Toddlers wait for nothing and no one, not even late-night drama."

Instead of laughing at her lame attempt at humor as she'd expected, a frown pulled the space between Finn's gorgeous eyes. "I'll come over in the morning and handle Noah for you. You need some sleep."

God, yes, she did. But that probably wouldn't happen if Finn showed back up at her house tomorrow morning. Besides… "He's not something that needs to be handled."

His frown deepened. "I'm aware of that. You know what I meant."

"You've already helped enough."

"No, I haven't." Shaking his head, Finn started for her front door.

"Wait." *Goddammit*. What was she doing? "It's late. And something tells me whether I want you to or not, you'll be on my front porch right about sunrise."

He shrugged his shoulders.

"Stay. I'll make up the guest room. It's the least I can do after your help tonight."

Finn had been exhausted, but it was difficult to drop into sleep knowing Genevieve was down the hall. Especially after being woken up by the feel of her soft body falling against his.

It had taken everything inside him to set her back on her feet and not strip her naked so he could explore the luscious curves of her body.

So, he'd been restless and horny as hell. Which explained why he was groggy and bleary-eyed when he finally woke up the next morning. He didn't mind losing sleep…when it was necessary and worth it.

Rolling out of bed, he pulled on the pair of jeans he'd been wearing last night, not bothering with his Henley. If he'd been a gentleman, he would have. But that wasn't something he'd ever aspired to being.

And maybe there was a small part of him that wanted to know if Genevieve would still react to seeing him half-naked as she'd used to. He'd never been the kind of man to ignore an opportunity.

Padding out into the hallway, he listened for noise of some kind. Didn't babies like to cry and laugh and play?

But the place was eerily quiet.

Sticking his head inside Noah's room, Finn registered that the crib he'd laid his son in last night was empty. So was the office and the living room as he passed through.

The kitchen was empty, as well, although there was a coffee maker with an empty mug and an assortment of pods sitting on the counter just waiting.

His eyebrows beetled in confusion—had Genevieve left? He walked across to pop a pod in and start the drip of coffee into the waiting mug. Not that it would necessarily matter. She'd have to come home at some point. He could wait.

It wasn't until he crossed to the fridge for cream that he found her. Sitting outside on her back patio, legs curled up beneath her as she moved lazily on a swing. Her own mug was cradled between both palms and pressed against her chest, forgotten as she stared out across her open backyard.

God, he hated that expression on her face. Pensive and entirely too troubled. He recognized it from before. Usually only after she'd had a run-in with her grandfather. The man had the ability to take every spec of light that Genevieve harbored inside and snuff it out with a single well-directed, disparaging remark.

Her grandfather wasn't part of her life anymore, though, which made seeing it now almost worse. Now, just like back then, Finn had the undeniable urge to make the expression disappear at any cost.

Stepping through the back door, he joined her outside. The morning was crisp and cool. A slight salty tang hung in the air. Genevieve's backyard was nice, if on the small side. It was clearly set up for a child, with a swing set in the far corner and a sandbox up closer to the stone patio.

Genevieve didn't bother turning his direction when he walked up, although he knew she was aware that he'd come out. Her shoulders tensed, as if preparing for a fight.

Which was the last thing he wanted.

Sitting down next to her on the swing, he let his legs sprawl out, crowding into her personal space. "Where's Noah?"

"Where's your shirt?"

A quick shot of amusement tugged at the corners of his mouth. "You go first."

"My friend came and picked him up a little while ago."

Disappointment shot through him. He'd been looking

forward to spending time with the both of them this morning. "Why?"

"It's our normal routine and I didn't see a reason to change it." For the first time since he'd walked out, she turned to him. Her gaze ripped down his body with the speed of a hummingbird's wings before jerking away again.

Interesting.

"Besides, I thought there were a few things we needed to discuss."

Without their son to distract either of them. Fine with him.

"I spoke with Nick this morning. He's preparing surveillance footage to give to the police."

"Excellent. I'll get my footage together, as well." Although he had every intention of keeping a couple of the cameras he'd installed to himself. The first rule of power was never reveal all your secrets.

This time when she looked at him her eyes were narrowed, but even as slits, Finn could see the shrewd calculation behind them. Genevieve might be naive, but she was far from stupid.

"And just why do you have footage to share? How did you know what was happening before Nick did?"

Finn took a quick sip of coffee and scalded his tongue. Stalling a little longer, he leaned forward and set the mug on the ground beneath them. "Do you really think I'd leave you and my son unprotected?"

She shook her head, her eyebrows crinkling with irritation and confusion. "What exactly do you think we need protection from? You're the most dangerous person in our lives."

That stung, although he really didn't think she'd meant it to.

"Obviously not, considering last night. You know better, Genevieve. You come from the world of privilege and money."

"None of that was ever mine."

"Maybe not, but not everyone understands. And plenty of people are aware who Noah's father is. If they weren't before, the public visitation proceedings fixed that. I might be a degenerate and an asshole, but I'm a filthy-rich one. And where there's money there are always people willing to take it."

"You'd certainly know," she mumbled under her breath.

If her words were intended to wound, they didn't. In fact, as far as he was concerned, she'd proved his point.

"Exactly. I take advantage of people's weaknesses. My philosophy has always been if you can't protect something, you don't deserve to own it."

"You don't own me or our son."

"No, I don't. But you and Noah are the most important parts of my life. And I won't let someone hurt you in order to get to me. I was never afraid of making enemies. I had plenty before I went to prison, and I made a few more while I was there."

Genevieve recoiled. "Are you saying Noah and I are in danger? Is there something I should be concerned about?"

"No, I'm just not willing to take any risks. I saw vulnerabilities in your security and I plugged the holes. And it turns out I was right, wasn't I?"

Finn watched Genevieve's jaw tighten and her eyes flash. "Instead of talking to me about it, you decided to take care of it yourself?"

He shrugged, unwilling to apologize for doing what he thought he needed to. "After the end run I had to do just to get a few thousand dollars into your hands…let's just say I didn't expect you to be receptive to either my observations or my footing the bill to correct the deficiencies. Like I said the other night, I have copies of your financials. You have no secrets from me, Genevieve."

Six

God, she hoped that wasn't true.

The last thing she needed was for Finn to know just how difficult it was to keep her hands to herself. Even pissed at him.

Damn him.

"Just because you might not like my answer doesn't give you the right to do whatever the hell you want, Finn. That's not how adult relationships work."

"Is that what this is, an adult relationship? Because if it is, I'd like to lodge a complaint. I'm not getting any of the adult perks."

How could the man make her body flush with heat at the same time she wanted to smack him across the face? "You know exactly what to say to get a rise out of me, don't you?"

"God, I hope so. Although I think you've gotten our anatomy confused again."

"You're incorrigible, and I'm still pissed at you."

Finn shrugged. "You can be pissed all you want. I won't apologize for protecting you and Noah."

Tipping her head back, Genevieve looked at the sky and prayed for patience. It didn't really help.

Pulling in a deep breath, she brought her focus back to Finn. "Were you going to tell me about the extra surveillance?"

"Eventually."

"Do I want to know when you thought that might be?"

"Probably not."

Well, she'd never said the man was stupid. In fact, he was too damn brilliant for his own good. Or hers, for that matter.

"But I need your permission to upgrade the system inside your studio, so sooner rather than later."

Letting out a frustrated sound, Genevieve gave up. Nothing she said would make a difference. Apparently, Finn could be stubborn as hell when he wanted to. Who knew?

"I think the words you're looking for are *thank you*."

"No, they really aren't." But weren't they? Even with his high-handed, sly tactics, Finn had saved her a lot of headache. Scrunching her nose up in distaste, Genevieve reluctantly said, "Fine. Thank you."

"Was that so difficult?"

Yes, it really was.

"You're welcome. While we're discussing security, I should probably also let you know that I have a couple people analyzing the surveillance footage. While I'm certain they do the best they can, I don't necessarily trust our police force to put a ton of effort into finding a burglar who didn't actually steal anything."

Did she want to know who these people of his were? Apparently, she must have voiced the thought aloud because Finn actually answered.

"There are only a few people I'd trust with those most important to me. Stone and Gray are at the top of that list."

"Stone and Gray?"

"Anderson Stone and Gray Lockwood."

Of course she'd heard of both men. Anderson Stone had been in the media recently because of the controversy surrounding his own incarceration for manslaughter. And Gray Lockwood's embezzlement conviction had been watercooler fodder a few years ago.

"They're both better men than I could ever aspire to be."

Genevieve was surprised at Finn's confession, but found that hard to believe. It wasn't a point worth arguing over, though.

"They recently opened a security firm. They're both rich enough to be picky about the clients they take on and the cases they investigate. Right now, you're their only client."

"What do you mean I'm their only client?"

"Well, aside from working to prove Gray's innocence. I hired them to keep an eye on you and Noah."

Pushing up from the swing, Finn walked a few steps away. As Finn leaned his back against her porch railing, Genevieve couldn't stop herself from noticing the wide expanse of his hands, or the strength and dexterity of his fingers as he wrapped them around the long plank of wood behind him.

She remembered how he could make her feel with those fingers. The pleasure and excitement. With nothing more than a molten glance, Finn could make her feel desired, wanted. Sexy.

When she was with Finn, she saw herself differently. Because he'd seen her differently.

He'd convinced her that she deserved better than her grandfather's constant disapproval and criticism. She was smart and talented, but Finn was the first person in her life to convince her that was true.

To show her she was strong when she'd always thought herself weak.

"Why would you do that?" she finally asked, unsure she really wanted to know the answer.

"Because you and Noah matter to me. What will it take to make you believe me?"

Air backed up in her lungs. She wanted to tear her gaze from his, find her equilibrium so she could feel in control again. But he wouldn't let her go. His gaze was magnetic. Imploring. Tempting.

"I know I hurt you, Genni. And I know it can't take that pain away, but if it helps, I hurt myself, too."

"You're just saying that because I'm the first woman who's ever told you *no*. I'm the first one to resist."

Finn's head tipped sideways. A flash of something crossed his face. It was so fast Genevieve didn't have time to analyze or name it. But her belly certainly managed an interpretation as it gave a slow roll. She was in trouble.

Before she could react, Finn was across the porch and in her personal space. Reaching down, he grasped her under the arms and lifted her up. His hard body pressed into her from shoulder to hip.

Yep, big trouble.

Her body melted, traitor that it was, sinking into his hold.

Leaning close, Finn brought his lips to her ear and murmured, "Baby, don't lie. We both know you wouldn't be able to resist if I put my mind to seducing you."

Her mouth opened to protest, but her brain shut down the words before they could leave her lips. Because he was right.

Even now, tiny tremors rolled through Genevieve's body.

Tipping her head back, she stared up at him. Torn by what she should do and what she wanted to do—which was grab him and kiss the hell out of him.

She'd spent so much of her life afraid to do anything but what she'd been told. She never broke the rules or took any risk.

Until Finn.

He'd given her the confidence to be herself. And for that

she'd always be grateful, no matter what else happened be-tween them.

But what good was that lesson if she chose to ignore it when she was scared?

And everything about Finn DeLuca scared the hell out of her. Because nothing with him was simple or easy.

Her grandfather had ordered her to leave Finn alone. But for the first time in her life, she'd disobeyed. And look how that had turned out.

The weeks they'd shared had been a whirlwind of amaz-ing. He'd made her feel special, powerful, beautiful. She'd taken a risk…and he'd betrayed her in the worst way.

After everything she'd been through, Genevieve had wanted to find a nice, quiet life with her son. No drama. No demanding men or complicated, forbidden love affairs.

She'd had that for the last couple years.

And she'd been bored out of her mind. She'd tried to convince herself that she hadn't needed or wanted the ex-citement Finn had shown her.

Such a lie.

Like a drug, she craved it. She craved him.

He'd awakened something inside her. And she was tired of denying what she wanted in order to do the right thing.

Who decided what was right, anyway?

Cupping her palms around Finn's jaw, she guided him down until their mouths touched.

And then she had no idea what to do next.

Finn's hands balled into fists at his hips. That was the only thing preventing him from snatching Genevieve up and hauling her hard against him.

But, God, he wanted to. He wanted *her*. And the fact that she'd been the one to initiate the kiss…amazing. And sexy as hell.

But a huge part of him wanted to see what she'd do next. How far would she take it?

Her hands landed lightly on his chest. She barely touched him, just skimming the surface as her fingers slid up his body. His dick shouldn't go half-hard from just that, but it did.

Rocking forward, Genevieve brought her body closer. Chest to belly, he could feel all of her soft curves and wanted them naked against his skin. Tilting her head, she changed the kiss, opened to him. Licked her tongue across his lips, asking for more.

He never wanted to deny her anything, least of all that.

Finn let himself sink into the kiss, although he was careful not to move. Because the minute he did...he didn't trust himself to keep control. He wanted her too much.

Instead, he watched her eyes drift shut. Her sigh brushed against his open mouth. Gorgeous. She was like the most precious work of art, vibrant and alive. He could stare at her for hours and never get bored. Not something he could say about much else in his life.

Most people bored the shit out of him. But never Genevieve, which didn't make any sense.

A tiny crease wrinkled the space right between her eyes. They fluttered open. She pulled back, breaking the physical connection between them. Her pale green eyes, huge and slightly unfocused, stared up at him as she asked, "What do you want from me?"

Everything. The word blasted through his brain. But he was intelligent enough to prevent it from spilling from his lips.

"Right now? I want you to kiss me again. I want to pick you up, carry you inside and make love to you until we're both so exhausted we can't see straight."

Her sharp intake of breath dragged over him. Her pupils dilated and her body swayed closer. Triumph thrilled through him. She was teetering on the edge.

"But more than that, I want you to trust me."

And just as quickly as the dewy, distracted, sexy expression on her face had appeared, it vanished.

Well, shit.

Blowing out an annoyed breath, Genevieve swept a hand through her messy hair and took a step back. "Why couldn't you just stop at the sex?"

Her honest words surprised him, although they probably shouldn't. But he'd match her frankness just the same. "Because there's more between us. We have a son together and I want to be a part of his life."

"So you've said."

Finn chose to ignore the rueful tint to her words. "As much as I want you right now—and every time I'm within ten feet of you—I need more than amazing sex."

Palm against his chest, Genevieve put more space between them. She sank back into the waiting swing and pushed off with her feet. Every inch between them felt wrong, but the fact that she was still on the porch… For the first time since he'd watched the hurt and disappointment fill her face as the officer snapped handcuffs around his wrists, Finn wondered if there was a way back to what they'd had together.

Genevieve watched him, her eyes sharp as they searched his face in a way that made his skin feel too tight for his body. Slowly shaking her head, Genevieve finally said, "The problem is, I never know when you're giving me a line and when you're telling me the truth."

"I always tell you the truth, and I always will."

"Sure, just like you told me you were watching me."

Crossing his arms over his chest, Finn gave her a disappointed look. "Genni, you didn't ask me."

"Because it never occurred to me I needed to."

"Then you weren't paying attention and don't really know me."

Her lips twisting into a rueful grimace, she mumbled, "That's what I've been saying."

"Then let's fix that. Spend time with me and I'll tell you anything you want to know." Or, at least, the pieces he wanted her to know. His life contained plenty of shit he didn't want touching her. Things he'd never let taint her or his son.

He'd have to be careful, because he truly meant what he'd said. Finn never wanted to lie to Genevieve, but he understood the valuable use of creative omission. Ultimately, the more time they spent together, the more opportunities he had to win her trust. To prove she could let him into her and Noah's life without fearing he would betray her again.

"Have dinner with me tonight."

Her mouth opened and Finn could see the protest sitting there, right on her lips. But she didn't give it to him. Instead, she waited for several seconds before finally nodding her head. "Okay."

Moving fast, before she changed her mind, Finn pushed away from the railing and started back inside. "Perfect. I'll send a car for you at seven. In the meantime, Stone or Gray will probably be contacting you about upgrading the security system here at the house and at the studio."

Moving through the kitchen, Finn dropped his mug on the counter and scooped his keys off the hook where Genevieve had obviously left them last night.

Following quickly behind him, she grasped his arm and pulled him around to face her. "Wait. What?"

"Now that I have full access to your security system, I want to upgrade everything. Your equipment is seriously out of date. You're vulnerable."

Shaking her head, Genevieve said, "I didn't say you could have full access to anything."

Finn gave her a half grin. "Ah, but you didn't say I couldn't. Be smart, Genevieve. I'm the perfect person to spot the vulnerabilities and help correct them. Let me do this."

He could see the gears turning inside Genevieve's head as she considered. No doubt she was trying to figure out what he might have to gain. It sucked that he'd put doubt into her head. But it was impossible to change the past.

All he could do was work on what came next.

What is his angle?

Genevieve studied Finn, her brain whirling as she tried to come up with something...but there was nothing.

They both knew if he'd wanted to rob her blind he'd had plenty of opportunity. So it wasn't money or the jewels in her safe. It definitely wasn't access to her grandfather's inventory since she no longer had that. He'd already won visitation with Noah and she'd been more than accommodating on that front.

She couldn't figure out how updating her surveillance system could benefit him.

Oh, she had no doubt Finn had a motive. He didn't do anything without a hidden agenda. She just hadn't figured it out yet.

Which scared her.

But she also couldn't argue with his logic. He was no doubt the best person to pinpoint her security weaknesses and suggest how to mitigate them. Hell, he'd probably logged at least a half dozen ways he could rob her blind after five seconds inside her studio.

She might not have known much about Finn DeLuca when he'd first come into her life. But afterward...she'd made it a point to learn as much as she could about her son's father. Her curiosity had nothing to do with the fact that she'd felt lost, vulnerable and idiotic after he'd used her. Nope, not at all.

But the information she'd uncovered—admittedly, with Nick's help—had been eye-opening. Stealing the Star of Reilly might have been the first time Finn had gotten caught, but he had quite the reputation within certain circles. Rumors and innuendo followed him right along with the trail of broken hearts he liked to leave behind.

He'd been on the radar of several law enforcement agencies, insurance companies and crime families. However, the DeLuca name, seamlessly limitless purse strings, charm and devil-may-care attitude seemed to protect him from actual prosecution.

And the man didn't give a rip about rumor or innuendo. He didn't give a shit what anyone else thought of him.

Which was one of the qualities that had intrigued her about him in the first place.

And it still did.

He was so different from her in that respect. She envied him that quality, even as she realized he often took it too far to the other extreme.

However, watching him now, she had to wonder if going to prison had really and truly changed him.

The Finn she'd known before wouldn't have hesitated to take advantage of what she'd offered him. It hadn't escaped her notice that he'd obviously been interested. The hard length of his erection had been pressed tight against her belly.

Not to mention, he'd single-handedly saved her collection last night. She'd invested everything she had into these pieces and this show.

Crap. "Fine. Have your friends contact Nick."

Finn's jaw tightened. "No, I want them working with you directly. I don't trust Nick."

"Why? I've known him for years. Certainly longer than you. He worked with me at Reilly. He quit his job and followed me when I left. He's been a good friend. One of a handful of people I know I can count on."

"Are you really that blind?"

What the heck was he talking about? "What?"

"He's in love with you."

Genevieve scoffed. "No, he isn't. He's like my brother."

"You might see him that way, but trust me, that man wants in your pants."

Nope. "You're wrong. He's never made a single move."

"Which just means he's not certain of his reception." Closing the distance between them, Finn cupped her jaw, angling her face up to his. "Trust me, I know people. That man fancies himself in love with you. He relishes his role of protector and he isn't going to appreciate you getting advice or assistance from someone else. Especially if that someone is me. Nick will stonewall my people."

"No, he wouldn't. He'll recognize the value and appreciate the help. He's been a one-man show for a long time."

His fingers tightened on her jaw, gently urging her up onto her toes as he brought his own mouth down to connect with hers. The kiss was quick, but full of heat, stoking at the embers and making need flare through her hot and hard.

Murmuring against her lips, he said, "You really are naive. Luckily, it's one of the things I appreciate most about you," before stepping back and letting her go.

Genevieve's brain reeled, from both the kiss and Finn's words. How could the man take something that was clearly not a compliment and twist it until it became one?

God, he confused her.

"Stone and Gray deal directly with you," he reiterated in a tone that left no room for argument.

She really didn't have the time for that, but clearly Finn wasn't budging. "Whatever. But I've got a lot of work to do."

"Don't worry. The disruption will be minimal."

Yeah, right. Something told her Finn's definition of minimal and hers were probably two different things.

Seven

"**I** need your help." Finn didn't beat around the bush as he walked into Stone's office.

First, he knew his friend was going to agree. He, Stone and Gray had had each other's backs long enough that there was no doubt he could count on his friend for anything.

What was up in the air was whether Stone would provide the help for free, or if he was going to use this opportunity to extract a little payment.

He was a businessman, after all. And a damn good one.

Besides, that's how their world worked. A favor for a favor, even among friends.

Plopping into the chair across from the large mahogany desk his friend currently had his feet propped up on, Finn waited to find out.

Stone watched him for several seconds, his standard, blank expression on his face. That poker face had been one of Stone's biggest assets on the inside. No one knew what was going on inside that scarily brilliant mind of his. Not even his best friends.

Finn was no slouch when it came to intelligence. He'd

received the best education money could buy. The rest of his knowledge he'd gained from hands-on experience. He was an excellent judge of character and understood how to intuit a person's desire to use it for his own advantage.

He'd never once been able to manipulate Stone. And it certainly wasn't for lack of trying. He did live for a challenge, after all.

After several seconds, a brilliant smile bloomed across Stone's face. "That's handy, because I need your help, as well."

So that was how he was going to play it.

"How did I know you were going to say that?"

"Because you're an intelligent man?"

"Uh-huh. Stop blowing smoke up my ass and tell me what this is going to cost me."

"Everything."

At least his friend was honest. That was one of the things he valued most about his friendship with Stone. He trusted the man implicitly, and that wasn't something he could say about many people.

Exactly three, in fact. Stone, Gray and Genevieve.

Finn let out a groan, already anticipating what Stone was going to say. "No."

"Yes."

"This is highway robbery."

"No, it's negotiation, and you're damn good at it. You walked in here fully aware of exactly what I was going to say."

That was true, but it didn't mean he couldn't protest. Loudly.

"You're being an idiot."

"No, I'm not."

"You know I want nothing to do with the business. You're going to extort—"

"Haggle."

Finn ignored Stone's interjection. "My participation. You realize that's a terrible way to gain cooperation. I have no incentive to care about the business. You're going to give me a chunk of your profits for nothing in return."

Stone laced his fingers behind his head and leaned farther back into his chair. A satisfied grin split his lips and Finn fought the very real urge to reach across the desk and deck him. The man could use a little crooked nose to make his pretty face less perfect.

"You forget, I know you better than just about anyone."

Oh, Finn wasn't forgetting anything.

"You like to pretend you're some debauched billionaire living the playboy lifestyle. However, we both know you work damn hard at something when you want to."

"Sure, but you fail to grasp that *I don't want to*."

Stone shrugged. "Then it's my job to bring you something that piques your interest. Luckily, I have just the thing."

Of course he did. *Dammit.*

Shooting forward, Stone dropped his feet to the ground with a resounding thud. With quick, efficient movements, he snapped open a drawer, pulled out a folder and slid it across the desk toward Finn.

"The document is pretty straightforward, but feel free to have your lawyer take a look before you sign it."

Yeah, right. Finn wouldn't bother wasting the time. He had no doubt Stone had covered everything.

"You had this just ready and waiting?"

"Let's say I'm optimistically prepared."

"Asshole."

Flipping open the folder, Finn's gaze scanned the partnership agreement making him one-third owner in Stone Surveillance. No doubt the rest of it detailed the role each partner would play in the business, but it didn't really matter.

He'd do whatever his friends needed him to, which Stone had already been aware of. Finn didn't need to be a partner in order to help. But Stone had a need for the world to be fair, which was why he'd been hounding Finn for months to join the company.

It wasn't like Finn needed the money, although he had no doubt Stone Surveillance would become highly successful.

Without bothering to read the rest of it, Finn snatched up the heavy gold pen sitting on the desk and scrawled his name across the bottom of the last page. Flipping the folder closed, he shoved it back across to Stone.

"Happy?"

"Yep."

Well, that made one of them, but Finn wasn't going to argue with him anymore.

"I need you to get a team over to Genevieve's studio and home. The technology on her security system leaves a hell of a lot to be desired. I also need Gray to see if he can scrub the footage from last night to get more information. I want to know who the asshole is so I can beat him into the ground."

Stone pressed a button on the phone sitting on his desk, and Finn heard a beeping noise from the outer office. A few moments later a woman in her late thirties slipped into the room. She was pretty. Dressed conservatively and with a pleasant, accommodating smile on her face.

"Yes, Mr. Stone?"

Holding out the folder, Stone said, "Please make a copy of the document and bring it back for Mr. DeLuca."

Losing patience, Finn said, "I don't give a shit about the paperwork, Stone."

"I know, but I do."

The woman didn't even acknowledge the conversation. With a nod, she took the folder and disappeared back out the door.

Flipping his wrist over, Stone glanced at the heavy platinum watch. "A team's been at Genevieve's studio for about two hours now. They should have the equipment installed by late this afternoon. We'll move to her personal residence tomorrow. Gray should have a preliminary report by the morning, although he's already warned me there's not a lot to work with."

Finn frowned. "That doesn't sound like an amateur smash and grab."

"No, it doesn't," Stone agreed. But he didn't add anything else. And he wouldn't until he had definitive information to pass along.

In the meantime... "Thank you."

"You're welcome. I know she's important to you."

Finn's gaze narrowed. "My son is important to me, so yes, her safety and livelihood are important."

Stone didn't say anything, just raised a single eyebrow.

Finn wanted to argue, but he couldn't. For the first time since he'd watched a shadowy figure appear on the screen last night, he finally let his body relax.

"We've got you, Finn."

You'd think after several years he'd be used to that fact. But he wasn't. It had been a very long time since there'd been anyone in his life who unconditionally had his back. Not since Sawyer...

"Now, let me tell you how you can help us."

Genevieve tried to concentrate on the stones spread in front of her. Frowning, she moved them around. Again.

An itchy, restless sensation crawled beneath her skin. It was part frustration with the design she was supposed to be working on. Pushed up against a timeline that couldn't budge, she'd forced herself to start the setting for several of the smaller stones. But she wasn't happy. It just didn't feel right.

Unfortunately, she didn't have a better plan so she was moving forward, anyway. But the tedious work of preparing the settings, molding the platinum and gold, polishing them, measuring, marking and scoring for the gems…it was all time-consuming and she couldn't help but feel the time was wasted.

Adding to her level of frustration was the extra layer of edginess Finn's presence was causing her. If she'd known he would tag along with the team his friends had sent to upgrade her surveillance system, then she might have found a good reason to stay home.

Not that she could afford to lose a day of work.

Genevieve was at the microscope, using it to prepare a halo she was creating for one of the stones when a tremor bolted through her body. Her hands, usually rock steady when she was working, shook. The delicate instrument she was using jumped, scraping across the polished surface of platinum and leaving a mark.

"Dammit," she growled, pushing violently back from the expensive piece of equipment before she did something stupid and regretful. The casters on the bottom of her chair rattled as she rolled across the floor, but stopped suddenly when she crashed into something unexpected.

Or someone.

Finn's hands settled over her shoulders. "Easy there. What's wrong?"

What was wrong? Everything. Looking down at her hands in her lap, she realized they were trembling. And she still held the instrument she'd been using in a too-tight grip. Twisting to the side, she gently set the thing on the surface of a worktable and then shook out her hand.

Pushing up from the chair, she pivoted and moved out from beneath Finn's grip. Right now, she didn't want him to touch her.

Or she wanted him to touch her too much. She was no longer certain which one.

"What's wrong?" she repeated his question, still uncertain exactly what to say.

She wanted to yell at him. To tell him he was the problem. He and his friends who'd been in her space for the last couple days. Disrupting her work, sending Nick into a tizzy and making her life generally more complicated.

But that wasn't exactly fair. Sure, the mistake she'd just made—one that would set her back several hours of work—wasn't his fault. Even if his presence had been the reason for the jolt through her body.

Genevieve had known the moment he walked into the studio. Her body responded. Wanted.

Damn him.

Licking a tongue across suddenly dry lips, she answered in the only way that wouldn't reveal too much. "Just a problem with the design."

Holding out a hand, he said, "Let me see."

"No."

A single dark eyebrow winged up and he waited, hand outstretched. Several tense seconds pulled between them. Finally, with a frustrated sigh, she reached behind her, snatched the piece up and slapped it against his palm.

Squinting, he brought it close so he could inspect the setting. His lips pursed as he turned it. Finally, he closed a fist around it and dropped it to his side.

"Aside from the scratch, it's good work."

Genevieve nodded, expecting nothing less. But he didn't stop there.

"Your heart isn't in this."

No, it wasn't. "I know."

"Then why are you working on it?"

"Because I don't have a choice. I need to finish the piece and there isn't enough time if I don't get to work on it now."

Reaching for her, Finn wrapped his hands around her arms and gently pulled her close. The warmth of his body was so tempting, especially when he just held her for several seconds. Tucking her head against his chest, he rested his chin on the crown of her head. Together, they stood there and breathed.

And for the first time in weeks a sense of calm washed over her.

Pulling in a deep breath, Genevieve held it for several seconds before blowing it out on a long streaming sigh.

Shifting, Finn pushed her out to arm's length and guided her over to one of the high stools she kept in the studio. Edging her down onto it, he said, "Show me the design."

Genevieve shook her head. "I don't have one."

"Why not?"

It was a valid question. Normally, she started with a sketch, transferred the idea into a program on her computer that set the dimensions of the entire piece and allowed her to make adjustments down to millimeters.

The problem was, none of the sketches she'd done had felt good enough to move to the program. But she'd been out of time so decided to use the old-school method and just wing it. Part of her had hoped inspiration would strike while she was working with the stones.

Clearly, that wasn't happening.

Finn watched Genevieve's internal struggle. Disappointment, desperation and anxiety crossed her beautiful face. His first thought was how he could fix the problem for her.

Finally, she shrugged her shoulders. "None of the designs felt right. But I don't have time to wait for inspiration. I need to get started on the piece or it'll never be ready in time."

"Show me."

Shaking her head, Genevieve said, "This isn't your problem."

Maybe not, but he wasn't about to leave her frustrated and unhappy when there was potentially something he could do about it. "Show me."

Wrinkling her nose, she finally turned to the large safe mounted on the far wall of her workroom. Finn didn't bother to look away as she entered the combination on the keypad. Mostly because knowing the code wouldn't make a damn bit of difference. If he'd wanted inside it would have taken him less than ninety seconds. Upgrading the thing was next on his list.

The heavy door creaked, metal scraping against metal, as Genevieve swung it wide. Inside, there were several shelves and drawers. Reaching for one in the middle, she pulled it fully out of the safe. Cradling it in her arms, she turned to the worktable and set it down.

Stepping closer, Finn peered down at the seven stones spread across the black velvet.

He wasn't sure what he'd expected, but the deep purplish-red of the alexandrite wasn't it. In artificial light some people mistook the gems for rubies, but Finn knew immediately what Genevieve had.

Grabbing the biggest stone—at least three carats and worth probably around thirty thousand depending on the gem's ability to shift color—he walked across the room. The stone was cool in his palm. He couldn't help but move his hand up and down in an unconscious attempt to pinpoint the weight.

Thrusting it into the natural light streaming in from the floor-to-ceiling window, the gem shifted to a deep turquoise color that had breath backing into his lungs. "Gorgeous," he breathed.

Alexandrite might not be as expensive as diamonds, but it was rarer. Especially at this quality.

Even engrossed in the stone, he knew Genevieve was standing right beside him. Her soft, floral scent washed over him, filling his head and making his blood whoosh. The need for her was always right there, churning beneath the surface.

"Do all the other stones have this depth of color?"

Reaching out, Genevieve ran a soft fingertip over the beveled surface. "Yes."

And he was immediately half-hard, needing her to touch him in the same reverent way.

Nope, now was not the time.

"The stones are gorgeous. Seductive. Why is it so hard to find the right design?"

Finn didn't think her distracted question was actually directed at him. It was clearly an internal one, and one she'd asked herself before with no real answer.

Closing his fist around the stone, Finn registered the way it absorbed his body heat, soaking in warmth just as it did the light.

Genevieve's gaze skipped up to his. The way she looked at him... Finn's chest tightened, trepidation and need twisting into a painful band.

"We'll figure this out," he promised, reaching up and running a finger down the soft slope of her jaw.

She blinked, unconsciously leaning into his touch. "I've had the stones for two months. I haven't figured it out yet."

"I wasn't here." Finn flashed her a self-deprecating smile and started walking backward.

Genevieve let out a groan and rolled her eyes. "Your ego is enormous."

Finn's grin grew. He kept backing toward the worktable and after several seconds she followed. When his back bumped against the edge, he turned to set the gem onto the black velvet.

Picking up each of the other stones, he studied them

for several seconds before placing them next to the largest. Genevieve slid up beside him, her tiny, talented hands gripping tightly to the edge of the table.

Once the gems were displayed, Finn tilted his head and looked at them as a whole.

"One piece or several?"

"The smart move is a necklace, earrings and bracelet."

"Sure." That made sense. She had enough stones of varying sizes to make a set. But it was expected and safe. Two words the world might use to describe Genevieve…but that was only because they didn't really know her.

Not like he did.

In many ways, Genevieve was just like the gems she worked with. Polished and perfect on the outside. But on the inside…only the best gemstones held fire.

"Why do you need to make the safe choice?"

"Because I have a business and brand to build. I have a son to support. I need to make smart choices."

Hearing her say those words made him cringe. Genevieve had spent a lifetime making smart choices. But that was such a bland existence. He better than anyone understood that living a perfect life didn't necessarily mean safety, happiness and longevity.

Sawyer had been the angel to Finn's devil. And look at what had happened to him…

"In this case, I think playing it safe is working against you. These stones scream for something outrageous and amazing. They need to be the jewels in someone's crown."

"I'm designing for the commercial market. Yes, these pieces are custom, but each piece will inspire pieces that can be sold and marketed in each of the Mitchell Brothers' stores. Not many women need a crown."

"I'm perfectly aware of how your arrangement is supposed to work." And not just simply because he'd gotten his hands on a copy of her contract with the brothers and had his own legal team review it. "But you already have several pieces that accomplish that goal. What you don't have is a centerpiece you can use to make a media splash at the premiere."

In the right design, Finn had no doubt these stones would make everyone salivate. They were unexpected, but so gorgeously seductive.

"I have so much money tied up in the stones. I need the piece to sell, not just cause a scene."

"How about this, I promise if no one else shows interest, then I'll buy it."

This time when Genevieve frowned, it was directed straight at him. He felt the impact of her irritation, but let it roll right off him.

"You promised you wouldn't buy any more of my pieces just for the sake of getting me money."

Shifting closer, Finn let his fingertips slip down the line of her jaw. Her skin was so soft and smooth. A warm contrast to the cool gem he'd held just moments ago. Using the pressure of his finger, he tipped her chin up.

Her eyes dilated and her pink lips parted. She unconsciously leaned closer, begging him to kiss her.

Instead, he maneuvered so he could stare straight into her pale green eyes. "When will you understand I don't do anything I don't want to? I want to take care of you and Noah."

"We don't need to be taken care of."

"I'm aware. Doesn't prevent me from wanting to do it. I also want these stones. They're gorgeous. I happen to have faith that the design you come up with will be amazing. If nothing else, purchasing them will be a wonderful investment."

"You have more faith in me than I do right now."

Eight

What was it about the man that cut straight through all of her defenses?

His fingers slipped across her skin, sending a wave of goose bumps down her arms. Genevieve stared up at him, utterly drowning in his deep brown eyes.

"Genevieve, I have no doubt you can accomplish anything you set your mind to. But if you need my faith in you right now until you can find your own...you're welcome to it."

Hell. The words coming out of his mouth were a line. But the expression in his eyes was pure sincerity. Her brain told her not to fall for it. The rest of her wanted to dive headfirst into him.

"If you weren't thinking about commerciality, what would you do?"

Genevieve stared at the stones, thoughts and ideas flying through her brain. As soon as one popped up, though, she automatically dismissed it without giving it voice.

"No, don't censor. Tell me."

"I could do a larger necklace with intricate filigree. Use

smaller diamonds to accent. Platinum and white gold for the settings. The metals would contrast the deep, rich colors in the stones."

"Yes, they would. Draw it up."

Genevieve shook her head. "No one needs a necklace like that. When I designed those kind of statement pieces at Reilly they were always commissioned. The cost of the materials is just too much without a buyer. Especially right now."

"You have a buyer. Draw it up."

What was she going to do with him? He was offering her the opportunity to do exactly what she wanted. If she was honest, the design had been in the back of her mind from the moment she first saw the stones. The reason no other design had worked was because they weren't *that* one.

She shouldn't want anything from Finn DeLuca. So why did she want to let him give her everything?

Making up her mind, Genevieve turned to him. "Fine. I'll draw it up tonight, show you tomorrow for approval."

"You don't need my approval for anything, Genni."

Yes, she did. She was going to treat this like any other commissioned piece. Because if she didn't, what she was about to do would make her feel…edgy and restless. "Maybe not, but since you're the buyer, you get approval."

"Fine."

That settled, she shifted closer. Going up on her tiptoes, Genevieve wrapped her hands around his face and tugged. His body bent as hers lifted, coming together with a whoosh of breath and an overwhelming feeling of right.

Her mouth found his, angling to give them both access. The kiss started out soft and hesitant. Because Genevieve was in charge and she wasn't entirely certain of her reception.

Sure, Finn had kissed her the other day, but since then…

he'd made no move to touch her again. His lack of interest had been frustrating, not to mention a little soul crushing. Part of her was waiting for him to pull back, set her away from him and gently tell her he wasn't interested in blurring the lines.

But she shouldn't have worried.

Sliding her hands down his body, over the tight expanse of chest, to rest on his hips, Genevieve relished the feel of him. She wanted more. Memories of their time together flashed across her mind. Hot, sweaty nights. The way he'd made her feel powerful, beautiful, alive. The expression on his face as his gaze raked across her naked body...like he couldn't breathe without her.

She wanted that again. Was greedy for it.

No one in her life had ever made her feel the way Finn DeLuca could. Maybe it was stupid, but she was going to grab that while she had the opportunity. For however long it lasted.

There'd be time enough to deal with the complications that came with her decision later. Right now, she just wanted him. Wanted them.

Gripping the hem of his shirt, Genevieve tugged it out of the waistband of his slacks so she could find his naked skin. A tortured hiss slipped from his parted lips when her hands found their target.

She relished the way his fingers flexed where they gripped her own hips. Involuntary reaction. Genevieve liked knowing she wasn't the only one a little out of control.

What she wasn't prepared for was for Finn to use the hold to lift her up into the air. She let out a yelp of surprise, scrambling for something to hold on to. Her hands landed on his shoulders, gripping tight. After a few seconds of air time Finn settled her onto the worktable.

Nudging her thighs wide with a knee, he stepped up against the table and settled into the open V. His hands tangled into the hair at her nape, using his hold to tilt her head for another kiss.

She didn't have a chance to take a breath before he was devouring her. Silently demanding she open to him and give him whatever he wanted. A thrill raced along Genevieve's skin.

God, he made her feel alive.

Reaching behind him, Finn gathered a handful of shirt into his fist and pulled it up over his head. Standing half-naked before her, she couldn't resist laying her hands on him.

The wide expanse of his chest and shoulders tapered down at his hips. The man had always been built, but clearly he'd put his time in prison to good use. He now sported layers of muscle that definitely hadn't been there before.

Running her hands over him, Genevieve let her fingertips explore the dips and valleys. Flicking a fingernail over the tight peak of his nipple, she relished the hiss he let out. Her gaze followed the trail of her fingers, studying, cataloging, exploring.

Leaning forward, she placed her mouth on his skin and let her lips join the fun. His skin was warm, the taste of him a combination of salt and spice that made her tongue tingle.

"God, you taste good," she murmured.

His grip on her tightened. Thumbs beneath her chin, he tipped her gaze up to meet his again. His body was still, but with her hands on him, she could feel the tension snapping through him.

Calculated exactly how much he was holding back.

"Now's the time to say stop."

No. The single word screamed through her brain. "Don't stop."

"No regrets."

It wasn't a question. He was telling her that whatever happened from here was her choice. At this moment the power was all hers.

Genevieve shook her head. "No."

Apparently, that was all the answer he needed. Reaching into the collar of her blouse, Finn pulled it in two. Buttons popped, pinging against the wall, table and floor. He didn't even bother to apologize for ruining it before he was pushing it over her shoulders and away. The soft fabric fluttered into a puddle on the table.

But Genevieve didn't have time to care. Reaching behind her, Finn popped the clasp of her bra, sliding it down her arms and tossing it behind them.

Cool air ghosted across her naked skin. Her nipples tingled and tightened, and not just from the change in temperature. The heat in Finn's gaze scraped across her exposed body, sending a rush of awareness down her spine.

His features sharpened with need. A need that reverberated through her own body.

Her fingers shook as she scrambled to find the opening to the fly of his slacks. With impatient fingers, Finn brushed her away and finished the job himself. The buckle of his belt clanged as it hit the floor. Genevieve watched him toe off his shoes and kick everything out of the way.

The hard length of his desire jutted out from his hips. Long, swollen and a dark, tempting red at the tip. Genevieve wanted to lean forward and suck him deep, but when she shifted to do just that, he stopped her.

Instead, he found the zipper to her own jeans. Leaning her back and supporting her with an arm at her back, Finn pulled her pants down and off, leaving her naked. Exposed.

Aching.

Using her prone position to his advantage, Finn used a palm to the middle of her back to hold her in place. His mouth found her, starting at the curve where her neck met her shoulder. Following the line of tendon, he nipped and sucked.

Genevieve's eyes closed at the pleasure.

But he didn't stop there. His lips trailed fire over her shoulder and collarbone. Circling and teasing down in a pattern that came close, but didn't quite touch where she wanted him most.

She fought the urge to squirm, but ultimately lost the battle. Panting and shifting, trying to move her body so he couldn't avoid her tight, achy nipples anymore.

An involuntary cry shot out when he finally gave her what she wanted. His lips closed around a tight bud, drawing it deep. His cheeks hollowed out as he sucked, using the edge of his teeth to scrape the sensitive flesh.

Transferring his attention to the other, he let his teeth close around the pouting pink nub. Gently, he tugged, applying the perfect pressure to have her head dropping back, enjoying the amazing sensations he stirred inside her.

But he didn't stop there. His mouth continued the trail down her body. A palm to the center of her chest, Finn urged her down. The black velvet felt soft, rich, decadent against her overly sensitized skin.

Using the flat of his tongue, he licked up the crease where her hip and thigh met. The unexpected sensation had her hips bucking off the table.

Dropping to his knees, Finn placed a hand on either knee and pushed gently until she opened wider. It wasn't the first time he'd had a front-row view to her sex. But it had been long enough that a moment of unease shot through her.

She'd given birth since the last time they'd had sex. Her body had changed in ways she hadn't even thought about until right now.

"Relax," Finn murmured, the single word brushing against her heated skin.

Easy for him to say.

But two breaths later her own self-consciousness melted away. Because his mouth found her.

The sharp tip of his tongue swiped across her sex. He

found her clit and, using the flat of his tongue, laved it over and over again.

Sparks shot through her body, repeatedly popping. Every muscle drew tight, straining closer and closer to the relief only he could give her.

Using his thumbs, Finn spread the lips of her sex wide, giving him better access to torture her. Genevieve bucked and whimpered. Finn growled, the rumble of sound vibrating through her in a way that left her gasping.

"Give it to me, Genni. Let me watch you come."

Her body had always been eager to do anything he asked. The tight rope of tension snapped. Her body spasmed. Pleasure washed over her, a wave that quickly pulled her under. Genevieve knew nothing except the feel of Finn's hands and mouth as he pushed her to ride out the orgasm, followed her down, chasing for more.

Reality returned slowly, in bits and pieces. Except that the world was still dark. It took her several seconds to realize her eyes were closed.

When they popped open it was to find Finn looming over her. Watching her. A satisfied grin curled the corners of his lips.

But his dark eyes… God, they made her sex clench again, another tremor rocking through her.

"Why do you look like the cat that ate the canary when I'm the one who just had a mind-blowing orgasm?"

"Mind-blowing, huh?"

Genevieve smacked his shoulder. "Don't be an ass. You know damn well you just rocked my world."

"Yeah, but a guy likes to hear the words, anyway. And just so we're clear, I'm not done with you yet."

Heat and need swirled through his expression, sending a thrill down her spine.

She wanted that. All of it. How could she crave more with the power of what he'd just given her?

* * *

Finn couldn't take his eyes off her. Genevieve was gorgeous. Flushed. Disheveled, and he liked knowing he was the reason she looked that way.

He couldn't help but compare the girl she'd been to the woman she was now. Three years could make such a difference. The first time he'd made love to her, she'd been shy and uncertain. Now, she was confident and unapologetic. Spread before him across her worktable, she didn't even attempt to cover her nakedness.

In fact, he watched her stretch, her back arching up and her breasts thrusting closer to his face. "You're not done with me yet, hmm?"

"Tease," he growled.

"I'm pretty sure you can only use that word if there's no follow-through."

She wanted to play games, did she? Games he enjoyed.

Backing up, he decided to see just where she planned on going with this. His little temptress.

"Feel free to show me your follow-through, sweetheart."

The view didn't suck, either, as he took several steps away. The black velvet beneath Genevieve's body made the alabaster of her skin glow. Yellow-gold light streamed down from above, highlighting the luscious curves of her body. Her red-gold hair shone like fire.

A knowing smile pulled at the corners of her mouth as she watched him back away. Her eyelids lowered, giving him a sleepy, sexy expression that immediately went to his dick.

The tempting pink tip of Genevieve's tongue slowly licked across her bottom lip. Excruciatingly slowly, she spread her thighs wide, inch by inch, revealing what he'd been dreaming about for the last three years.

His memories didn't do her justice.

Genevieve's sex glistened with the evidence of her orgasm. She was slick and swollen. And he wanted to sink into her. To feel the tight walls of her grasping at him, pulling him deeper.

Bracing on one arm, she let her hand drift across her body. Her teasing fingers plucked at the tight pink bud of her nipple before trailing down her belly, over her hips and back up the inside of her thighs.

She was teasing them both.

Her head dropped back, but she didn't break eye contact with him. She wanted him to watch.

Stroking the lips of her sex, she let out a tiny gasp when she found the sensitive nub of nerves. Her hips jerked as she rolled her thumb over and over that perfect spot.

Finn wasn't certain at what point he'd gripped his aching cock, but the sensation of his own palm rubbing up and down the hard length was both excruciating and heaven.

Because it wasn't enough.

And he wasn't about to go off in his own hand when he had Genevieve spread like a gift in front of him.

A strangled sob caught in her throat as she plunged two fingers deep inside her own sex. Her eyes slid shut. That broken connection was enough to have him moving.

In two strides, he was back between her spread thighs. His hands were probably rough as he grasped her hand, flinging it away from her body. She didn't seem to care. And he was fresh out of finesse.

Genevieve reached for him, her fingers digging into his hips as she urged him closer.

"Please, Finn," she whimpered.

The sound of his name on her lips in that begging tone did wicked and weird things inside him. He'd do anything she wanted. She made him want to be a better man. The kind she deserved.

But she also made him want to growl and shout from the

highest rooftop that she was his. She made him sloppy. She made him give a damn, which was dangerous.

How could she make him want to be both the best and the worst versions of himself at the same time?

Not that it really mattered. It simply was. Genevieve was complicated, and his reaction to her was even more so.

Caught up in her own cloud of need, she reached for him. Her fingernails dug into his skin. The pinch helped to center him, bring him back to the here and now.

Curling his body over hers, Finn placed his palms on either side of her. Finding her mouth, he pulled the taste of her deep inside.

His dick throbbed with need, but he had to ask a couple questions first.

Staring into her glassy eyes, he asked, "Are you on something?"

"Huh?"

"Birth control. As much as I want you pregnant again so I can experience everything with you this time, I think probably not a smart move."

"Oh." She blinked, the haze clearing a little. "Yeah, I'm on the Pill."

Thank God. "Obviously, I'm clean."

She blinked again. "Oookay."

Perfect. Bending his head, Finn tugged the bud of her nipple into his mouth. Grasping her hips, he pulled her to the edge of the table so that he could align his cock with the tight, wet entrance to her body.

Genevieve's hands curled over his shoulders. "Wait. Wait."

Finn stilled, the head of his dick kissing the moist heat of her pussy. It was torture to stand there, so close to heaven, but he did.

Closing his eyes, Finn started to back away, but Genevieve's legs wrapped around his hips tightened, keeping him in place.

"You aren't going to ask me if I'm clean?"

That's what she was worried about?

Finn could count his own heartbeat as it pulsed through his cock. The opening to Genevieve's sex fluttered around the tip. She pulled his hips closer, and it was just too much.

Using his grip on her, Finn pulled her forward at the same time he thrust deep. He slipped inside her body like he was born to be there. A groan of relief rumbled up through his chest. Genevieve let out a matching sigh.

The walls of her sex clamped down around him, squeezing tight and stealing his breath.

"Holy shit." The words just popped out.

Wrapping his hands around her face, Finn said, "Look at me."

Genevieve's heavy-lidded gaze snapped to his.

"I didn't ask because I already knew the answer. How many times do I have to tell you that I know exactly what you've been doing for the last three years? Genevieve, you and Noah matter. You have from the moment I laid eyes on you."

She shook her head. "Too much."

She was wrong. "Not enough," he countered.

This was a discussion they could have later. Right now, he needed to feel her fall apart in his arms.

Using his leverage, Finn began to thrust in and out of her body. Slowly at first, relishing the pleasure he found from her. The excruciatingly satisfying scrape and pull of friction.

Genevieve whimpered. She spread her thighs wide, rocking her hips in time with his movements. Gripping his shoulders, she held on.

It had been a damn long time since he'd had sex. Since the last time he'd touched her. Before, a dry spell for him had been going three days without a woman in his bed, let alone over three years.

"This isn't going to last long," he warned.

Her response was to lean forward, sink her teeth into his shoulder and shatter around him. The wave of her orgasm broke over him, sucking him under.

The world spiraled down into a darkness that left only Genevieve at the center. His own release started at the base of his spine and shot straight out in hot spurts that left him gasping and weak.

His knees sagged against the table and his arms collapsed out from under him. If it wasn't for Genevieve's thighs wrapped tight around his body he might have hit the floor. Instead, he ended up draped half across her body and half across the table.

His harsh breathing mixed with hers. Her head was buried against the column of his throat.

He was aware enough to register the flutter of her mouth as she placed a kiss against his skin.

Yes. This was right.

Finding strength from somewhere, Finn rolled back up onto his feet. He scooped her into his arms, spun to find the office chair on the far side of the room and collapsed down, cradling her naked body against his.

After a few seconds, Genevieve stirred. Shifting, she looked up at him, an impish grin tugging at her lips.

"You finished with me now?"

"Not even close."

Nine

Genevieve woke up alone. She knew Finn was gone before she'd even opened her eyes. Dread curled through her belly, but she forced it down. Nope, she wasn't going to let herself think the worst.

But instinct had her hand moving over to where he'd been sleeping to test if the sheets held any residual warmth. They did, although what did that prove?

Nothing really, except that she needed to get a grip on herself. She was either doing this or she wasn't, and if she was she couldn't live every day waiting for the other shoe to drop.

That wasn't fair to Finn, but it also wasn't fair to Noah. Or herself.

Rolling onto her back, Genevieve pressed the heels of her palms into her eyes and rubbed. It had been two days since the studio. And since then, Finn had been at her side. Which was amazing, but it was also overwhelming.

She hadn't had a chance to catch her breath. To reason her way through what was happening and just how she needed to handle it all.

Maybe she needed to send Finn home for a while.

Grabbing her phone from the nightstand, Genevieve looked at the screen through bleary eyes, but that all changed when she registered the big numbers glaring at her. 9:18.

Bolting out of bed, she was halfway down the hall, her heart thudding for a completely different reason. No toddler slept until 9:18. Something was wrong.

It didn't help to find her son's room empty. Or for the rest of the house to feel eerily quiet. Darting through the house, she skidded to a halt at the kitchen. The empty kitchen.

Spinning in a circle, the dread that had churned her belly minutes before was now making it a whirlpool. Until something out of place caught her eye. A white piece of paper in the middle of the counter.

Snatching it up, her eyes raced over the words, just starting to digest them as the garage door began to rumble.

Yanking open the door, she raced into the garage. Even though, thanks to Finn's note, her brain knew what was going on, the rest of her needed to feel Noah's little body cradled in her arms.

Finn had barely stopped the car before Genevieve popped open the back door. Noah grinned up at her, chocolate smeared across his angelic face.

"Doughnuts, Mama."

Her precious son took the smashed-up treat gripped in his tight fist and shoved it against her lips.

Her hands shook as she unbuckled him from his seat. Her arms felt weak, but she wasn't about to let him go once she'd scooped him up. Hugging him close, Genevieve pressed a kiss to his head and breathed in his toddler scent.

Rounding the car, Finn gave her a huge grin and leaned in for a kiss. But after touching his lips to hers he suddenly pulled back. His eyebrows beetled with confusion.

"Hey, what's wrong?"

With his arm wrapped around her body, there was no way she could hide the tremors still working through her.

"I woke up and you were both gone." She should have stopped there, but words tumbled out. "He's my whole world and I don't know what I'd do if you took him away from me."

Finn jerked backward as if she'd hit him. Which only made the sludge of nasty emotions in her belly worse.

Shaking his head slowly, he said, "I would never take him away from you. Not ever, but definitely not like that."

"I know." The minute the words were out of her mouth, she realized they were the truth. Finn was a con artist and a thief. But he had his own twisted sense of honor. He'd done nothing but help her since he'd forced his way back into her life. And while she might not trust him implicitly, she did trust him to protect their son.

Closing her eyes, Genevieve realized how terribly she'd just screwed up. Reaching for him, she placed her hand along the hard ridge of his jaw. "I'm sorry. You didn't deserve that reaction."

"No, I didn't." His words were harsh, but the hand he pressed into the small of her back was gentle. "But I understand."

She seriously doubted that he did. But even if so, that didn't make what she'd just done any less regrettable.

It was clear, by the expression in his eyes, that she'd hurt him. Something she wouldn't have thought possible.

Finn DeLuca didn't let anyone matter enough to inflict pain. Or he hadn't before. Even when she'd thought he was letting her in, it became obvious to her in hindsight that while she'd opened up to him about her worst fears, deepest secrets and most private desires…he'd given her absolutely nothing. In fact, he'd used what she had shared with him in order to get exactly what he wanted.

For the first time, Genevieve stopped being pissed because that reality had left her vulnerable, devastated and feeling like a stupid idiot. Instead, she started to wonder *why*.

What had happened to make Finn DeLuca the man he was? A charming, egotistical, devilish loner?

She had no idea what this was between them, and wasn't willing to even ask the question at this point. But what she did know was that this time she wasn't going to let him get away with keeping himself separate and walled away.

Genevieve had every intention of demanding more.

It was the middle of the night. Finn, Genevieve and Noah had spent all day together. After the rocky start in the morning, it had turned into an amazing day.

Made even better by the fact that Genevieve was naked, spread out diagonally across the bed, her hair a mess, her skin flushed from pleasure and a relaxed smile on her face. The orgasms he'd had didn't suck, either.

Propped up on an elbow, she watched him. "Tell me something I don't know."

Such a typical Genevieve demand. "That's a pretty wide area to cover. And a difficult order to comply with. I don't know everything you know so I can't fill in the gaps."

She kicked out, her foot connecting lightly with his shoulder. "You know what I mean."

"No, I really don't."

"Tell me something about you I don't know. Before, you didn't share anything. You've said several times that I have no secrets—which is creepy, by the way. You have nothing but secrets. I know you're wealthy, but I don't know how or why. I know you like jewels and art, but I don't know where that desire started from. I don't know if you have any family. Brothers, sisters, parents?"

A frown tugged at the corners of her mouth. She rolled,

grabbing the sheets and tucking them around her body. As if cataloging all the things she didn't know about him made her feel exposed.

Nope, he wasn't going to let her start hiding from him now.

Reaching out, Finn grasped the edge of the covers and yanked. They dragged against her skin, slithering against her body as he tossed them onto the floor beside them.

"Hey," she exclaimed, leaning up and chasing after them.

Finn snaked an arm around her waist, tugging as he tumbled them both back to the bed.

She struggled for a few seconds and he let her, waiting until she'd calmed again before rolling them so she was tucked into the curve of his body.

"I have family money. My great-great-grandfather owned a plantation. He grew cotton and tobacco. But my great-grandfather wanted to move away from agriculture and slavery, and he wanted to be more powerful and influential. He used the family connections to build an import/export business, eventually building a transportation conglomerate. Shipping, rail, trucking, each generation managed to grow the business...until it became a multi-billion-dollar corporation."

Genevieve's fingers began to play against his chest, lightly stroking his skin in a way that was soothing and arousing at the same time.

"My father was no exception. He spent his entire life devoted to growing the company. However, his focus was on expansion, which meant he was always traveling. Gone for months at a time as he opened a new hub in Europe or Asia. Or acquired some tiny warehouse in Africa. My mom went with him."

Finn heard the bitterness in his own voice and hated himself a little for it. You'd think after so many years he would have gotten past the anger. Apparently, not so much. "They were rarely home, and when they were they spent most of their time at the office. The business was their life."

"Is that why it's not yours?"

"Partly." No, that wasn't true. "Absolutely. I didn't learn much from my parents, but I did learn that life requires balance. Sawyer and I decided early on we weren't going to let the company—or any job—consume us the way it did my parents."

"Sawyer?"

Tension tightened his shoulders. Finn consciously tried to relax it away, but it didn't help. "My little brother."

"Where is he? When do I get to meet him?"

"He's dead."

Genevieve shifted, trying to move so she could look up at him. Tightening his arms around her, Finn kept her right where she was.

"How?"

Of course she'd ask. Finn fought against the rage that always tried to swallow him whole whenever he thought about Sawyer. The problem was that whenever he won the battle, that just left the guilt. The guilt he'd never be able to get rid of.

"I was an adrenaline junkie when I was younger."

Genevieve tipped her head sideways. The fingers that had been playing across his skin stalled for several seconds. No doubt she was confused how his statement answered her question.

"The problem with having no goal in life, but enough money at your disposal to buy whole islands, is that you get bored."

"Not necessarily. *You* got bored."

"Fair enough. I got bored. It didn't take me long to figure out adrenaline cured the boredom. Around seventeen I started racing cars. Not legally, mind you."

A huff of sarcastic laughter puffed against his chest. "What would be the fun in that?"

"Exactly. The more dangerous, the better. Some of my degenerate friends turned to drugs for adventure and the high, but I never found that satisfying."

"You like to be challenged, not to be out of control."

"Pretty much. Street racing, skydiving, BASE jumping. You name it—if I could get a hit of adrenaline, I was in."

"What does this have to do with Sawyer?" There was the question he'd been expecting.

"Sawyer was the angel to my devil. Studious and serious. While I had no intention of working at the company at all, he always planned to take over. My parents recognized that and began grooming him for the position at an early age."

"Did that bother you? Them choosing him over you?"

"Not at all." Bitter laughter squeezed from his chest. "I felt sorry for Sawyer, although I know he didn't dread the idea of it as I did. The thing was, since our parents were always gone, the two of us pretty much only had each other. We were very close, even though we were very different."

"Not surprising."

"But we also fought. All the time."

"Also not surprising. You were brothers. And young."

"Maybe so. The older I got, the worse it became. Because Sawyer didn't approve of any of the things I enjoyed doing. He was constantly harping on me that I was going to die young."

What irony that Sawyer had been the one to fulfill that prophecy.

Caught up in his own misery and memories, Finn hadn't realized he'd stopped talking until Genevieve asked, "What happened?"

"He followed me to a race one night, pissed that I was going. There was a rumor the police had been tipped off about the intended track, so the location changed at the last minute. Somehow, he got word the new location had been compromised, as well. He followed me to stop me, but I wouldn't listen. We argued, but I got in the car, anyway."

God, he would never forget the utter anger on Sawyer's face as Finn had driven to the starting line and roared away.

"I didn't see the accident. I just heard about it later. The cops did show up. There was a scramble as people left. And somehow, Sawyer was hit. They told me he died on impact."

Finn shrugged, words backing up into a lump in his throat.

"That doesn't change the fact that he's gone." Genevieve's soft voice washed over him.

"No, it doesn't. He shouldn't have been there. It's my fault."

She stirred again, trying to move so she could see him. Finn tightened his arms around her, but this time she wouldn't be put off. Wiggling free, she pushed up so she could look at him.

"You're smarter than that, Finn. You know it's not true."

"Maybe."

Grasping his face, she brought them nose-to-nose. "No. You didn't hit him."

"It should have been me."

"That's not how life works. I lost my parents when I was so young that I don't have a single memory of either of them."

"I wish I didn't have a memory of mine. I identified Sawyer's body. I was nineteen. Our parents let their staff make the arrangements for his funeral. They flew in that morning and flew out again that night. Some business deal in Hong Kong that couldn't be postponed."

"Jesus. My grandfather is a demanding, dictatorial asshole, but your parents might be worse."

Finn shrugged. "They're gone now. Died in a plane crash in Thailand nine months after Sawyer."

Genevieve made a strangled sound in the back of her throat.

"Trust me, it wasn't a loss."

Her eyes were damp. Finn stared at Genevieve, taking in the sadness that filled her. For him. He didn't think anyone had ever cried for him.

"I'm so sorry," she whispered.

"Not your fault."

"No, but that doesn't stop me from caring you've experienced that pain. Thank you."

"For what?"

"Giving me this piece of you."

Dropping back down onto the bed beside him, Genevieve wrapped her arms around him and squeezed. She simply held him, soothing away something that wasn't her fault or responsibility.

Giving him peace he hadn't known he'd desperately needed.

Finn stared at the imposing structure of the museum across the street. The soaring columns were impressive, not to mention the history of the building itself. Once a church used as a hospital during the Civil War, now it housed the largest private collection of historic manuscripts.

Most people would be surprised to discover Finn had an affinity for "old paper." But the documents, manuscripts and scores housed inside the building held history, revolution and humanity. They were the memory of mistakes and triumphs. Lessons the rest of the world needed to remember so as not to repeat.

Not to mention, manuscripts and historical documents could be quite valuable.

But this place had one piece that always held a special

place in his heart—the stage version of Twain's *The Adventures of Tom Sawyer.*

Standing out front, it was child's play to catalog the weaknesses in their security. It wouldn't take much effort for him to take ownership of the piece. Only one thing kept him from following through—he appreciated the ideas the museum had been founded on.

Not to mention, he had a hard and fast rule about stealing from nonprofits. Taking something from a private collector who got off on keeping precious works of art hidden behind walls and barriers for the sole purpose of ownership...that was reprehensible.

This was just him getting itchy.

He'd been restless since his conversation with Genevieve. Opening up to her about Sawyer had left him feeling...uncomfortable.

He'd pulled his first job weeks after Sawyer's death. Planning the heist had been a distraction from the grief and guilt. The ultimate high to drown out the pain when it had gone flawlessly and he'd walked away with a priceless work of art.

Standing outside the museum—effortlessly formulating a plan he had no intention of using—was a needed reminder of just who he was.

Someone who would never deserve to be a part of the happy family Genevieve would someday have.

Hell, it had been less than two weeks and he was already straining beneath the mantle of domesticity. Ignoring the urges deep inside him, pretending to be the man she wanted and needed, was exhausting. Not to mention, doomed to failure.

Deep down, he would always be a criminal. Dangerous to those around him that mattered.

Maybe it would be better if he admitted that right now. Reminded them both that he wasn't a good man.

He wasn't who Genevieve wanted him to be.

The rub was, a huge part of him wanted to be who she saw when she looked at him. But Finn had no idea how to do that.

One thing was for certain, walking inside that museum and stealing a historically valuable document simply because it reminded him of his brother wouldn't accomplish anything.

Ten

Finn turned from the museum and headed back to his car, restless energy still humming seductively beneath his skin. Slipping into the soft leather seats, he connected his phone to the Bluetooth and hit one of the few numbers programmed in.

He slammed the gas pedal to the floor and roared out of the parking lot, uncaring for the nasty looks he received on his way out—a guy needed to get thrills where he could—just as the call connected.

"Finn," Stone's dry voice answered.

"I'm itchy as hell and about to do something stupid." That was as close to a cry for help as he was going to get.

"Where are you? I'm coming to you."

This was why Stone was one of his best friends. No hesitation, question or censure. Just support and immediate action.

"No need. I'm coming to you."

Hitting the button to end the call, Finn let the force of the car push him back into the cradle of the expensive leather seat. His fingers wrapped tightly around the steering wheel, not just gripping for control of the car.

Ten minutes later, he walked in the front door at Stone Surveillance and straight back to Stone's office. Knocking the door closed behind him, he sprawled into the waiting chair across from his friend's glossy desk.

Stone didn't bother to ask questions. He walked to the sideboard, poured two fingers of Scotch into cut-crystal glasses and handed him one. "Talk to me."

Frowning into the amber liquid, Finn stared at it for a few seconds before knocking it back and swallowing it in one gulp. The liquor burned down the back of his throat, but he welcomed the pain of it.

"I can't do it," he finally murmured.

"Do what?"

"Go straight." Finn dropped the glass onto the top of Stone's desk and then stared up at his friend. "It's only been a few weeks and I'm chafing against the perfect family picture Genevieve is painting me into. We both know I'm not a nice guy and I've never professed to be one. Eventually, I'm going to screw up, man."

Stone crossed his arms over his chest, leaned his hips back against the edge of his desk and pulled his lips into a frown. "From everything you've told me and the reports I've read, Genevieve strikes me as a pretty practical woman. Not to mention intelligent."

"She is."

"Something tells me she's perfectly aware of the kind of man you are and doesn't expect you to be anything you're not, including perfect."

"For someone so smart, you can be incredibly stupid" was Finn's dry response.

"Funny, Piper likes to tell me the same thing. I think you're both wrong. But I'm absolutely certain of it where

Genevieve is concerned. Have you talked to her about any of this?"

"Hell, no. Given our history, I'm certain the last thing she wants to hear about is my struggle to go straight."

"I don't know. I have a feeling she'd be pretty supportive."

Finn scoffed. "You know nothing about women."

"Bullshit. I'm the only one of us who's currently planning a wedding." Stone waved a hand, cutting off any rebuttal Finn could make. "None of that matters. I have a solution that might get you the adrenaline fix you need in a way that's perfectly legal."

Finn was pretty certain nothing legal could provide him the same challenge or gratification that stealing could.

"Whatever."

"No, seriously. Listen to me."

Finn shrugged. He didn't have much choice. He'd come to Stone, after all.

"Why do you think I've been pressuring you to join the company?"

"Because you're an asshole." And a good friend. "But you've gotten your way." As usual. "So what does that have to do with anything?"

"I have a client I think you can help."

Finn scoffed. "You have someone who needs a painting stolen?"

"Yes."

"Yeah, right." Stone was as straight a shooter as Finn had ever encountered. He might have spent ten years in prison, but he was hardly a criminal. In fact, the time he did break the law was in defense of his fiancée, killing her rapist. There was no way in hell Stone would agree to take on a client who wanted them to steal something. Stone had too much honor for that.

"Actually, our client already had a priceless artifact stolen from his office."

No doubt the idiot had displayed the piece in an attempt to make himself feel powerful and in control, but failed to protect the item. "I'm going out on a limb to suggest he deserved to lose it."

"Probably."

"So you and Gray are helping to recover the piece." Finn didn't bother to ask the question, he already knew that's what his friends were going to do. Because their sense of honor where this kind of thing was concerned happened to be a bit different from his own.

"Yes."

"Great, you know that's not something I'm going to help with."

"I know."

"Exactly what do you need me for, then?"

"He's also asked us to assess his security around the rest of his personal collection."

"And you want me to point out where his holes are."

"Yes. But I want you to do more than just observe and assess. I want you to break in and steal whatever you can get your hands on."

Finn tipped his head sideways, staring at Stone and trying to figure out if he was being serious. "What does that accomplish? Just assess his system, tell him where the weaknesses are and get him to sign off on the upgrades."

"He wants a more hands-on approach."

Well, bully for him. "People in hell want ice water."

"Let's just say this guy has enough money to purchase your specialized skill set."

"Too bad I don't give a shit how much money he has. I don't need it." Finn lasered Stone a pointed glance. "Neither do you."

His friend shrugged. "True, but Stone Surveillance does need the funds."

"Bullshit."

"How about we need the word of mouth in order to build the business? We're not planning to advertise. We're only looking to take on niche clients."

"Or bleeding-heart stories and clients who need real help." Because that was his friend. Stone had billions of dollars and could spend the rest of his life sitting on the sand somewhere with a cold drink in his hand. But that wasn't Stone.

"We're lucky, Finn. You, me and Gray. We've all had our problems, but at the end of the day our bank accounts afford us access to resources that allow us benefits others don't have."

Apparently, not enough benefits since all three of them had spent plenty of time in prison. Although he had to admit that, out of the three of them, he was the only one who'd actually deserved to be there. Stone had been defending someone he loved from a monster. And Gray... Finn had no doubt Gray was innocent of the charges he'd been convicted of.

And that was a puzzle he'd happily spend the rest of his life helping his friend solve.

But in the meantime... "This client of yours sounds like he has plenty of resources all on his own. Why does he need our help?"

"He's a close family friend. A man I've known my entire life."

"Ahhh." There was the connection.

"And taking paying clients allows us to help the ones who can't afford help on their own. The ones who really need us."

"You're going to keep talking until I agree to do this, aren't you?"

"Remember that agreement you made when you signed the ownership paperwork? Let's consider this your contribution to the company."

"Asshole."

Stone grinned at him. "Do you wanna see the specs on his system or not?"

Finn let out a low growl, but waved his fingers, indicating Stone should bring it on.

"What the hell does this guy own, anyway?"

"One of the largest private art collections in the South. He has several paintings from Rembrandt, Degas, Pollock, van Gogh and Basquiat. He also fancies himself an amateur archaeologist and likes to purchase artifacts from ancient civilizations. He's not selfish, though, and regularly loans his pieces out to museums around the world."

"Jesus," Finn grumbled. "Sounds like a guy with more money than sense."

"No, he's simply a collector who likes to believe he's preserving art and history for the next generations."

"Without spending the time and money he needs to protect that history."

"That's where you come in. He recognizes the need to up his game. And he's willing to invest in the best. Use your expertise. Get up close and personal with his systems. Tell us what he needs so we can help him preserve that culture for others."

Finn didn't like this. Something about it felt wrong, but he also couldn't fault Stone for his argument.

"You've known this guy for a long time?"

"Yes. He's given his permission for us to have unfettered access to whatever we need. And he's aware we might have unconventional methods for assessing his current security."

"Well, that takes all the fun out of things, doesn't it?"

A wicked half smile tugged at Stone's mouth. "Not really. We won't tell him what you're doing. I might be able to get you out of jail after the fact, but if you get caught breaking in, you're likely going to spend some time behind bars again."

"Not to mention give my probation officer heart palpitations."

"So don't get caught."

For the first time since walking into Stone's office, excitement began to bubble through Finn's veins. "Oh, I have no intention of getting caught, my friend."

Genevieve pushed back from the microscope she'd been using to create the setting for the alexandrite necklace. The platinum filigree and brilliance of the tiny diamonds she was using as accents would be a perfect contrast for the deep, rich colors of the bigger stones. Ever since talking with Finn about the pieces a week ago, things had started to fall into place. This felt right, when everything else she'd attempted had felt oh-so-wrong.

Inspiration was a fickle and amazing thing.

It was also an unrelenting taskmaster. She'd spent more hours in the studio over the last week, driven to finish the piece as quickly as possible, than she had in the last month. When she wasn't in the studio, she was cramming in as much time with Finn and Noah as she could.

There was no hiding the fact that she was exhausted. There just weren't enough hours in the day, which made her feel guilty. The only thing that held the guilt at bay right now was the idea that it would all be over in just a few weeks. After that, she was going to take a long break and make it up to her son.

Rubbing at her eyes to try and get them to refocus after being tunneled down to just the piece, Genevieve let her body sag against the chair.

"You're working too hard."

She jumped, the rolling casters on the bottom of her chair rattling as it moved several inches before being caught and stopped.

Craning her head around, she stared up into Nick's face. "You startled me."

"I'm sorry. I didn't mean to. I was just coming to let you know I'm heading out for the night. And suggest you do the same. You've had your head stuck in that scope for hours."

Shifting his hands, Nick brushed the hair away from her neck and began digging his thumbs into the top of her spine. "Your neck has to be killing you after sitting hunched over like that for so long."

Genevieve didn't realize the ache was even there until he started rubbing. Letting out a deep groan, she sank into the relief his capable hands were giving her.

But after a few minutes, once the initial pain had subsided, a sense of unease trickled through her. Damn Finn and his poisonous thoughts. Nick was a friend and nothing more. He'd rubbed her neck this way before, countless times. In her own studio and when they'd both worked at Reilly.

It meant nothing.

Still, twisting, Genevieve stood up and offered Nick a grateful smile. "Thanks. I didn't realize how tight my muscles were."

"No problem." Taking a step toward the door, Nick said, "I'm heading out. Why don't you leave, too? I can lock up for you."

Genevieve looked longingly at the door. A part of her wanted to do just that. Go home, scoop her son up into her arms, feed him dinner and give him a bath. Then curl up beside Finn on the couch and neck like teenagers in front of the TV, watching a show neither of them cared anything about.

But there was also a part of her that didn't want to go

home. Because home was complicated and uncertain. What the hell was she doing with Finn?

Anyone looking in would say they were in a relationship. A family. But…she wasn't sure that's what was really going on. Or what she wanted.

Could she ever let herself trust Finn again? Or trust herself around him?

Sure, Finn challenged her. He'd been the first person to recognize who she was, and tell her there was nothing wrong with being that person. Even if her grandfather had always told her she was stupid, useless and wrong.

And then, by his actions, Finn had managed to taint the self-discovery that had started to make her feel empowered. Sure, over the last three years she'd found her own inner power, but now that he was back in her life…

Bottom line was, she didn't trust her own instincts around Finn. He clouded her judgment. He made her reckless.

If it was just her, she might enjoy the ride and deal with consequences later. But it wasn't just her. Unfortunately, the same thing that made her cautious was the same thing that would keep Finn in her life for a very long time. It wasn't as simple as trying to resist.

She'd already proven she sucked at resisting Finn De-Luca.

So, giving in to what was between them was inevitable. But she needed to find a way to keep pieces of herself safe and protected, even as he became a bigger part of her life.

"No, I need to get more done."

While that was true, part of her just needed some distance…because after the last couple weeks, all of her defenses were sorely close to crumbling.

Nick left. Alone, Genevieve rolled back to her equipment and began working the delicate filigree. It was intri-

cate work that required her full attention. She had no idea
how long she stayed that way, although her shoulders were
aching again, when an unexpected sound broke through
her concentration.

Pulling back, she listened for it again. It didn't take long
to hear a rattle at the back door. Her heart lurched into her
throat and she jumped out of her chair, simultaneously grabbing for her phone. Without thinking, she pulled up Finn's
number and punched the call button.

What she didn't expect was to hear the echoing sound of
his ringtone faintly coming from the other side of her back
door just before it opened. If she hadn't heard his phone,
she might have screamed. Although most burglars didn't
come burdened down with enough bags and boxes that they
could barely see over the stack.

"What the hell?" she asked, not sure what she wanted
to know more: why he was there, what he was carrying or
what his plan was.

Because there was no question Finn DeLuca was up to
something.

Ducking sideways, he flashed her that mischievous,
charming smile that always made her knees weak. "I come
bearing gifts."

"Obviously. Why?"

"A surprise."

Because suddenly showing up at her studio wasn't surprise enough? "I'm not particularly fond of surprises."

Which wasn't entirely true. But she wasn't exactly a
fan of Finn's surprises. So far, not many of them had been
happy.

"You'll like this one. I hope."

"Hmm," she hummed, unconvinced.

Kicking the door shut behind him with the heel of a
shiny dress shoe, Finn strode across the room and dumped
his armful of packages onto an empty worktable.

That's when she realized he was dressed in a tux.

"Hot damn." It was unfair how good the man looked all dressed up. He reminded her of some dashing Victorian duke.

Finn flashed her a knowing grin, smoothed his hands over the sides of his jacket and said, "Glad you approve."

Egotistical ass. The man knew exactly how amazing he looked, which was both charming and frustrating at the same time. "A little overdressed for a night watching TV, don't you think?"

"Probably, so it's a good thing that's not what we're doing."

"Oh, no? I don't know about your plans, but that's exactly how I intended to spend my night. Besides, someone has to get back to our son. The babysitter would probably appreciate going home."

He cut her a wounded look. "What little faith. I've arranged for Maddie to get Noah. He's spending the night with her and excited about the idea, I might add."

Genevieve wasn't sure how that should make her feel, a little excited and sad at the same time apparently. Conflicted, which is how Finn often made her feel.

"All right," she responded, pulling the words into multiple syllables, waiting for the rest of the information. When Finn wasn't forthcoming, she finally asked, "And just why did you go to all the trouble?"

"Because I need to attend a benefit gala tonight and I'd love for you to accompany me."

"A benefit gala?" Dread and irritation mixed in her belly. She'd attended her fair share of fancy events. Been hostess for her grandfather at several. None had ever been a fun experience. She'd rather enjoyed skipping them the last few years. "These kind of things don't just spring up overnight. Why are you telling me about this now?"

"The invitation came in weeks ago, but I wasn't planning to attend."

"What changed?"

He shrugged. "A friend asked me to go."

Grabbing a garment bag from the pile, he spread it across the table. "Before you protest that you don't have anything to wear, I've obviously taken care of that."

Pulling open the zipper, he revealed a breathtaking emerald green lace gown. Genevieve couldn't help but step closer so she could run her hands over the material. The lace was so intricate and delicate, soft beneath her fingertips.

She had to admit the only benefit to the events had always been getting dressed up. Putting on beautiful clothes had always made her feel elegant and pretty, something that didn't happen often.

Until Finn. He always had the ability to make her feel gorgeous with nothing more than a hot, burning glance.

Reaching inside the bag, Finn lifted the gown out so she could get the full effect. It was strapless with a corset bodice that three years ago would have made her feel naked and inappropriate. But the way Finn was watching her right now made her think he was already imagining her in the dress.

And out of it.

Gesturing to the bags still strewn across her table, Genevieve said, "I hope you had the forethought to bring undergarments."

A wicked grin crinkled the corners of his eyes. Finn tossed the dress onto the table and grasped her instead. Pulling her close, he brushed his lips against the sensitive shell of her outer ear and whispered, "Sweetheart, what makes you think I want you wearing anything beneath this dress?"

Genevieve pulled in a sharp breath, a little because she

was scandalized, but mostly because her body warmed to Finn's outrageous words.

Pulling back, he grabbed the dress, draped it over her arms, spun her around and gave her a gentle shove. "Go put it on."

Genevieve found herself walking across the studio toward the tiny attached bathroom. It wasn't until she'd closed the door and began taking her clothes off that she realized he hadn't actually given her anything to put on underneath.

Eleven

Eleven

Finn waited impatiently for Genevieve to emerge. She was going to look amazing in the dress. If there was one thing he recognized, it was beauty.

Genevieve Reilly was gorgeous inside and out.

Needing something to keep him busy, Finn started pulling the rest of the things he'd brought from the bags and boxes. Yes, he'd included panties—and made sure they were tiny and lacy—although a huge part of him hoped Genevieve let her inner vixen out and decided not to wear them.

Knowing she was walking around, hobnobbing with the Charleston elite completely naked under the dress he'd bought her...not only would he find that amusing, but he'd most definitely need to find some quiet alcove to pull her into so he could take advantage of her naked state.

He'd brought a couple pairs of shoes, makeup and an assortment of hair products. The last thing he pulled out was the case for the emerald pieces he'd bought. He tucked the box out of sight, wanting to save that surprise for last.

He couldn't wait to see their gorgeous color against her

creamy skin. He'd purposely picked out the dress to complement the pieces so that he could show off Genevieve and her skills as an artist.

The door slowly creaked open. Genevieve stood, framed by the doorway, a complete vision. Finn's dick went half-hard and his heart thumped erratically against his chest.

"You're stunning," he whispered.

The answering smile that dawned across her face made his heart kick even harder. *Crap.* He wanted to be the reason for that expression every day for the rest of her life.

And he had no idea what to do with that revelation.

"Thanks."

Swiping an arm over the table, he said, "You should have everything you need."

Walking across the room toward him, Finn couldn't help but appreciate the way the dress clung to her luscious curves. He knew there was a fine layer of beige mesh beneath the lace covering her body, but the illusion that she was naked between the intricate work made his brain threaten to explode.

Walking close, Genevieve let her body brush against his. She watched his reaction from beneath her lashes, the little vixen.

His straitlaced rule follower was feeling a little wild. And he was happy to encourage that kind of behavior.

Wrapping an arm around her waist, Finn pulled her tight against his body. He strategically placed her so the edge of her hip rubbed right against the erect ridge pushing against the constricting teeth of his zipper.

Finding her ear, he murmured, "Yes, there are panties somewhere in this pile. My question is, are you brave enough to leave them here?"

Shaking her head, Genevieve stretched out, rummaging through everything until she found the panties he'd bought. Just like the dress, they were a deep emerald green, silk and lace.

Fingers tucked inside the waistband, she pulled until they went taught and then flipped them around so she could see the tiny string that constituted the back. Pursing her lips, she turned her head and looked him straight-on.

He expected to get a lecture on how inappropriate they were. So he was surprised when, instead, Genevieve neatly folded them into a little fan, yanked out the square of material tucked into the pocket of his jacket and replaced it with the panties she obviously wouldn't be wearing.

God, this woman was amazing. A constant surprise.

"You're trying to kill me, aren't you?"

"Nope, that would be stupid. I really want you to make love to me later. Hard to do if you're dead."

What he wanted to do was shove the skirt of her dress up and sink into her body right now. But if he did that, they'd never make it to the gala. And he really needed to be there tonight.

The gala was being held at Dennis Hunt's home. Hunt happened to be Stone's client. This was the perfect opportunity to survey the estate, review the security measures and find some vulnerabilities.

Seeing Genevieve all dressed up was simply the cherry on top of the sundae.

"As much as I'd like to show you that playing with fire gets you burned, we don't have time. The car will be here in twenty minutes." Sweeping a hand over the table, he continued. "You're perfect just the way you are, but if you want makeup and hair now's the time."

Genevieve quickly picked through the products, gathering a few in her hands. Tossing a saucy smile over her shoulder, she headed back to the bathroom.

This time she didn't bother shutting the door. So Finn followed, leaning a shoulder against the jamb so he could watch. With a few sure strokes, she applied just enough makeup to highlight her face. Then with nothing more than a band, some pins and a curling wand, she managed to put her hair up in some elegant twist that made her look both sexy and sophisticated.

Less than fifteen minutes later, she was shooing him out of the doorway so she could pick out a pair of heels. He'd brought several options, not just so she could have color choices, but because he wasn't certain what heel height she'd be most comfortable wearing.

He was slightly surprised when she picked out a pair of strappy sandals about four inches high. But he was grateful when she walked across the room in them, her hips swaying seductively.

Reaching behind him, Finn pulled out the case he'd stashed. Genevieve faltered, her steps stuttering in a way that had him extending his arm to her because he was afraid she was falling.

But she wasn't. She was solid on her feet, her eyes trained on the box in his hand.

Nerves suddenly fluttered deep in his belly. Finn couldn't remember the last time he'd been nervous about anything.

Opening the lid, he held the jewels out to her.

"I wanted you to wear these."

Her eyes drifted across the pieces nestled against the black velvet inside. Pride, peace and happiness flitted across her face.

But she didn't move to touch them.

Dropping the box onto the table, Finn lifted out the necklace. It was light and cool against his hands, just as it would be until the heat of her body warmed it.

Stepping up to her, he waited until she spun so he could place the necklace around her neck. The teardrop settled into the valley at the center of her throat. It moved as she swallowed.

The backs of Finn's fingertips brushed across her soft skin. Genevieve shivered. Following the line, he worked the clasp and then reluctantly dropped his hands away.

And waited for her to spin around.

He wasn't disappointed with the vision she made when she did. But he didn't speak. Not yet. Reaching back into the box, he pulled out the set of earrings, handing them to her one at a time as she leaned sideways to put them in. The matching bracelet followed.

Only then did he take a step back so that he could appreciate the full impact of her.

"You are beautiful every minute of every day, but right now...you glow. The jewels around your neck pale in comparison to your fire and light."

Genevieve's eyes sparkled and shimmered. For a moment he was worried she might start crying, but instead a radiant smile curled her lips. Closing the gap between them, she placed both of her palms against his chest and leaned close.

"You make me feel beautiful, Finn. And you always have. You've always been happy to share your own intense fire and excitement for life." Touching her mouth to his, she whispered, "Thank you."

Finn wasn't certain if she was thanking him for tonight or for something else, but it really didn't matter.

He was just about to say to hell with the gala, he'd find another way to survey Hunt's estate, when his cell buzzed letting him know the car had arrived.

"Perfect timing," he mumbled irritably, before sweeping a hand toward the back door. "After you."

Genevieve was familiar with the world she'd just entered. It had simply been a long time since she'd been back.

The imposing brick mansion, lights blazing out over a forecourt lined with towering oaks, didn't impress her. It did remind her of movies like *Gone with the Wind* and *Midnight in the Garden of Good and Evil*, though.

Uniformed employees opened the doors as they approached, revealing a sweeping double staircase framing the entrance to a ballroom filled with elegantly clad people. Everything sparkled and shimmered, especially the women milling about.

This was definitely something she hadn't missed for the past few years. These kinds of events had been regular affairs in her life with her grandfather. She was expected to be the perfect companion, quiet and unimposing. Demure and obedient. An example he could point to when he wanted to praise his own parenting skills and a disappointment and burden he could reference when he wanted to play the martyr.

She'd hated every minute, usually finding the events boring and tedious.

Something told her tonight would be much different.

Proving her point, the material of her dress brushed against the naked mound of her sex, sending a thrill racing through her blood. Finn didn't help matters any when he let his hand drop from the dip of her hip to the rounded flesh of her rear…and gave her a hard squeeze.

Elbowing him in the side, Genevieve cut him a disapproving glance. His response was an impish grin that suggested he planned to ignore her hint.

Letting his hand slide into hers, Finn led her to the heart of the ballroom, sweeping past people, uncaring when they attempted to stop him and speak.

Genevieve had no doubt one of the things that drew people to Finn was his complete lack of caring about what others thought…or wanted. At least generally speaking. If someone wasn't important to him, their opinion or needs mattered not at all.

That attitude came with an air of confidence that was attractive and seductive. She'd seen the phenomenon before. People were drawn to Finn. And it was no less true tonight.

Of course, it didn't hurt that he had a reputation for being outrageous and an air of danger because of his history. People delighted in gossiping behind his back, but wanted to be able to say they knew him for the shock value it could provide.

Finn didn't give a rip about any of it.

Over the next thirty minutes or so Finn kept a tight arm around her shoulders or waist, ensuring she stayed close. He spoke to a handful of people, carrying on banal conversations that he was very careful to be sure included her.

He made it clear—to her if not to anyone else—with his actions and words that as far as he was concerned, she was the most important person in the room.

Which eventually had a flock of women surrounding her as they attempted to figure out how she fit into things. Several of them she'd been acquainted with through her grandfather and her work at Reilly, although none were what she'd consider friends.

Needing a break, she was about to excuse herself and find a ladies' room where she could hide for a few minutes when she registered a change in Finn's tone of voice. Before, his words had held a clipped, bored undertone. Now, whoever he spoke with actually mattered.

Genevieve turned her attention back to Finn, closing the small gap that had developed as they engaged with different conversations. Coming up beside him, she realized a gorgeous couple stood across from him.

What struck her immediately as she slipped her hand

into his was how relaxed his body was. Until that moment, she hadn't realized the thin layer of tension snapping through him. His expression now was free and easy. Comfortable.

She'd seen Finn interact with many people—tonight and several years ago. He was always in complete control, of himself, of the situation and of the people around him. But in order to be that way, he had to constantly be on.

With the couple in front of him, she realized he didn't feel that need. Which intrigued her.

Turning her attention to them, Genevieve immediately began cataloging them both. The man was a couple inches over six feet. Just like Finn, he was obviously fit beneath the layers of polish and expensive clothing. His facial features were sharp, and not simply because he had an aristocratic heritage. His personality and demeanor added even more of an edge. Without the smile on his lips and the crinkled edges at his eyes he could have been austere and intimidating.

Genevieve had no doubt there were times that's exactly how he came across. Because he could be when necessary.

But not with Finn.

The woman standing beside him was stunning in a girl-next-door way. Tonight she was wearing a couture gown that was simple even as it showed off her petite frame. She didn't need beads, sequins or crystals because they would have appeared garish next to her elegant beauty. Her blond hair was pulled back into a demure knot at the base of her head. She could have come across as aloof and snobbish, except that her eyes glowed with joy and genuine interest.

Separately they would have been intimidating. Together, their love for each other was so obvious that you couldn't help but want to bask in their happiness so some of it could rub off.

Genevieve was about to introduce herself so she could learn who they were to Finn, but he beat her to it.

Wrapping an arm around her waist, he pulled Genevieve against his side.

"Genevieve, let me introduce you to Stone and Piper, two of my closest friends."

By his own admission Finn allowed few people close enough to call friends. So it was easy to make assumptions about who Stone was. Not that she'd needed the deduction once she'd heard their names.

Anderson Stone and Piper Blackburn had been in the news several months ago. Genevieve might not know the intimate details of their situation, but she understood enough.

Holding out a hand, she said, "Wonderful to meet you both."

Stone accepted her offering, giving her hand a squeeze. Piper, though, didn't bother. She moved straight past Genevieve's outstretched hand to pull her close and wrap her in a tight hug. Pulling back, she gave Genevieve a brilliant smile. "We need to get together for drinks and dinner soon. I want to get to know you better."

In that moment, Genevieve decided that she really liked Piper. "That would be great."

Piper drew her a few steps away from the men, sharing a little about herself and asking questions of her own.

"How's your son?"

At first Genevieve was taken aback that the other woman seemed to know more about her than a stranger normally would. Until she continued.

"I've seen pictures. He's adorable, by the way. And heard plenty of stories. Noah is one of Finn's favorite topics. He's such a proud daddy."

Placing a hand on Genevieve's arm, Piper leaned closer. "I know it's none of my business, but I just want to say that from a professional standpoint, I admire your ability to separate your personal issues with Finn and let him be a father to Noah. I have plenty of patients still dealing with the aftermath of an absent father."

Genevieve blinked, uncertain how to respond.

Piper pulled a grimace. "I'm sorry. Stone's always telling me I need to keep my psychologist firmly locked away during these events. I just know it couldn't have been easy at first to let Finn back into your life given the history between you. I'm impressed. And it says a lot about you as a person and a mom."

Well, okay. "Thanks?" Was that the proper response when someone praised you for being a decent human being? "I admit I wasn't thrilled and tried to stop Finn from being involved at first. But once I had no choice…finding a way to interact became important for Noah's happiness. And the first time I saw Finn with him…"

How could she not have allowed him into Noah's life? No matter what else happened, Genevieve knew Finn loved their son and would do anything to protect him.

That was all she could ask of him.

Waving a hand to change the subject, Piper said, "No more of that. Finn said you're a jewelry designer. Did you make the pieces you're wearing?"

"Yes."

"They're stunning."

"Thank you. Finn bought them from one of my consignment clients."

Genevieve couldn't stop her gaze from dragging across the space to find him. At some point he and Stone had moved several more feet away. At the edge of the room, they were standing half in shadows, heads bowed together in conversation.

Finn was relaxed. Stone, on the other hand, was frustrated and irritated. Leaning into Finn's personal space, he was attempting to make a point with whatever words he was using. While Finn was clearly unswayed.

"What are they talking about?" she found herself asking Piper.

The other woman shrugged. "Who knows. Those two are the best of friends, but Finn delights in irritating Stone. I'm pretty sure it's a game to him. One I keep pointing out to Stone that he's letting Finn win."

Piper shifted, turning her back to the men again. Genevieve couldn't pull her gaze away from them, though. Something about the conversation made her uneasy. To anyone else watching, Finn most likely appeared to be unaffected by what his friend was saying. But Genevieve knew him better than most.

He was upset.

"I wish Gray was here. He's usually the peacemaker between them. I've learned from experience not to get between them when they get going. It doesn't do much good."

"Gray?"

"The third member in their little trio. All three met in prison, but I assume you already knew that."

Genevieve nodded.

"Gray was convicted of embezzling forty million, although all three of the guys contend he was framed. They've been working together for months to try and find proof to back up their claim."

"Any luck?"

"Not so far."

"Because there isn't any evidence or because they haven't been able to find it?"

Piper's gaze cut to hers. Her head tilted sideways as she studied Genevieve for several moments. Genevieve fought the urge to squirm beneath the sharp, intelligent, all-too-seeing gaze.

After several seconds, she finally said, "My money's

on they just haven't been able to find it. Yet. Everyone in prison claims to be innocent…except Stone and Finn. They both readily admitted to doing what they were convicted of. Gray's always maintained his innocence."

Twelve

"You brought her with you to rob the place?" Stone asked, a frown pulling his brows into an unhappy V.

"No, I brought her to a benefit gala for a charity I'm happy to support."

"Bullshit."

Finn shrugged his shoulders. "You asked me to take on this project. Let me do it."

"Oh, I have no qualms with your ability to successfully complete the assignment. I do, however, question your judgment in bringing Genevieve into it."

"Really? She's the perfect cover for a little theft."

"Sure. Until she figures out you've used her and then she's gonna be pissed."

"She'll never know."

"Uh-huh. Man, if there's one thing I've learned it's that women always find out." Stone sent a sardonic expression in Piper's direction. If Finn was a better friend, he might ask questions about what Stone was talking about.

But he wasn't a good friend.

Finn shrugged. "I'll take my chances."

"You'll have a preliminary report tomorrow?"

Business concluded, Finn was eager to get back to Genevieve. He wanted to enjoy the party for a little while longer before using the cover of the crowd to slip off and see what he could haul home with him.

Returning to the women, the four of them chatted for several minutes. Piper invited Genevieve out for lunch next week and he was happy when she agreed. Lackland had isolated her so much that she'd never really had the opportunity to build strong friendships.

Piper was the kind of woman who liked to take on the wounded and lost. While Genevieve didn't quite fit into that category, he had no doubt Piper would sense her need for friendship and attempt to fill the role. If for no other reason than she liked him and Genevieve was important to him.

Leaning into her personal space, Finn drew her close. "Dance with me," he murmured against her temple.

Her answering nod was slow and deliberate. Leading them out onto the floor, Finn spun her around and into his arms.

Together, they moved with smooth, sure steps. The melody of the music pulsed beneath the surface of his skin. Finn relished the brush of her body against his. The delicate feel of her. The rough brush of lace as his palm slid across her hip. The heat of her melting deep into his blood.

Finn closed his eyes, soaking up each moment.

Which was why he missed the sneak attack.

"I'll have to speak to Hunt about his guest list. Obviously, he doesn't realize that he's let the serpent into the garden."

His arms wrapped around her, Finn couldn't miss the way Genevieve's body stiffened. She couldn't even see the man standing behind her, but it didn't matter. The voice was obviously enough.

Finn tightened his grip on her, maneuvering them both so he could tuck her protectively against his side.

"Grandfather," Genevieve finally spoke, her voice cool and remote.

"Granddaughter," Lackland countered, his snide voice full of disdain. "I see you haven't gotten any smarter. I can't imagine why you'd let this man anywhere near you given what he did the last time you spread your thighs wide."

Finn took a menacing step forward. Lackland didn't flinch. In fact, he moved closer, raising his chin in a taunting invitation to make a spectacle in the middle of the crowded ballroom.

Genevieve was the one who stopped Finn. A cool hand on his arm, she squeezed. "He isn't worth it."

Finn's gaze was hot when he turned to look at her. Her face was pale and drawn, her jaw tight from grinding her teeth.

"Maybe not, but you are and I won't have him making malicious remarks about you."

"Nothing malicious about my remark, DeLuca. You seduced an innocent woman to gain access to my family vault, stole from us and then left my granddaughter alone and pregnant."

"Every sin you just named was mine, not hers."

"She let you do it. I raised her to be smarter than that."

"You raised her to be an obedient servant. But she isn't. She's a human being with feelings and needs."

"And you had no problem exploiting those needs."

Seriously, if Lackland didn't get out of his sight, Finn was going to deck the man. Spectacle be damned. "You better watch your words, old man. Speak that way about her again and you'll regret it."

"The only thing I regret is that you didn't spend more time behind bars. But I'm certain you'll land yourself back there soon enough. A leopard doesn't change its spots."

Finn balled his hand into a fist. Genevieve yanked hard on his arm. "Walk away, Finn. He's goading you into making a scene."

Logically, he knew Genevieve was right. But he wasn't certain it made a difference. Someone needed to put the bully in his place and Finn had been itching to do it for a very long time. If they'd been anywhere else, he wouldn't have hesitated.

But he still had a job to do.

"Fine," he ground out. Turning to Genevieve, he cupped her face in his hands and brought her close enough that he could stare straight into her eyes. "You and Noah do not need this man in your life. He's poison and has nothing to offer anyone. You, on the other hand, are one of the kindest, most talented and beautiful people I've ever met. I have no idea how you managed to flourish when this man did everything in his power to snuff out your light, but I'm grateful that you did."

Genevieve's eyes widened and her mouth opened and closed. He didn't wait for her response, mostly because he didn't want one. What he'd wanted to do was replace her grandfather's toxic words with something more uplifting.

Arm around her waist, Finn turned his back on her grandfather and led them both across the ballroom and into a hallway off the far side.

The first few rooms had blazing lights and knots of people inside. A game room, a drawing room. What he wanted was a few quiet minutes with her.

Farther down the hall, the noise of the party faded. The bright lights were replaced with muted lamps and sconces. Peeking into a room to the left, Finn found a sunroom. Another door down was an office with an imposing desk and a tufted leather sofa.

He made a mental note to come back in a bit, assuming this was the perfect place to hide a safe.

Another two doors down revealed a smaller, intimate room. The far wall was floor-to-ceiling windows that looked out over the rolling lawn of the estate. The other three walls contained soaring shelves of books with several groupings of furniture clearly designed to curl up and relax.

Tugging on her hand, Finn pulled Genevieve inside and shut the door behind them. This was perfect.

A few feet in, she pulled to a stop. "We shouldn't be here."

"Yes, we should."

"No."

Finn reeled her in, using his hold on her hand to draw her to him. So small, she settled into the shelter of his body. Even reluctant, she didn't hesitate to let herself relax against him.

Her trust was a gift, one he never wanted to screw up again.

Bending his knees, Finn brought his mouth to the naked line of her shoulder. Placing gentle kisses along her skin, he followed the curve up to that sensitive spot on the side of her neck.

The sharp inhale of her breath when he nipped right there sent a surge of need thundering through him. The erection he'd been fighting since she walked out of that bathroom came back full force.

Genevieve's fingers, buried beneath his suit jacket at his hips, curled into his body. Her head dropped sideways, giving him better access to tease her with his mouth.

Finn wasn't the kind of guy to let an invitation like that go unaccepted.

Walking backward, he pulled them both farther into the room until a patch of moonlight, streaming through the gigantic windows, fell across Genevieve's pale skin.

Dropping to his knees at her feet, Finn looked up at her. She was gorgeous, but what sent his heart fluttering was the unguarded way she watched him, her eyes filled with hope and something deeper.

Hands braced on his shoulders, she waited.

Slowly, Finn began to gather the hem of her dress in his hands, revealing her ankles, calves and thighs.

But the real jewel was the dark apex of her sex.

"Lean back and grab the table behind you," Finn ordered. He didn't wait for Genevieve to comply before moving in, murmuring, "I've wanted to do this since you stuffed those panties in my pocket."

Spreading the lips of her sex wide, Finn found her warm center glistening with the evidence of her desire. Genevieve's body rocked backward when his mouth latched on to her. Licking, sucking, using every part of his mouth, Finn relished the explosion of her taste across his tongue. The muffled sound of her whimper as she tried to be quiet.

Her hips moved in time with his motions, rocking harder against his mouth, trying to find more. But he wasn't ready to let her go.

Finn kept her teetering on the edge of release, bringing her close and then moving back. He relished the way her wild hands found his hair, tangling in the strands and using the hold to try and get what she wanted.

"Finn," she finally breathed. "Please."

He couldn't deny her anything.

Adding a finger deep inside her body, Finn ran the flat of his tongue across her clit several times. Adding a second finger, he pulsed them in and out, finding the spot that had her whimpering.

Her body drew tight right before the explosion of her orgasm erupted around him. Finn rode it out, milking her body for every speck of pleasure she could give him.

But the moment she went lax, he shot to his feet and began undoing the fly at his pants. His cock pulsed with the need to feel her warm, wet heat. He wanted to be buried inside her. As close as he could possibly get to her.

Picking her up, Finn flicked the tail of Genevieve's gown out behind her as he set her onto the surface of the table. She hissed at the unexpected cold, but didn't stop him. Instead, she took up the task of freeing him.

Her palm was hot as she stroked up and down his throbbing shaft. "I'm not going to last long if you keep doing that," he breathed.

"Who said anything about lasting long?"

She scooted to the edge of the table. Spreading her thighs wide, Genevieve drew him closer to the waiting heaven she was offering.

Finn bit back a belly-deep groan when he sank inside. She was so wet and warm. Her body fit his like a glove, opening up and welcoming him home. Every time he touched her, he wanted more. Tonight, the need for release was pounding against his brain, but he would have been just as content to stay like this, connected to her in the most primitive and fulfilling way.

But she had other plans.

Hands on his waist, she started guiding him in and out. Finn let her set the pace…for a minute or two. But then it became too much.

Using his grip on her hips, Finn held her steady as he began to pump in and out. Long, even strokes that made his eyes want to cross.

"So damn good," he whispered.

Urging her backward, Finn placed his hands on the tabletop. His thrusts became harder, a rhythmic snap accompanying each as the table tapped the wall behind them.

"Someone's going to hear," Genevieve protested.

"Let them. I want everyone in that ballroom to know you're mine."

Genevieve's eyes sharpened and glittered like the jewels circling her throat. Dropping her head, she exposed the tender underside of her jaw. Finn leaned forward, finding the pulsing vein running along the side and sucked hard.

Her body bowed up and her gasp echoed through the room. Her sex fluttered and tightened around him, another orgasm slamming into her.

And that was all it took for him to topple over. The explosion of pleasure rocked through him, blacking out everything except her.

He was breathing hard several minutes later when his brain clicked back on and everything came into focus. Genevieve had collapsed onto the table beneath him, but she was staring up at him with a sleepy, satisfied expression.

Her hair was messy and her necklace was twisted sideways.

"You look like you just had sex."

A wry grimace pulled at her mouth. "Go figure."

Pulling away, Finn grasped her hands to pull her up. "I've already said it, I don't care what anyone else thinks of us. And I don't mind them knowing we just had sex. But I know you do. So, stay here. I'll go find something to clean us both up."

Quickly working the fly of his pants, Finn strode out into the hallway, but didn't get very far.

His feet faltered halfway past the doorway to the office. It would only take a few moments to do a little reconnaissance.

Genevieve would never know.

Genevieve had no idea how long she stayed in the room. It probably wasn't more than five minutes, but it felt like forever. She was rumpled and clearly sexed up. If anyone walked in right now...

Looking around, Genevieve was hoping to find a mirror hanging on one of the walls that she could at least use to repair her hair. No such luck.

A few more minutes had an anxious sensation pulling at the muscles between her shoulder blades. Maybe Finn had been caught by someone in the hallway and he was attempting to extricate himself from a conversation so he could return to her.

Either way, she was tired of waiting. Surely there was a bathroom somewhere close.

Returning to the hallway, she began moving down, peeking into each room she passed. One door was partially closed so she started to ignore it, but halfway past a noise from the inside caught her attention.

Something made her turn. When she pushed against the door, it didn't even creak as the well-oiled hinges gave way, revealing a large room with an imposing desk prominently displayed.

The piece was massive and intricate. She didn't have to touch it to know it would be heavy. The wood gleamed with the patina of age and the color reminded her of the tobacco leaves she'd once seen on a documentary about Southern plantations.

This room didn't benefit from a massive wall of windows overlooking the back of the estate. The natural light from the few high panes of glass weren't enough to beat back the gloom of darkness that shrouded the edges of the room.

She wasn't supposed to be there.

Genevieve might have backed out, except a movement off to her right caught the corner of her eye. It took her several seconds to register the shape of a man in the shadows, but the minute her eyes picked out the image, the hair at the back of her neck stood on edge.

And not because she was scared.

She didn't need to see clearly to recognize Finn. She'd know the lithe, controlled way he moved anywhere.

Genevieve watched him as he ran his hands along the large frame of a painting mounted on the wall. When that one revealed nothing, he moved to another. The muffled sound of triumph that fell from his lips as he found the catch made her throat ache. The frame swung away from the wall revealing the huge face of an inset safe.

Finn didn't hesitate, but quickly pulled a set of tools out of the pocket of his jacket. How the hell had she missed those? She'd had her hands all over him tonight and hadn't felt them.

He'd brought her here for cover.

Hell, sneaking off to have sex with her had no doubt been another layer to that subterfuge.

He'd used her. And she'd blindly let him.

But she was done accepting that kind of behavior—from him and herself.

The plush carpet silenced her heels as she crossed the room. But something must have tipped him off because he spun around just steps before she could reach him.

"Genevieve," he said, the single word as grim as his expression.

His gaze skipped up and down her body, settling squarely on her face. No doubt she looked like she was pissed. Because she was.

"This isn't what it looks like."

"Oh, you didn't use me so you could break into Hunt's estate and rob him blind?"

"No."

"Bullshit."

"I mean, yes, I am here to rob him, but you weren't cover for that."

Genevieve's head threatened to explode. "I wasn't cover? So I'm just an accomplice instead? Sure, much better. This way our son can lose both his parents when they go to jail."

"Neither one of us is going to jail."

"Because you're going to put—" Genevieve waved her hand toward the tools still clutched in his hands "—whatever those are away, lock the painting back over that safe and we're going to walk out of this room together."

The expression on Finn's face went even grimmer. "I can't do that."

"Oh, yes, you can. If you want to be part of my life, you can."

Closing his eyes, Finn pulled in a deep breath, held it for several seconds and then let out a soul-deep sigh.

"I'm working for Stone."

Seriously, he kept saying things like the words were supposed to make things better, but they just didn't. "I don't care if the queen of England hired you to rob Hunt blind. I won't let you do it."

"The queen of England didn't hire me to rob him, but Hunt did."

Genevieve blinked once. And then again. "Excuse me?"

"Well, technically, he hired Stone Surveillance, but since I'm one-third owner and the resident expert on relieving people of their unprotected valuables, this assignment fell to me."

Seriously. "Are you speaking English?"

"Apparently, Hunt isn't just a longtime friend of your grandfather's. He's known Stone all of his life and been in business with Anderson Steel for years. He approached Stone about beefing up his security, but when Stone made several suggestions, he didn't see the value. They made an agreement, allowing me to break in to take whatever I could."

Genevieve's mind spun with the information. "Why

didn't you tell me you'd taken an assignment with Stone? Or that you're part owner in the company?"

"Because until a few days ago I wasn't. Stone's been trying for months to get me to join the team, but I really didn't want to do it."

"Why not?"

"Because I thought it would be boring. I already own a company and don't enjoy being involved with it. Why would I want to take on the responsibility of another? Especially one that needs to be built from the ground up?"

After meeting him, something told her Anderson Stone would have no problems building the business into whatever he wanted it to become.

"What changed?"

"You did."

For the second time tonight Genevieve found herself asking, "Excuse me?"

"I needed Gray's expertise and Stone's resources in order to get the security at your studio and house upgraded quickly. Stone drives a hard bargain."

"You agreed to something you didn't want to do, something you've been telling your closest friends no about for months, in order to protect me and our son?"

"Of course."

How could she go from wanting to strangle the man to wanting to jump his bones in the space of five minutes? One thing was for sure, Finn DeLuca definitely made her react.

But he wasn't finished shocking her.

"I had every intention of just being a silent partner, in name only." Suddenly, Finn shifted, running an agitated hand through his hair. For the first time since she'd caught him, he began to look guilty. "I'll be honest, I've loved spending the last few weeks with you and Noah. But I was starting to get restless, chafe at the normal. I went to talk to Stone and he suggested I take this job. Use my skills in a way that might scratch the itch without jeopardizing everything."

Genevieve watched him, trepidation churning sickly through her belly. She *had* to ask the question, but she really wasn't sure she wanted to know the answer.

"And?"

A smile tugged at the edges of his mouth. "I thought knowing it was legit would take the edge off, but it didn't. Or at least, there was enough left to make the experience an interesting challenge."

That's what Finn needed and why he did the things he did. Not because he wanted the things he stole. But because he wanted to feel alive. Needed to feel alive.

In a way that wouldn't cost someone else their life, like Sawyer.

God, what was she going to do with him?

Shaking her head, Genevieve was at a loss. She believed him. Maybe she was stupid to, but she did.

Before she could regret it, she grumbled, "Hurry up. I have your come dripping down my thighs and would really like to go home."

The shocked laughter that burst from Finn was totally worth it.

Thirteen

The last few days had been a whirlwind of activity. Genevieve had been in the studio all hours of the day and night working on the finishing touches of her collection. Finn had taken to staying at her place, spending time with Noah so she could do what she needed. Aside from playing with his son, the best part of his day was when Genevieve walked through the back door.

He'd finished up his work for Hunt, submitted his report and eventually returned the items he'd taken from the safe. It had actually been more gratifying than he'd anticipated to help design the system and protocols Stone and Gray were implementing to protect the estate.

Tonight, he'd convinced Genevieve that she needed a break. He'd pressured her to leave the studio early. After running by to see Stone, he'd stopped by his place to pick up a few things.

Finn wondered how long it would be before he could convince Genevieve to move in with him. Her place was nice enough, but it was small. His had more room, although he'd need her help to baby-proof it for sure.

He was halfway back to Genevieve's when an alert went off on his phone. He pulled over to the side of the road, looked at the screen and swore beneath his breath.

An alarm was going off at her studio.

Swiping to open the app, Finn pulled up the video feed. Flipping through the cameras, it took him several minutes to find the shadowy figure creeping through the office and into Genevieve's work area.

No doubt Stone was on it, but he punched in his friend's number, anyway.

Stone didn't bother with a greeting when he answered. "Yeah, man. I see it."

"I'm three minutes away," Finn answered, pulling a U-turn in the middle of the road and heading back in that direction. "I can get there faster than anyone else."

Stone's voice was grim when he said, "I'm calling in reinforcements."

"Thanks," Finn responded, ending the call and tossing his phone onto the seat beside him. He wasn't going to call Genevieve until he knew exactly what they were dealing with. No reason to upset her just yet.

Rushing into the back lot, he parked sideways in front of the back door.

"Dammit," he muttered when he realized it was hanging open several inches.

He was not going to let this happen. Genevieve had worked too hard.

But he also didn't want to alert whoever was inside that they'd been caught. Easing the door open, he slipped inside the studio. The place was pitch-black so he stood for several seconds, letting his eyes adjust to the darkness.

It was difficult to wait, especially when he heard a loud scrape of metal against metal coming from deep inside Genevieve's workroom.

Dread and white-hot anger curled through his stomach.

Slipping into the room, he expected to find some asshole standing in front of the open safe, rummaging through the drawers of jewels.

He was partially right. The doors to Genevieve's vault hung wide open. Several of the drawers were pulled out. But they weren't empty. Pieces spilled haphazardly over the lip of the drawers. A few jewels winked from the floor, scattered like a rainbow crumb trail across the room toward the front door.

Maybe he hadn't been as quiet as he'd thought and had startled the thief.

The good news was several of Genevieve's pieces were still there. The bad news was that the few jewels on the floor were by themselves, which meant they'd been broken apart from the rest of the design.

A string of curse words blasted across Finn's brain.

Torn between wanting to catch whoever was ransacking Genevieve's hard work and not wanting to let something valuable sit vulnerable on the floor, Finn dashed across the room.

But he scooped up the pieces on the floor as he went, stuffing them into the pockets of his slacks.

Bursting into the front room, the sound of sirens in the distance finally registered. Stone must have called the police along with the private team he employed.

He hated that Genevieve was about to spend her night talking with officers. Again. But that process would be easier and better if he could hand them a suspect.

Unfortunately, when Finn reached the front room, no one was there and the door leading onto the sidewalk was standing wide open.

A handful of police cruisers peeled up to the front of the building at the same time he raced out onto the sidewalk. Red-and-blue lights flashed right in his face, making him squint. Finn spun, first to the left and then to the right. The asshole couldn't have gotten far.

But no one was there.

"On the ground," one of the officers shouted.

Finn turned his attention back to the front of the store. Four or five cars were parked in an arch around the building, blocking off the street. A handful of cops had positioned themselves behind the open doors, guns drawn and pointed straight at him.

Well, that was enough to give any man pause.

"On the ground," one of the officers shouted again.

Realizing he didn't have much choice until he could explain the situation, Finn slowly raised his hands up over his head. Folding, he knelt onto the sidewalk.

"Let me explain."

One of the cops holstered his weapon and walked behind him. "You'll have plenty of time to explain."

Finn ignored what they were doing as the officer grabbed his wrists, pulling them behind his back. His words were fast, trying to talk before the cuffs came out.

"The thief is getting away. I work for Stone Surveillance. We got an alert on our security system for Genevieve's Designs. I was close so came to investigate. The back door was wide open. I chased someone through the building, but they slipped out the front door before I could catch them."

Cold metal kissed his skin. The snap around his wrists was a sensation he'd promised himself he'd never experience again.

"The only person we saw in front of the building was you."

Finn turned his head, looking again in both directions. He didn't understand and couldn't explain how that was true. The thief couldn't have moved that quickly. How had they just disappeared?

Urging him up onto his feet, the officer led him over to

one of the cruisers. "I'm going to search you now. Anything I need to know about? Weapons? Needles? Anything sharp?"

What the hell did the man take him for? "No. I did scoop up some of the jewels the thief had scattered across the floor. They're in my pockets."

A skeptical expression crossed the officer's face. "Jewels, huh?"

"Look, I knew they weren't safe just sitting on the floor. I needed to secure them."

"Sure, you were just securing them."

Frustration bubbled through him, eating at his patience like battery acid. "Call Anderson Stone. He'll corroborate my story."

"Oh, I'm certain he would. Being a convicted murderer."

"He killed his fiancée's rapist," Finn growled.

The cop shrugged. "Doesn't change the facts. But if what you say is true, we'll sort things out soon enough. Until then, you're being detained for questioning."

How had the night gone so terribly sideways?

He'd planned to spend it at home with Genevieve and Noah. Listening to the belly-deep giggle his son made when he tickled him. Watching the light in Genevieve's eyes when she looked at Noah. Making love to her until they were both exhausted.

Instead, he found himself ducking into the back of a cruiser for the second time in his life.

The worst part was looking through the chaos to find Genevieve standing on the sidewalk, once again watching him as he was carted away.

Pain and devastation stamped across every feature of her face.

How could this be happening again?

Genevieve watched as the officer pulled several gems

out of Finn's pockets and placed them inside an evidence bag. She'd gotten a call from Nick saying an alert had come up on the security system.

In between loading up Noah, she'd desperately tried to get in touch with Finn. But he hadn't answered any of her calls.

Now she understood why.

Scenes from the last several weeks flashed through her mind. Conversations they'd had. Moments they'd shared.

Pain and hope twisted inside her. This couldn't be right. She didn't want to believe he could have done this. There had to be another explanation.

Like at Hunt's.

But the evidence before her was hard to refute.

A huge part of her wanted to trust. Wanted to believe, like with the Star, that there was more to what was going on than met the eye.

Although one irrefutable fact about the Star was that he *had* stolen it. By his own admission he'd had it several days before returning it.

She didn't trust her own judgment when it came to Finn DeLuca. Was she clinging to hope simply because she wanted to? Was she being blind and stupid, ignoring the evidence in front of her?

Watching the officer duck Finn's head down so he could be loaded into the back of the cruiser didn't help at all. In fact, it made her sick to her stomach.

The officer obviously thought there was enough evidence to take him in.

"Genevieve," Nick said, coming up behind her. Wrapping his arms around her, he gently turned her away from the scene. Urging her into the shelter of his arms, he held her tight. "I'm so sorry."

Stroking his hands up and down her back, he murmured, "I watched the feed on my way over. So pissed. Because there was nothing I could do but watch as he popped open the safe like it was nothing and took everything you'd worked so hard for."

"You saw the video? Clearly? It was him?"

"No mistake at all. I'm going to turn it over to the police, although I'm not sure they'll need it. You saw. They caught him with some of your pieces in his pockets."

The sick, hollow sensation spread from her belly to her chest. The show. "I need to see."

She needed irrefutable proof.

Pulling free, Genevieve spun on her heel, heading straight for the front door. A gentleman there attempted to detain her, until she explained the studio was hers.

Walking inside was like waking up in the middle of a nightmare. The heavy safe doors stood wide open. A couple of her pieces spilled over the edge of the drawers. But she could see where the settings had been snapped.

Swallowing the lump in her throat, Genevieve refused to cry. It wouldn't do any good. She needed to assess the damage and see if there was anything salvageable.

Her equipment had been moved, tables pushed out of place and a couple chairs overturned. Picking her way through the rubble, she pulled open the drawers in the safe, one after the other, devastated at what she found.

Dropping to a crouch, she pressed the heels of her hands against her stinging eyes.

Nick's hand landed on her back. She knew he was trying to give her support, but right now, the last thing she wanted was to be touched.

But because she knew he meant well, she didn't shake him off.

"It's ruined. Everything," she finally croaked out. Her mind spun. In a matter of days, she was going to be in breach of contract with Mitchell Brothers. Legitimately, they could come after her for everything she had. They'd sunk a lot of resources into the release of her collection and in anticipation of selling the pieces in all their stores for the Christmas shopping season.

She had nothing to give them.

"I'm ruined." The words were out of her mouth before she realized they'd formed in her mind. "What am I going to do? How am I going to provide for Noah?"

Goddamn Finn!

"Why? Why would he do this? He doesn't need the money. Hell, he doesn't even need the challenge. It doesn't make sense."

Nick's fingers squeezed her shoulder. "Who knows how the man thinks? He's never needed the money from the things he's stolen. You know that's not why he does it. He's sick. He has a compulsion he can't control."

No, that wasn't true. Although Finn's words from several days ago rang in her ears. He went to Stone, *itchy*, he'd said. Stone had provided him a legitimate outlet.

Maybe it hadn't been enough?

But why *destroy* her pieces? She could understand Finn taking them—no, *understand* was the wrong word. She could have dealt with him taking them. But ripping her work apart?

It made no sense. He had nothing to gain from doing that. He'd bought three of her pieces, dammit. What purpose would this serve?

None that she could think of.

But the evidence was hard to ignore. And she'd always said Finn DeLuca had a purpose for everything he did. Maybe she just didn't have all the pieces yet to understand.

Slowly, Nick folded down so he was crouched beside her. Looking her straight in the eye, a sad expression pulling against the corners of his eyes, he said, "As much as I hate to say it, maybe it's time you called your grandfather. He could help you."

Oh, wouldn't Lackland simply love that.

The memory of his sneer and disparaging words from the gala ran through her head. When she'd left to live on her own, she'd promised herself that no circumstance existed where she'd go back. Not only did she deserve better than the toxic, abusive environment her grandfather created, but so did her son.

Unfortunately, her son also needed to eat and have a roof over his head. And if Mitchell came after her for what they could...even those basic necessities were in jeopardy.

Once again, she'd been naive. Obviously, there was a circumstance where she would go back to her grandfather.

Providing for her son would be worth anything, including subjecting herself to that environment.

Lackland was going to relish not only that she was crawling back, begging. But that she was doing it after Finn had ruined her.

Again.

Genevieve stared at the phone sitting on the kitchen table in front of her. She'd spent hours at the studio, evaluating exactly where she was and speaking with the officers.

After viewing the video Nick showed her...it was difficult to remain hopeful that there was an explanation.

While she hadn't seen his face—because he wouldn't be that sloppy—Finn had made one mistake. The shadowy figure had been wearing the same clothes Finn had been when he'd run out the front door of her studio, her jewels stuffed in his pockets.

There were two phone calls she needed to make, both of which she was dreading. Mitchell Brothers and her grandfather.

If there was one thing Lackland had taught her, it was to get the task you were dreading the most out of the way first.

Snatching up the phone, Genevieve flicked open the screen and quickly scrolled to her contacts. And the number she'd hoped never to need again.

Hitting the button, she dialed her grandfather, dread and disappointment churning in her belly.

"Genevieve."

Even the sound of his voice made her want to vomit.

"I hear you've had some excitement today."

Of course he'd heard. Her grandfather made sure he was aware of everything important that happened in the city.

"Yes."

"Such a shame your collection with Mitchell has been ruined."

He didn't even attempt to hide the pure glee filling his voice.

Genevieve desperately wished she could tell him that everything was going to be fine. That she had the situation well in hand. But she didn't. And years of dealing with the man had taught her, it was easier to keep her words simple and short. To let him gloat and believe he'd won. It made the unpleasant experience end faster.

And right now, that's what she wanted. To get through this conversation so she could take the next steps forward.

"I assume you're contacting me, for the first time in three years, to ask for my assistance."

Genevieve gritted her teeth, wishing she could keep the word behind her teeth. Unfortunately, that couldn't happen. "Yes."

"Hmm. I wonder, my dear, if you remember my words when you left, pregnant and disgraced?"

Of course she remembered his words. He'd been bitter and mean. Telling her that she was destined to fail at any attempt to be self-sufficient because she was stupid, incompetent and untrustworthy.

But it wouldn't matter what she said at this point. Lackland was going to delight in reminding her. No doubt that was part of what he was most looking forward to.

"I told you that you'd fail on your own. No matter what, you'd manage to screw things up and would need to come crawling back to me."

"Yes, Grandfather."

"And here we are. Exactly where I said you'd be."

Genevieve closed her eyes and waited for him to make his demands, because there was no denying that he would.

"And if I remember correctly, I promised you that I wouldn't lift a hand to help you at that point."

Of course he had, but Genevieve knew he'd never stick by that statement. Not when he had the perfect opportunity to have her back under his thumb, a puppet he could control.

Her grandfather liked nothing more than controlling people.

"However, three years is a long time and perhaps I was a bit hasty back then. I'd welcome you back into the family and at Reilly, but I have a few demands."

Of course he did. Genevieve had expected nothing less.

"I refuse to accept the son of that thief as my great-grandson."

Genevieve sat straight up in her chair. What exactly was he saying?

"However, I recognize that he's your son. So, I'm willing to accept you back on the condition that your son is sent to boarding school. Your focus should be on Reilly and the designs you'll be creating for our company, anyway."

No, there was no way Genevieve would ever agree to send her toddler to boarding school. "He's not even three yet," she ground out.

"I'm aware. I'm certain I can find a school willing to accept him despite his age. Better he grow up in that environment, anyway. The sooner he realizes that he's alone in the world and won't be accepted as part of this family, the better."

She wanted to scream. She wanted to cry. She wanted to curse both her grandfather and Finn for putting her in this position.

Lackland didn't even wait to hear her response. "Those are my terms. Take them or leave them," he said, before cutting the connection.

The dial tone buzzed through Genevieve's head, along with anger and despair.

Fourteen

Genevieve pulled Noah tight into her arms. Her son squirmed, pushing against her, wanting down so he could toddle over to the pile of toys in the corner and play.

He was completely innocent and oblivious to everything going on around him. To the changes that could potentially rock his world.

Genevieve set Noah on his feet, and he didn't even look back at her before tearing across the room. If she did go back to her grandfather—and that was a big if—she'd find some way around her grandfather's demand.

She had to.

Luckily, she didn't have to make that decision tonight. Or even tomorrow. The Mitchell brothers had generously given her a few days to figure everything out and evaluate what could be salvaged.

Right now, her focus was Noah. Partly because that was easy.

"Noah, you want some chicken nuggets?" The thought of food might make her stomach turn, but her son still needed to eat.

Abandoning his toys, Noah shot back across the room. Bumping into her knees, he wrapped his arms around her legs and looked up at her with a huge smile on his face.

Chicken nuggets were his favorite.

"Dinosaws?" he asked.

"Of course. Go play. I'll get them ready."

Confident she was going to get him what he needed, her son went back to his toys. Genevieve went into the kitchen. Keeping an eye on him, she pulled the bag from the freezer and preheated the oven.

The moment was normal and domestic. Something she'd done hundreds of times. But right now, it felt wrong. Because she shouldn't be doing it alone.

She'd just popped the pan into the oven when there was a loud knock on her door.

With a sigh, Genevieve dropped her head and squeezed her eyes tight. She wasn't in the mood to deal with anyone, not even well-meaning friends. She'd already called Nicole to say she wasn't going into the studio tonight.

Standing in the middle of her kitchen, Genevieve contemplated ignoring the knock. Everything inside her balked at the idea of being impolite, but she really didn't have the energy to deal.

Honestly, she was afraid that at the first well-meaning word from anyone's mouth she was going to lose it. Right now, she was holding it together for Noah.

But when the polite knock morphed into an insistent pounding that rattled her front door, Genevieve decided it would be easier to open the door and pointedly tell whoever was there to go the hell away.

Whether she would have actually said that or not was a moot point because when she opened the door, she was shocked silent.

Anderson Stone asked, "Can we come in?" but didn't

bother waiting for her answer before scooting by her into the foyer.

The man with him followed silently behind, pausing long enough to shut her front door with a quiet click. It didn't take a genius to figure out this was probably Gray Lockwood, the third musketeer.

Shaken from her stupor, her words dripped with sarcasm as she swept an arm wide indicating her den. "Make yourselves at home."

Stone gave her a long look before the corner of his mouth quirked up into a little grin. "Look at that, the mild-mannered thing has teeth."

"I don't know what you want or why you're here, but I'm really not in the mood right now."

For the first time, Gray spoke. "You're going to want to see this, I promise."

His voice was smooth and deep. For some reason it made her think of smoke-filled rooms with brocade wallpaper and filigreed sconces. A twenties speakeasy with gangsters, beautiful women and rich Scotch.

Blond and polished, he was the contrast to Finn's swarthy, mischievous demeanor. He was also quieter and less assuming than Stone, who always seemed to be up front and in charge.

Not that she particularly cared, but staring at the two men standing in her den, she wondered how the prison they'd been in had survived all three of them. At once. They were gorgeous, cunning and autocratic. Together, she had no doubt they'd been a force to be reckoned with.

They still were.

Turning her attention to Gray, she asked, "What do I need to see?"

Walking into the kitchen and over to the table, Gray set down a laptop she hadn't even noticed he'd been holding. Popping it open, he clicked a few buttons and began playing a video. Stepping back, he waved her forward so she could get a better look.

A frown pulling at her mouth, she did as he'd indicated. It took her several moments to orient herself to what she was watching. Some context might have been helpful, but probably would have blunted the impact of the images on the screen.

The video was perfectly clear, no doubt because the men standing behind her could afford to buy state-of-the-art equipment. But that didn't negate the fact that it had obviously been dark whenever the footage was taken.

Despite that, it was easy to identify Nick and her grandfather leaning close and engaging in an intense conversation.

She didn't need to hear the words being spoken to know that Lackland Reilly was pissed. Mostly because she'd been the recipient of the expression on numerous occasions.

Nick wasn't exactly happy, either, but he was clearly deferring to her grandfather.

Genevieve understood what she was looking at, but not the implications Gray and Stone were obviously trying to make. She needed more information. Turning, her gaze bounced between the two men as she asked, "What is this? When was it taken? What are they talking about?"

Before they could answer, Noah came bouncing into the kitchen. He gave both men a cursory glance before making a beeline for Genevieve.

"'Saws?"

She'd completely forgotten about the nuggets in the oven. "Yes, baby. I'll get them out."

Making a move around the men, she started into the kitchen, but Stone stopped her. A hand on her arm, he said, "I'll get it. Let Gray explain."

She watched as one of the wealthiest men in the South scooped her son up, lifted Noah over his head and plopped him down onto his shoulders. Noah squealed, wrapping his chubby fingers in Stone's hair.

She watched Stone's tight grip around her son's back, holding him securely in place. Twisting his head so he could talk up at her son, he said, "Your daddy asked me to keep an eye on you while he's gone for a little bit. Let's get you those nuggets, little man."

Watching the scene before her, it was difficult to reconcile the elegant man in the expensive suit she'd met just a few days ago with the one letting her toddler's diaper-clad rear bounce up and down against his shoulders as they went to get chicken nuggets out of her oven.

"Cut them up into little pieces and make sure they're not hot enough to burn his mouth," Genevieve said, a little bemused.

Stone tossed her a big grin. "We got this, Momma. Listen to Gray."

Gray took that as his cue. Tapping a few keys on the computer, he pulled up another video feed and pressed Play. A man of few words, he again didn't bother to tell her what she was about to watch.

The screen was split between two feeds, both of which were of her studio. One camera was clearly pointed directly at her safe, although she'd never seen footage from this angle. The other had a wide view of her back door and the hallway leading into the workroom.

"Finn asked us to set up a couple additional cameras that he didn't mention to you or Nick."

"Why?"

Why would he do that? So he could have access to watch the studio that no one else was aware of? But, obviously, *someone* had been aware of it since Gray was showing her the feed.

His friends had been in on the plan the entire time. That

was surely the more logical explanation. However, that didn't explain why they were both in her house right now.

Unless they were upset that all their hard work had yielded nothing and were hoping to play some other angle.

God, Genevieve was confused. And conflicted. None of this made any sense. Both of the men in her home had enough to money to buy everything she owned, including the jewels Finn had attempted to steal.

Hell, *Finn* had enough money to buy everything she owned.

And that's what she kept circling around in her brain. None of this made sense.

So she watched the feed, trying to find some clue that would answer all the questions that kept swirling inside her head.

It took her several moments to realize a dark shadow was lurking in the hallway by her back door. As she watched, it shifted and flowed into her workroom. Her eyes immediately jumped to the second half of the screen, waiting to see what would happen next.

The slim shape paused in front of her safe. The doors quickly swung open. "That was fast."

Gray hummed, "Almost as if someone had the code."

She'd given Finn a lot of access, but she hadn't shared the code for the safe with him. Mostly because it hadn't occurred to her that she'd need to and he hadn't asked for it. But he had been in the room when she'd opened it on several occasions. He was smart and observant enough to memorize it if he'd wanted to.

She expected to see the shadow reach inside and start taking pieces. But that's not what happened. Instead, the person pulled out a tool, the metal glinting for a moment through the darkness, and began systematically ripping her pieces apart.

That had been bothering her from the very beginning. The

stones were valuable, but they were already set. Why destroy the pieces? It wasn't like any of them were notorious—like the Star of Reilly—or would be difficult to fence just as they were. Perhaps down the road it would make sense to separate the stones so they'd be more difficult to trace, but why take the time to do it in the middle of stealing them?

She didn't understand.

But then, she wasn't a thief. So maybe Finn had a reason?

Her confusion thickened, though, when the thief took a handful of the gems and sprinkled them across the floor and her worktable like a trail of bread crumbs from a fairy tale.

Then, without taking a single stone, the shadow slipped back out into the hallway. And waited.

What was frustrating was that, even though the surveillance equipment was high quality and the feed clear, the person managed to keep their face hidden by twisting and melting into the shadows.

But that wouldn't be difficult to do for someone who knew where every camera was placed.

"What's he waiting for?" Genevieve finally asked, after staring for a couple minutes at footage of the thief simply standing there.

"Wait."

Suddenly, the shadow moved. Fast. Darting back through the hallway and into the workroom. This time, he didn't stop at the safe, but ran through, knocking over one of the tables, pulling a rolling table with equipment out into the middle of the room and overturning a couple chairs before racing into the front.

At the same time, motion at the back door caught her attention. Turning her focus, Genevieve let out a gasp when Finn came through. He wasn't even bothering to hide his face from the cameras. Instead, he was intent on getting into her workroom as quickly as possible.

She watched him survey the damage. His body jerked,

as if he'd been punched, and his mouth moved, although she couldn't hear what he said. She could guess, though.

Racing through, he stopped long enough to scoop up several of the jewels scattered across the floor, stuffing them into the pockets of his pants. He took the same path as the shadow, pushing chairs, table and equipment out of his way.

The feed cut off, but Genevieve continued to stare at the blank screen for several moments, her mind spinning.

Could they have doctored the footage?

She absolutely believed they had the expertise and equipment to do it. But to what end? What did Stone and Gray have to gain from showing this to her?

Other than freeing Finn.

But what did any of them have to gain from stealing her pieces? No, from destroying them?

Nothing. That was the logical answer.

Which left her with the question, who did have something to gain?

Turning slowly, she faced Gray. Arms crossed over his chest, he'd simply been standing and waiting.

"Explain what I just watched, please."

A frown pulled his brows into a tight V. "Finn didn't break in and steal from you."

"Obviously. I mean, what else? Who did break in?" She had no doubt Gray and Stone knew more about what was going on than they were saying. They might be keeping it to themselves because they weren't certain what her reaction would be, but they were going to have to get over that. "Why did you show me the first video and what does it have to do with everything else?"

"Finn asked us to put Nick under surveillance. He's had Lackland watched since before he got out of prison."

Later she'd address why he'd felt the need to do that—and not mention it—but right now it was immaterial.

"How long?"

"Almost a year."

About the time Gray had been released and several months before Stone and Finn. She'd done her research on all three once she'd realized who they were to him.

"It wasn't until the last few weeks, though, that we placed Nick under the same scrutiny. Or learned that he met with Lackland. It's possible—probable—they communicated the whole time. We simply can't prove it."

"What can you prove?"

Gray reached over and began clicking a few keys, shutting off the computer. He didn't look at her as he said, "What you probably suspect. Nick has been giving your grandfather information. He's also been working with him the last few weeks to sabotage the release of your collection. Reilly is hurting. The last few collections they've released haven't performed as well as anticipated. Competition from companies like Mitchell Brothers hasn't helped. Your grandfather has been leveraging assets to maintain his lavish lifestyle, anticipating the market would bounce back."

"Which hasn't happened." Genevieve was fully aware of the reputation Reilly had. The company was known for being old-fashioned. However, that wasn't always a bad thing. It also maintained a reputation for quality and excellence. "I didn't realize."

"No one does. He's worked hard to keep the truth from the board. The problems started about the time you left."

Which made sense. Up until that point, she'd been the one designing collections, for both their major commercial clients as well as any VIPs.

Genevieve stared at Gray for several moments, letting everything sink in.

"Finn didn't do anything wrong." Relief flooded through her.

Finn hadn't done anything wrong. She'd been right to question the evidence in front of her.

She should have trusted him. Trusted her own instincts more. She owed Finn a huge apology. And she needed to stop questioning his motives and trust he only had her and Noah's best interests at heart.

She simply wasn't used to anyone else caring enough about her to place her needs first. Or hell, second or third.

"Nope, he didn't do anything wrong."

"I heard that cop. They're not going to listen when he tells them the truth."

"Nope."

"I assume you're going to use this to prove he's right?" Genevieve asked, waving her hand at the computer on the table beside them.

"Yep."

"I want to come with you. I want to be there when they let him go."

Gray nodded. "You realize this implicates Nick and your grandfather. I have other evidence I plan to turn over."

"Good."

"They're both going to prison, but the police will want you to press charges."

"Happy to."

"Nick's been one of your closest friends for the last several years."

"Apparently not." Genevieve's face scrunched into a frown. "Are you trying to talk me out of doing this? Do you think it matters to me? My grandfather is a despicable man and always has been. And if Nick let him influence his choices, then he has to deal with the consequences."

In the kitchen, Noah's peel of laughter pulled her attention for several seconds. Watching her son, light filling his perfect face, her chest tightened.

"Despite everything, I love Finn. Sometimes I think I shouldn't, but I can't help it. He's charismatic, charming and mischievous. He has this uncanny ability to draw people to him. And more importantly, he recognizes strength inside of me when I can't see it for myself."

Gray's hand on her shoulder startled her. His gaze was steady and calm when Genevieve looked back to him. This man had deep wells of patience and understanding. The intelligence behind his eyes would have been intimidating if his demeanor wasn't so calm and assured.

"I know."

A relieved smile curled her lips. "So let's go save his impulsive ass."

Fifteen

Finn stared at the blank walls of the cell and tried not to let claustrophobia win.

He'd been grilled for the last several hours. Rapid-fire questions designed to trip him up and poke holes in his story. Unfortunately for the investigators, his story was solid. Because it was the truth.

Not that they'd been willing to listen.

They were still convinced he was lying. And based on several of the questions they asked him, their conviction was supported by something more than what had happened at Genevieve's studio. Obviously, they weren't revealing their information to him, but from what he could piece together, it had something to do with Hunt.

He needed to get in touch with Stone to clear up this whole mess. But what he needed more was to speak with Genevieve. Although from the expression on her face, he wasn't sure she'd be willing to listen to anything he had to say, either.

How was he about to lose everything when he hadn't done a damn thing wrong?

For the first time in his life, he'd attempted to follow the rules. And everything was turning to shit. Only learning of Sawyer's death had ever left him feeling this hopeless and helpless.

He'd spent the last few weeks proving to Genevieve that he'd changed. He'd made an effort to earn her trust, and he'd been certain those efforts were paying off.

Apparently not.

At the first sign of trouble, she'd believed the worst. She didn't question what was happening or whether he was innocent. She definitely hadn't offered her support. From the devastation on her face, it was clear she'd believed he'd stolen from her.

Which hurt most of all.

Finn had no doubt that eventually, with Stone and Gray's help, he would clear up the misunderstanding.

But he could see now that no matter how straight and narrow he attempted to live his life, it would never be enough. Genevieve would always be waiting for him to screw up.

And even if he deserved it, he couldn't live his life that way.

Rubbing a hand over his tight chest, Finn wanted to scream and throw something. But everything in the cell was bolted down.

Dropping his head back against the wall, he shut his eyes and let his body sag. Bone-deep exhaustion pulled at every muscle.

He had no idea how long he sat in the cell, but a while later an officer showed up outside. The door slid open and he gestured for Finn to follow.

"You know, it doesn't matter how many times you ask the questions, my answers aren't changing. I didn't steal anything."

The officer frowned at him. "This time."

Leading him through the sterilized hallways, it took Finn a few seconds to register what he'd actually said. "What do you mean, this time?"

"We know you didn't take anything from Ms. Reilly. All charges have been dropped."

"They have?" Finn tried not to sound incredulous, but failed. This was too easy.

Or maybe it wasn't. He'd assumed it would be morning before Stone could get things straightened out, but maybe he'd worked a bit faster.

That had to be it.

The officer led him to a woman, who processed his release. She gave him back the personal belongings that had been cataloged when they'd booked him. And then directed him through double doors and out of the station.

Freedom was a beautiful thing.

Until he walked out and found Genevieve waiting for him on the other side.

The sight of him was overwhelming.

Genevieve didn't realize just how scared she'd been until he pushed through those doors. She wanted to rush over and grab him. Put her hands on him and make sure he was there and unharmed.

But she didn't deserve that yet and wasn't sure what her reception would be. He definitely hadn't greeted her with his mischievous, open smile. She moved closer anyway, unable to stay away from him.

She wanted to reach for him, but stopped herself. Instead, she led with, "I'm sorry."

It hurt that he didn't reach for her, either. He stood in front of her, his expression shuttered and remote in a way that left a pit in her belly. "For what?"

"Doubting you, even for a little while. I realized nothing made sense pretty quickly, before Stone and Gray came to me. But I let my doubt and fears convince me that you must have done *something*."

His voice was flat when he said, "It's okay."

"It isn't."

"You know what? You're right. It isn't. I've changed who I am for you and Noah, Genevieve. I've given up a piece of me. After Sawyer died, I turned to stealing as a way of blocking out the pain, but also reminding myself of just how shitty a person I could really be. Good people don't steal."

Genevieve stepped closer. "Stop. You're a good person, Finn. One of the best men I've ever met."

"Bullshit. The expression on your face when they put me in that cop car said everything. You don't believe that. And no matter what I do, you never will."

"That's not true." She took another step, trying to bridge the distance between them in more ways than one. "You deserve my faith. Not simply because you've earned it, but because deep down I know the man you are. I *know* you have a code of honor you live by. It might not be the same one everyone else follows, but it's hard and fast for you. Unshakable. Even discounting the fact that you don't want or need anything I own, you'd never hurt me. Or use me. You're right. I should have trusted you. But I'm human, too, Finn. And I made a mistake."

Finn stared at her for several seconds. Genevieve had no idea what was going on behind his closed expression. Which scared the crap out of her.

But finally, Finn moved. Closing the gap between them, he ran the pads of his fingers across her cheek. "God, I can't stay mad at you, no matter how much I know I should. Of course I'd never hurt you or Noah. You two have become everything to me."

Leaning into his caress, Genevieve soaked up the warmth of his palm against her skin.

His mouth twisted. "I've given you reason to question me. I recognize that. Regret it every single day."

Shaking her head, Genevieve wrapped her fingers in the soft fabric of his shirt and tugged him closer. "It's not fair to continue to punish you for a single mistake that you've acknowledged, apologized for and done everything you could to atone for. That's all I can ask of you."

But it was more than that. "By every word and action, you've shown nothing but support for me. You accept me exactly as I am. Want my happiness and success. You're an amazing father to our son. We're both lucky to have you in our lives."

Slipping her hands up his chest, Genevieve cradled them around his jaw. "I love you, Finn. I have since the moment I met you. You're dynamic, challenging and the most accepting person I've ever met. You don't always make it easy—"

Finn laughed, the sound coming out a little strangled.

"—but you do make it worth it. You put up a good front, pretend to be this wicked soul, but deep down you're a good man with a beautiful heart."

She would have said more, but suddenly she was crushed against Finn's body. His mouth was on hers, kissing the hell out of her. The moment was filled with heat and promise. Someone behind them cleared their throat. Another person whistled.

Genevieve didn't care.

She was out of breath when he finally pulled back, murmuring against her lips, "Hush, woman. Give a guy the chance to say I love you, too."

Finn stared deep into her eyes. "I don't know what I did to deserve you and Noah, but I plan to spend the rest of my life appreciating the gift I've been given. I can't promise I'll never screw up."

Genevieve couldn't stop a huff of laughter. "I have no

doubt." They were confessing their love in the middle of a *police station*, after all.

"I can promise I'll always put you and our family first. And I'll do everything in my power to protect that. Working with Stone and Gray will help."

This was the one thing that worried her. But she had to place her trust in Finn. "Just promise that if it's ever not enough you'll talk to me. I won't judge, Finn. I want to give you the same level of support you've shown me."

"That's an easy promise to make."

Pulling her in, Finn kissed her again. Genevieve let out a sigh, of happiness, relief and pure joy.

Wrapping an arm around her shoulders, Finn turned to lead her out of the station. "Let's go home to our son."

Epilogue

Finn hung back, watching Genevieve. She stood in the middle of the conference room, her gaze wandering around the empty space.

He knew she was nervous because they'd talked about it this morning, but he also had no doubt she was going to be the best CEO Reilly International ever had.

Her grandfather and Nick had both been arrested. In exchange for a reduced sentence, Nick had testified against Lackland, explaining her grandfather's intricate plan to ruin Genevieve and leave her no choice but to crawl back to him and Reilly. They'd both spend several years behind bars. As far as Finn was concerned, that wasn't enough time for what they'd attempted to do to Genevieve, but no one had asked him.

Her grandfather's arrest had left a hole at Reilly. After much discussion, the board had voted her in as CEO. After several protests, Genevieve had agreed to take the position, as long as it was understood her focus would be on designing.

She was going to kick butt. She had a lot of hard work

ahead of her to bring the company back from the brink, but everyone had faith in her ability to do it.

The Mitchell brothers had been understanding, allowing her time to re-create the pieces Nick had destroyed. The collection launch had been pushed back and they'd missed the Christmas window, but in the end it hadn't mattered. Publicity had been wonderful and the collection was selling well. Not only that, but Genevieve was already speaking to them about a partnership with Reilly.

People slowly started trickling into the room, including Stone and Gray. She'd consulted with both men before agreeing to take on the role of CEO. Finn wasn't entirely certain what had happened while he was being questioned, but whatever it was had brought the three most important people in his life together.

Genevieve trusted Stone and Gray, and given their business backgrounds, Finn thought it was a great idea to use them as resources while she figured out how to run the company.

Hanging at the back of the room, Finn wasn't surprised when Stone and Gray slid up on either side of him.

The side-eye they gave him had him asking, "What've I done now?"

"Nothing," Stone said, a little too quickly.

"Then what do you want?"

"Nothing," Gray answered.

Nope, Finn wasn't buying it. "Bullshit."

Shrugging, Stone said, "We're just wondering how long it's going to take you to convince her to marry you."

Finn twisted, looking from one to the other. A knowing smirk played at the corners of Stone's mouth. He had to fight hard against the urge to smack it off. Gray, on the other hand, simply stared straight ahead. His expression grim and remote as usual.

"You guys are hilarious."

Stone's eyes danced. "She doesn't have any family. We're just looking out for her."

This was going to be fun. "For your information, we got married last week."

That got a reaction out of both of them. "Wait. What?"

"With everything going on, she didn't want a big event. And the moment we realized she was pregnant again, I wanted my ring on her finger."

Gray leaned sideways, looking around the people milling in the room. "Which she still doesn't have."

"Oh, she has it. We're waiting until after today to make the announcement."

"Pregnant, huh?" Stone clapped him on the back. "Congratulations, man. On both counts. You deserve to be happy."

"Until I met Genevieve, I wasn't sure I did." Finn couldn't fight the blooming smile. "But I'm not going to question it, I'm simply going to accept it and enjoy."

"Amen, brother," Stone drawled his agreement.

In unison, he and Stone turned to look at Gray. Their friend didn't even shift his attention as he responded, "Don't even go there."

"Any movement on your end?"

Gray's eyes narrowed, crinkling at the edges. "As a matter of fact…there is. With any luck, I'll have some new information in a few weeks."

"That's great news," Finn said. "Anything you need, you let us know."

Gray nodded, murmuring something under his breath that sounded strangely like *bail money*.

But before Finn could ask, the board meeting was called to order. There'd be plenty of time to interrogate his friend later and figure out just what was going on with Gray. Now that Finn and Stone were settled, it was long past time to focus on getting Gray's life back for him.

Together, they were going to solve the mystery and figure out just who had framed Gray.

* * * * *

AFTER HOURS REDEMPTION

KIANNA ALEXANDER

For Tameya. It was written in the stars.

My humblest thanks to my writing buddy Kaia for the intel and the encouragement. I'd also like to thank my Destin Divas, who are a constant source of inspiration and always give me the extra push when I need it. Thanks to the readers who continually support my work—I truly appreciate y'all. And thanks to the producers, the songwriters, the artists, the sound engineers—all those people who make it possible for us all to enjoy so much great music.

One

First, I didn't get a contract. Now I'm stuck driving home in a monsoon.

Peering through the water streaming down the windshield, Eden Voss kept an eye out for the turn going into her southwest Atlanta neighborhood. Typical of any Tuesday night, city traffic had been akin to driving in a demolition derby, and the rain only exacerbated that. The farther she got away from the city proper, the more she relaxed. She'd just spent three hours sitting in a smoky hookah lounge in Midtown with a producer and his newest act, discussing whether her songwriting might be a good fit for them. If the young artist had been as decisive as he'd been flirtatious, the meeting might have actually led to something concrete.

She wondered what she would have been like if her dreams of singing stardom had come true. Those ambitions were long ago laid to rest. However, she knew that if she had made it, she wouldn't have been so disrespectful as to ogle another industry professional, especially during what was supposed to be a business meeting.

Eden pushed those thoughts away, concentrating instead on making it home intact. Even with the wipers going full blast, visibility was limited at best. Carefully navigating the streets of her subdivision, she turned into her driveway just as another bright flash of lightning illuminated the sky. She shook her head, grateful she'd bought a house with a garage. After she'd pulled inside it and closed the shutter on the storm raging outside, she wrinkled her nose at the lingering smoke clinging to her clothes.

Moments later, she unlocked the side door and entered the house through the kitchen. She could see the glow of the television as she approached the living room. A smile curved her lips. *She waited up for me...again.* Her older cousin and roommate had a protective streak that still lingered from when they were kids.

She kicked off her shoes and padded into the room. "Ainsley, you didn't have to wait up."

Her cousin was stretched out on the couch, tucked beneath her favorite oversize throw emblazoned with the cover of OutKast's classic album *ATLiens*. "I know, I know. But I was already watching a *Law & Order* marathon."

She chuckled, seeing the familiar program on the TV. "Okay, Mom. Coop's upstairs asleep?"

Ainsley nodded. "You know my son. He treasures his sleep above all else." At ten years old, sleep and *Minecraft* were Cooper's two favorite pastimes. She shifted around a bit until she sat up. "How did the meeting go?"

Thinking back on the meeting made her cringe. "Girl, I don't even know. The producer seemed into it, but I think the singer paid more attention to my boobs than my pitch."

"Oh, what a creep. Is this a singer I know?"

"Levi Duncan. Newer artist, supposedly the second coming of Usher."

Ainsley's brow cocked. "Second coming? Please. Usher's had like ten 'second comings,' plus he's still around. These R & B dudes now are a dime a dozen. Very few stand out."

"You're right about that. Have you ever heard of him?"

"Nah." Ainsley shook her head. "Sounds like a real character. If that's how he acts, he'll fit right in with the rest of the jerks in the music industry."

She felt her lips stretch into a thin line as the memories of those days rose within. Late nights in the studio, poring over the lyric sheets with Blaine Woodson. The man who'd crushed all her hopes and dreams. She could still smell his woodsy cologne. Handsome, talented...and duplicitous. He'd brought her into the music business, along with Ainsley and their friend Cambria. He'd praised their talents, filled their heads with fantasies of what could be.

She'd fallen for his words, and in the process, fallen in love. But when the time came for him to really show he believed in her, he'd disappointed her in the worst way.

"Scoot over." Eden flopped down on the sofa next to her cousin. "Anything interesting happen at the studio today?"

"I heard one of the newer artists in the booth today, laying down backing vocals. Brought back memories, ya know?"

Eden laughed. "I bet." She leaned in close, even though there was no one else in the room, her tone conspiratorial. "I heard a rumor that T.I. was coming by. Did he?"

Looking amused, she shook her head. "No. Somebody from his label was there, but no action in the booth just yet."

"Well, keep me posted. When he's there, I might just have to drop by and bring you lunch."

Ainsley laughed. "You're a mess. But I'll let you know if I spot the Rubber Band Man."

She fist-bumped her. "My homegirl."

A brilliant flash illuminated the room, followed by a loud crack of thunder reverberating through the house.

Ainsley cast a wary eye toward the window. "It's a mess out there."

A memory popped into her mind then, and she asked, "Remember how Mom and Aunt Mimi would call it 'good sleeping weather'?"

"I remember." Ainsley's expression took on a wistful tone. "I miss them."

She squeezed her cousin's shoulder. "Me, too." It had been three years since the bus accident had claimed the lives of their mothers, who'd been traveling together for a church trip. Eden felt the tug in her chest, the same tug she felt whenever she thought of how much she missed her mother and her favorite aunt. Their deaths had forged an even closer bond between her and Ainsley. Eden yawned. "I'm beat, Ains. I'm going up to bed."

"I'll be up after this episode."

She extricated herself from the soft cushions and headed toward the foyer.

More lightning flashed, and before she could reach the staircase, another wall-rattling boom of thunder swept through the house.

This time, a huge, splintering crash followed.

Eden's head jerked toward the upper floor of the house, where it seemed the sound had come from.

What the hell was that?

"Mom!" Cooper screamed from his upstairs bedroom in the far corner of the house. "Help!"

Oh no.

Ainsley jumped up from the couch, and she and Eden raced up the stairs, their hearts pounding.

"We're excited to welcome your newest artist, Blaine." The voice of Rupert Wright, A&R director for Hamilton

House Records, broke through Blaine Woodson's thoughts. *Damn. I should've had that second cup of coffee.* It was just before ten Wednesday morning, and he had some serious midweek doldrums going on. Straightening in his stiff-backed chair at the conference table, he smiled. "I'm glad to hear that, Rupert. I think it's going to be an amazing partnership."

"Wonderful." Rupert redirected his attention. "And Miss Brown, let me be the first to welcome you to the Hamilton House family."

"Thanks. And you can call me Naiya." Twenty-three-year-old singer Naiya B. sat next to Blaine in a matching chair. Her gaze shifted around the room as if she were studying the wall displays. "I see you've got quite a few plaques under your belt."

Blaine gave Naiya's shoulder a quick pat. "And soon your platinum plaque will be up there with the rest." Her viral videos, featuring her singing covers of classic songs by the likes of Phyllis, Whitney and Toni, had first attracted Blaine's attention two months ago. She possessed a stunning vocal talent. He'd reached out to her, and she'd signed to his boutique label, Against the Grain Records. His subsidiary status under AMGI/Hamilton House provided most of his operating budget.

Naiya's warm smile conveyed her delight. "I'm really excited about all this. I have so much I want to say, and I appreciate this chance to express myself."

Seeing that sparkle in her eyes, Blaine couldn't help smiling. She reminded him of someone else. A curly-haired young woman with cocoa eyes lit up like the Vegas Strip. Sharp, witty, beautiful and wildly talented. *Eden Voss.* She'd been a part of the very first group signed to his label, and he'd shared a unique connection with her. But their chemistry extended far beyond music. He'd let her go in order to grow his label. It had been less than ideal, but Hamilton House held the purse strings, and he'd had to follow their edicts.

Rupert's bushy gray brows furrowed slightly. "What's your vision for your first album, Naiya?"

She brightened and gave a brief account of her plans. She wanted to sing about love and breakup, and the hardships faced by those in her Capitol View neighborhood.

"Hmm." Rupert appeared taken aback.

Blaine felt a twinge as he watched the light go out of Naiya's eyes. "I'm sure Naiya isn't planning to go on a diatribe on wax, right?"

She shook her head. "No, it was nothing like that."

Blaine let his eyes dart from Rupert to Naiya. *I hope she knows I'll fight for her to be able to say what she wants to say.* He hadn't fought for Eden back then, and regret had been his constant companion. Fate had seen fit to give him a second chance, perhaps one he didn't even deserve, by sending Naiya his way. *I won't make the same mistake again.*

"Believe me, I understand. We all have things dear to our hearts." Rupert leaned over his desk. "But in this business, it's best not to burn bridges before we've started the journey."

Naiya's voice was quiet. "I understand."

"I'm sure we'll come to a compromise, Rupert. Naiya and I will work with a songwriter to bring out the nuance of her message without getting too controversial."

As Naiya and Rupert walked toward the door, Blaine stood.

Rupert held up his hand. "Hang tight. Marvin wants to speak with you. You can meet Naiya and me in the lobby afterward."

"Sure thing." He watched the two of them disappear into the marbled corridor, wondering what Marvin wanted to talk to him about. As label liaison, Marvin Samuels stayed in frequent contact with him, and Blaine assumed it was that way for all the smaller labels under Hamilton House's umbrella.

Thinking back on his promise to Rupert to get the right songwriter for Naiya's album, he realized he'd not been completely honest. He'd said he had several songwriters in mind, but in reality, there was only one name rolling around in his mind.

Eden Voss.

She'd been dominating his thoughts, and not just because of his fascination with her. Eden was as brilliant a songwriter as Naiya was a vocalist, having written a few charting R & B and hip-hop songs. He'd followed her career closely, because he and Eden had a history—although not one he was entirely proud of.

Years ago, Eden and the members of her girl group had been on the brink of stardom, and he'd been guiding their career. He'd genuinely liked and respected all three young women, though what he'd had with Eden had been different. Special. Their creative synergy had been nothing short of magic. But their attraction to each other had been even more captivating. His heart had opened to her in a way it hadn't to any other woman, before or since.

I ruined their group. But worse than that, I hurt Eden.

Eden had reminded him of his father, set in his ways, immovable in his opinions of the way things "ought to be." His father's rigidity was the main reason Against the Grain existed. Blaine was the second of Caleb and Addison Woodson's five children, the odd one out. He was the goof-off, the one who could never live up to his father's legend or his elder sister's obedient perfection. So rather than join up with the family business at 404 Sound Recordings, one of Atlanta's oldest and most successful recording studios, he'd struck out on his own to form a small label.

He'd made a selfish choice, driven by his need to be independent of his father. His choice had altered all their futures. Cambria had gone on to solo stardom, but that wasn't the case for Eden or her cousin Ainsley.

Marvin entered, dressed in his usual black slacks and dark blue button-down shirt with the record company logo on the front. "Morning, Blaine. Good to see you again."

"Always a pleasure, Marvin. So, Rupert said you wanted to speak to me." Whatever was up, Blaine wanted to get right to the point so he and Naiya could make their flight back to Atlanta after lunch.

Marvin slipped into the chair next to him. "Right. I wanted to congratulate you. I think Naiya is a great fit for the label."

"I appreciate that." *Okay, so why are we really here?*

"While we're pleased to have Naiya on board, we also have very high expectations for this album. It's been over a year since you've had a top-selling album."

He held back his sigh. The ever-changing nature of the music business forced him to keep up with the tastes of a very fickle audience. Sometimes it felt like trying to take down a buck with foam darts. "We had a lull, but things are coming around again."

"I hope you're right. AMGI is making cutbacks, and the first things to go in times like these are underperforming subsidiaries."

The temperature in the room seemed to climb, and Blaine loosened his tie. "Is that where things stand, Marvin?"

The older man looked solemn. "Unfortunately, yes." He stood, gave Blaine a friendly pat on the back. "I have faith in you. You know what you're doing. But I didn't want you to leave without knowing what's going on."

He released a breath. "Thanks for being candid with me."

Marvin's lips curved beneath his bushy blond mustache.

"You can count on me to keep you informed." He glanced at his gold wristwatch, headed for the door. "I've got another meeting. Good seeing you again, Blaine."

"Likewise," he murmured as Marvin exited.

Shit. There goes my plan to slowly work my way back into Eden's good graces. Now it wasn't just Naiya's budding career that was on the line. The very future of Against the Grain, his baby, his livelihood, also hung in the balance. He needed to talk to Eden, and fast.

But after what I did...will she even take my call?

Two

Friday afternoon, Eden breezed into Blaine's office. She was determined he wouldn't see her sweat, so she kept her outer manner as calm and cool as possible, despite the tangle of emotions raging inside her.

When his receptionist had called her yesterday, she'd been tempted to hang up once she learned the call was on Blaine's behalf. She'd decided against it, however, since the woman had only been doing her job. It didn't surprise her that Blaine hadn't had the guts to call himself. He was the last person she wanted to work with, but she wasn't in a position to be picky about the jobs she took on right now.

She'd just left home, where Cooper lay with a broken leg and lacerations to his torso. Ainsley was taking good care of him, but she still felt terrible about what had happened to him. The storm that passed through earlier in the week had sent a tree crashing through the roof onto the foot of his bed. She was grateful he'd avoided more serious injury.

The house hadn't been so lucky. It would take a hell of a lot of money to fix the gaping, tarp-covered breach in her roof.

So here I am, going into a business meeting with the man who broke my heart and ended my singing career. Even Hitchcock couldn't have come up with a twist as epic as this.

The moment she saw Blaine, he commanded her full attention. He stood as she entered the space, adjusting his blazer. She couldn't tell if he was straightening it or taking it off; she felt a little disappointed when she realized it was the former. She would have welcomed a better view of his broad shoulders. The disappointment didn't linger, though; she was too busy letting her hungry eyes devour him like a delicious feast. He'd grown into his handsomeness over the past few years and was even more attractive now. *Wonder if he's grown more selfish, too?*

She was intimately acquainted with the ways of a selfish man…her own father had abandoned her and her mother when she was still very young. The scars of that abandonment still remained, and she tended to mistrust men until they proved themselves.

His edgy sense of style remained, as indicated by his clothes. The metallic silver blazer and crisp white shirt whose top two buttons were left open revealed a thick, beaded silver chain with a lion's head as its centerpiece. Distressed gray jeans sat low on his waist, displaying the outline of the powerful thighs beneath.

She swallowed. She'd come here with so many things on her mind. Now it was all she could do not to drool.

Damn. Even after what he did to me, I'm still fantasizing about him.

Her gaze swept up again, to his rich brown face and the chin-length black dreadlocks he'd bound in a ponytail at his nape. Above a pair of full lips framed by a neatly trimmed beard, his amber eyes sparkled with the flame of youthful passion.

Forget a snack. This man is a whole meal.

"Eden. It's great to see you." His deep voice seemed to fill the whole room.

"Same here." She knew she should move, but her feet were rooted to the spot. She closed her eyes for a moment, willed herself to take a step. *Get it together, girl. Get it together!*

"Come in, sit down." He gestured, welcoming her into his domain.

His invitation seemed to relieve her immobility. She crossed the room and took her seat in the chair positioned near his desk, trying to shift her gaze. She refused to get caught staring at him. Lucky for her, his walls held plenty of interesting portraits, plaques and other things she could look at other than his face. *He's really updated the decor in here.*

Despite all the room's new trappings, Blaine remained the true showpiece.

Retaking his seat in the big leather chair, he said, "I really appreciate you taking my call—"

She interjected. "You mean, your receptionist's call." If he thought she was going to let that slide, he had another think coming.

He cleared his throat as if he were uncomfortable. "I thought if I called, you'd hang up before I could invite you here."

"I probably would have." She folded her arms over her chest.

A slight frown came over his face, though it didn't detract from his magnetism. "You're not going to make this easy, are you?"

She shrugged. "Why should I?" She cocked her head to the right. "I'm older and wiser now, Blaine. I know exactly what you're capable of, and I'll govern myself accordingly." He had no idea how hard she and Ainsley had to work to hold their little household together. He was born into money and had no clue what it was like to struggle.

He dropped his gaze, shuffling through some papers on his desk. "At any rate, thanks for agreeing to meet with me. I know we didn't part on the best terms the last time we were in this office."

She kept her tone even. "I see you've updated things in here. It looks nice."

"Thank you." He pointed at the window behind him. "Finally got some curtains. You were always on me about it."

She sat back in her chair, resting her purse in her lap as she glanced at the gray-and-white-striped curtains. "It's definitely an improvement."

He watched her for a few silent moments. She met his eyes, camouflaging her true emotions so he wouldn't see how out of sorts he made her feel. He dragged the contact on just long enough to make her squirm inwardly before he spoke again. "Before we get into the details, I feel like I should start with an apology."

She shook her head. "That's not necessary."

"Just let me explain—"

"I don't want to talk about that." She wasn't going to do this with him today. His betrayal still stung, despite the passage of time, and being in his presence again made her feel as if her fragile heart could shatter again at any moment. But there was no way she would ever reveal that to him. "We're not going to talk about the past, Blaine."

One of his thick brows lifted. "Eden, what happened with you and Ainsley back then…"

She held up her hand to stop him, not wanting to hear whatever weak excuses might come next. "It's ancient history. I'd really prefer to just iron out the details of the job at hand, if you don't mind."

"Okay…if that's what you really want." He reclined in the chair, rubbing his large hands together as he asked, "Have you ever heard of Naiya B.?"

She squinted, turning the name over in her mind. "The name sounds familiar, but I can't place it."

"She's an internet celebrity."

Recognition sparked in her brain, and she snapped her fingers. "I think Ainsley showed me a video of her singing 'Greatest Love of All.'"

He nodded. "That video had over eight hundred thousand views in a week. Anyway, I've recently signed Naiya to Against the Grain, and we're looking for a songwriter to work with her on her first album."

She tilted her head, frowned. Usually an album was a team effort, involving many writers, along with a bevy of producers, musicians and more. "A songwriter? Why not several?"

"Naiya's voice and her brand demand something truly cohesive. We think we can best accomplish that by having a single songwriter work on the entire album—though we may vary the production team a bit here and there."

"And you think I'm the person for the job."

"Absolutely," he replied. "Naiya has a very clear vision of the sound she wants to achieve, a vision I share. And I can think of no one better to help us bring that sound to life than you."

Eden couldn't deny how his words flattered her. She drew a deep breath and instantly regretted it. His woodsy cologne flooded her senses. The scent, familiar and scintillating, made her think of things she shouldn't be thinking of in a serious business meeting. Like what it would be like to be in his arms, to have that scent clinging to her clothes…her bedsheets…

She exhaled, hoping to quell the effects of the fragrance, and the wearer. "May I ask why you feel that way?" *If he's being honest, he'll have no trouble backing up what he says.* His fineness, delicious scent and sweet words awakened her inside, but that didn't mean she trusted him.

He chuckled. "Fair enough. I've been following your career over these last several years, since we parted ways."

"Oh, have you?"

"Yes. And that's how I know you've written three top-100 songs on the R & B and hip-hop Hot 100 charts, just in the last four years. You've worked with both music legends and young artists. And you can record demos in full voice, which saves me the trouble of getting a studio singer to do them." He pressed his broad shoulders back, holding her gaze. "You're the total package, Eden. Everything we need to generate brilliant lyrics for Naiya lies within you."

Her mouth fell open, and she snapped it shut. "Wow. You've really been keeping tabs on me, huh?"

"In a sense." He gave her a long, speaking look.

She averted her gaze, not wanting to delve into what his eyes were saying that his mouth wasn't. "I have to be honest with you, Blaine. When I walked out of this office all those years ago, I had no intention of ever working with you again."

His jaw hardened. "Eden, I'm sure you understand my decision was a business one. It wasn't personal."

A bitter laugh echoed inside her mind. *That's precisely the problem with you, Blaine Woodson.* She waved her hand dismissively. "It's water under the bridge. Despite what I intended back then; I have good reason to take this job. That's why I took your call."

"I see. Care to elaborate?"

She shook her head. "I see no reason to go into that. After all, this is a simple business transaction." That's what her head said. Other parts of her said something altogether different, but she ignored those parts—for now. "As far as I'm concerned, a professional arrangement is all we can ever hope to have."

Watching Eden from across his desk, Blaine wondered what was going through her head. He knew damn well what was going through his: wonderment.

How did she get even more beautiful?

Seven years ago, she'd been a young woman in her early twenties, with an easygoing manner and grandiose dreams of music stardom. She had to be about thirty now, and she seemed to possess poise and maturity that amplified her natural outer beauty. She was of average height, though her strappy heels made her a couple of inches taller. As she sat across from him in the curve-hugging red dress, with her luscious lips painted to match, her femininity captivated him. She'd worn her dark, auburn-streaked hair loose, falling in large ringlets around her heart-shaped brown face. With those glittering cocoa eyes locked on him, he found it difficult to focus on business.

"Blaine, did you hear what I said?"

He reached back, wrapping his hand around the base of his bound locs for a moment while he gathered his wits. "Forgive me, I'm about a quart low on caffeine. What did you say?"

She narrowed her eyes. "I said, as far as I'm concerned, a business arrangement is all we can have."

"Ouch." He heard her loud and clear that time, and her words stung. He wasn't sure why; this meeting was supposed to be about business. Yet there was no denying how she moved him. He felt his brow crease. What had possessed her to say that to him? Was she talking about the past? Or was she picking up on how he felt right now? Blaine had always known her to be perceptive. "Where did that come from?"

"I just want to make sure that we're clear, right from the start. Mixing business with pleasure never works out the way it should. I'm not sure if you remember how it went down the last time, so we're just not going to do it."

He tried not to linger on the regret her words dredged up. "Of course, I remember." How could he forget the way she'd affected him; the way goose bumps had risen on his skin when he heard her sing? The way his blood had raced when she kissed him?

She pursed her lips, as if unconvinced. "Then you should be willing to keep things professional between us."

"I respect your stance, Eden."

"Good." She released her grip on her handbag, setting it on the desk before flexing her fingers. "Because if you want to work with me, those are my terms."

He knew she was still displeased with his decision to dump the group and elevate Cambria to the ranks of solo star. *If only there was some way I could make her see, make her understand that I did what I had to do.* He cleared his throat. "Eden, I'm just going to say it. I really need you."

Her eyes widened, her ruby lips forming an O shape.

He continued his declaration before she could read too deeply into his meaning. "This album, and its success, are of particular importance. You are the key to that success. Make no mistake, everything that happens between us will be on your terms."

She huffed out a breath, crossing one long leg over the other. "Really? And why should I believe that? You've blindsided me once before." Her shoulders were tense, her chin lifted in defiance.

"I've never denied that."

"I have to be careful about the projects I take on, Blaine," she told him. "My creativity suffers if I'm not."

"I hear you. And I understand why you might be hesitant to work with me. But there's a lot riding on this album,

and I can't afford to act in a way that would jeopardize it."
He didn't elaborate on the reasoning behind that; there was
no reason she needed to know his company could end up
being dropped from Hamilton House.

She shook her head, pressing her lips into a rueful half
smile. "There was a lot at stake for me back then, too. But
I'll take your word for it."

He sighed. She had good reason for mistrusting him,
and they both knew it. His hand had been forced, and he'd
tried to explain as much to Eden and Ainsley on that fate-
ful day. But emotions had been too high, and both women
had left his office visibly upset.

"I assume you've drawn up a contract?"

He opened his desk drawer and took out the document,
sliding it across the desk to her. "Let me know if you need
an explanation of anything."

He watched as she perused the document. Moments
later, a shocked look passed over her face, but it was gone
as quickly as it had appeared.

Silence fell between them while she finished reading
the contract, and he used the time to respond to a few messages on his smartphone. When she looked up, he slid a
gold-plated pen toward her.

Shaking her head, she said, "I'll need some time to consider the offer."

His brows hitched. "How much time?"

"Give me a week. I'll definitely make a decision by
then." She used her fingertips to roll the pen back toward
him.

He reached for the pen before she moved her hand, and
their fingers brushed momentarily.

A buzz, like the kick of a finely aged whiskey, fired
through his blood. Her skin was as smooth and soft as
satin. Even the brief connection was enough to remind
him of those long-ago nights they'd spent together in the

studio. He hadn't forgotten what they'd shared, and despite her cool manner, he could tell she hadn't forgotten, either.

She drew her hand away, tucking it into her lap and looking away from him.

She felt it, too.

He returned the pen to his drawer. "If you decide to sign the contract, we'll be able to give you a check for half the fee."

She nodded, dropping her shoulders, her rigid posture relaxing. When she spoke again, her tone had softened, lacking the earlier edginess. "Sounds good. If I take the job, when do we get started?"

It pleased him that she seemed more at ease. "I'd like to have you meet with Naiya and me next Monday, if possible. Would that work?"

"That would be fine. What's the time and place?"

"Here, in the conference room, about ten."

She stood. "Is there anything else?"

There's plenty. But now wasn't the time. She'd placed a wall between them for her own protection, and despite his fierce attraction to her, he'd always respect her boundaries. "No, that's all. Thank you again for coming, and for considering the offer."

"Just don't make me regret it, Blaine." She gave him a soft smile, turned and walked out of his office, leaving her parting words hanging in the air like a fog.

Three

Saturday morning, Eden sat beside Ainsley in the waiting room of the children's specialty clinic. On the opposite side of Ainsley, Cooper dozed, his head resting on his mother's shoulder.

"He's been in and out of sleep since we left the house," Eden noted, gesturing to her slumbering little nephew. Normally Cooper was a ball of unfettered energy, so seeing him napping in public like a worn-out toddler was a bit jarring for her.

Ainsley nodded. "It's the pain meds they gave him. The ER doc said they'd make him drowsy, remember?" She didn't remember, actually, but didn't see the need to say that aloud. Between the tree falling on the roof, spending the better part of Saturday at the emergency room with Cooper and then meeting up with Blaine on Friday, the last several days had been a blur of unpleasant surprises.

"You never really told me about your meeting with—"

Ainsley fluttered her lashes dramatically "—Blaine yesterday."

She rolled her eyes. "Why are you saying his name like that?"

"I'm just teasing you, girl." She giggled. "I know you hate his guts."

"Don't you?" She gave her cousin a penetrating stare. "I'm sure you remember him holding your child against you."

Ainsley shrugged. "He's not my favorite person in the world, but I don't hate him, either. And if I had to do it all again, I'd still choose my son over a music career, so…"

Eden shook her head. "You've got Aunt Mimi's forgiving spirit."

"And you've got your mama's sass." Ainsley winked. "But seriously, how did the meeting go?"

"I don't really want to talk about it." She had no interest in telling her cousin that she'd spent the better part of their meeting willing herself not to drool over Blaine's dreadlocked handsomeness. Or that he'd smelled like freshly minted cash and great sex. Nope, she'd keep that to herself. At least for now.

"Oh, come on." Ainsley nudged her with an elbow. "At least tell me if you took the gig."

She sighed. "I asked him to give me until next Monday to make my decision. But—"

A loud voice called out Cooper's name, effectively ending the conversation. Ainsley raised her hand, waving the scrub-clad nurse over. Silently blessing the timing, Eden helped rouse Cooper and hoist him to a standing position. Between their supportive arms, the nurse holding doors and his crutches, they finally got him back to the examination room.

Eden settled into a chair across from Ainsley after they'd helped Cooper onto the bed. Immediately taking out her phone, she gave rapt attention to her social media feed, as a sign to her cousin that she didn't want to talk.

Soon, Dr. Celia Fordham entered the room. Petite and slender, she wore her dark hair in a bun low on her nape. Adjusting the oval frames of her glasses, she asked, "How are you feeling today, Cooper?"

"My leg itches," he groused. "I can't scratch it 'cause of the cast."

Dr. Fordham smiled. "Don't worry, that's pretty typical." Giving him a pat on the shoulder, she asked, "Any pain?"

Cooper nodded his head. "How long will I have to wear this thing, Doc?"

"I'm afraid it could take about six weeks for your leg to fully heal."

Cooper's eyes grew round. "Six weeks? But baseball tryouts will be over by then!"

Dr. Fordham turned to Ainsley. "Tryouts?"

"He's going to middle school this year, and he wants to try to make the team. It's all he's talked about for the last two years."

Cooper nodded. "Yeah. That's why I gotta get out of this cast."

Eden sighed. The timing of this little disaster couldn't have been worse. Money was lean around the household, and now Cooper was faced with missing out on something he desperately wanted.

"I'm sorry, Cooper. But with this cast on, you won't be able to…"

Tears gathered in his eyes. "But I have to! I've been waiting forever to play on the baseball team."

Ainsley, visibly emotional, went to her son's side. Draping her arm around his shoulders, she asked, "Isn't there something else we can do for him, Dr. Fordham?"

"Yes, actually, there is another option. For the type of fracture Cooper has, surgery is a possibility. With him being as young and healthy as he is, I don't see why he couldn't get back on his feet in time for his tryouts." Dr. Fordham took the clipboard from beneath her arm, flipping through the pages. "If you like, I could put in a recommendation for the procedure."

"What would it entail, exactly?" Eden asked.

Dr. Fordham gave a brief rundown of what the surgery would involve.

Ever practical, Ainsley queried, "Will insurance cover this?"

Dr. Fordham appeared thoughtful. "It should cover at least a portion, but you'll have to check with the insurance clerk at checkout to be certain."

Ainsley looked thoughtful for a moment, but by the time they left the clinic, Dr. Fordham had put in an order for the procedure.

Eden drove her cousin and nephew home. The silence that had stretched on for the ten minutes since they'd left the hospital was starting to get to her. Her mind kept drifting to Blaine, and he was a distraction she just didn't need right now. So, she asked, "When are we going to talk about this surgery, Ainsley?"

"What about it?"

She scoffed. "Come on, Ainsley. You heard the clerk. We have to meet a two-thousand-dollar deductible in order for insurance to pay for the surgery. How are we gonna afford that?"

"I'll figure it out. Besides, I've already paid five hundred."

"No, we will figure it out, stubborn. That's still fifteen hundred dollars, and I'm not going to let you try to come up with all that cash on your own. We're family, and I'm here for you."

Ainsley blew out a breath. "I couldn't say no to him, Eden. Not with him giving me those big sad puppy eyes."

She nodded. "I know. As I said, we'll figure it out together."

Decision made, silence fell between them. Her eyes on the road, Eden thought back to her meeting with Blaine. She had not given him a definite response, but there was no turning down the gig now, no matter how much she disliked being in Blaine's company. The fee she'd make would cover Cooper's medical bills, and hopefully, the roof repair.

"So, is this a better time to ask what happened with Blaine?"

She sighed. "No. But I don't think there ever will be."

Ainsley chuckled. "Just spill it already."

Reluctantly, she recounted the details of their meeting. "Anyway, I'm looking forward to working with Naiya. She's very talented."

"Mmm-hmm."

She eyed her cousin. "What, Ainsley?"

"Well, you left out the most important part." Her cousin scratched her chin. "Is he still as fine as he used to be?"

"Honestly? He's finer." She turned the wheel to the left, navigating into their driveway. "Not that it matters. All interactions between Blaine and me will be strictly business. We've already discussed it."

But even as she said the words, deep down she knew that arrangement might be hard to keep.

Holding his briefcase over his head to shield himself from the pounding rain, Blaine dashed into the Bodacious Bean Thursday morning. Once inside, he scanned the interior while walking toward the counter. His younger brother Gage was due to meet him there for a quick chat, and he didn't want to spend too long lingering in the coffee shop. Despite the colorful HBCU-themed decor, friendly staff and inviting atmosphere, Blaine had far too much work to do in preparing for Naiya B.'s album to be hanging out here all day. Grabbing a few napkins to wipe the droplets clinging to his face and his briefcase, he stepped up to place his order.

By the time the barista set to work on his large French vanilla latte, the bell rang over the door, indicating the entry of another patron. Blaine turned toward the sound and smiled when he saw Gage shut his umbrella and shake it before ducking inside.

"How you doing, bro?" Blaine asked.

Shaking his head, Gage wiped a hand over his damp forehead. Dressed in a charcoal-gray suit, crisp white shirt and purple tie, he didn't look too pleased about the numerous wet spots covering his clothing. "Pretty good, considering this torrential downpour." He gestured to the window, where rain continued to pelt the glass.

"Gotta love that ATL weather. One day chicken, next day feathers." Blaine chuckled as he took his drink from the barista. "I'll grab us a table in the back." He walked away, leaving his soggy brother at the counter.

The place was pretty empty for a weekday morning. *Guess the rain kept them away.* Blaine usually got his coffee to go, because open tables were scarce most workdays. Finding a suitable two-top table near the establishment's rear window, he sat down, easing the briefcase beneath the table. Watching the falling rain, he sipped from his sleeve-wrapped paper cup, enjoying the feel of the warm, slightly sweet beverage as it washed over his tongue.

Gage set his cup down. "So, what's going on? I figured you needed something when you asked me to meet in the middle of the workweek."

"I do need a favor, but we'll get to that." He rested his hands on the table, lacing his fingers together. Despite the tense relationship he had with his family, he still cared about them. "How's the fam?"

Gage rolled his eyes. "Our siblings are fine. It's pretty

much business as usual with them. Dad's been complaining about his tennis elbow acting up for almost two weeks but refuses to go to the doctor. That leaves the rest of us stuck listening to his gripes."

He wasn't surprised by his brother's observation. Their father wasn't one to admit defeat, and he'd likely go on bearing the pain until it became so bad he was forced to seek medical attention. "Dad's always been like that. What about Mom?"

"She's great. Still all about fitness. She's vegan now, did you know that?"

He shook his head. "How long has that been a thing?"

"A month or so. And she's moved on from step aerobics to kickboxing." Gage snorted a laugh, took another sip of his coffee. "We all try to stay on her good side because it's pretty obvious she can kick all of our asses."

Blaine couldn't help smiling at his brother's words. *Mom's always been a pistol.* "She may just outlive us all." He finished up his drink, setting the empty cup aside. "So, what's up at 404? Everything good business-wise?"

"Yeah. We're still solidly in the black. We're looking to update some things, though. First is that equipment in Studio A. I think Dad kept it so long because it was his first soundboard—you know, sentimental attachment or something. But that thing's long overdue for an upgrade."

"And as head of operations, that falls under your jurisdiction." He watched his brother intently. "What are you going to do with the old equipment?" He was somewhat surprised his father had agreed to part with it, though he assumed their brother Miles, who served as finance officer, had explained how new equipment would bring higher profits into the studio.

Gage tilted his head to one side. "For right now, it's going into storage. After that, who knows? We may donate it to a museum, though Mom's been talking about setting up a display in the building to commemorate the thirtieth anniversary. So, we'll see."

He nodded but remained silent.

"You know, you could always come by the offices and *see* your family, instead of always asking me how everyone is." Gage gave him a pointed look.

"And you know why I can't do that." He was in no mood to talk about the rift between him and his family. He was the black sheep, the wayward son who'd gone off on his own instead of joining the family business. He missed his mother, and would occasionally text her, as well as his baby sister, Teagan. But everyone else sided with his father, so what was there for them to discuss? "I'm not into drama, Gage. So, I avoid it whenever possible."

"Hmph." A slight frown tilted his baby bro's lips, but it disappeared as quickly as it had shown itself. "Anyway, let's get to the matter at hand. What's going on with you? Because I hear you're doing big things."

His brow furrowed as he asked, "What have you heard?"

"I heard you nabbed that hot viral video singer for your label."

Blaine smiled. "Oh, so you heard about Naiya B.? I'm glad she's a hot topic around town."

"I've heard her sing, and I must say, she's quite a score. Congrats, bro."

"Thanks. She's got an amazing voice. Songwriting isn't her strength, but I've come up with a brilliant solution to that problem."

Gage's expression morphed from curiosity into a knowing grin. "I heard about that, too. When were you going to tell me you had a meeting with Eden Voss?"

Blaine let his head drop back. "Damn, bro. You're really all up in my business like that?"

He shrugged. "Come on, B. You know how word gets

around in southwest Atlanta. I'm just mad I had to hear it in these SWATS streets instead of from you."

Blaine groaned.

Gage leaned in, his tone low and conspiratorial. "So, y'all just working together? Or are y'all...*working together*?" He waggled his brows to accentuate the last two words.

Blaine resisted the urge to pop his brother upside the head. "Ugh, Gage. You're so freaking annoying. It's a business arrangement, bruh. I offered Eden a contract to write some songs for Naiya. Hopefully she'll sign, and we'll all get paid. That's it."

Gage gave him that familiar head tilt/side-eye combo, the one that meant he didn't believe what he'd heard. "Oh, really?"

"Yes, really. It's. Strictly. Business. Case closed."

"You're awfully touchy about it for that to be true...but I'll take your word for it." They chatted for a few moments about Blaine's possible use of 404's live band recording studio, and how Blaine could do his usual "wear a hoodie and use the rear entrance" routine to keep his father from being aware of his presence.

"Yeah, yeah." Gage crushed his empty paper cup, tossing it into the nearby trash can. "You know, you and Dad are going to have to iron things out eventually."

"I know, I know." *But not yet.*

Four

Eden entered the modest one-story building that housed Against the Grain Records on Monday morning, carrying her leather-bound notebook and purse. Inside, she took a few steps toward the waiting area, consisting of chairs and a low black enamel coffee table. Resting her palm on the cool steel frame, she took a seat in one of the sleek black leather chairs, intent on mentally preparing herself for the day ahead.

She crossed one leg over the other, taking a good look around. She'd been anxious the first time she met Blaine here, so she relished the opportunity to evaluate his domain. The roomy space, with its stained concrete floors, soft gray walls and black lacquer furniture, was an obvious reflection of his tastes. Framed black-and-white prints of musicians playing instruments adorned the walls, and the reception desk was flanked by two polished pewter sculptures: one of a bass clef, the other, a treble clef.

She liked the decor; it was simple, well-coordinated and

reflective of the type of business conducted there. Back in the day, Blaine's studio had been little more than a desk and chair surrounded by blank walls. Now he had made the space his own. He'd obviously experienced some degree of success during their time apart.

If only he'd afforded Ainsley and I that same chance at success. After all that had transpired between them, she never would have expected to find herself working with him at this point in her life. But fate obviously had other plans.

Back then, she'd been so enamored with him that she could never have anticipated his betrayal. He'd seemed so perfect, so loving and so into her. He'd taken her hand and touched her soul.

She sighed as the image of his drop-dead-gorgeous face floated through her mind. As enticing as he was, however, she knew she had to get her mind right for the task ahead. Daydreaming about Blaine simply wouldn't do.

I've got to get focused. There's so much at stake.

Her professional reputation aside, she had about as much motivation to succeed at this job as a person could have. She'd agreed to split the fees for Cooper's surgery with Ainsley, and she knew she'd need to replace the $1,250 she took from her savings. Beyond that, the damage to their roof was so extensive, she'd need an entirely new one, to the tune of $6,500 above what her homeowner's policy covered.

She massaged her temple, blowing out a breath. *It's not just about Naiya's album anymore. I need to do well with this project because if I do, it will open up the door to so many more opportunities.*

The door swung open then, and she turned her head. As the blast of humid August air ruffled her bangs, Blaine strode in.

Her breath caught in her throat at the sight of him. He

wore a loose-fitting pair of blue jeans, a black Goodie Mob tee, and black-and-white leather sneakers. A denim jacket was draped over his broad shoulders, Georgia heat be damned. His dreads were in a bun atop his head, and dark sunglasses obscured his eyes.

No one had a right to be so freaking handsome. And yet there he stood, looking like temptation personified. Liquid desire pooled low in her belly, the warmth spreading through her body. She took a deep breath. *Gather yourself, girl. He's just a man.*

She stood, brushing remnants of this morning's biscuit from the front of her dark skirt. "Good morning, Blaine."

He smiled, teeth glistening. "Good morning, Eden." He leaned down, and before she could react, pecked her on the cheek. "So, I'm assuming you decided to sign the contract?"

Heat bloomed beneath her skin. Doing her best to shake off the effects of his disarming smile and his surprise kiss, she handed him the document. "Yes. I'll do my best to live up to your expectations."

"I have no doubt that you will." A sparkle lit his dark eyes.

Naiya entered the room then, a bright smile on her face. "Morning, folks."

Gathering her wits, Eden moved past Blaine to greet the vocalist. Sticking out her hand, she said, "Naiya, I'm Eden Voss. It's nice to finally meet you in person."

Naiya offered a small smile and handshake. "Thanks. Nice to meet you, too."

Dressed in a simple green sundress and a pair of tan sandals, with her flowing, blond-streaked brown waves of hair hanging loose around her shoulders, the petite young woman appeared somewhat nervous. Eden noticed the way her eyes darted around the space, never settling in any one place for long.

Blaine removed his shades, his dark eyes shimmering

with a mixture of confidence and mischief. "Now that you two ladies have met, let's get to work on this album, shall we?" He winked, then began walking past the reception desk and down the hall.

Eden swallowed. Those piercing eyes...deep brown, flecked with gold. They'd been her downfall once before, and she couldn't afford another fall. Not now. She dragged her gaze away from him, focusing on Naiya. Looping her arm through the younger woman's, she asked, "Tell me about your vision for this album."

A few minutes later, they were settled into the recording studio. Blaine sat at the control board, while Naiya and Eden sat facing each other inside the booth. As Naiya relayed some of the topics she wanted to explore on her album, Eden took notes. Listening to Naiya, Eden found herself increasingly intrigued by the young singer's words. Not only was she a talented vocalist, but she possessed great intellect, as well as a surprising level of awareness of the world around her.

"I have to tell you, Naiya. I was impressed with your singing, but now that I've heard your thoughts, I'm even more impressed with you." Eden closed her notebook, resting it on her lap. "You're so tuned in to everything."

Naiya tilted her head to one side, releasing a brief giggle. "I know people like to think that the younger generation is too self-absorbed to notice such things. But not all of us are that way."

Eden winced, noticing the way Naiya had subtly quashed her preconceived notions. "I can see that. And I'm honored to help you realize your vision with this album."

Naiya snapped her fingers as if remembering something. "I almost forgot. I brought my journal." She reached into her purse, taking out a small spiral-bound book and passing it to her. "I don't know what your process is like, but I thought it might help with the lyrics."

Accepting the journal, Eden smiled. "It absolutely will help. Thank you for trusting me with it."

Blaine's voice filled the booth as he spoke into the mic. "Okay, ladies. Have you had enough time to chat?"

They both nodded.

"Good," he continued. "The bigwigs at the label want us to turn around a first single pretty quickly, so we need to get cracking on that. After that's done, we'll tackle the rest of the album."

Naiya's grin revealed her excitement. Standing, she slipped on a headset and spoke into the mic. "Do we have a beat yet?"

"Yep. Just got one in from Jazzy." Blaine flipped a few switches on the soundboard, and the sounds of the track filled the space.

Eden was bobbing her head and tapping her foot almost immediately, and she felt the smile sweeping over her face. The track sounded unique and fresh, yet reminiscent of nineties hip-hop. "This is fantastic."

Naiya, snapping along with the beat, said, "You can't go wrong with an 808. I love this! It's retro but it's current at the same time."

Eden had to agree. The Roland TR-808 drum machine had played a seminal role in hip hop and R & B music, starting with its release in 1980. While it was only in production for three years, the 808 had been used for countless hit songs, and even today's music software often emulated the patterns the legendary drum machine had created. The track the producer had created for Naiya had just enough instrumentality to give it a classic sound and used the 808 to lay down a trap drum line popularized by some of the hottest recent rap acts.

Blaine's million-dollar smile beamed through the glass partition. "Great. Then it'll give y'all the perfect jumping-off point. I'll just let it loop." He slid back from the board and stood.

Eden turned his way, and their eyes connected.

He offered her a smile tinged with wickedness.

Her breath caught in her throat. She could remember him smiling at her, just that way, one night when they'd been working together. She swallowed, recalling how that smile had set off a chain of events that had ended with them making love. Her tongue darted over her lower lips as she recalled the way he'd bent her over the conference room table and lifted her skirt...

His voice cut into her memories. "I'll be in my office. I've got a call to make." Taking off his headset, he exited the studio with a wave.

Eden watched him go, feeling a mixture of relief and disappointment as his overpowering male energy left the space. She knew she needed him gone so she could concentrate, yet less logical parts of her wanted him nearby.

In the quiet of his office, Blaine sat down at his desk and sighed. He hated to leave the studio, because he loved watching the creative process in real time. It was like being present for a birth, metaphorically speaking. There was nothing else quite like watching a musician bring forth a new song. The music became a living thing with a bass line for a pulse, a lyrical heart and a body made of sound. Out in the world, that music could change someone's mood, their day or even the trajectory of their life.

He believed in the transformative power of music. To him, it was just as tangible and present as the air he breathed or the water he drank. That was why he'd entered the music business. It wasn't about the storied Woodson family and their history. It was about him, pursuing his true calling, on his own terms.

And now, to be working with Eden again felt amazing.

She'd been his muse in the past, and he knew she'd be able to create something truly special with Naiya. A tiny part of him still held out hope that she'd create something special with him, too, something as beautiful and as timeless as a classic love song. He knew it would take work to get back into her heart, but he was willing to do whatever it took.

Marvin's cryptic warning from their meeting in New York had been echoing in his head. In order for him to move forward with Naiya's debut, he needed to know the whole story. Parts of him were ill at ease, and he hesitated over the keypad of his phone.

But he pushed past his apprehension and dialed his boss's direct number.

A few moments later, he ended the call. Leaning back in his chair, he released the groan he'd been holding back for most of the call. In a way, he'd expected bad news. But he'd never thought it would be this serious. The sweeping changes being made by AMGI made him nervous. And even if Against the Grain survived this round of cuts, what guarantee did he have that he wouldn't be facing the same situation again at some point in the future?

The other blow from the call was Marvin's admission that label management wasn't fully on board with his decision to have Eden do all the songwriting. According to the suits, Eden didn't have a consistent enough track record for writing chart toppers.

He sighed. *What I really need is a massively successful album. With that kind of money, I could cut ties with the corporate world of music, and Against the Grain would become a truly independent label.*

Maybe Naiya's album would be just what Against the Grain needed.

He thought of the other three artists he was currently working with, but none of them seemed more likely than Naiya to deliver the powerhouse content he needed.

You could just ask your father for help, a voice in the recesses of his mind chided.

He frowned, rejecting that voice. He'd made it this far without his father's money, and there was no way he'd ask for it now.

Pushing his chair back from the desk, he stood and stretched. Eden and Naiya were probably well into their process by now, and even though he wasn't in the best mood, he wanted to observe as much of it as he could. Pocketing his phone, he left his office.

Instead of returning to the studio, he exited the building via the rear door and headed for the small courtyard. After the conversation he'd just had, he needed some fresh air and some time to clear his head before he went back to working the controls. As he moved toward the wrought iron bench beneath the old poplar tree, he noticed someone sitting there.

Eden. The sight of her made his pulse race.

A smile turned up the corners of his mouth as he approached her. "What brings you out here, Eden?"

She looked up from her phone, a soft smile on her face. "I…couldn't focus. So, I decided to come outside and get a little fresh air."

He chuckled. "What a coincidence. I'm in need of a little decompression myself."

"The music biz." She shook her head, her gaze directed upward, as if she were studying the canopy of leaves above her head. "It's not for the faint of heart."

"That's for sure." He moved closer, gesturing to the empty spot next to her. "Mind if I join you?"

She was quiet for a moment. Just before the silence became uncomfortably long, she said, "Go ahead."

He sat next to her, leaving only a sliver of space between them. Draping his arm over the back of the bench, he asked, "How far have you two gotten on the single?"

"Not very. I know the direction for the song, but I was feeling a bit stuck." She ran a hand over her loose curls. "I thought it would be better to just take some time and get myself together, rather than try to force the process, ya know?"

He nodded. "I get it." He scratched his chin with his free hand. "Do you remember that time back in the day when you had writer's block? We were working on that song 'Love by Night.'"

She tilted her head, looked thoughtful. A moment later, she snapped her fingers. "Yeah, I remember. That's the time we went for that run around Piedmont Park, right?"

"Right."

She let her head fall back against his arm as she laughed. "Oh, man. I had forgotten about that."

"You wanna go for a run now?" He gave her a teasing look.

She rolled her eyes. "You know the answer to that." Gesturing to her body, she said, "I don't run, and it's probably obvious."

"I can tell you still work out, though." He winked. "I know it takes effort to maintain a shape like that."

Her cheeks reddened as she changed the subject. "How long is that trail loop? Three miles?"

"Closer to four. It was a hell of a workout."

She laughed. "You're telling me. I remember going back to the studio sore and sweaty."

He leaned in, unable to resist. "Do you think that was because of the actual run? Or what we did on the trail?"

She dropped her gaze to her lap.

"Remember? We found that little wooded nook just off the path…" He traced his fingertip in a circle over her thigh.

Her hand went to her chest, and she swallowed hard. "I remember, Blaine."

"Standing in that position for so long might have made

you sore," he announced. "But I never heard any complaints."

"I didn't have any," she admitted softly. "It was amazing…you were amazing."

Their gazes met, and the heat of the memories they'd made in that little corner of the park passed between them. He could still hear her soft moans, feel her hands grasping his shoulders for purchase as he tasted the sweetness flowing between her thighs.

He picked up her hand, raising it to his lips. Placing a soft kiss against her palm, he released her. "We'd better go back inside." It was true…he knew that if they remained out here much longer, he wouldn't be able to resist dragging her soft, curvy body into his lap.

She stood, appearing a little shaky on her feet, but only for a moment. "Agreed." After a moment's hesitation, she added, "Blaine, we really shouldn't dwell on the past now. Let's just keep things professional, okay?"

He offered a quick nod in response.

Seconds later she walked past him. Enjoying the view of her backside, he followed her back into the building.

Five

The next day, Eden was back in her seat on the stool inside the recording studio at Against the Grain. Her leather notebook on her lap, she absently flipped through the pages. Naiya's journal had proven to be a valuable resource for Eden when it came to writing lyrics for her debut single.

I just hope I'm going in the right direction for Naiya. She certainly has a lot to say.

With the wealth of information she'd gleaned about the singer's inner life, she felt confident that she'd written a solid draft for the single. Now it was simply a matter of whether Naiya and Blaine agreed.

Thinking of Blaine brought a slight smile to her lips, despite her better judgment. She still remembered the day they'd met on the campus of Atlanta Tech. He'd been charming, funny and easygoing, and at the time, she'd thought him the perfect counter to her studious, hardworking, straitlaced self. Blaine Woodson wasn't like any other man she'd ever met, and he'd fascinated her from the very start. What followed could only be described as a passionate affair. While they worked on music in the studio, their hearts entwined like the treble and bass lines of a song. Their song was beautiful, yet tragically brief.

With time came wisdom, though, and she'd since learned the folly of her ways. What had seemed like an ideal match had only led to heartbreak for her, both romantically and professionally. Shaking her head to cast off those wayward thoughts, she stood. Leaving her notebook on the stool, she left the studio and went across to the ladies' room.

When she returned to the studio and opened the door, she detected a familiar woodsy and decidedly masculine aroma. As she entered the space, a small creaking sound near the board drew her attention. She glanced in the direction of the sound and saw Blaine sitting there, his back to her as he spun the chair slightly from side to side.

She cleared her throat, and as he pivoted to face her, plastered on a congenial smile. "Hi, Blaine. How are you?"

"I'm fine. Much better now that you're here." He grinned. "I'm excited to see what you've come up with, and I'm sure Naiya is, as well."

She answered only with a smile and a nod. She didn't open her mouth, to avoid saying something foolish. What was it about his presence, the sound of his voice, that made her knees go weak? She looked through the glass partition, and seeing no one in the booth, asked, "Where is Naiya, anyway?"

"Caught in traffic. She texted me to let me know she's on her way."

She chuckled. "Gotta love Atlanta traffic."

"Yeah. Where the rush hour is from midnight to 11:59 p.m." He scoffed. "I've been late to many an appointment trying to navigate through Midtown."

"You've actually got a better shot getting places on time if you walk." As much as she loved the city and her fellow "ATLiens," she didn't think she'd ever get used to the frenetic pace of traffic, especially 85 where it cut through the heart of the city.

He rubbed his hands together. "So, you ready to get this single done?"

"I am, assuming you and Naiya like the lyrics I've come up with."

"Can I take a look?"

She shook her head. "I always let the artist lay eyes on my lyrics first. After Naiya's seen it, then you can take a look."

He looked surprised but seemed to take it in stride. "Okay. Can't blame me for being curious, though. There's a lot riding on this album."

She watched him silently, noting the way his entire demeanor changed when he uttered the last few words. *There's a lot riding on this album.* Was that indicative of the way he felt about every album his label released? Or was there something more to the story, something she wasn't privy to?

Before she could ask any more questions, a smiling Naiya entered. Her hair was in a ponytail hanging down the back of her pink-and-white maxi dress. "Hey, y'all."

"Hi, Naiya." Eden turned her full attention to the young singer. "I'm really excited for you to see what I've come up with for your first single."

She clapped her hands together. "Me, too. Let's dig in."

The two women entered the booth and took their seats. Eden hazarded a quick glance through the glass partition and saw Blaine leaning his elbows on the soundboard surround. The expression on his face looked as if his mind was elsewhere. Returning her focus to Naiya, Eden handed over her leather notebook. "Here's the song. After reading your journal, I thought your first love might be a good place to start."

Naiya blew out a breath. "So, we're going for drama, eh?"

"Sort of. Anyway, I think the things you wrote about your first love and the subsequent heartbreak were very compelling. Audiences are pretty likely to relate to that, regardless of their age."

"I hope you're right."

Eden watched as Naiya read through the lyrics. "Trust me on this one. Love songs usually take one of two paths. Romantic and sentimental, or bitter breakup. What I've tried to do is create a third path. 'It didn't work out, but I don't hate you, and you gave me some good memories.'"

Naiya nodded. "Nice."

Silence fell between them, and Eden thought about the lyrics she'd written. The story had not only been inspired by the words in Naiya's journal, but by her own experience with Blaine. They'd had a great time way back when, and though she doubted she'd ever fully trust him again, she didn't hate him. On the contrary, she wished him happiness.

I just wonder if he could ever find that happiness with me. Thinking about all she'd shared with him was bittersweet. There were parts of her heart, hidden deep down where no one could see, that still craved his love. But logic and common sense told her to steer clear of him. Working with him, while keeping things strictly professional, proved more challenging than she would have expected.

Naiya looked up from the notebook, her eyes wide.

Eden watched warily, unsure of what her expression meant. "What do you think?"

"Wow." Naiya shook her head from side to side. "This song…is fantastic."

Releasing a pent-up breath, Eden remarked, "Awesome. Your expression had me a little worried there."

"I'm just amazed at how accurately you captured my sentiments about my first love." She held up the notebook.

"It's not sappy and fake, nor is it ragey and bitter. It really toes the perfect line."

Placing her hand over her heart, she smiled. "Thank you. It means a lot to me that you like it."

"We're going to work great together." Naiya's gaze dropped to the handwritten lyrics again. "I can tell."

Eden spun halfway around on the stool, intent on knocking on the glass to get Blaine's attention. When she faced the partition, she saw him standing near the studio's open door, talking animatedly to a very familiar-looking man.

Naiya asked, "Who's that Blaine is speaking with?"

Eden shrugged. "One of his brothers, though I'm not sure which one." She watched the exchange, and even though the booth's soundproofing prevented her from hearing their conversation, she could tell by their body language that their discussion was heated.

Blaine threw up his hands and returned to the soundboard. Engaging the mic, he said, "Ladies, I need to go to my office for a bit. I'll be back as soon as I can."

Without waiting for a response, he switched off the mic and strode from the room.

Eden blew out a breath. *What's going on with him?* When they'd been in the studio alone, she'd had his full attention. Now it was obvious something else was at play, and she couldn't help feeling frustrated. "Okay, then. I guess we're working on paper for a bit. Any tweaks you want to make to the lyrics?"

Stalking down the hallway toward his office, Blaine stopped near the benches outside his door. Gage, following close behind him, nearly collided with him.

Fixing his brother with a hard stare, he asked, "Why in the hell would you do this, Gage? Why would you bring Dad here?"

"Because he asked me to." Gage shook his head. "More like he demanded it. What did you expect me to do?"

"Show some backbone and tell him no," he groused. "We're not kids anymore, Gage. We don't have to do everything he says."

Gage ran a hand over his close-trimmed fade. "Maybe you aren't, bro. But in case you forgot, my office is two doors down from his. The only way I was going to be left alone to get my work done was if I did what he asked."

Blaine sighed. "Thanks a lot, Gage."

"You're welcome. He's in your office, and I'd suggest you don't keep him waiting much longer."

Groaning, Blaine went to his office door. He leaned forward, peering through the small tempered-glass window.

Just as Gage had said, Caleb Woodson sat in the guest chair near Blaine's desk. Blaine could see his father's sour disposition displayed on his bearded face. Caleb wore one of the charcoal Italian-cut suits he favored, and his arms were folded over his chest.

Pausing to take a deep, steadying breath, he turned the knob and pushed it open. "Good morning, Father."

"Hmph. What's so good about it?" Caleb's gruff tone communicated the same level of dissatisfaction as his expression. "Come on in here. I need to talk to you."

Blaine let the door shut behind him, seeing no reason to subject the whole building to their discussion. Walking around the desk, he took a seat and faced his ornery father. "Well, it must be important. I never expected you'd lower yourself to visit me here." He knew his words were harsh, but they were also true. His father had basically disowned him when he'd opened Against the Grain. "You could have called, so you wouldn't have to sully yourself."

"Trust me, son, I don't want to be here any more than you want to see me." Caleb leaned forward, placing his hands atop the desk and lacing his fingers together. "The only reason I came here instead of calling is that I wanted to see your face when I asked you this question. That way I'll know if you're lying to me."

He wanted to roll his eyes but refrained. "Go ahead. Ask away."

"What do you know about Hamilton House putting in a bid to buy out 404 Sound?"

Blaine furrowed his brow. "Dad, what are you talking about?"

Caleb watched him intently, his dark eyes boring into his son's. "You mean you haven't heard anything about your principal backers trying to take over my life's work?"

He sighed. "No, Dad. I don't know anything about it."

"Are you sure? Weren't you in New York at the headquarters not too long ago?"

"Yes, I was in New York recently," Blaine retorted. "But I don't know anything about this whole buyout situation. What you just told me is the first time I've heard it."

Caleb watched him for a few seconds more. Letting his shoulders droop, he took his hands off the desk and sat back in his chair. "I see."

"I'm not sure what kind of relationship you think I have with Hamilton House, but it's not like I'm privy to every decision they make." Blaine rubbed his temples, feeling a headache coming on. "They help fund my business, and in exchange, they get a cut of my profits. That's the entire extent of our relationship."

Caleb rubbed his hands together. "Would you have told me if you knew about it?"

He shrugged. "I don't know. It's not really my place."

His father shook his head, his expression grim. "You're such a disappointment, Blaine. I wanted so much more for you."

There it is. Dad can't talk to me for more than five minutes without taking a shot at me. Shaking his head at the patronizing tone his father had taken, he sighed. "I know, Dad. And I'm sorry I can't be as perfectly organized as Nia, or as obedient as Gage and Miles, or as creative as Teagan. I'm the family screw-up, and if I ever forget that, I'll always have you to remind me, won't I?"

"Not always, kid." His lips twisted into a grimace. "But that's neither here nor there."

"Nice use of guilt there, Dad. You missed your calling as an actor on a daytime soap."

Caleb slammed his fist on the table. "Watch your tone, Blaine. I'm still your father."

He averted his eyes, remaining silent. As strained as their relationship was, he didn't set out to purposely disrespect his father.

"You listen, and you listen good. Addy and I raised all our children with good manners and good sense. You're grown now, and your choices are your own. But don't you sit there acting like you sprouted up from the earth fully formed. Show some damn respect."

"I'm sorry, Dad," he murmured. "It's just that I did all this for myself." He gestured around the office. "I did it on my own, and you never give me credit for it."

"Yes, son, you did do this on your own. Against my advice and without my blessing. And I admit you've done all right for yourself. But had you stayed with 404, stayed with the family, you'd be doing better."

Blaine blew out an aggravated breath. "Okay, Dad. I've answered your question, so can I get back to running my business now?"

Caleb stood. "You do that. But I have a message for those cronies at Hamilton House, and I want you to give it to them."

"I'm listening."

His father leaned forward, resting his palms on the surface of the desk. "You get on the phone, and you tell them this. Addy and I will never sell 404 Sound. It's our legacy, and we worked too hard to build it up to just hand it off to someone outside the family. And even if we did sell, there's no way in hell we'd ever sell to Hamilton House."

Blaine quipped, "Should I use those exact words, or is it okay if I paraphrase?"

Caleb scowled. "Tell them however you want, smartass. Just make sure they get the message, you hear me?"

"I've got it, Dad."

With a huff, Caleb turned on his heel, slung the door open and marched out.

Left alone in his office, Blaine dropped his head against the backrest of his chair and let out an audible groan.

Six

Eden slipped into the recording studio Wednesday around 10:00 a.m. She looked around the empty space, seeing no sign of Blaine or Naiya. She glanced at the time on her phone. *I'm a little early. He should be here soon.* She could remember many slights Blaine had dealt her, but he generally didn't keep her waiting.

She scoffed, shaking her head at the direction of her own thoughts. *What do I know about Blaine, really?* She had only her past interactions with him to go on. She'd thought she knew him well then, which had led to her being blindsided by his betrayal.

She entered the booth, leaving the door ajar so she could hear him when he came in. Hanging her woven purse from the doorknob, she sat down on the stool. In the quiet surroundings, she let her mind wander.

She recalled those days when she was a fresh-faced twentysomething, dreaming of singing superstardom. She, Ainsley and Cambria had pulled many long days and nights in the studio, working on what was supposed to have been their debut album as Swatz Girlz. As a songwriter for the group, Eden had probably put in more hours than her cousin and their good friend.

She'd been spending so much time in the studio with Blaine that, looking back on it now, it seemed only natural that they'd become romantically involved. She remembered the way he watched her when she sang, as if her voice were the most beautiful sound he'd ever heard. She could still feel the warmth that flooded her body whenever he smiled at her, her breath catching when his hand brushed against hers, the way tingles of excitement ran down her spine whenever he kissed her.

She sighed aloud.

Those were the days.

When I was trusting and full of hope.

When I was too young and naive to see what was coming.

The memories of what she'd shared with Blaine seemed so long ago, and simultaneously, it seemed like only yesterday. Her life had changed so much since then. One thing that remained unchanged was her love of music, hip-hop and R & B in particular. It was that love of music that had helped her survive the crushing heartbreak of Blaine's betrayal.

She turned her head to the left, eyeing the instruments occupying one corner of the recording booth. Spying a keyboard sitting on its stand, she scooted the stool up to it. Turning it on, she set the keyboard to piano mode and plucked out a few notes. There had been many times when she'd written songs just this way—by picking out the basic tune on the keyboard while working out the lyrics in her head. As the verses became more solid, she'd start vocalizing to get the cadence just right. It wasn't usually until the second or third draft that she put the words on paper. Her process was a bit unorthodox, but it worked well for her.

She ran through the scales a few times, then paused, her fingers still poised over the keys. The urge to sing overtook her, and she felt her fingers change position. Soon, she segued into the opening notes to a classic tune by Xscape, "My Little Secret." The song, from their 1998 album *Traces of My Lipstick*, was one of her favorites of the last two decades. Knowing that group members Tiny, Tamika, LaTocha and Kandi were fellow Atlanta natives only made her love their work more.

Singing through the opening verse, she could feel the smile coming over her face. Singing gave her a special kind of joy, a feeling she didn't get from anything else. Watching Ainsley and Cooper interacting was a close second, because it touched her heart to see the genuine love between mother and son. But there was nothing quite like opening up her mouth and letting her voice soar.

She was rounding the second chorus when she noticed Blaine standing in the open door to the booth. Surprised, and a bit embarrassed, she stopped mid-note.

His face filled with earnest admiration, he spoke into the awkward silence. "Please, Eden. Don't stop."

Heat flared in her chest, and she could feel it rising into her cheeks. "Blaine, I..."

"It's been so long since I've heard you sing." He took a step closer. "I don't want it to be over yet."

Swallowing her nervousness, she picked up where she'd left off. Now that he was in the room, the lyrics, about a secret romance between two people with plenty of baggage, suddenly seemed much more potent.

And personal.

Suddenly, this song, which she often sang in the shower or while driving, simply because she found it catchy, became almost autobiographical. Under the intense, watchful gaze of the man she'd once loved, every word took on new meaning.

She sang the song to the end, then eased her fingertips away from the keys.

Blaine burst into applause. "You've still got it, Eden."

"Thank you," she said, her tone softer than she'd intended. She looked away, reeling from the intimacy of the moment. Having him as a spectator to her impassioned singing felt too familiar, too reminiscent of a time she'd fought hard to forget.

"I'm not just gassing you up, either." His tone quiet, almost reverent, he took a few slow steps until he was right next to her. "I hear singing all day, every day. But I've never, ever come across another voice like yours."

She sucked in a breath, and his rich, woodsy cologne flooded her senses, threatening to undo her. Blowing the breath out, she struggled to find words to articulate her feelings. "I appreciate the compliment, Blaine. I really do. But..."

"But, what?" He watched her intently. "Is something wrong?"

She tucked in her bottom lip. *How can I tell him that being this close to him ruins my concentration? That I can't focus on my work because all I want to do is climb him like a tree?*

"Eden?"

"I'm fine." She shifted on the stool, angling her face away from him in hopes that she might regain some of her faculties. His physical size, combined with his overt masculine energy, seemed to fill the space around her, making the booth feel even smaller than it actually was.

He reached out, his fingertips brushing lightly over her bare shoulder. "Are you sure?"

She trembled, reacting to the tingling sensation brought on by his electric touch. For a moment, she wanted him to continue, wanted to feel his kiss. Soon, though, common sense took over, and she shook her head. "Yes, Blaine. I'm positive."

Blaine took a step back from Eden, concerned he might be invading her space. Even though she insisted she was fine, he sensed the discomfort rolling off her. Clearing his throat, he said, "Feel free to speak honestly with me, Eden. We've known each other too long to be dishonest with each other."

"If I had something to say, trust me, I'd say it." She tossed the words over her shoulder, still not facing him.

He sighed. "Well, I do have something to say." He jammed his hands into his pockets, trying to get the words to line up in his mind. She looked so beautiful today, in a sunny yellow sleeveless blouse and a pair of wide-legged white linen pants that hugged her hips like he used to when they were making love. "I've…missed you."

She glanced over her shoulder at him, her eyes wide.

He cleared his throat, trying to cover what had been too honest an admission. "I meant… I've missed working with you." He could feel his blood warming. No other woman had ever left him so discombobulated.

She did a slow turn on the stool, facing him again. Her hair, tied back in a low ponytail, highlighted the beauty of her bronze-skinned face. Her expression held a mixture of surprise and annoyance. "Oh, really? You've missed working with me, but you never called on me to write for you before now."

He missed more than just working with her, but something told him now wasn't the time to mention that. "Just like your voice, your writing talents are unique, special. Up until now, I haven't had an artist I felt could carry what you bring to the table."

"Laying it on pretty thick, huh?" She chuckled, shaking her head. "If you say so."

"It's true." And it was, partially, at least. He did think Naiya was perfectly suited to Eden's songwriting style. But he'd also stayed away from Eden because she'd made it clear she didn't want him around. After he'd been forced to cut her and Ainsley from his roster, things had soured between them in a major way. Both their personal and professional relationship had been flushed down the toilet that day, and he didn't know if they'd ever get back to a good place. Still, part of him wanted to try.

"Why are you staring at me, Blaine?" A curious half smile came over her face.

He sensed her goading him. Still, he decided to take a serious tack. "Eden, you do realize I didn't have a choice, right? I had to do what I did."

"Oh, boy." She shook her head. "Here we go."

"Honestly. I had a lot of faith in Swatz Girlz as a group. But I had to make sure I had funding to make my business successful."

She laughed, slapping her thigh. "Do you realize you said the same thing back then? It's the same old line about how you didn't have a choice. But the thing is, you did. It's *your* business, Blaine. You always have a choice." She fixed him with a look, her eyes slightly narrowed. "You chose."

That's easy for her to say. She could never understand what it was like to be him. People tended to assume that because of his family's money, his whole life had been some sort of leisurely stroll through the garden. Nothing could be further from the truth. "Come on, Eden. You're not being fair here."

She snorted. "I think it's a very fair judgment. You did what was best for you, I get that. But you have to admit to not giving much thought to what would happen to us. You know, you and me? The relationship we were building? Did you give any thought at all to the future we could have had?"

He shoved his hands into the pockets of his jeans. "Why can't you see things for what they are? Why do you insist on thinking the worst of me?"

She rolled her eyes. "I can only go by what you've shown me. You'll have to excuse me for not seeing you as some kind of saint."

He groaned. "I never claimed to be a saint, but…" He stopped mid-sentence.

Their gazes locked, and silence fell.

Seeing the fire dancing in her dark eyes made his body temperature rise. All he wanted was to hold her, to possess her as he once had. In an instant, his anger melted away, replaced by a consuming desire to pull her into his arms. What was it about this woman that had him vacillating between wanting to verbally spar with her and wanting to ravish her? Before he could stop himself, he grasped her hand.

"Blaine?" Her lips were slightly parted, begging to be kissed.

Giving her a gentle tug, he growled, "Stand up."

She did as he asked. "Why?"

"So, I don't have to kneel to do this." He grazed his fingertips along her jawline.

Her eyes closed briefly, then popped open again. "If you kiss me, I'll box your ears."

"You can't even reach my ears," he teased.

"I'll get a step stool."

"If you do, I'll take my lumps like a man." He eased the tip of his index finger over her lips. "Just let me have this one kiss."

A soft chuckle escaped her throat. "Damn it, Blaine." She angled her face up, pressing her lips together in a soft pucker.

Moments later, he kissed her. The contact, heady and all

too fleeting, sent sparks of desire dancing down his spine like electricity moving along a fallen power line. Her lips were soft and yielding, just as he remembered them. After a few more soft brushes, he deepened the kiss. Sweeping his tongue over her lower lip, he thrilled when she opened her mouth for him. As he slipped his tongue inside, a soft moan escaped her throat, and he nearly came undone. He knew that if they continued, he'd be laying her down on the sofa and taking her until she cried out his name. Reluctantly, he eased away.

"You're made of temptation, Eden Voss."

She placed her fingertips against her lips. Her eyes were glazed with desire, but as always, she deflected with her trademark humor. "I should have made you kneel."

Now it was his turn to chuckle. "Maybe I'll kneel for you later."

"Hey, guys."

A third voice entered the conversation, and he turned toward the sound.

Naiya had appeared in the doorway. She leaned against the doorframe, glancing back and forth between them. "Sorry, am I interrupting something?"

Blaine shook his head, tearing his gaze away from Eden. "No. We're just talking shop." He kept his tone even, not wanting to reveal the delicious tension of the preceding moments. "So, Naiya, how are you feeling about the single so far?"

"It's great. I'm ready to move forward with the process."

"Ready enough to lay down some reference vocals on your single?" he asked.

Naiya smiled, her excitement apparent. "Let's do it."

He looked her way again. "Eden, you can stay in the booth with Naiya and give her delivery tips as we go along, okay?" He tried to direct his thoughts back to business, but it was all he could do to stand up straight after how hard she'd made him. She glanced down, a ghost of a smile crossing her face.

She nodded. "Sure thing."

She knows. He thought about the frigid snowfall from his last winter vacation in the Colorado mountains until his ardor finally calmed enough for him to walk.

He left the booth, letting the door close behind him. Moments later, he was at the soundboard. Giving them a thumbs-up through the glass partition, he put on his headphones and started the playback of the track.

While he bobbed his head along with the music, he did his best to shake off the memory of Eden's kiss. But just like any great composition, the melody of her was impossible to shake.

Seven

Friday morning, Eden stifled a yawn as she entered the Bodacious Bean. The air-conditioned interior provided immediate relief from the sticky August air, and she sighed as soon as the door shut behind her. The combination of the oppressive humidity, high temperature and a lack of quality sleep the night before had left her feeling like a zombie, and she desperately needed a caffeine pick-me-up.

She'd spent the better part of the night tossing and turning, unable to sleep. And when she had finally drifted off, Blaine and his magnificent kisses were waiting for her in dreamland. She just couldn't seem to shake her desire for him. She craved his touch the way flowers craved sunlight.

Ponying up to the counter, she greeted the barista and ordered an iced coffee with two shots of espresso. Once she had the coffee and a blueberry muffin in hand, she slunk to a table near the back. As she sucked down the first sip of her drink, her phone buzzed. Picking it up, she glanced at the screen before answering. "Hey, Ainsley. What's up?"

"What's up with you? You barely said two words to me last night when you came in, and then you bounced this morning before I even got up."

She stifled another yawn. "Sorry, girl. I was exhausted."

"You sound like you're still tired. What's going on with you? Didn't you sleep last night?"

She drank a bit more coffee before answering. "Not as well as I would have liked."

"Mmm-hmm."

She rolled her eyes even though she knew her cousin couldn't see it. "Mmm-hmm, what?"

"There's something you're not telling me, Eden. I just know it." Ainsley's tone dripped with suspicion.

"Dang, Ainsley. You're always grilling me. Even my mama didn't get in my business as you do."

"Well, my mama did. I'm just picking up where she left off."

Shaking her head at how much Ainsley reminded her of Aunt Mimi, she sighed. "Fine. I got to the studio a little early Wednesday, so I sat down to the keyboard… Anyway, Blaine walked in on me playing and singing."

"Were you singing that Xscape song? The one you're always belting out around the house?"

She laughed. "Yes, I was. Anyway, it's been so long since I got to play and sing like that. And it really reminded me how much I miss singing professionally…"

Ainsley interjected. "Boo, we both know you miss singing. But it ain't never been serious enough to keep you up at night. So why don't you stop beating around the bush and tell me the real tea, okay?"

Yikes. She chewed on the plastic straw. "Ainsley, you're killing me."

"Then let's make it quick. Or would you rather drag it out and lengthen your suffering?"

Annoyed as she was, she couldn't help laughing at her

cousin. "Okay. Blaine started talking about how he missed working with me, and I fussed at him a little."

"So, you couldn't sleep because y'all argued?"

"No, that's not it. And I wouldn't call it an argument, it was more of a heated discussion. Even though we were having a pretty heavy conversation, somehow, he…ended up kissing me." Retelling the tale to her cousin forced her to relive those torrid moments wrapped in his arms. She could still smell his cologne, still feel the strength of his arms enfolding her…

"I knew it!"

She dropped the phone on the table. Picking it up a moment later, she groused, "Can you not shout in my ear? It's way too early for these shenanigans."

"I'm not gonna say I told you so."

"You literally just did."

Ainsley laughed. "Well, I'm not gonna say it twice. Anyway, I knew that as soon as y'all got in that studio together, the sparks would start flying."

"Don't you have something to be doing right now?"

"I'm in the kitchen making Cooper some breakfast."

"Good. Well, I'll let you go so you can focus on cooking before you burn the house down. We're already paying for the roof, and I don't need any more mishaps."

"But…"

She hung up on her cousin, laying her phone face down on the table. Part of the reason she'd left so early was so she could get her coffee and have it quietly, giving the caffeine time to do its magic before she had to be at the studio. No way was she about to give up that peaceful start to her day to play a game of twenty-one questions with her well-meaning but nosy cousin. She was still processing what had transpired between her and Blaine and discussing it with Ainsley certainly wasn't helping her achieve clarity.

After draining the contents of her cup, she popped off the lid and headed back to the counter for a refill. Just as she got her filled cup back, the bell above the door sounded and she turned.

Blaine walked in.

She nearly dropped her coffee. Snapping the lid back on, she swallowed. *It's too early for anybody to be looking that damn good.*

True to his usual style, he wore a pair of distressed black jeans, black leather sneakers and a black T-shirt bearing the Against the Grain logo in metallic silver. The signature large sunglasses once again obscured his eyes, and his locs were tied in a haphazard knot atop his head. His lips tilted into a smile when he saw her. "Morning, Eden."

"Good morning." Her voice squeaked out, barely above a whisper.

"You've...got a little something..." He gestured, pointing toward her face. "You know, right around your mouth."

She brushed away the crumbs of blueberry muffin clinging there, then blew out a breath. "Ever had the muffins here? They're pretty great."

"Yeah, they are." He advanced toward the counter. "You okay?"

She ran her free hand over her hair, hoping it resembled something like a style. She spoke again, a bit louder this time. "Yes, I'm fine. I'm just low on caffeine."

"Me, too. But at least you came to the right place."

She eased back toward her table, and part of her hoped that he'd get his drink to go, and that would be the end of their interaction, at least until she made it to the studio. She sat down, pretending to scroll through her phone while taking surreptitious glances in his direction.

When she saw him walking toward her, coffee in hand, she knew her hopes of him leaving her to finish her coffee alone had been dashed on the jagged rocks of reality.

Drawing a breath, she braced for his entry into her personal bubble.

He paused near the empty chair across the table from her. "Mind if I sit with you for a bit?"

While this wasn't what she'd planned, she could think of far worse company to be in. With a soft smile, she said, "Have a seat."

"Thanks." He set his paper cup down on the table as he eased into the seat.

Silence fell between them for a moment, and she tried not to look at his lips. She failed, and the memory of his kiss rose to the surface. Looking at him only made her remember the delicious pressure of his lips against hers. She took another sip of her drink, noting the way he rubbed the back of his neck. With his eyes still hidden behind the dark lenses, she couldn't fully read his mood. "Is there something you want to talk about?" She realized too late that the question had been too open-ended, but since she couldn't take it back, she just hoped for the best.

He cleared his throat. "There is, actually. I was wondering if there's anything we could do to speed up the process of completing Naiya's album."

She picked up on something in his voice, something she wasn't used to hearing from the confident label head. *Is he nervous about something? Is it because he kissed me, or is it business-related?* "I've already started drafting the second song, if that's what you mean."

"No. I mean, can we speed up the timeline for the project as a whole? I'd really like to get ten solid tracks done in less than a month, if possible."

She contemplated his words for a moment. While she was glad he hadn't taken her question as an invitation to discuss kissing, she couldn't help feeling curious about his sudden rush to finish Naiya's album. "I suppose I could.

However, debut albums can be tricky, and I want to do my best work for her."

"I understand, and trust me, I appreciate that. But I'm on a bit of a time crunch, though I'd rather not discuss why."

She wasn't thrilled that he seemed to be hiding something from her, but this was Blaine Woodson, after all. "I think it might help my process if I could see her perform live. Just to get a better feel for her style and how she interacts with a crowd."

He brightened, clapped his hands together. "Great! Then you can come with me to her open mic show at the Bass Line Lounge tomorrow night."

She studied his face, trying to ascertain his intent. "Are you asking me on a date, Blaine?"

He chuckled. "No. It's not a date. It's business. I'm simply giving you what you say will help your process."

"Good. So that means there won't be any flirting, or kissing…"

He chuckled again, a deep, rumbling sound that seemed to reverberate through his broad chest. "Don't worry. I won't kiss you again until you ask me to."

She swallowed hard. It was impossible to miss the teasing in his tone, yet she knew he meant what he said. She also knew that the odds were pretty good that she would cave and ask for his kisses again…she just wasn't going to tell him that now.

She rolled her eyes. "Awesome. That means it will never happen again."

That afternoon, Blaine retreated to his office while Naiya and Eden worked in the booth. He'd left Trevor, his engineer, to operate the soundboard while he handled some of the tasks he'd let pile up on his desk over the last few weeks. He didn't relish this mundane part of the job, but after he delegated as much as he could to Leanna, his assistant, he had no choice but to complete the rest.

He slid aside a small stack of completed paperwork and set his pen down, flexing his fingers to relieve some of the stiffness in his joints. With the papers tucked away in a folder, he dropped his head back against the headrest of his executive chair. His gaze was on the ceiling, but his mind was on the morning encounter he'd had with Eden.

He hadn't been expecting to run into her at the coffee shop but seeing her had given his day an instant lift. Since his mind had been on his problems with Hamilton House, he hadn't been able to take the conversation in the direction he'd have wanted. He'd wanted to talk about kissing her, specifically, about how soon he could kiss her again. The memory of her soft, yielding lips and the way her skin felt beneath his fingertips made him yearn for more.

Instead, he'd steered the conversation to work. He'd asked her to work harder, faster, to produce the lyrics for Naiya's album. It wasn't ideal, but he didn't have much of a choice. *If I want to remain competitive, keep Against the Grain on the cutting edge, and most of all, keep my main source of funding, I've got to level up.*

He didn't want to put pressure on her, professionally or personally. But he wanted Eden, in all the ways a man could want a woman. And though she would probably rather get a root canal than admit to it, she wanted him, too. So, he'd wait. Patience had never been a strength of his, so he knew it wouldn't be easy.

The struggle is real. But she's absolutely worth it.

His stream of thought was interrupted by the intercom chime on his desk phone.

Leanna's voice came over the speaker. "Blaine, Pierce Hamilton is here."

He felt his brow crinkle with annoyance. He'd only had a few interactions in the past with Pierce, the son of reclusive company owner, the widowed Everly Hamilton. None of them had been particularly positive. Pierce came across as an arrogant, entitled, self-absorbed man who'd gladly step on someone's throat to get his own way. "I don't want to deal with him right now…tell him I'm unavailable."

"I told him that…unfortunately he's already on his way down the…"

Before Leanna could complete the sentence, Blaine's office door swung open. Pierce strode in, his fingertips attached to the lapels of his expensive sports jacket as if he feared the jacket might fly away if he didn't hold on to it. "Greetings, Blake."

"It's *Blaine*." He emphasized the word through his tightly set teeth. Pierce never seemed to get his name right, and while he wasn't surprised, he still found it grating.

"Oh, yes, of course." Pierce took a seat in the guest chair across from him, settling in as if he planned to stay for a while. "So, tell me. How are you? How have things been going?" He laced his fingers together, watching Blaine as if awaiting his answer with great anticipation.

Blaine responded with an icy half smile. "I'm fine, thanks for asking. But I'm sure this isn't a social call." He leaned back in his chair. "So, what can I do for you, Mr. Hamilton?"

He waved his hand. "Pshaw. Mr. Hamilton was my father, God rest his soul. Call me Pierce."

I'd call him an asshole, but I'm sure that wouldn't fly. "If you insist. So, what motivated this little impromptu visit?"

Pierce leaned to the right, resting his chin in the crook between his thumb and index finger. "Quite frankly, I'm surprised you don't know. I hear our label liaison is a real chatterbox."

Blaine felt the tightness build at the base of his spine, crawling up his back like a spider. *I can see where this conversation is headed. No need to put all my cards on the table, though.* "I'm not big on gossip. So why don't you just tell me?"

"We've been talking about expanding the Hamilton House empire." Pierce offered a sly smile that showed off the diamond set in his upper left incisor. "We're looking at creative ways to be the biggest, most comprehensive music production company in the American South…and then, in the whole country."

Blaine kept his tone even, training his expression to remain flat. "Sounds like you've got big dreams."

"You're right. But it's not just me. Mother and my dear sister London are also on board with this vision for the future."

"This all sounds very exciting, Pete."

His eyes flashed. "It's *Pierce*."

"Of course. My apologies." It pleased him to give the man a taste of his own medicine. Still, this back-and-forth banter had started to lose its luster. "I'm still not seeing how this relates to me."

The flash of anger disappeared, replaced by a smug grin. "We've got our eyes on 404 Sound. It's the perfect addition to the brand, and it would give us control of one of the most state-of-the-art studios in this part of the country."

His shoulders stiffened as the spiderlike legs of tension spread. So it was true. "That seems to have more to do with my parents than it does with me. As you know, I'm not affiliated with 404."

Pierce chuckled. "Oh, it has more to do with you than you think. Because if we're going to buy out 404, we'll need an infusion of capital. Mother hates to come out of pocket on these things if it can be avoided." He leaned forward in his chair, his gaze focused squarely on Blaine's face. "And the best way to get that capital, at least as far as I can see, is to stop funding Against the Grain. That way, we can easily redirect those funds to this new endeavor." He scratched his chin. "I suppose we'd hold on to your label if your performance improved dramatically…but I don't really see that happening."

The tenuous hold Blaine had over his expression slipped. Pierce must have seen the change because he immediately straightened in his seat, putting more distance between them. "It's really strange that you came by, Pierce. Because my father was here a few days ago. Apparently, he'd already heard about this little buyout plan, and he left a message for me to convey to Hamilton House."

Pierce laced his fingers together. "I'd love to hear it." His tone held both challenge and thinly veiled contempt.

Blaine stood, towering over Pierce. "I'll paraphrase for you. My parents aren't selling 404. And even if they did, they'd never sell it to the likes of you." He gestured to the door. "Now if you'll excuse me, I need to get back to work. Have yourself a great day."

Pierce stood quickly, nearly toppling the guest chair in the process. "We'll see each other again, Woodson." He slid his gaze upward since Blaine towered over him by a good five inches.

"I'm sure we will." He continued to gesture to the door.

Pierce narrowed his eyes but said nothing. Moments later, with his fingertips locked on his lapels again, he strode out.

Eight

Saturday night, Eden handed her ticket to the gargantuan bouncer. Once he'd nodded his approval, she entered the dimly lit Bass Line Lounge. The club, spacious and open, had foregone the typical setup of crowding the floor with a lot of tables. There was a glossy marble bar that occupied the wall directly in front of her, the gleaming mirrored shelves stocked with liquor of every variety. Cozy booths lined the east and west walls, providing seating as well as a modicum of privacy for those who desired it. Centering the space was a stage, with the DJ spinning records on an elevated platform. Just below the booth were drums, a keyboard and speakers.

Circling past the stage and to her right, she glanced around the place. *I'll head to the bar. That way he won't have to search for me when he comes in.*

Maybe Blaine was already in the building. She imagined him somewhere backstage, giving Naiya a pep talk as she prepared to go onstage. What kinds of things would he say to the talented young singer? She slid onto an empty barstool, feeling her jaw tense as she followed that line of thinking. Would he smile at her? Remind her of her talent? Praise her? *Is he telling her all the things he used to say to me?*

"Miss?"

The voice dragged her out of her own head and back to reality. Looking up, she saw the bartender standing nearby. He slid her a cocktail napkin. "Anything to drink?"

"Just a ginger ale for now, thanks."

He moved away to get her drink, and she released a quiet sigh. Thinking about those days always made her a little melancholy, so she avoided it most of the time. Like most of her recollections, these had a soundtrack. J. Cole, Kendrick Lamar, 2 Chainz. Miguel's impassioned crooning accompanying Wale's rhymes, Elle Varner craving a little more of that good conversation.

Swept up in the moment, the floodgates opened, and she let herself be carried away by the deluge of memories.

Those nights in the studio, the booth dimly lit. His hands working the controls at the soundboard while she sat on a stool by the microphone, pouring her heart out in song. Sitting next to him, their hips barely touching, while they bopped their heads to the playback. He'd smelled of expensive cologne, the light watery scent blending with the jasmine incense she still burned when she sat down to write.

The bartender set her ginger ale down, jarring her out of her thoughts, and she thanked him as he moved away with a smile. Sipping from the glass, she turned on her stool.

Blaine stood there, less than two feet away. He wore a metallic gray button-down shirt dotted with dark blue feathers, the top two buttons left open. A black sport coat, slacks and polished loafers completed his ensemble.

His locs hung down around his shoulders, unbound.

Their gazes met, and the moment that wicked smile tipped his full lips, something inside her clenched, then unfurled.

The glass slipped from her hand, clattering to the carpeted floor with a clanking thud. Only the splash of ice-cold liquid hitting her bare thigh made her draw her eyes away from Blaine's blinding fineness.

Entering her space, he stooped to pick up the glass and set it on the bar. "You okay, Eden?"

She nodded, unable to speak for the moment.

"You sure?" He took a small step back, his gaze appreciative as it swept over her body. "Because you certainly look fantastic."

Her cheeks warmed, and she cleared her throat. "I'm fine, Blaine. And thanks for the compliment."

He sat down on the stool to her right. "Been here long?"

Just long enough to have impure thoughts about you... She shook her head. "Just a few minutes."

"Do you wanna stay at the bar? Because I reserved us a prime booth so we can get a good view of the show." His eyes connected with hers. "And...so we can talk."

She swallowed, her throat dry. "We can go to the booth. Just let me replace this drink." Gesturing for the bartender, she got a new ginger ale, then followed Blaine to the booth.

As he'd promised, their position gave them a great view of the stage. The intimacy of the booth, with its high backed, U-shaped bench upholstered in black leather, made him seem even bigger than his usual tall, broad-shouldered self. He eased close to her toward the center of the bench but left a respectable space between them. With any other man, she'd have considered his nearness an imposition on her personal space. But since this was Blaine Woodson, she scooted nearer to him, stopping when his muscular thigh brushed against hers.

"This is cozy," he remarked with a wink. While watching her, he tossed his arm casually around her shoulder, as if waiting to see if she'd move away.

She didn't. The voice of logic, the one that told her she was treading on thin ice by getting this close to him, was increasingly drowned out by another, more assertive voice. The one that had awakened the moment she'd entered his office and seen him for the first time in seven years.

This man is too gorgeous for you to be fronting like you don't want him. She almost chuckled aloud, because it sounded like something Ainsley would have said.

"What's on your mind over there, Eden?"

She smiled, but before she could open her mouth to answer, the house lights were turned out, signaling the start of the show. A short Black man in a cherry-red suit stepped into the spotlight on stage, bowing graciously at the applause that met him.

"Welcome, y'all, to the Bass Line Lounge's New Artist Showcase." He paused for a second wave of applause. "For those of you that don't know me, I'm Ray Price, owner of this fine establishment. Tonight, we're proud to welcome two upcoming acts from right here in the ATL. First up, singer Naiya B. Come on up, Miss Naiya." He gestured to the area just to the left of the stage.

Eden watched as Naiya climbed the two metal steps up to the stage. After exchanging a hug with Ray as he exited, she approached the stool and the microphone stand, offering a curtsy in response to the cheers in the room. She wore a strapless black one-piece pantsuit with wide legs. An ankle-length white floral kimono covered her arms, the fabric billowing around her as she moved. Her mass of curls cascaded around her shoulders, and huge silver hoop earrings peeked out from among the ringlets. An acoustic guitar, mounted on a tan leather strap, hung on her back.

"Good evening, y'all. I want to thank Ray and Neil for having me tonight. My name is Naiya B." She paused for another smattering of hoots and hollers. "Some of you may know me from the videos I've posted on Beyoncé's internet."

Laughs sounded throughout the room, and Eden found herself chuckling as well.

Naiya sat down on the edge of the stool, swinging the guitar around to the front. "What you might not know is that I'm currently in the studio, recording my very first album. I'm excited to share a little something from that project with you later on tonight." She plucked a few notes on the guitar. "But before we get into that, let's start out with a classic, shall we?" She played a few more notes, segueing into an emphatic cover of Lauryn Hill's hit "The Sweetest Thing."

I love this song. Eden found herself swaying in her seat, her body moving of its own accord. A quintessential late-nineties ballad, the song spoke of the bittersweet memory of young love, bursting with hope and passion, but finally falling victim to the harshness of reality. Naiya's cover paid homage to Hill's original without being a direct imitation and showcased the young singer's incredible vocal range.

By the time Naiya hit the soaring notes of the vamp, Eden's hand went to her chest. "She's magical." Turning toward Blaine, she found him staring at her. The intensity of his gaze shook her to the core.

He reached out, gently cupped his hand around her chin. "I know. I'm very familiar with magic."

Blaine stared into Eden's dark eyes, reading the wonder they displayed. He'd struggled to hold back from touching her, and now that her silken face rested on his hand, he knew he wanted to do so much more. That decision wasn't his to make, but he'd plead his case as earnestly as he knew how.

She looks so beautiful tonight.

Dressed in that hot little one-shouldered white mini-dress, paired with metallic gold high-heeled sandals, she was a stunner. No other woman in the club could hold a candle to her. And while his main purpose in being here tonight was to support his newest artist, he had a difficult time taking his eyes off his gorgeous companion.

"Blaine." She whispered his name.

Still cupping her chin, he said, "Yes?"

"People are staring at us."

He didn't bother to verify what she'd said, because it didn't matter to him who saw them. "I don't care. But if I'm making you uncomfortable..."

"It's not that." Her cheeks were warm and slightly reddened. "It's just... I'm trying to focus on Naiya's performance. That's why I'm here, remember?"

He released her, nodding. "Of course." Though parts of him were bereft at the loss of contact between his hand and her scented skin, he knew she was right. He turned his gaze back to the stage.

She shifted on the bench. "That doesn't mean we can't continue this later, after the show."

He glanced her way, and she gave him the sauciest little wink. His heart skipped a beat. *Is she finally softening up?*

Grinning, he looked again toward Naiya, illuminated by the spotlight. Applause filled the space as she ended the song. "Thank you so much. Next, I've got another familiar tune some of you might know." Two black-clad female background singers eased into position behind her, their microphone stands flanking Naiya's stool. She strummed her fingers over the strings again, this time easing into India.Arie's "Steady Love."

Eden watched, her expression conveying her awe. "Look how easily she segues between eras. She's so fluid, so versatile." She leaned forward, tenting her fingers as her elbows rested on the table. "That's definitely going to help with the songwriting for her album."

"She's really in her element up there, isn't she?"

She nodded. "Yes, she's a dynamic performer. But what I'm really getting is a good sense of her range as a singer. She's already given me her journal, so I know what's in her heart. Seeing her on stage like this will help me translate her thoughts and feelings into lyrics more effectively."

"Great. I'm glad this is helpful for you." He scratched his chin, wondering what kind of things the two women would come up with once they returned to the studio. He was anxious to hear the outcome, and not just because of the added pressure placed on him by recent happenings at Hamilton House. He only took on artists if he felt fully invested in developing their careers, so he truly wanted to see Naiya showcase her vocal prowess on her debut project.

He did his best to pay attention for the rest of Naiya's forty-five-minute set, and he caught most of it. But sitting so close to Eden had his mind slowed and throwed, as if DJ Screw himself were inside his head, working the crossfader back and forth. He found that focusing on anything other than her brown-skinned beauty required a hell of a lot of effort.

"So it's time for my last song, folks." Naiya leaned into the microphone, her voice rising over the quiet din of conversation and clinking glasses. "It's the first single from my upcoming album *Capitol View Soul…*" She paused, smiling out at the audience as a cheer went up at the mention of her neighborhood. "Oh, I see y'all. We in the building? Capitol View, stand up!" A few more hoots and hollers followed her acknowledgment. When the room quieted, she spoke again. "This song is called 'The Way It Was,' and I hope y'all like it."

The DJ dropped the needle, and Naiya set her guitar and

stool aside, standing at the microphone. While her background singers provided harmonious accompaniment, she belted out the song, her love letter to the neighborhood that had nurtured her. She and her singers even threw in a few simple, choreographed steps, upping the entertainment value. Folks clapped along, and Blaine felt his foot tapping beneath the table. Looking around the room, he noted the bobbing heads, the pumping fists.

People are feeling the vibe. This is definitely a good sign.

By the time Naiya hit the song's soaring final note, most of the crowd was on its feet. A rousing round of cheers and applause shook the club as Naiya and the two singers took their bows. Blowing kisses to her audience of new fans, she jogged out of the spotlight and off stage.

Blaine tapped Eden on the shoulder. "Come on, let's go congratulate our superstar." He slid out of the booth, then held out his hand to help her to her feet.

She slipped her hand into his, smiling. That familiar electric charge snaked up her arm in response to his touch, and she relished the sensation. Slinging her purse strap over her bare shoulder, she maintained the contact as they navigated through the crowd toward the stage area.

They found Naiya standing among a tangle of enthusiastic admirers. Blaine stood back, watching as people jockeyed for selfies with the young singer or asked her to sign various items. Then he spoke with his artist briefly, offering his congratulations on a great performance. Naiya then left to celebrate her accomplishment with a few friends. As soon as she was gone, Blaine turned back to Eden. "Now. About what you said earlier..."

Her expression turned coy. "I'm not sure what you're referring to, Blaine."

He feigned distress. "Come on, Eden. What do I have to do to get you to spend some time with me? You want me to grovel? Get down on my knees and beg like Jodeci?"

He held his hands up. "What's a brotha gotta do to get on your good side, girl?"

She laughed, shaking her head. "You're crazy, you know that?"

"Yes. I also know that most of the reason I'm acting this way is you." He moved a bit closer to her. "So what do you say? Give me a shot?"

She sighed, but a slight smile tipped her glossy lips. "Let's go for a walk."

He frowned, confused. "Now?" It was after ten on a Saturday night, after all.

She nodded. "Yes. Take me to Piedmont Park." She folded her arms over her chest.

He cocked his brow. "Piedmont Park, eh? I know you remember what happened the last time we were there."

"How can I forget when you keep bringing it up?"

He chuckled. "Don't act like you don't like it."

She rolled her eyes in an exaggerated fashion. "Whatever, Blaine. Do you want to go, or not? Unless you have something else you'd rather be doing right now?" He eased closer to her, dragging his fingertip over the satin line of her jaw. Then he leaned close to her ear, his voice low as he spoke. "I can assure you, the only thing I want to be doing right now is you."

She gave him a wicked smile. "Then let's go."

Nine

A half hour later, with the moon sitting low in the sky, Eden walked hand in hand with Blaine through the Twelfth Street Gate at Piedmont Park. She'd brought her trusty blue twill blanket from the trunk of her car, and had it slung over her bare shoulder. The night had given way to a cooler, breezier atmosphere, a welcome respite from the day's oppressive heat and humidity.

There weren't many people out this time of night, save a few folks walking their dogs or taking an evening jog. The subtle song of crickets, grasshoppers and frogs mingled with the whir of passing traffic whizzing around Midtown.

"It's so nice outside," she remarked as they strolled down the concrete path. The city light shimmering beyond the treetops only added to the beauty of the night. This was the city she'd grown up in, the place she loved. And while some might crave the wide-open spaces of the plains or the sandy beaches of the coast, she loved her hometown, the crown jewel of the southeast.

"It is." Blaine squeezed her hand. "Company's not bad, either."

She winked as they passed the I-shaped structure of the Ladies Waiting Room.

"Mind telling me why you insisted on coming here?" He eyed her curiously.

She tugged him along by the hand, around the circular path leading to the Clara Meer Dock. When they came to a stop, she pointed. "This is why I wanted to come here."

He looked out, his eyes scanning the dark, glassy surface of Lake Clara Meer. "I'm guessing you come here often?"

She nodded. "This is my thinking spot. Whenever I'm working on lyrics and I can't quite get it right, I come here. I spread my blanket out on the grass, sit down with my notepad and work it out."

He looked at her skeptically. "So, did we come here to work?"

"Nah." She shook her head. "It's Saturday night, after all. I brought you here to talk."

He frowned. "I'm still confused."

She started walking over to the grassy patch overlooking the water and the dock and spread out the blanket there. "Something about this place always seems to bring me clarity. It's a little slice of heaven, right in the middle of the city. It's bound to inspire some pretty deep conversation between us." She sat down, careful not to let her dress ride up till heaven and earth were filled with her glory. Then she patted the empty spot next to her.

He hesitated, standing there on the concrete path, looking a bit baffled.

"You scared, Blaine?" She faked a pout, sticking her lip out as she teased him. "Of little old me?"

He rolled his eyes, but his smile was evident as he joined her on the blanket. "You're too much, Eden."

"So, we're basically alone now." *Or at least as close to*

alone as we're gonna get without me crawling into your lap. She watched him, taking in his moon-dappled handsomeness. The dim lighting seemed to enhance his features, especially the golden flecks in his dark eyes. He was temptation in the flesh; her body craved him even though her mind knew better than to get lost in him again. The question was, how much longer would she be able to lead with logic? "What do you want to talk about?"

He cleared his throat. "If I'm being honest…"

"Please do," she encouraged.

"I want to talk about kissing you again." His deep baritone had each word dripping with sensual energy.

Warmth raced through her body, and she felt it pool in her cheeks, her chest and a bit farther south. "Blaine." She meant it as chastisement, but it came out sounding far sultrier than she'd intended.

He shrugged. "Can't blame a brotha for shooting his shot."

"I guess not." She chuckled, from both amusement and nerves. "I don't know if we should lead with talking about kissing, though."

"Why not?" He gave her a wicked look. "Did you enjoy the kiss?"

She swallowed and needing a respite from the intensity of his gaze, she looked down at her lap. Her dress had crept up her to mid-thigh, so she tugged the end a bit. "I'd be lying if I said I didn't enjoy it. But that's beside the point."

"If you say so."

She shook her head. *Same old Blaine. Always charming, never reflective.* "There's too much in our past that you're not considering, Blaine. We can't just ignore our history."

"Who said I'm ignoring it?" He traced a finger along her lower leg, trailing from her knee to the top of her sandal-encased foot. "What I know about you, our 'history' as you call it, is precisely why I want you."

She drew a deep breath. Was he misremembering? Or was he really so clueless that he didn't understand where she was coming from? "You know your decision to cut Ainsley and me from the group effectively ended both of our singing careers, right? Not to mention how much it hurt me personally. You have to realize the impact of that."

He tilted his head to the side. "We talked about this, Eden. Do I have to remind you again that my hands were tied?"

Now he was just being obtuse. "You keep saying that as if you truly had no other options. I never understood why you were so determined to do things on your own anyway. Why couldn't you have just joined up with your family at 404?"

"Dad and I were…not on good terms. He wasn't exactly pleased when I left the family business to strike out on my own, and his disappointment has only grown since then."

"You should have tried to repair the relationship. Who knows? Maybe he would have helped you achieve your vision for the group."

"I doubt it. We were barely speaking then, and not much has changed."

Her expression earnest, she said, "Family should always come first, Blaine. You should have reached out to him. If he's holding on to anger, you should try to make up with him."

His brow creased into a frown, and he withdrew his touch. "You wouldn't understand. It's more complex than it seems on the surface."

He's right. I wouldn't understand. His family is still intact. My father walked out on my mother before I took my first steps, and now my mother is gone. Ainsley and Cooper are the only family I have left.

She sighed. "I didn't bring you out here to argue. It goes

against everything I love about this place. Let's just agree to disagree for now."

"Can we still kiss? You know…while we're disagreeing and all?" A glimmer of hope shone in his eyes.

She pursed her lips. "Honestly, Blaine…" The thought of kissing him appealed to her like a decadent dessert, but risking her heart again wasn't something she wanted to do.

"Listen. What happened in the past isn't nearly as important as what's happening right now." He reached out, enfolded her hand inside his own. "And what's happening now is that I'm attracted to you, Eden Voss. If you truly feel I wronged you in the past, then please, give me a shot at making it up to you. That's why I brought you on for Naiya's project."

"So, you hired me to pay penance for your actions in the past?"

"Only partly." He held her gaze, hoping she could see his sincerity. "I also believe in your talent. The label wasn't thrilled about my plan to bring you on. But I have absolute faith in you."

It's a start…that's probably the best I'm going to get out of him for now. She'd held on to her resentment like a favorite accessory for so many years. But ever since he'd been back in her life, the part of her that still cared for him, still found him irresistible, threatened to snatch that bitterness away.

"You got quiet," he said, his voice just above a whisper. "What's on your mind?"

She drew a shaky inhale, then let the words fall out. "I want to kiss you again, Blaine. So, help me, I know it's a terrible idea. But I…"

He silenced her by dragging her close and pressing his lips against hers.

A soft moan escaped her mouth, flowing into his, and he deepened the kiss in response. Leaning into him, she opened her mouth. Their tongues mated and played, while his hands roved over the sensitive flesh of her shoulders, her arms, her thighs. His hot mouth and his skilled caress fired her blood. She could feel her heart thumping, hard and fast, while the thrill of his touch reverberated through her body like sound waves.

Blaine held Eden's soft body close to his, drawing out the kiss for as long as she'd allow. What had been a cool, breezy night had now become humid again, and this time, it had nothing to do with the late-summer Georgia temperatures.

By the time he eased away from her lips, he almost expected a puff of steam to escape his shirt collar. "Eden..." He ran his fingertips over her satin jawline. "I want you so badly."

She trembled beneath his touch but remained quiet save for her quickened breaths.

He toured her body with a gentle, questing hand. First, he trailed his fingertips down the bare skin of her arm, then let his open palm caress the fullness of her thigh just below the hem of her dress. She writhed, a soft whimper escaping her lips.

She shifted a bit, tucking her legs beneath her. "Blaine... we're playing with fire here."

"You're telling me." The fire had been smoldering inside him since the moment she'd walked into his office and accepted his offer of work. There would be no putting this fire out, and truthfully, he wanted it to blaze until it consumed them both. He continued to circle and tease the exposed skin of her thigh. "Your thighs are magnificent. What do you do at the gym...squats?"

She blushed. "Yeah... I do a lot of side-to-side lunges, too."

"It's working for you."

She closed her eyes, sucking in her lower lip as her skin tingled beneath his touch. "You're too much, Blaine."

"I know I'm a lot." He chuckled. "But I also believe you'll be able to handle me just fine."

She leaned in and kissed him, and moments later, they were caught up in the throes of passion again. His tongue tangled with hers as he explored the sweet cavern of her mouth. By the time the kiss ended, he could feel his blood rushing toward his lower half.

"If memory serves, you have a sweet spot right...about... here." He slid his index finger up the side of her throat, swirling it over her skin just beneath the tip of her diamond-studded earlobe.

She gasped.

He leaned in, flicking his tongue over the sensitive spot. He repeated the gesture until her soft sighs rose on the cool night air.

She shifted, moving out of his reach for a moment. But before he had a chance to miss her, she slid into his lap, her full, lush hips resting atop his pelvis. By now he was so hard he could drive railroad spikes without a hammer, and he knew she could feel it.

He looked into her eyes in the moonlight.

She offered him a sultry smile. "You seem...excited."

He cleared his throat. "No hiding that. Especially not with you sitting on my lap like this." Running his hand over her silken waves, he growled, "Look what you're doing to me, Eden."

She winked. "I can do even better than that...but not here." She gestured around with her hands, reminding him of where they were.

"You're right." He gave her hip a firm squeeze. "I'm pretty sure getting busy in the park is a quick way to get arrested."

She giggled, and the tinkling sound of her laughter

warmed his heart. "Why don't we head over to my place, and we can…" The loud ringing of his phone, accompanied by its insistent buzzing, cut him off midsentence. Annoyed, he shifted and dragged the phone out of his back pocket, careful to keep Eden in her position on his lap. Looking at the screen, he frowned. *Geez. Nia's timing is absolute garbage.* His eldest sister rarely ever called him, and even when she did, it wasn't this late. Thinking he'd better take the call, he swiped the screen. "Hello?"

"Blaine, it's Nia. Stop what you're doing and come to Emory hospital right away."

He sat up straight, feeling the prickles of worry racing up his back. "What's going on? Has something happened?"

"It's Mom," Nia blurted, her tone grim. "She's been in an accident."

"What? How did it happen? And is she okay?"

"Blaine, I don't have time to give you a lot of detail right now. Just get down to the hospital as soon as you can, all right?"

He heard something in his sister's voice he'd never heard before. *Panic.* "I understand. I'll be there right away." Disconnecting the call, he looked at Eden and found her watching him, her expression etched with concern.

"I wasn't eavesdropping, but I can tell by your face that something's going on, something you need to attend to. Am I right?"

He nodded. "Yes. It's an emergency."

She slipped from his lap, then stood, straightening her dress.

He was on his feet moments later. "You've gotta know that nothing else short of an emergency could have pulled me away from you. You do know that, right?" She gave a small nod, her gaze soft and sympathetic. "I believe you, Blaine."

"It's my mom. She's been in some kind of an accident,

and my sister is playing it close to the vest. I need to get over there and check on her." He grasped her hand, brought it up for his kiss. "Come on. I'll walk you back to your car."

After navigating the gauntlet of parking in the deck, he headed straight for the hospital information desk, hoping to find out more about his mother's condition.

Gage stood near the desk, his expression serious. "Hey, B. Nia sent me down here to meet you."

"Where's Mom?"

"She's in a room on the seventh floor. Get your visitor's pass and I'll take you up there."

He turned to the desk attendant, and after presenting his driver's license and posing for a rather drab-looking photo, he slapped on his adhesive visitor badge and followed his brother to the elevator.

On the ride up, Blaine asked, "Gage, what happened to Mom?"

He frowned. "You mean Nia didn't tell you?"

"You know how she is. She just ordered me to get my ass over here, without telling me anything except that Mom had been in an accident."

Gage rolled his eyes. "Same old Nia. Anyway, Mom was out running and took a pretty bad fall. Her left ankle is totally screwed up, and she's got quite a few scrapes and scratches."

He cringed. *Sounds like she had a rough day.* "How is she now?"

"She seems to be doing okay. They've patched her up and given her pain meds." The elevator dinged, and Gage stepped out, holding his hand out so the doors wouldn't shut before his brother exited. "I'm sure she'll be glad to see you."

He wanted to protest but managed to hold back.

They walked down a quiet concourse, where the only

sounds were the footsteps of scrub-clad nurses and the occasional blip emanating from a machine until they approached an open door. Gage stepped back to let Blaine enter first.

Inside the small room, he found his entire immediate family. All his siblings were crowded around his mother's hospital bed, while a tired-looking Caleb sat in the blue recliner wedged between the bed and the wall. There were Teagan and Miles, the babies of the family, fraternal twins who both possessed their mother's sense of humor and her zest for life. Hovering beside them was Nia, the eldest, whose personality echoed her father's serious, regimented nature. And then there was Gage, who was only eleven months younger than Blaine. They were the closest in age and the only two of the kids who seemed to take their traits almost equally from both parents.

In the center of it all, Addison Woodson lay dozing in her bed. She was attached to a heart monitor, and the steady blips coming from the machine gave Blaine a measure of comfort. But the various bandages covering her arms, legs and the left side of her face, as well as the contraption stabilizing her ankle, were a worrisome sight. Not wanting to frighten her, he approached the bed quietly, easing in between the twins to get closer, and called out softly. "Mom?"

She opened her eyes slowly, and a smile spread over her face. "Blaine. Hi, baby."

Emotion welled in his chest. "Mom, are you all right?"

"I'm fine," she insisted in a sleep-heavy voice. "Should have turned down my music. Didn't see that cyclist coming until he was about to hit me." She yawned. "Dived out of his way—and right into a sticker bush."

He sighed. "Mom, you're a real pistol."

"You bet your ass. And don't you worry... I'll be back

on the trail in no time." No sooner than the words left her mouth, she drifted back off to sleep.

Spotting an empty folding chair in the corner of the room, he took a seat. Now that he knew she was okay, he planned on staying put to hear what the doctors had to say.

His thoughts shifted briefly to Eden. His ardor for her would have to be set aside for the moment, but he planned on rectifying that as soon as possible.

Ten

Sunday evening, Eden chewed her lip as she knocked on the front door to Blaine's Ansley Park condo. The complex he lived in was less than ten minutes away from Piedmont Park; she'd been passing his place for ages without even knowing he lived there.

Ever since he'd buzzed her in at the gate, she'd been nervously fidgeting, wondering what tonight might hold. Would he really want to pick up where they'd left off the night before? Or would he still be distracted by whatever emergency had called him away in the middle of their rendezvous? She willed herself to stop overthinking. *Guess I'll just play it by ear.*

She took a deep, soothing inhale, detecting the subtle but delectable aroma of garlic and herbs coming from his unit. Just as she released her breath, his door swung open.

"Hi, Eden." A welcoming smile stretched his full lips, revealing his pearly white teeth.

He looked comfortable but put together in a charcoal-gray button-down, dark slacks and black loafers with a silver chain detail across the toe box. The top three buttons of the shirt were left open, and the short sleeves revealed the muscled beauty of his biceps. His locs were piled on top of his head in a messy bun-slash-ponytail.

"Hey, you." She extended the silk pouch holding the bottle of merlot she'd brought. "A little gift to thank you for inviting me over."

"Thanks." He took the bag, then stepped aside and gestured her in.

She entered his domain, letting her gaze move around the interior. *Wow. This place is stunning.* The open floor plan gave her a wide-angle view of the polished oak floors and cabinetry, contrasted against the gray marble countertops and stainless appliances in the generously sized kitchen. He'd furnished the living room with a sleek but comfortable-looking camel-colored sofa, two matching chairs and a low-profile glass coffee table. "Nice place."

"Thanks. Bought it a few years ago." He walked around the tall granite-top bar that represented the only separation between the living room and kitchen, gesturing her to follow him. "It's close to the studio, spacious, and best of all, I don't have to cut the grass." He positioned himself by the stove, tending to something sizzling in a cast-iron skillet.

She chuckled as she eased onto one of the two upholstered wrought iron barstools. "I can see the appeal of that. I usually get one of the teenagers down the street to mow ours."

"Dinner should be ready in about fifteen minutes." He used his spatula to flip whatever was in the skillet.

"What are you making, anyway? It smells heavenly."

He used a mitt to grasp the pan's handle and gently shook it. "My vegan soul food specialty. Salisbury steak and mushroom gravy."

She pursed her lips, contemplating that. "Vegan steak? What's in that? And when did you become vegan?"

His deep rumbling chuckle preceded his answer. "The base for the steak is chickpeas and lentils. Don't worry, you'll love it. And I'm not vegan, but I try to eat three to four plant-based meals each week."

"I see." She looked down, suddenly self-conscious about her little lower-belly pooch. "So that's how you maintain that glorious physique, huh?" If eating fake steak made from legumes kept his body looking like it was carved from marble, she certainly wasn't going to knock it.

"I don't think I've ever heard my body called 'glorious' before. You flatter me, Eden." He tossed a wink over his shoulder.

She rolled her eyes for show. But deep inside, she fought off the urge to grab a handful of that magnificent ass of his.

"But, nah. I work out to keep my body in shape. The way I eat is more about how I feel. I'm too old to be eating garbage, you know. Can't digest it. It's just not worth having an upset stomach."

"Relatable. I gave up fast food a few years back, and my insides are sincerely grateful." Giving up fast food, along with her regular strolls around the neighborhood, had helped her shave off a few pounds. Still, her curvy frame always seemed to hold on to a nice layer of padding, and she'd long since accepted the fact that she'd never be skinny. And that suited her just fine. "I'm looking forward to trying your creation."

"You're gonna love it. It's a big hit with Gage, and he loves meat to an almost frightening degree."

She nodded. As he worked at the stove, she couldn't help noticing the slight slump to his broad shoulders. "Hey, I'm not trying to get in your business, and you don't have to tell me anything if you don't want to. But what happened last night? Is everything okay?"

He turned off the burner and set down the spatula, facing her. "I don't mind telling you. My mother took a bad fall while out running yesterday evening."

She frowned. "Oh, no. Is she going to be all right?"

"She'll be fine. She's a real pistol, my mom. She's pushing sixty and you can't tell her anything." He shook his head, wearing a rueful smile, and quickly relayed how his mother had gotten hurt.

"Well, damn." Since she frequented the city's trails, she could easily imagine having such a run-in with an oblivious cyclist. "How's she holding up?"

"Other than being mad she can't run for a few weeks, she's in pretty good spirits. They kept her overnight because her pulse was erratic and the doc wanted to observe her, but they cut her loose this morning." He opened the fridge, pulled out two bottles of water and slid one to Eden. "Sent her home this morning with a cane, meds and orders to take it easy for a while." He cracked open the bottle, taking a big swig of water.

"How's the family handling things?" She opened her water and let its cold freshness quench her parched throat. Her other thirst, however, could only be satisfied by the man standing just beyond her reach.

"As well as can be expected. Nia's gone into 'bossy-britches' mode, but then again that's her default setting."

She snorted. "Bossy-britches?"

"If you ever meet my sister, trust me, you'll see what I mean." He took another sip from his water. "The twins are waiting on Mom, babying her the way she's always babied them. Gage, he's a little standoffish. I think it's hard for him to see Mom laid up like this. As for my Dad, he's giving her moral support."

"What about you, Blaine? How are you holding up?"

His eyes met hers. "It's not an ideal situation. I was pretty freaked out by Nia's cryptic call. But now that I know Mom will be fine, I feel better." He stifled a yawn. "I'm just a little tired and achy. I stayed at the hospital with Mom last night, and those damn hospital recliners will have your whole body in knots."

"I'm familiar." A memory passed over her mind like a storm cloud, of sitting at her aunt's bedside after the bus accident. Her mother had perished in the ambulance, but her aunt had held on for a few hours after the crash. Her final words still echoed in Eden's mind.

Take care of my Ainsley.

Shaking the memory off, she said softly, "Is it ready? I'm eager to test your skills in the kitchen." There was a double meaning there, and they both knew it.

He watched her, letting her remark hang between them for a moment before replying. "It's ready. I was just letting it cool off." He held her gaze for a long, smoldering moment. "We wouldn't want to get down before it's time, right?"

She sucked her lower lip between her teeth as a tingle of anticipation danced down her spine.

Seated at his beautifully set dining room table, she watched as he placed the finished plate in front of him. The pristine white bone china plate held the whipped mashed potatoes, running with mushroom gravy and topped with his vegan steaks. A pile of bright, crisp green beans, sautéed with shredded carrots and red onion, accompanied the main course. "Wow. This looks amazing."

He grinned as he took his seat across from her. "Wait until you taste it."

She dug in and soon found herself groaning with delight as the flavors collided on her tongue. "Blaine. You're a fantastic cook. This is really delicious."

His smile widened. "I'm glad you like it."

"I love it." She forked up more of the scrumptious offerings.

As they ate, they chatted about their day, the weather and the horrors of Atlanta traffic.

Before she knew it, she'd cleaned her plate. Setting her utensils down, she noted how she felt full, but not stuffed. "What a meal. I can't even imagine what you came up with for dessert."

"Oh, it's definitely the sweetest, the creamiest, the most delicate thing I could think of."

Her mouth watered at the prospect of whatever culinary delight he had in store. "Ooooh. What is it?"

Their gazes connected across the table.

"You."

Blaine felt the change in the atmosphere as soon as the word left his mouth. The air between them seemed to vibrate, saturated with the electric charge of their attraction.

Ever since she'd stepped over the threshold in that long, flowing fiery red dress, with slits on either side that parted to show off her luscious legs as she walked, he'd been keeping a tenuous hold over his hormones. She made him feel like a young man just discovering the birds and bees… and she was the only flower in the garden he wanted to buzz around.

Eden's eyes widened for a moment, then surprise melted into seduction as her glossy lips parted. She pushed her plate away, easing her chair back from the table. "Oh, really? And what makes you so sure I'll agree?"

"If you don't, I'll be devastated." He spoke softly as he stood and rounded the table. When he reached her chair, he knelt at her feet. He lifted one, observing the jeweled sandals she seemed to favor as he held her ankle in his hand. "All I ask is that you let me plead my case as to why you should."

Her tongue darted out, slid over her bottom lip. "And will I like the way you plead, Blaine?"

She was teasing him, and they both knew it. As hard as he was, he still savored every moment of this banter, this delicious back-and-forth. He caressed her ankle, then let his fingertips trail up to her calf. "You'll love it. I promise."

"Mmm." The low moan escaped her throat, spurring him onward.

He stroked her soft-skinned legs, grazing his open palms from her calves to the tempting fullness of her thighs. "You're so beautiful...so soft."

She let her head drop back.

He unfastened the jeweled sandals and set them aside. Sitting down, he took her bare feet into his lap and began massaging them with slow, methodical purpose. He worked each gold-painted toe in a small circle, then moved on to knead the instep of each foot.

She crooned in response. "Oooh. How did you know I needed a foot rub?"

"Psychic, I guess." He continued his work, feeling her muscles loosen beneath his touch. Her hips edged forward on her seat as she arched her back in response to his ministrations. Watching and feeling her reactions made him feel powerful...with each moment, he grew more confident that he'd be able to please her in all the ways she craved.

He stopped a moment before she would have slid off the chair, and her body made a slow return to its original positioning. She looked his way with passion-hooded eyes. "You make a very convincing argument," she whispered, reaching out to stroke his jawline.

As she leaned forward, the tops of her full breasts moved into his direct line of vision, and his dick pulsed with need.

He placed his hand atop hers. "I'm just getting started, baby."

She gave him a wicked smile. "Well, don't let me stop you."

He leaned forward, placing a series of soft kisses on the exposed swell of her bosom, enjoying the way she hummed with pleasure. "May I?" He grasped the thin straps of the dress, and she nodded. Letting the straps fall, he tugged the top of the dress down until the fabric bunched around her waist. His breath escaped in a whoosh as her full, naked breasts were revealed to his appreciative eyes. Unable to hold back, he took one rounded globe in each hand, giving them a gentle squeeze before devouring one taut, dark nipple.

Her small, sharp cries punctuated each suck, each lick, each pass of his thumb over her berried flesh. He kept his eyes open, thrilled by the sight of her, arched and trembling as he pleasured her.

He moved away for a moment, stood to kick off his loafers.

She was on her feet a moment later, tugging at the buttons of his shirt. A couple of them flew off, but he couldn't have cared less.

There in his dining room, with the moonlight streaming in through the window, they undressed each other. She undid the clasp of his pants as he tugged down her dress; undergarments followed, adding to the pile of fabric he kicked under the table. Once they were both as nude as the day they'd been born, she reached out, running her open palms over his abdomen.

His skin burned at this first tentative touch. She was gentle, tenderly caressing him, driving him mad with wanting. He pulled her into his arms, weaving his fingertips through her silken tresses as he lifted her face to his kiss.

Long, torrid moments passed as he savored the sweetness of her mouth. Yet there was another treat he wanted to taste, to devour. So he eased her back into her chair and knelt before her again. Hands guiding her into the proper positioning, he eased her hips forward and her thighs apart. He could see her glistening with wetness in the shadowy light, and he trailed his index finger over her hardened clit.

She gasped. "Blaine…"

"Don't worry, baby, I'll take care of you." He circled the taut bud, teasing it with his finger as he planned to do with his tongue. Moments later, he cupped the undersides of her thighs, raising and opening them further as his outstretched tongue delved between her slick folds.

She cried out, then dissolved into melodic moaning as he feasted on her. She was dripping with honey and tasted much sweeter than anything he could have concocted in his kitchen. There wasn't a finer dessert to be had anywhere in Atlanta, or the rest of the world, for that matter. While she writhed and sang her pleasure, he sucked, he teased, he enjoyed. Only when her orgasmic shout sliced the air did he stop.

He sat on the floor, watching her shiver and listening to her heavy breaths for a few moments before he stood. Grasping her hand, he asked softly, "Can you stand?"

"Mmm." Still trembling, she shook her head.

"I got you." He lifted her naked frame into his arms and carried her to his bedroom. Then, laying her atop the comforter, he sheathed himself with protection and eased between her parted thighs.

She grasped his hardness, her eyes locked with his as she guided him inside her warm, slick passage.

He groaned as he entered her fully. She was so hot and so gloriously tight. Her body gripped his shaft as he began to move, sliding in and out of her. Her fingernails dug into his back, but he ignored the sting as he worked his hips forward, then back, then forward again. Being inside her again after all this time felt so amazing, so right…he never wanted this to end.

"Oh, Blaine…" Her voice cracked as she called his name.

He couldn't recall ever hearing a sweeter sound.

And there, fourteen floors above the jewel of the South, he made love to her until exhaustion forced them to seek sleep.

Eleven

Monday morning found Eden standing in the studio at Against the Grain. Arms folded over her chest, she stood behind Trevor as he worked the soundboard. Next to Trevor sat the legendary hip-hop producer Jerome Dupois. Wearing a red-and-tan leather letterman jacket emblazoned with his famous label's logo, Jerome scribbled notes onto a notepad he'd brought in with him. Glancing his way, Eden wondered if and how the brotha could see more than a few inches in front of him, considering the dark sunglasses obscuring his eyes.

On the other side of the glass partition, Naiya sat atop the wooden stool inside the sound booth. Wearing the special noise-canceling headphones that allowed her to hear playback of the track unencumbered by outside interference, she shuffled through the pages of her lyric sheets.

Trevor, the engineer, was a laid-back dude with a close fade dressed in his standard uniform of white polo and khakis. Holding down the intercom button on the panel, he asked, "Naiya, you ready in there? I'm gonna feed the playback into your headphones, okay?"

She gave him a thumbs-up, straightening her posture on the stool.

Eden took a seat on the plush sofa behind the board, and the playback started just as she settled in. The mid-tempo track, featuring Dupois's signature funky bass line and rocking percussion, provided the perfect backdrop for the song. Eden's lyrics, inspired by the words in Naiya's journals, recalled the giddy excitement of the singer's first love.

She felt the smile tugging the corners of her lips as she heard Naiya's delivery. Her vocal talents were impressive, and she delivered a great first run-through of the song. As the track came to an end, Eden returned to the board and held down the intercom button on the soundboard.

"Wow, Naiya. You really can blow, girl!"

Naiya blushed. "Thanks, Eden."

She smiled. "I only have a few pointers for this next take. We'll run through the main melody once more before we move on to recording the harmonies." She checked her phone for the time. "We've still got about forty-five minutes before the backup singers get here, which should give us plenty of time."

"Okay, what do you need me to do?" Naiya lifted the left earphone, propping it haphazardly atop her head.

"Stretch that initial note just a little bit. When you get to the bridge, take it up a half an octave. And keep emoting— you're doing great putting your feelings into the music, okay?"

"I got it." Naiya returned the earphone to its proper position. "I'm ready."

Jerome raised his index finger and made a circling motion, signaling Trevor. The engineer restarted the playback, and Naiya leaned into the mic to belt out the song for a second time. Save for a random sneeze that caused one

section to have to be rerecorded, she delivered a flawless second take.

Eden applauded as Naiya hung up her headset and exited the booth. "Amazing. Absolutely amazing. You've made light work for the backup singers."

Naiya stood in the doorway of the soundboard vestibule. "Thanks." She slipped her phone from the back pocket of her jeans. "You think I have time to run down for a quick coffee and a snack before the other girls get here?"

Eden nodded. "Sure. Besides, you've earned a break."

"Cool." Naiya called out to the producer, who was scrolling through his phone. "Yo, JD, you want anything?" Moments later, after promising the producer an herbal tea, she left.

Eden exited the studio soon after. Her mind wandered to Blaine, and the amazing encounter they'd had. She'd remained in his arms all night, and it was some of the best sleep she'd had recently. She smiled at the thought of the way he'd worked her body...and the way he'd greeted her the next morning with kisses and that beautiful smile. There was none of the awkwardness she'd been afraid of, but she hadn't been thrilled to hear him talk about how being with her brought back sweet memories. It made it seem as if he'd been reaching for the past, instead of working toward a future with her. Whatever the case, she knew she wanted to experience his lovemaking again, as soon as possible.

It took considerable effort, but she turned her thoughts back toward the work at hand.

I can't wait to tell Blaine about the amazing progress we're making on Naiya's album. Even seasoned music veterans often needed several takes to record a song; despite her young age and relative inexperience in a professional studio, Naiya consistently delivered her vocals in three takes or fewer. This was the third single they'd recorded so far, and if they could maintain this pace, they might actually be able to meet Blaine's rather unreasonable demand to finish the album before the month ended.

She walked down the hallway toward Blaine's office at the end. His door stood slightly ajar, and as she approached, she slowed. The sound of his voice filtered through the gap between the door and the frame.

She raised her hand to knock, but let it drop when she heard a familiar name.

Cambria. He's talking to her on the phone.

Resting her back against the wall, she felt the cool painted concrete against her bare shoulders. She shivered, wishing she'd brought a sweater to wear over her favorite pink T-strap maxi dress. Wondering what reason Blaine had to be talking to her former groupmate, she folded her arms and listened.

"I'm glad you called, Cambria," Blaine said, then paused, probably to listen to Cambria's reply. "Yes, actually, your timing is great. Guess who I'm working with?"

Eden frowned. *I've got a pretty good idea where this is going.* But would he really take it there? Or was she just projecting her worries onto him and his conversation?

"No. Nope. Listen, you're terrible at guessing so I'll just tell you." His tone held unveiled amusement. "It's Eden… yes, that Eden." He laughed. "No, no. All is forgiven. We're both mature adults, you know." He laughed again, this time more heartily. "I'm not going into details, Cambria. But trust me. We're definitely back on great terms. Probably even better than before." Her chest tightened, and a sense of dread rolled over her like a fog.

"No, no, it's true," he continued. "Listen, if you don't believe me, you can always slide through the 404 and see for yourself. When's the next time you're free to come down south?"

Eden sighed, her frown deepening. Turning away from the door, she went back toward the studio. She'd heard quite enough of Blaine's overblown characterization of their current partnership. From their chat the morning after they'd made love, she gathered their lovemaking was a means to relive the old days…to experience the heady sensations of their former relationship, for old time's sake. That's where he stood…and she told herself she could accept that. But could she?

Back then, he'd held the promise of a solo career over her like the proverbial carrot. But when the management decided Cambria was their golden girl instead, she'd been tossed aside. Eden had found it very karmic that Cambria had taken an offer from another label and gone on to stardom.

She walked into the studio long enough to grab her purse and strode right back out. As she headed outside to her car, her annoyance grew with each step. Not only was Blaine on the phone evangelizing about how great things were between them, but it seemed like he was using her and their so-called "great relationship" as some kind of weird bait to get Cambria to come to Atlanta. By the time she flung open her driver's-side door and climbed into her car, she could feel her body vibrating with hurt and anger.

Naiya, in her little blue two-door coupe, pulled into the spot next to Eden. Letting down her passenger-side window, she cast a confused glance her way. "You leaving already? I thought we were going back to work on the backing vocals?"

She blew out a breath, trying to calm herself. There was no reason to take her bad mood out on Naiya. "Sorry, but I need a little break. JD and Trevor are still in the studio… I'm sure they've got it covered."

"Okay." Naiya's expression showed her lingering questions, but thankfully, she refrained from asking any as she got out of her car. "I'll see you later."

Eden watched as Naiya went inside the building with

a cardboard carrier holding several drinks. She stuck the keys in the ignition but didn't start the car...she didn't even know where to go. Dropping back against the headrest, she let her mind wander back to those old days. Back when she, Ainsley and Cambria had been thick as thieves, a nearly inseparable trio. From the day they'd met at the beginning of their first year at Atlanta Tech, nothing had ever managed to come between them.

That was, until Blaine. He'd gotten them to record together the first time by capitalizing on their obvious closeness. Then, just as everything had seemed to be coming together for Swatz Girlz, just when they thought their careers were about to take off...he'd hit them with a ton of bricks.

And all these years later, he still couldn't seem to acknowledge the betrayal he'd dealt her, the way he'd shattered the heart of an idealistic, starry-eyed young woman. It wasn't just the end of her singing career; it was a death of her younger, more trusting self, an end to her naïveté.

A tear slid down her cheek, and she angrily swiped it away. *He's caused me enough pain. I'm not about to let him cause me any more.*

Blaine absently spun his chair from side to side, holding his phone to his ear as he listened to Cambria rambling on about her hectic schedule. He chuckled. "Okay, I get it. You can't get down here over the next couple of weeks, it's cool. Just hit me up when you get ready to come through."

"I will," Cambria insisted, "because I still don't believe you're on all these wonderful terms with Eden."

"Why not?"

She chuckled. "If you were a woman, you wouldn't even be asking me that question. You'd know the answer, man."

He rolled his eyes. "Whatever. Anyway, I'll let you get

back to work. I'm gonna head down to the studio and look in on what's happening with Naiya B.'s album."

"Later, Blaine." Cambria disconnected the call.

He pocketed his phone, shaking his head. *Cambria Harding...the one that got away.* Professionally, at least. He'd harbored no romantic interest in her, but he'd known from the moment he'd met her that she possessed an amazing voice and incredible stage presence. Her star had risen quickly as a solo artist, and after her first album, she'd moved on to a larger label, one that could get her the kind of wide exposure she sought. He couldn't hold that against her. After all, her talent warranted the kind of massive backing she got from her internationally known label. She performed in huge arenas, drawing crowds of thousands of screaming fans wearing her custom-designed merchandise. As hard as he worked, he knew he simply didn't have those kinds of resources.

Standing up, he stretched his arms above his head before leaving his office. A few long strides carried him to the studio, and when he opened the door, he saw the work on Naiya's album continued. Naiya was on the couch, while JD and Trevor sat at the soundboard. Inside the booth, two backup singers were recording vocals as the track playback echoed through the room.

However, he couldn't help noticing one rather conspicuous absence. "Where's Eden?"

Neither Jerome nor Trevor knew where she was. So he turned to Naiya. "Do you know where our songwriter is?"

She shrugged. "Not really. I ran into her in the parking lot, on my way back from the coffee shop. She said she needed a break."

His eyes widened. "I'll be back." He left the studio and jogged out to the parking lot. For some reason, the idea of her leaving in the middle of the day upset him. He hadn't gotten to spend very much time with her outside of the studio, and since they'd made love yesterday, she haunted his mind like a specter.

Outside, he stepped off the sidewalk and saw her sitting in her car, her eyes closed. Was she taking a nap? Part of him didn't want to disturb her, but he also wanted to know what had brought her out here in the first place, just in case he might be able to help. He tapped the glass, and her eyes popped open.

He saw the sheen of wetness in her eyes, and it tugged at his heart.

Her expression flat, she rolled the driver's-side window down.

"You okay? It's too hot outside for you to be sitting out here like this."

She frowned. "You picked a fine time to be concerned about me."

He felt his brow furrow. "What do you mean by that?"

She scoffed, shaking her head. "Why bother?"

"Eden, tell me what's wrong. If there's something I can do to fix it, I'll do it."

She gave him a sidelong glance. "Oh, really? Then explain to me why I heard you on the phone telling Cambria that we're besties now?"

He swallowed hard. "You were eavesdropping on my phone conversation?"

She pursed her lips. "No. Your office door was open and you're a loudmouth. I can't be blamed for you not knowing how to use your inside voice."

His hands clenched. "Whatever the case, you had no right to be listening in on my..."

"Whatever, Blaine. I couldn't care less who you talk to on the phone. The problem I have is what you're saying about me, about us."

"And what exactly did I say that you have such a problem with?"

"Why were you telling Cambria that all's well between us now? And from what I heard, it sounded like you were using our new 'liaison' as bait to lure Cambria back to Atlanta."

He thought back to his conversation, and it occurred to him that what he'd said might have sounded flippant and dismissive of her feelings. "Eden, I don't know what to say that's going to satisfy you. But I really thought we were making great progress."

She released a bitter chuckle. "Why? Because we made love?"

He wondered if his expression conveyed his confusion. "Wow. Really, Eden?"

She sighed. "Yes, really, Blaine. You really haven't been listening to me all this time, have you?"

"I've heard everything you've said."

"But you haven't listened. Because if you had, you'd know where I'm coming from." She shook her head.

He shifted his weight from foot to foot, crammed his hands into his pockets. This again? Hadn't he told her more than once that his hands had been tied? That he'd had to make a hard decision for the sake of his business? "You can't still be talking about being cut. It's been years, Eden."

She fixed him with a hard stare. "Blaine, you're treading on thin ice. Do you really wanna keep going down this road?"

He sighed. "No, I don't. At least not now."

She pursed her lips. "I didn't think so."

"Don't get me wrong, Eden. I'm not avoiding this argument you seem so determined to have with me. All I'm doing is postponing it because now isn't the right time."

"Oh, really? So tell me, Blaine. When exactly *is* the right time?"

He shrugged. "I can't give you an exact date. All I'm

saying is, can we please, please finish Naiya's album before you proceed with chewing my head off?"

She scowled.

"I know you don't think I deserve the courtesy, and maybe you're right." Part of him still couldn't grasp what had her so irrationally angry, but after hearing the same thing from her so many times, he was beginning to wonder if there might be things he hadn't considered. Still, he didn't want to see Naiya's project flushed down the tubes because of whatever personal drama existed between him and Eden. "But Naiya does. She's been working so hard, grinding day and night so this album can finally come to fruition. Don't do it for me. Do it for her, okay?"

Eden's expression softened, and she appeared thoughtful for a moment. Finally, she spoke. "Fair enough. After all, it was work that brought me here, and if I want to keep my reputation as a songwriter intact, I have to remain professional, no matter what."

"Thank you." He pulled the handle to open her car door, then bowed.

She stepped out, rolling her eyes. "Okay, Mr. Dramatics. Let's get back inside and check on Naiya's progress. It'll be lunchtime soon, and we need to see if Jerome is hungry. He's been with us all morning."

He chuckled. "Somebody's gonna have to go down to Midtown for him. You know he's vegan, right?"

"I didn't know that." She walked ahead of him toward the door, and he found it hard not to stare at her ass, the curve of which he could see through the flowy fabric of her dress.

"Yep. I'm full of fun facts. You'll learn a lot of stuff if you just hang around me a while longer." He reached out and opened the door, holding it so she could enter.

"We'll see, Blaine. We'll see."

Twelve

Eden spent the rest of the day keeping her distance from Blaine and focusing on her work. Jerome left a little after lunch to go about the rest of his day, while Trevor worked his editing magic on the backing vocals recorded by the two hired singers. Eden remained on the sofa behind the soundboard, observing Naiya's work and giving pointers whenever necessary. Blaine came into the room a few times to converse with Trevor, but each time he looked her way, Eden made a point of turning her gaze elsewhere.

Around five thirty, with one finished track and the rough cuts of two more committed to digital memory, Trevor stifled a yawn. "Okay, folks. Let's pack it in."

"You don't have to tell me twice." Naiya took off her headset and placed it in its cradle. "I'm so hungry you may have to edit my stomach rumbling out of the music."

Eden chuckled. "Same. Come on out of there. You've done fantastic work today."

After the equipment had been shut down and secured,

and the lights turned off, Naiya and Trevor left the building. Eden stopped by the restroom and was on her way out the door when she caught a whiff of expensive cologne. She stopped mid-step. Feeling a familiar presence entering her space, she slowly turned—and came face-to-face with Blaine. She let herself drink in the sight of him, for the first time today. He wore a crisp white button-down, top button undone, beneath a studded leather jacket. Fitted black jeans sat low on his hips, and the black motorcycle boots on his feet were tipped with silver toe caps. His shades were perched atop his head, and his amber eyes burned into hers.

"What is it?" She was perturbed at being waylaid from going home to curl up with a mug of tea and a good book, and she didn't bother to hide that from her tone.

"Remember what I said earlier? About putting off arguing until later?"

She narrowed her eyes. "Yeah, I remember."

"Well, it's later." He stood there watching her expectantly.

"Blaine, not now. I'm too tired to fight. I just want to go home."

He reached out and grasped her hand. "You don't have to fight. I just want you to give me a chance to try to smooth things over between us."

She pursed her lips. "And just how do you plan on doing that?"

He smiled as he guided her down the darkened hallway toward his office. "You'll see."

She sighed but followed him anyway. Something about him drove her wild, made her cast aside her good sense in favor of spending time with him. He'd worked his way into her heart again, despite all the barriers and obstacles she'd erected to keep him out. And as much as she wanted to fight it, she knew it was a losing battle.

Blaine Woodson had a hold on her, one she couldn't seem to shake.

He turned the knob with his free hand, pushing open the door to his office and gently tugging her inside. He'd cleared his desk, save for his thin keyboard and flat-screen computer monitor. Patting the edge of the desk, he said, "Have a seat."

She did as he asked, perching her hips on the desk surface. "Is there anybody else in the building?"

He shook his head, then leaned in and kissed her, a soft, fleeting brush of his lips against hers. "There's no one here except you and me. That means we can settle this right now, without being disturbed."

"Blaine, whatever you're going to say, make it quick. I'm really worn out."

He released her hand then, sitting down in the guest chair. "Who said I planned on saying anything?"

Her eyes widened as he scooted the chair forward, his shoulders coming in line with her hips.

His fingertips grazed the bare skin of her ankles, then crept slowly upward as he moved up the fabric of her dress. "My mouth will be too busy for me to talk."

"Blaine." His name escaped her lips on a breathy sigh as his palm blazed a hot trail over her thigh. Her legs widened of their own accord in response to his touch.

"Yes?" he murmured into her thigh as he kissed it.

"Oh…" A tremor worked its way down her spine.

"Do you want me to stop, baby?" He swirled his tongue over her knee.

Her heart thundered in her ears, and the rising passion made her whimper, "No, don't stop…"

As he bunched the fabric of her dress around her waist, he eased aside her silky panties. Questing fingers stroked her, teased the bud of her womanhood until she flowed

sweet and wet. Moving her hips in tandem with his ministrations, she felt herself slipping off the edge of the desk.

He steadied her with his free hand, and moments later,
she felt his kiss between her thighs. She shuddered as he
followed with a series of slow, deliberate licks and sweet,
gentle sucks. He tossed one thigh over his shoulder, his
tongue delving deeper. Her hips bucked, her back arched,
and as the sensations grew to a crescendo, she screamed
his name while the spreading warmth engulfed her entire
being.

She returned to awareness, finding herself laid out
across his desktop, her dress in disarray. When she looked
down, she saw him sitting back in the chair, looking rather
satisfied with himself. Sitting up, she straightened the garment and met his eyes. "Though they lack substance, your
arguments are very convincing."

He grinned. "Thank you."

She shook her head, smiling in spite of herself. "Damn
it, Blaine. Do you have a serious bone in your body?"

"Of course, I do." He gave her a wicked look and an exaggerated wink.

She licked her lips. The remnants of his masterful oral
"argument" were still reverberating through her body, and
she couldn't deny that she wanted more.

"I'll take that as a yes." He stood then, reaching for the
zipper of his jeans.

She felt her breath catch in her throat. "You're not serious. We can't really…"

"What? Fuck in my office?" He tilted his head to the
side. "Well, since I own this building, and everything in it,
I'd say we can do whatever we damn well please."

A shiver tripped down her spine, and she bit her lip.
"Oh, my."

By now he'd undone the jeans and pushed them down.
His boxers quickly followed, and he left the fabric pooled

around his hips. Moving forward, he grasped her hips, tugging her toward the edge of the desk.

She gasped when his hardness bumped against her inner thigh.

He worked the dress up around her waist again. Licking his lips, he leaned forward, his breath warm on her face. "Tell me again what we can't do in here?"

Her arousal level increased tenfold just from his tone of voice. She knew she couldn't form a coherent sentence, so she simply purred into his ear.

He pecked her on the lips, then hurriedly fished a condom out of his back pocket. The moment he'd covered himself, he slipped his hands beneath her ass, cupping it as he raised her hips. Then he slid inside her in one long, delicious stroke.

She groaned, her back arching in response to him filling her so erotically. Her hands wrapped around his strong shoulders, she held on as he rocked his hips, each thrust sending her closer and closer to ecstasy.

"Eden...baby." He ground out the words in time with his thrusts. "So tight."

The shaking began then, beginning in her thighs and spreading through her whole body, as an orgasm sprouted and bloomed. Soon her impassioned cries and his rough grunts echoed through the empty building.

In the aftermath, he righted their clothing and pulled her into his lap, holding her close while she tried to slow her breathing.

"You're amazing," she admitted with a contented sigh.

"Does that mean you're not mad at me anymore?"

"It means what I said. I do need to get home, though." She knew what he was trying to do, and now that she had her wits about her, she wasn't about to play this game with him. Yes, Blaine was a magnificent lover. But that prowess wasn't a get-out-of-jail-free card he could use to erase his mistakes. *Maybe that's how he is with other women, but he's not going to do that to me.*

She knew she wasn't perfect. Hell, nobody was. Growing up without a father in her life had made her somewhat cynical. She held on to things like the proverbial dog with the bone, and she made people work hard to earn her trust. Still, how could she be blamed for protecting her heart? If she didn't do it, who else would?

She stood, and finding her legs a bit wobbly, she waited for her knees to quit knocking together. Once she felt she had steady footing, she started walking. "Bye, Blaine. I'll see you tomorrow."

His exasperated groan followed her, but she didn't look back.

When Blaine walked into his condo Thursday night, Gage was already seated on the sofa in the living room. Their typical game-time snacks were artfully arranged on the coffee table, and Blaine could tell his brother hadn't seen fit to wait for his arrival before digging in.

"You're late," Gage called around a mouthful of popcorn.

"Good evening to you, too, bro."

Washing down the popcorn with a swig of cola, Gage chuckled.

"I never should have given you a key to my place." He shut the door behind him and hung his keys on the hook near the door. "Flattening out my couch cushions…eating my snacks…"

"You know you love me."

Snorting, Blaine joined his brother on the couch. "Why are you such a pain in the ass, Gage?"

"When we were kids, we went to the state fair one year, and you tried to trade me in for cotton candy. Do you remember that?"

He frowned. "Not really." *Though I do love cotton candy, even to this day.*

"Neither do I, but ever since Mom told me the story, I've been looking for subtle ways to pay you back for it." He winked.

Blaine groaned. *Leave it to Gage to hold something like that against me.* "What did I miss?"

"The whole pregame show and kickoff, but not much else." He scooped up more popcorn from the ceramic bowl. "But I have to ask you a question."

"What?"

"Why haven't you been to the house to visit Mom? Ever since she got out of the hospital, she's been asking about you."

"I stayed at the hospital all night with her Saturday. Doesn't that count for something?"

Gage munched for a moment before speaking again. "Of course, it does. But she still wants to see you."

"I know Nia, the twins and Dad have probably been smothering her with attention." He turned his gaze toward the television, not wanting to meet his brother's accusing stare. "She doesn't really need me there."

"Oh, so now you get to decide what Mom needs?" Gage shook his head. "Why are you being so stubborn?"

Blaine twisted his mouth into a frown. "You'll have to excuse me for not wanting to be around the rest of the family. They're all judging me any time we get together, and I just don't want any part of it."

"Who says anybody is judging you?"

He scowled. "Oh, please. Nia told me as much herself, and I can tell the twins are judging me by the standoffish way they act. Trust me, I'm our parents' biggest disappointment."

Gage shook his head. "Blaine, you are way too dramatic. Anyway, I'm just passing a message along. If you don't go see Mom in the next three days, she said she's going to pluck you like a chicken."

He cast his brother a sidelong glance.

Gage shrugged. "Don't look at me like that. That was a direct quote."

He almost wanted to laugh, but he knew their mother was quite serious. Addison Woodson loved her children fiercely, but she never made idle threats. "I got it. I'll go visit her soon, I promise."

"Meanwhile, we need to talk about the real reason you're so distracted."

"What's that?" He braced for one of his brother's leaps to a conclusion.

"It's Eden, isn't it?"

He shifted uncomfortably in his seat. "Eden? What does she have to do with anything?"

Gage snickered. "Oh, please! I know you're involved with her."

"You don't know as much as you think you do, Gage."

"Whatever. I know that when I called you yesterday, you were at lunch with her."

"So? That doesn't mean…"

"And the day before that? Trevor told me you were locked in your office with her for at least two hours, and that when he left Monday, the two of you were still at the studio…alone."

Blaine rolled his eyes. "You pressing my employee for information now, Dick Tracy?"

"No, I'm not. But since Trevor and I play poker together on Tuesday nights, we talk." Gage fixed him with a penetrating stare. "It doesn't matter where I'm getting my information, we both know it's true. It's so obvious you're trying to pick up where y'all left off back in the day."

"If you're trying to make a point, just get to it already."

"Listen, I like Eden. We all do—she's a great person."

Gage poked him in the shoulder with his index finger. "Don't screw her over this time, Blaine. Don't break her heart."

"You don't honesty think I'd set out to hurt her, do you?" He ran a hand through his locs. "Things just didn't work out, that's all."

Gage sighed. "I'm going to get some more soda." Standing with his empty glass in hand, he said, "You've got a lot of things going for you, bro. Self-awareness ain't one of 'em."

Blaine watched his brother walk away, shaking his head. *What is he going on about now? Sure, I made some mistakes the first time around with Eden, but who hasn't? Plus, I'm older and wiser now.* Gage was the middle child in every way possible: always analyzing his siblings' behavior, trying to outsmart them or trick them into holding hands and singing "Kumbaya." *As much as I love him, he is way too extra sometimes.*

Nevertheless, he thought about his brother's declaration that he lacked self-awareness. What did he mean by that, exactly? He considered himself very thoughtful in general, but especially when it came to his personal relationships and his business dealings. *Could a man without self-awareness have achieved this level of success in the music industry?* Especially one who'd eschewed his family's fortune and power to make his own way?

As for Eden, she was a grown woman, and capable of making her own decisions. *What's happening between Eden and me is none of Gage's damn business. So what if I don't know exactly where we're headed just yet? We'll figure it out.*

Thirteen

Friday morning, Eden sat next to Trevor at the soundboard, watching proudly as Naiya recorded her fifth single for the album. Hearing the way Naiya delivered her lyrics delighted her; every songwriter dreamed of working with someone with talent of this caliber.

Swaying along with the lilting music of the ballad, Eden couldn't help smiling. *This album is going to be a huge hit. I can feel it.* Though her relationship with Blaine still had its ups and downs, she didn't regret taking this job. In addition to being able to cover the cost of her roof in full, she knew working with Naiya would end up being very positive for her career. Then there was the glimmer of hope that she and Blaine could rekindle their romance. There was something especially sweet about the second time around… Shalamar had written a whole song about it. But she needed to know he'd changed, that he understood how to really care for her heart.

As playback ended on the first run-through, Trevor

turned on the intercom to communicate with Naiya in the booth. "Awesome take. Let's run it back a couple more times so you can record your harmonies. You want the high road or the low road first?"

"I'll do the soprano, then the tenor." Naiya adjusted her headphones, then gave the thumbs-up.

Just as Trevor restarted playback on the track, the studio door swung open. Blaine strode in, and Eden could feel her body aligning with the frequency of his presence in the space. This was her first time seeing him today, and she swallowed the warmth of arousal rising in her chest. He wore a pair of tight black jeans adorned with thin silver chains draped through the belt loops like a metallic bunting. His black shirt was printed with white music notes, and the buttons were open to reveal the yellow tank beneath. Black motorcycle boots on his feet and the ever-present lion's head necklace completed today's look.

As he moved into the soundboard suite, the scent of his cologne awakened her senses. Notes of wood, citrus and musk curled up her nostrils with each inhale, effectively undoing her concentration. She was so distracted by his handsomeness and his heady aroma; it took her several moments to realize he hadn't entered alone.

Blaine's companion was a stout, pale man in a black suit. The man had blue eyes and dark blond hair combed over in an attempt to conceal a receding hairline.

Eden stood from her chair as Blaine came near, with the stranger close on his heels.

"Morning, Eden. I want you to meet Marvin Samuels. He's the label liaison from Hamilton House."

He stuck out his hand. "I'm pleased to meet the songwriter Blaine's been going on about. How are you?"

She felt her cheeks warm when he mentioned Blaine's praise. "It's lovely to meet you as well, Mr. Samuels."

"Call me Marvin." He gave her a friendly wink.

With the introductions made, she watched as Blaine and Marvin took seats on the sofa. Returning to the soundboard, she asked, "So, what brings you to Atlanta, Marvin?"

"I had a few meetings in town, and I wanted to swing by and see our newest star in action." He gestured toward Naiya, who sat inside the booth, silently mouthing the words as she read over her lyric sheet.

"I see." She returned her attention to her own copies of the lyric sheets. In the back of her mind, she wondered what Marvin would think of Naiya. He seemed to be in a position of reasonable power at the label, and she had to assume his opinion would have some influence. Still, if he had any real experience in the industry, she figured he'd have to be pretty damn jaded to be unimpressed by Naiya's raw, natural talent.

She also noticed the way Blaine seemed to be reacting to Marvin's presence. His usual relaxed posture and easy smile had been replaced by a serious, businesslike expression and ramrod-straight posture. *Considering how deep and fluffy the couch is, it's got to be taxing for him to be sitting up that straight.* She smiled at the thought of the core strength he was building…strength she hoped to put to good use later.

The four people in the soundboard suite watched silently as Naiya worked through the song. This particular track had a higher level of complexity than the ones she'd previously recorded, requiring her to record several takes of each verse. While the music played, Eden made notes on the elements of Naiya's delivery that she picked up on.

Blaine seemed to be enjoying what he heard. Nodding his head along to the music, he remarked, "This ballad is fantastic. She's really bringing out all the feels on this track."

Eden had to agree. "She amazes me every time she steps in the booth."

As the session drew to an end about ninety minutes later, Naiya left the booth and came over to the soundboard suite. She walked over to the sofa and stuck out her hand. "Marvin. It's great to see you again."

"Likewise." He gave her a broad smile.

"Me and Trevor are going to grab lunch at the deli. Does anyone want anything?" Naiya took her purse from the hook by the door and slid the strap onto her shoulder.

They all shook their heads.

After Naiya and Trevor left, Eden went back to her notes. Behind her, she could hear Blaine and Marvin chatting. Listening to the way he talked about Naiya, the album and her lyrics made her feel wonderful.

"What did I tell you, Marvin? Isn't Naiya amazing?"

"That she is. Very impressive."

"I'm really excited about her project in general," Blaine announced. His eyes were alight, his hands gesturing as he spoke. "She's on the brink of something major—we could be looking at the beginnings of a stratospheric career. And I'm not just talking about the R & B market, either. She could go so much further than that, especially with a talented songwriter like Eden working with her."

"Hmm." Marvin nodded but said nothing.

Eden wasn't sure what to make of his reaction, but something about it stood out to her. She couldn't understand why Blaine's passion didn't seem to be rubbing off on the label exec. *Is it just me, or does Marvin seem a lot less excited about all this than Blaine does?*

"I really feel like Naiya could go mainstream if we just…"

Marvin cleared his throat loudly, effectively cutting him off in mid-sentence. "I wouldn't worry about all that right now, Blaine. You're broadcasting too far into the future. For now, just focus on helping Naiya do her best work and getting this album finished as quickly as possible, without sacrificing quality."

Even as he maintained a congenial smile, Blaine's shoulders slumped, and the sparkle faded from his eyes. "Sure thing, Marvin. Don't worry. I've got it covered."

The exec stood then. "I need to get going. I've got a few more meetings and then a late flight back to New York."

Blaine got to his feet as well, shaking hands with Marvin. "Thanks for coming by."

"No problem. I look forward to hearing the finished product soon." Marvin turned and tipped an imaginary hat in her direction. "Lovely meeting you, Eden."

"Same here. Safe travels." She offered a small smile.

Not long after that, Marvin left. Alone in the soundboard suite with Blaine, she watched him. He stood in the middle of the room, staring off into space.

"Are you okay, Blaine?"

"Huh?" He glanced her way, his expression absent-minded.

"I asked if you were okay." She watched him, awaiting his response.

He remained silent for a few moments, and even though he looked in her general direction, he almost seemed to be looking through her instead of at her. Finally, he shrugged. "I'm fine." Without any further explanation, he turned and left the suite.

Standing alone in the empty room, Eden felt her doubts resurface. She'd just watched as Blaine went from total rapture over their joint project to utter indifference. It was as if Marvin's lack of enthusiasm had effectively killed Blaine's.

Pulling the front door shut behind him, Blaine stepped into the grand foyer of his parents' Buckhead home. The palatial home of his youth, with its marble floors, Yoruba and Xhosa art pieces, and polished wood looked as immaculate as Lourdes, the housekeeper, always kept it. He stopped for a moment, listening for sounds that might indicate the presence of his father or siblings. He didn't hear any chatter or footsteps, so he assumed his family members were out and about, doing whatever they did on Saturday mornings. Leaving his shoes on the rack, he headed up the wide staircase to the second floor.

Turning left at the top of the staircase, he headed toward the open door of his mother's study. The soft sounds of jazz wafting from within gave away her probable presence there, and when he rapped softly on the door and peeked into the room, he confirmed his guess.

There she is.

Inside the small room, decorated in shades of melon, peach and pink, Addison Woodson reclined on her favorite embroidered chaise. She wore her favorite pink satin robe and a matching marabou slipper on her uninjured foot. Most of her body from chest down was adorned in one of her old, but clean, colorful afghans; her short gray curls were similarly wrapped in a blue silk scarf. A fragrant mug of jasmine tea on the table and a magazine in hand, she looked up at his entrance. "Blaine. I assume you got my message from Gage?"

He nodded. "Yes, Mama. And I had no desire to be plucked like a chicken."

She smiled. "Then you made the right decision in coming to visit me." She gestured to the armchair to the left of her. "Come here, honey, and sit with your mother for a little while."

He did as she asked, taking a seat in the plush chair. The soft cushion immediately sank beneath his weight, enveloping him. "How are you feeling, Mama? You're looking much better."

"Thank you, son." She yawned. "Now, once I get this ugly boot thing off my foot, I can go back to wearing the fashionable footwear I'm used to." She gestured down at her feet. "This one-shoe look is not hot."

"How long will you have to wear it?"

"Another month or so, depending on how well it heals." She sighed. "I miss going to the gym, running. Not to mention being able to dress up and put on a pair of nice pumps and go dancing with your father."

He noticed that a few of the bandages on her face were gone, and the remaining cuts and bruises were on their way to healing up. "I know it's hard, Mama. But try to be patient."

She set her magazine aside. "I *am* being patient. But a girl's got things to do."

"Like what? What's so pressing that Dad or one of us can't take care of it for you?" Blaine gave his mother a pointed look. "Now isn't the time to be overtaxing yourself."

"Fair enough, Blaine. I promise to rest…if you promise to answer one question for me."

One thing I know about Mama—she's unpredictable. He leaned back in the chair, bracing for whatever she might throw his way. "Sure. What do you want to ask me?"

"When were you going to tell me that Eden is back in the picture and that y'all are seeing each other again?"

His mouth fell open, and he blinked several times. "What? Who told you that?"

She pursed her lips. "I'm not about to reveal my sources. Anyway, who told me is beside the point. Why didn't you let me know she was back in your life again?"

He sighed. "Mama. It's not like that. She's a songwriter, and I asked her to work with me on a debut album for a new artist. That's it."

She folded her arms over her chest and gave him that knowing look only Black mothers gave their children. "Boy, do you think I just fell off the turnip truck? I know good and well that if she's been in your space, you've been in her face."

He closed his eyes, shaking his head. *She knows me so well she can rhyme about me like Dr. Seuss.* "Yikes, Mama. You gotta step on my throat like that?"

"Right now, I'm only stepping on your throat metaphorically, on account of this bad foot." She pointed at her boot. "But if you don't come clean, so help me, I'm gonna give you a swift kick with my good foot."

He blew out a breath. "I guess I'm busted."

"Very much so."

"Okay, Mama." He knew better than to keep denying her the information she sought. "I really did ask her to work with me on the album, and she's done a fantastic job with the lyrics. She's really captured Naiya B.'s essence as a singer and infused it into the music. It's amazing to see."

Addison rolled her eyes dramatically. "Yeah, yeah. I know Eden can run circles around a lot of these folks out here writing songs. That's not what I asked you about though, is it?"

Seeing that his mother planned on giving him no quarter, he said, "Fine, Mama. Yes, I'll admit it. The chemistry we had between us is still very much alive."

"Mmm-hmm."

"Come on, Mama. How much detail do you expect me to go into here? This is getting embarrassing." If he said much more, he feared she might wash his mouth out with soap. No way would he be filling his mother in on the impure thoughts—and actions to match—that he'd had pertaining to Eden.

Her expression changed for a moment, into sort of a half frown. "You know what... I'm fine with that. Let's just say you're in love with her and leave it at that. Spare me the gory details."

He frowned. "Who said anything about being in love with her? All I said is we had chemistry."

She snorted a laugh. "Boy, you are hilarious. You can tell me you don't love her till you're blue in the face. Put it on a billboard. Have it written in the sky if you want. But it ain't gonna change reality."

Blaine dropped his face into his hands. He couldn't think of anything scarier than one of his mother's "declarations." She'd made plenty of them in his day, and he couldn't recall even once when she'd been wrong. Family lore had it that all the women on his mother's side were soothsayers. His great-grandmother, his grandmother and now his mother. Nia and Teagan seemed similarly gifted—if one could call it a gift—and he assumed that should he father a daughter, she'd continue the family tradition.

"Don't get quiet on me now, son."

"What can I say? We all know about your predictions, Mama."

"It's very mature of you not to fight it." She took a long sip from her mug of tea. "Very mature."

He sighed, rubbing a hand over his temple. Yes, he was attracted to Eden. And yes, making love with her felt like a taste of heaven. But…love? What he'd felt for her all those years ago had certainly been love. He'd assumed the passage of time had effectively ended his feelings. Perhaps he'd been wrong. He couldn't imagine that being a good thing.

Emotions only served as distractions, or weaknesses to be taken advantage of. If he let his heart get involved, he knew for certain his feelings would be used against him.

And he simply couldn't let that happen.

Not now, not ever.

Fourteen

"Aunt Eden, did you hear me?"

"Huh?" Eden snapped back to reality at the sound of Cooper's voice insistently calling her name. "Sorry, honey, I wasn't paying attention. What did you say?"

He shook his head. "Auntie, do you need some coffee? You look kinda sleepy."

Stifling a yawn, she nodded. "Yes, sweetie. I could use some coffee." She had a serious case of the Mondays. She'd spent a good portion of the night tossing and turning instead of sleeping. And the few times she had drifted off, her dreams were filled with visions of Blaine, doing all kinds of naughty things to her. Now, even though she wasn't going into the studio until later, she was sitting in the lobby of her nephew's physical therapist, waiting for his name to be called. Ainsley couldn't get the day off, so despite her drowsiness, she'd driven him here. After his appointment, she'd deliver him to school, as any aunt worth her salt would.

"You know they have coffee over there." Cooper raised his small hand and pointed to an out-of-the-way alcove across the lobby.

Her eyes widened as she climbed to her feet. She'd been so focused on getting him here early, she hadn't even noticed the coffee station. "Bless you, Cooper." A few minutes later, she returned with a steaming cup of Colombian roast, doctored with her preferred amount of cream and sugar. Sliding back into her seat, she took the first long sip and groaned in delight. "Listen, I'm taking you for ice cream this weekend."

A broad grin spread across his face, and he started doing the Milly Rock right there in his seat. "Thanks, Auntie."

She winked, going back for another sip of coffee. The warm liquid trickled down her throat like velvet. She felt energized as the coffee slowly began to take effect. *Sweet, sweet caffeine.*

After another few minutes of her guzzling coffee and Cooper playing some kind of puzzle game on his phone, the nurse called his name. Grabbing her purse, Eden stood and extended her hand to Cooper.

"Ah, come on, Auntie. I'm too big for that now." He glanced around the lobby as if he were looking for someone.

"What, are you afraid one of your little friends is gonna just appear here and see you holding my hand?" She chuckled. "You're still not one hundred percent stable on your feet yet, Champ. Once you're steady, I'll let go, okay?"

He gave her a sheepish look. "Okay." He took her offered hand, and she helped him to his feet. His first few steps were a bit wobbly, as had been the case ever since his injury. But after ten or so, he seemed all right on his own, so she released his hand.

The nurse led them down the hallway to the gymnasium, where Dr. Lexi Madison, his therapist, waited. A petite black woman with an Afro, she wore her signature royal-blue scrubs embroidered with her name and the alphabet soup of all her various degrees.

"Morning, Cooper. How are you?" She walked over and extended her fist.

Cooper smiled and bumped fists with her. "I'm fine, Dr. M."

"Ready to get started on your exercises?"

He nodded. "Yeah. I've been practicing at home with Mom and Aunt Eden, too."

"Awesome." Lexi caught his arm and began leading him toward the obstacle course she'd set up for him.

Eden took her seat in one of the plush chairs bordering the space, where family members waited for the patients to complete their appointments. Phone in hand, she was scrolling through social media when she got a text from Blaine.

GM. Where are you?

She dashed off a quick reply. I'm at the PT with my nephew, remember?

I forgot. My bad. What time are you coming to the studio?

She rolled her eyes. *I told him all this Friday, but I guess he wasn't paying attention. He's awfully good at pretending to listen.* Around 11, after I take him to school.

I really want to see you.

She sighed. What did he mean by that? *I'm not about to ask him.* You will. In a few hours.

He responded with a "heart eyes" emoji, and she sucked her lip. *This man is gonna be the death of me.* Things between them had become so much like they'd been back in the day, and she found it both exhilarating and terrifying.

Yes, she loved the way he made her body feel—the stolen kisses, the shared looks, the lovemaking. But her memory of what they'd shared back then would always be tainted by the reality of his betrayal, a reality he had yet to fully acknowledge.

Another text came in. Hey, what are you wearing? ;)

Wait and see, crazy. She tucked her phone away, determined not to answer any more of his cheeky texts. Instead, she focused on watching her nephew work through the tasks Dr. Madison had set out for him. He climbed up and down stairs, wove his way between cones and hula hoops, and rode the stationary bike. He'd healed well from the surgery and made it just in time for the last day of baseball tryouts. Now that he'd made the team, he worked even harder at his therapy exercises. It made her happy to see him so excited about playing baseball, and the way that excitement seemed to fuel his progress. *Pretty soon, he should be ready for prime time.*

At the end of the hour, Dr. Madison walked Cooper over to the chair where Eden sat. "He did very well today, Ms. Voss. I'm really pleased with his progress."

"Great." She brushed a fallen lock of hair away from her eyes. "Do you think he'll be ready to start training with the team in November?"

She nodded. "I don't see any reason he couldn't. As long as he continues to do his exercises and is careful not to re-injure that lower leg, he should be just fine."

"Yes!" That news had Cooper dancing again.

Eden laughed at her nephew's exuberance. "Thanks, Dr. M."

"No problem." She fist-bumped Cooper again. "See you next week, buddy."

After they left the office and she'd delivered her nephew safely to school, she headed back toward the studio. The benefits of two cups of coffee were flowing through her veins, and she finally felt awake. Still, she didn't know what to expect when she walked into the studio. She'd seen her share of famous folks coming and going, so she tried to make sure she looked presentable at all times. At least that's what she told herself, because she didn't want to accept that she might be spending so much extra time on her appearance because of Blaine.

She swung by the restroom just inside Against the Grain's building. There, she adjusted her navy slacks and the dolman sleeves of her white blouse, then checked her reflection in the mirror. Smoothing her hair behind her ears and adjusting her headband, she walked out of the bathroom…

And nearly crashed into Cambria.

Blaine trailed behind Cambria by a few steps as they left his office. He saw Eden headed in their direction, though she appeared to be looking at something on her phone as she walked.

A moment later, her head jerked up. "Oh!" She sidestepped at the last possible second, narrowly avoiding the collision. "Cambria?"

Blaine watched as the two women stood there, assessing each other.

Cambria bounced on the balls of her feet. A caramel-skinned beauty, she was tall, lean and leggy. Her long jet-black hair hung down her back, and her wide-legged denim jumper looked both comfortable and fashionable. "Eden?" It was more a squeal than a greeting. "I haven't seen you in ages!" She pulled her in for a hug.

"It's good to see you, Cambria." Eden returned the hug. "When did you get into town?"

"Like an hour ago. I promised Blaine I would come by the studio the next time I made it to town."

As the two friends stepped apart again, Eden's gaze

drifted to meet his, and she narrowed her eyes just enough for him to see.

He frowned. *What's that about?*

"What?" Cambria tilted her head, her expression conveying confusion. Obviously, she'd noticed it, too.

"Nothing, nothing." She linked arms with Cambria, leading her away. "What brings you to town?" He watched their retreating backs as they headed back toward the studio, chatting and giggling. He stood there a moment, trying to parse out what was going on. Eden seemed happy to see her friend, if a bit surprised. *So why did she cut her eyes at me like that?* He leaned against the wall, and as if on cue, Eden glanced back his way, a sour look on her face.

She did it again! Now I'm really confused. This was the thing about women that he didn't like. Their ever-changing emotions perplexed him. It seemed he often got into trouble with them but had no idea what he'd done wrong.

Not wanting to be on the receiving end of any more attitude from Eden, he shook his head and retreated back into the quiet of his office. There, he sat down at his desk, started up a Ludacris playlist on his phone and navigated to his email. He clicked through while bopping his head to the music, clearing out the clutter of unread messages and replying to those that required his attention. *I gotta stop letting my inbox get so out of hand.*

The music stopped, replaced by the sound of his ringtone. Swiping over the image of Marvin's business card on the screen, he answered the call. "Hi, Marvin. What's up?"

"Hey, Blaine. You doing all right? How's life in the Dirty South?"

He chuckled, as he always did whenever Marvin tried to sound hip. "It's all good, can't complain. But I'll be even better once you tell me what you thought of Naiya's album. It's amazing work, right?"

Marvin cleared his throat, remaining silent.

Blaine waited, leaning back in his chair and looking up at the ceiling. *He's hesitating...it's making me nervous.* But he didn't dare reveal that to his higher-up.

Marvin broke his silence. "This album is… Well, we know you worked super hard on it, with Naiya and Eden and the producers. And we absolutely think that 'The Way It Was,' 'Kisses at Dawn' and 'Look My Way' are absolutely fantastic tracks. Especially 'Look My Way.' How did you nail down Antoine 11 for that guest verse? He's pretty elusive these days."

Apparently, he's leading with the positive, so I'll just go with it for now. "Oh, a friend of mine knows one of Antoine's favorite producers. We hit him up, he hit up Antoine, and the rest is history, as they say. He's up in New York now, and since he couldn't make it down to the ATL, he just recorded his sixteen bars up there and we mixed it with Naiya's vocals after the fact."

"Awesome. Great job on securing the verse. It's a hot track, and everyone at Hamilton House agrees that having Antoine on the song will play very well with the fan base."

"Yeah, I agree. That's why we decided to approach him. It's sort of a hometown tag team, ya know? Antoine and a lot of that crew grew up in Atlanta. I think that's why he was so willing to work with Naiya, even though she's pretty new in the industry."

"Nice." He paused. "So, you're definitely on the right path with this album. However…"

Blaine frowned. *Here it comes.*

"…the other tracks on the album, are, well, not what we're looking for."

"Meaning? If you're going to say something like that about seventy percent of the album, I'd like to gain a little clarity here, Marvin."

He cleared his throat again. "Sure, sure. Absolutely. So, when we're looking at subject matter for the remainder of the album, you've got to admit the topics Naiya's singing about are pretty heavy."

Blaine rotated his chair so he could look out the window behind his desk. The gray sky and fat dark clouds indicated a coming storm. "That's a fair enough assessment, but that was done on purpose. What specifically do you have a problem with?"

"It's not me, Blaine. It's the team. I just want to be clear on that."

He flexed his jaw. "Then what is it that *the team* doesn't like?"

"Well… I mean…for instance, there are two songs about race stuff."

"You mean anti-Black bias?" Blaine gritted out.

Marvin coughed. "Yes, that. And then she's singing about how men are trash and rich whites are ruining the historically Black neighborhoods in Atlanta…"

He wanted to laugh but held back. "You mean misogyny and gentrification? Women do have to deal with a lot of crap from men on a daily basis, and gentrification is a problem in cities all over the country, not just in Atlanta." He paused, tapping his chin. *I can't pass up this chance to troll him a little.* "I've known you a long time, Marvin. And I know you're an intelligent, culturally aware person. You can't be telling me you're unfamiliar with these concepts."

Another series of coughs followed that.

Blaine tucked in his lower lip to hold back his chuckle.

"Yes, well, of course, I'm aware of these things," Marvin said once he got himself together. "Still, we don't think these are appropriate topics for Naiya's album. Especially not on a debut."

"Okay. And why is that?"

"You see, we want to put out music that counters the current toxic climate in media. You know, some positive vibes to cut through the negativity. We think Naiya's talents are well suited to the feel-good album of the year."

He shook his head. It was easy to see where this conversation was going. *I've got a choice here. I can cut my losses and agree with him now, or I can sit through twenty more minutes of corporate BS, just to end up with the same result.* "Level with me, Marvin. What does the team want us to do moving forward?"

"As I said, you're on the right path. We'd like you to keep the three standout tracks just as they are and revisit the creative process for the other tracks."

Blaine's mouth fell open for a moment. Snapping it shut, he asked, "Are you telling me we need to rework seven songs, seventy percent of this hard-won album, and rerecord them?"

"No, no. Of course not. What I'm saying is, just scrap the seven songs and start over. Build new songs, from the ground up."

He felt his jaw clench. "And is there another alternative here?"

"Not one that involves us funding the project." It was the bluntest statement Marvin had made for the entire conversation.

He blew out a breath. "I understand. Thanks for letting me know."

"I'm happy to help. Well, I'm due at a meeting soon. Have a good rest of your day, Blaine."

"You, too, Marvin." The words tasted like sour milk in his mouth, but he ground them out anyway. And moments later, he ended the call.

Shit.

Fifteen

A few minutes before nine Tuesday morning, Eden strolled through the open door of the small conference room at Against the Grain. The room, sparsely decorated with a few framed album covers, held only a few items. A mounted whiteboard took up one entire wall, and the opposite wall held only windows. Centered between the two walls, a rectangular table with seating for eight people took up most of the floor space.

She slipped into a seat on the side of the table closest to the door, tucking her purse into the chair next to her. She didn't think Blaine had any solid dress code for the meeting, so she'd kept it simple by wearing a silver silk blouse and wide-legged black slacks with her favorite low-heeled black leather loafers.

She'd been sitting there a minute or two, scrolling through her phone, when Blaine strode in. He looked handsome as ever, wearing a pair of navy slacks; a button-down shirt featuring navy, hunter-green and white zigzags; and a pair of navy wingtips with a gold toe box. His locs were tied at his nape, and his favorite pair of dark sunglasses was perched atop his head.

Have mercy. Why does he have to be so fine? I could just stare at him all day. He always looked like a snack, no matter what he wore. But when she looked up at his face, she didn't see the mischievous smile she'd become accustomed to. Instead, she saw a guarded, taut expression that gave her pause. *Damn. What is he about to say?* She'd come into this meeting expecting to hear some good news about the album. Now that she'd seen his face, though, tiny needles of tension began to prick the base of her spine.

"Good morning, Eden." He greeted her as he took a seat at the end of the table to her right.

"Morning." She would have said more, but she was too busy worrying about what he might say.

She held his gaze for a second, and he winked at her.

"You all right down there, baby?"

She swallowed, knowing full well she wasn't okay. Because every time she looked at his handsome face, she felt her body temperature rise. "For now. I'm just…wondering what's about to happen, that's all."

Naiya breezed in a few moments later, clad in a floral sundress and flat nude sandals. Her wavy hair pulled back into a ponytail, she looked put together yet approachable.

Eden smiled and waved at Naiya, who waved back with a grin of her own.

Blaine cleared his throat. "Okay, ladies. Time to get down to business."

"Yes, let's," Naiya said, shifting from side to side in her seat. "What did the label team say about my album?"

Eden swallowed, bracing for whatever was about to spill from between the full lips that had kissed her senseless on more than one occasion.

He rested his elbows on the table, tenting his fingers. "I

got some very positive feedback from Marvin. The team is especially fond of 'Look My Way'..."

Naiya grinned. "I knew they would be. That Antoine 11 verse is fire. I'm so glad he agreed to collab with me."

Eden nodded. "Yes. I mean when you combine his bars with Naiya's vocals...it's magic, really."

A slight smile tilted his lips. "I agree completely. The team also had a lot of great things to say about 'The Way It Was' and 'Kisses at Dawn.' Great work there as well, ladies."

She felt her brow crinkle. *He's said a lot of good things... about three out of ten tracks. What's he holding back here?* "Okay. This is all great to hear, but... I feel like you're leaving something out, Blaine."

"Yeah," Naiya interjected, running a hand over her hair. "Don't keep us in suspense. What was the feedback on the rest of the album?"

"Well..." He hesitated. Instead of saying more, he opened the leather portfolio. Taking out some documents, he slid copies to both of them. "In terms of feedback on the other seven tracks, I'd like you to take a look at this."

Eden scanned the top of the thin stack of papers, reading the headline on the first page. "'Official Correspondence. Hamilton House Recordings, a subsidiary of American Music Group Incorporated.'" Her eyes narrowed as she read further.

Naiya read along in silence, her lips flexing in time as her eyes perused the words on the page.

Eden got halfway down the first page before she saw a string of words that gave her pause. *Creative Revision Request.* Followed by another phrase that stopped her in her tracks. *Mandatory Change.* She looked up at Blaine, who avoided her gaze by pretending to look at the papers. *I'm sure he's already read them. That's probably why he can't look me in the eye.*

Naiya looked up, her eyes wide. "Blaine, what does all this mean? What are they asking us to do?"

He cleared his throat. "Well, Naiya, what the upper management team would like us to do is rework the seven remaining tracks on the album."

A few long, slow blinks later, Naiya said, "What?"

"Well, if you think about it, it's really a chance to dig deeper into your creative vision." He turned toward Eden. "The management team had its doubts about bringing you on for this project. But this allows you to keep your role as songwriter, as long as you're willing to make a few changes."

"Is it really, Blaine?" Eden, now reading through page three, held the document up as she read aloud. "'Clause C. Pursuant to the terms of this document, the following subject matter has been deemed "off-limits" for tracks on the album. Gentrification. Misogyny and Misogynoir. Rape Culture. Racism. Anti-Black Bias. Political affiliation'?" She dropped the papers on the desk. "That's only the first half of the list of things I'm not allowed to write about as lyricist, and that Naiya isn't allowed to sing about."

Naiya's mouth dropped open.

He held his hand out, open palm facing them. "Now, ladies. Think about how this could benefit album sales. We want to keep the subject matter light and…"

Naiya slowly shook her head, tears springing to her eyes. "No, Blaine. You told me that if I signed with you, you'd help me see my vision through to the end. You *promised* me."

He slumped, his head dropping to one side. "Don't you see, Naiya? That's exactly what I'm trying to do…deliver on that promise. I want to see your album in the hands of music lovers just as much as you do." He held up the document, flipping through the pages. "And to make that happen, all we have to do is sign on page five, agreeing to the terms that Hamilton House has set for us."

Eden closed her eyes, blew out a breath. "You don't even realize how you sound right now, do you?" She gestured to the crestfallen Naiya, who sat in stony silence, tears coursing down her cheeks. "Look at her, Blaine. She's a true talent. Passion. Stage presence. Vocal ability. And she actually has something meaningful to say."

"I agree, but—"

She held up her hand. "Let. Me. Finish. She has all those things going for her, and here you are trying to get her to go for the okey-doke. To record another cookie-cutter album, something that could be interchangeable with a thousand other female R & B albums. You're sitting here asking her to give up everything that makes her special." She looked over at the young singer. *I'd hug her if I thought it appropriate. She looks so sad.* "You've been here, you saw how hard we both worked on this. How could you, Blaine? How could you do that to her? To both of us?"

"Listen, I agree with everything you're saying. Naiya's talent, and her awareness of her surroundings, are so, so special. But Marvin is forcing my hand here. If we want to get this album out, we've got to make some sacrifices."

Naiya stood slowly, still shaking her head. "I... I can't do this."

Blaine stood, as well. "Naiya, wait. Let's talk about..."

"No." She dashed away her tears with her hand. "I'm leaving." Looking her way, she said, "Thank you, Eden. Thank you for seeing my vision."

Giving her a solemn nod, Eden watched as Naiya strode out the door. Then she looked at Blaine, not bothering to hide the hurt in her gaze. "I can't believe this is happening. I was so invested in this project... I feel like you're betraying me, all over again."

Left alone in the conference room with Eden, Blaine ran his hand over his eyes. *I haven't even gotten to the heart of the document, and things have already gone to the left in a major way.*

No, he hadn't expected that Naiya and Eden would be thrilled about the prospect of all this extra work. But he also hadn't thought they'd take the requests from Hamilton House as some kind of personal affront.

He shook his head. Upper management was accustomed to giving mandates and having them followed, most of the time without questions or pushback. That obviously wasn't going to happen in this instance, and he knew they wouldn't like it. *I'm royally screwed here.*

"Did you even hear what I just said, Blaine?" Eden's anger-laced voice cut through his thoughts like a chain saw taking down a tree.

He looked her way and found her watching him, her eyes narrowed, and her mouth twisted into a frown. He gave a nervous little chuckle, hoping to soften her mood. "Sorry, I checked out for a minute. What did you say?"

Her eyes narrowed further, indicating his attempt at humor hadn't moved her. "I said, you haven't changed, Blaine."

Leaning back in his chair, he held out his hands in defense. "Whoa, whoa, whoa. This doesn't have anything to do with me being selfish or whatever. This is simply business, Eden."

She scoffed, shaking her head. "Are you really that thick-headed? You really think 'business' is the only thing at play here?"

He felt his jaw tighten. The insinuation that he lacked intelligence hit him in the gut like a punch. He'd heard that all his life…even his own father chastised him for leaning on his charm and good looks instead of using intelligence to get ahead. "Just because I can't read your mind or do some brainiac job in a lab somewhere, that doesn't mean I'm stupid."

"Blaine, I'm sorry. I'm not trying to insult your intelligence. I just need you to understand the stakes here."

"I didn't hear any complaints when we were making love."

She let her head drop back. "I can't. I can't with you."

"Maybe that's the problem here, Eden." He pushed his chair back from the table but stayed seated. "You can't open up to me. You've been talking about me being selfish, thoughtless and uncaring ever since you came here... yet you haven't told me why."

She sighed aloud, her fingertips rubbing her temples. "Why did I even come here? Why did I expect anything different from you?"

He shrugged, feeling his annoyance rising. "I don't know. You tell me."

She blew out a breath, pushed back from the table and stood. "You keep saying your hands are tied. That you don't have a choice. That it's all just 'business.' But none of that is true, Blaine. It's not true now, and it wasn't true seven years ago, either."

He threw up his hands. "Oh, boy. Here we go..."

"Hold up. I'm. Not. Finished."

He clamped his lips shut, though he wasn't thrilled about her tone or the direction she was taking the conversation.

"You made all these promises to Naiya. Told her you'd look out for her, make sure her album was true to her vision. Yet the very first time the suits in New York dispute what we worked so hard on you cave. Then you expect us to just go along with it."

He folded his arms over his chest but said nothing. *She's gone off and there's no need for me to speak. Anything I say right now will just be used against me.*

"Seven years ago, when the suits told you to disband Swatz Girlz you promised me a solo career. But when the label decided to ditch me and make Cambria a star, you caved then, too." She propped her fist on her hips, fixing him with an accusing stare. "Tell me, Blaine. How much pushback did you give them back then? Did you voice any opposition at all? Or did you just gleefully discard me like yesterday's trash?"

He cringed. "I think you're being unfair. These are two different situations."

She chuckled bitterly, with a slow shake of her head. "That's just it, Blaine. They aren't different, and I'll tell you why. You didn't stand up for Naiya." She looked away from him. "And you didn't stand up for me, either."

"Eden, I…"

"I don't want to hear it, Blaine. You keep acting as if I'm being unreasonable, as if it's all business and nothing personal. But in reality, it's very, very personal." She leaned over the table, placing her open palms on the tabletop. "You want to know why I don't fully trust you? Why I'm not open with you? Why I should never have let you into my bed or my heart?"

He swallowed.

"I'll tell you why. All the problems we've had, now and in the past, can be traced back to one thing. Your absolute inability, or at least refusal, to stand up for someone else. To do what will be best for someone other than yourself."

He frowned. "That's a sweeping statement. I don't think it's accurate, either."

She scoffed.

"No, Eden. I'm not going to let you accuse me of being this callous jerk. I cared about you then, and I still care about you now. Whether you believe it or not, it's the truth."

"Fine." She slapped the table. "I'll make it more specific. You didn't stand up for Naiya. And it just serves to remind me of how you didn't stand up for me back in the day." She stood, her chin stuck out defiantly. "I can't do this with you, Blaine. I won't."

"You won't what? Make changes to the album?"

"Ugh." She sounded disgusted. "Fuck those guys at Hamilton House. I don't care about their demands or their stupid contracts. And as for you and me, it's over. I'm not going to keep being involved with someone who doesn't have my back when it really counts."

"What about us? What about everything we've shared?"

"I'm not gonna deny the connection we share, Blaine. But I have to be careful when it comes to my heart. I can't risk the pain of having you betray me again."

That stung, and he felt his heart clench. "I care about you. I feel like…like we have something special between us."

"Bullshit. I don't want to hear declarations like that when it's so obvious you're not going to do anything to prove it."

He stood and walked around to where she was. Grasping her arm, he pulled her toward him, letting his lips crash against hers. For a few fiery moments, she leaned into him, their tongues tangling like the ball of emotions rolling around in his stomach.

Then she snatched herself away from him. Her expression was strained, tortured. "Don't, Blaine."

"Eden, you can't just walk out like this."

"Watch me." Shooting him one last hard, cutting look, she snatched up her purse, turned her back and strode out of the room. Her echoing footsteps sounded on the concrete floor as she retreated, moving farther and farther away by the second.

Alone in the room, he rested his elbows on the table and dropped his head in his hands.

Sixteen

Stretched out on the sofa in sweatpants and an old tee, Eden flipped absently through the pages of one of her fashion magazines. The flat-screen television, tuned to one of those home renovations shows, provided little more than background noise. And while the house was quiet for now, she knew Cooper and Ainsley were due home soon from his baseball practice.

It was Wednesday evening, the middle of what seemed like the longest week of her life. This time last week she'd been on a high. She and Blaine had been making sweet love and creating music together, and Naiya's project had been on the cusp of wrapping up.

Now everything had crashed down around her. *I always sucked at Jenga. Always pulling the wrong block, or not keeping my hand steady enough. Now my life is scattered just like those wooden blocks.*

She let her head drop back against the cushion, staring at the ceiling. She knew how cliché it was for her to be lying here like this, pining over a man who'd shown himself to be unreliable on more than one occasion. Yet she couldn't shake the feeling. Because there was more to him. There was a sweet, loving side to him...a man who held doors and pulled out chairs, whose smile lit up a room, who made love to her like a champion. And knowing all the goodness inside him only made this situation harder to take. All she wanted to do was lie there, like a bump on a pickle, kicking herself for getting involved with Blaine in the first place.

She heard the front door open and turned her head.

Ainsley entered, her arms laden with grocery bags. Cooper came in right behind her.

"Hey, Auntie," he shouted as he shut the door behind them.

"Hey, Coop." She sat up on the couch, righting her disheveled clothing a bit. "How was practice?"

"Good. I got to work on pitching today." He jogged past her, setting a paper grocery bag on the counter in the kitchen before returning. "Coach says I've got a pretty good arm."

"Of course, you do." She flexed her biceps. "It's in your genes, kiddo."

He laughed. "Auntie." Shaking his head, he disappeared up the stairs.

Ainsley, who'd muscled her bags into the kitchen, stood in the doorway, shaking her head. "You two. Meanwhile, why don't you get up and help me put these groceries away? Obviously, Cooper has a more pressing engagement with *Minecraft*."

Eden frowned. "I guess I should. I've probably been vegging on the couch way too long." She stood, stretching her arms above her head.

Ainsley cocked a brow. "Girl, what's going on with you? You didn't come home from the studio yesterday, then I come home today and find you here, leaving an Eden-sized divot in the sofa. This ain't like you, E."

She shook her head as she entered the kitchen. "You're telling me." As she and Ainsley plucked items from the bags sitting on the counter and the island, tucking them into their designated spots, she related the story of what had happened during yesterday's meeting at Against the Grain.

"But where'd you go after that?" Ainsley hung a bunch of bananas on the little silver hook stand she kept on the counter solely for that purpose. "Why didn't you come home last night?"

She shrugged. "I just… I don't know. My emotions were high, and I wanted to be alone. So, when I left the studio, I called Naiya to apologize to her. Even though it's not my fault, I know what she's going through, and I sympathize."

Ainsley nodded.

"Then I headed down to the park. Sat on the dock by the lake for hours, then checked into a hotel when it started to get dark. I couldn't come home. I couldn't face you and Cooper knowing how angry and hurt I was. I would never want to take it out on the two of you, my only real family."

Ainsley made a face. "Oh, damn. I'm sorry, girl."

"Yeah. I feel like hell. No appetite, can't sleep." She dropped her gaze. "That's on top of feeling like Boo Boo the Fool."

"No, I mean, I'm sorry you felt you couldn't come home." She placed her hand atop Eden's. "We love you no matter what. We love you at your best and at your worst. I'm just upset you suffered alone."

Eden felt the smile creep over her face, despite her mood. "Thank you, Ainsley. I really appreciate that."

"And if you want me to go over there and kick Blaine's ass, just let me know." She balled up her fists and positioned herself in a fighting stance. "I've got a clean record; I probably won't get in too much trouble for putting him in traction."

She giggled. "You're the best."

Ainsley chuckled, too. "Guess what I brought home from the store, cousin?"

"What?"

"Triple fudge brownie ice cream. Nuts. Whipped cream." She extracted each item from a bag as she called them out. "You down for a sundae?"

"Do you really have to ask?"

A few minutes later, they were both on the couch with their bowls and spoons.

"So, what are you going to do about Blaine?"

She shrugged. "Go back to what I was doing before, I guess. Pretend he doesn't exist."

"What about Naiya's album?"

"I held up my end of the deal. I wrote ten solid songs, based on her own words and feelings. I got paid for my work."

Ainsley scoffed. "Yeah, yeah. We both know you ain't gonna leave that girl hanging. She could have been me back in the day. Or you." She gave her a pointed look.

She sighed. "You're right. I definitely see my younger, more idealistic self in her. I'd hate for her to give up or change herself to try to fit into the industry." She scratched her chin. "I'll reach out to her in a few days, see what she wants to do moving forward."

"Fair enough." Ainsley set her empty bowl on the coffee table. "Now, about Blaine…"

She shook her head. "No. I don't want to talk about him."

"Eden, you're not going to be able to forget him or pretend he doesn't exist, and you know I'm right." She touched her shoulder. "You're just not that kind of person. You're going to care about him no matter what."

The last spoonful of ice cream lost some of its chocolaty flavor when she heard those words. "Damn it, Ainsley. Stop telling me the truth and tell me what will make me feel better."

"Girl, stop whining. You know I'm all about keeping it one hundred." Settling back against the cushion, she tossed one leg over the other. "Here's what's real. You love him. And even though you're mad at him, and rightfully so, that's not gonna negate your feelings for him. You are gonna have to figure out a way to make it work."

"Ugh." She ran a hand through her messy hair. "That was physically painful to hear."

"Like our queen, Lizzo, said, truth hurts." Ainsley shrugged. "So are you gonna call him or what? Odds are he's just as miserable as you are."

She shook her head. "No way. After what he did, he'll have to call me." She wasn't about to let him off easy, not after he'd given her a repeat performance of his self-centered ways. As badly as she wanted to call him, if only to hear his voice, she knew she couldn't do it. She'd simply have to set her intense longing for him aside…as best she could, anyway.

"All right, I guess that'll do." Ainsley wrinkled her nose, the way she did when in deep thought. "I know he's gonna call you. It might take him some time to get his head out of his ass, though."

"Whatever." Eden yawned. "I'm tired of talking about him."

Grabbing the remote, Ainsley searched through the on-screen guide. "Looks like *Idlewild* is coming on."

Eden chuckled, then settled in for her fiftieth viewing of her cousin's favorite film.

Thursday night, Blaine reclined in the engineer's chair in the soundboard suite of his studio. The room, darkened except for the electronic glow emitted by the controls, matched his mood. His very soul felt shrouded in black, and the few points of light he could see all pointed back to one thing.

Eden.

No one had been in the studio since Monday, as no one had booked studio time this week. He'd asked his receptionist to leave the schedule open, just in case work on Naiya's album took longer than expected. He only had one studio in his building, though he dreamed of one day building a state-of-the-art facility with at least three recording suites.

For now, though, all the dreams he held dear faded into the background, overshadowed by the immense pain of Eden's absence from his life. He'd tried calling and texting her all day and into the night Tuesday; she'd ignored every attempt. By Wednesday morning, he'd given up on getting back into her good graces. Then he'd trudged here, to his big empty workplace, come into the studio and plugged in his headphones to hear the one sound he craved more than any other.

Blaine had not left the studio last night; he'd only left the room to go to the bathroom or grab the occasional beverage. His appetite was nonexistent, and he hadn't eaten a substantial meal in the last thirty-six hours. Still, he didn't want to leave, didn't want to set his headphones aside.

I want to be here, where she was. I need to be near where this began, where I can still feel her energy.

He leaned the chair back as far as it would go without unplugging his headphones. Stretched his stiff legs out in front of him. Focused only on the sweet, sweet sound filling his ears. Music always salved the wounds of his soul... this time was no different.

The door of the soundboard suite swung open, and the motion in his periphery made him jerk his head in that direction. He could make out a figure in the dim light but couldn't yet see the man's face. He rubbed his tired eyes, but that didn't help. Straightening up in the chair, he called out, "Who's there?"

The lights flickered on, and he closed his eyes against the brightness. He looked again, seeing his brother through his bleary eyes. Gage's mouth was moving, but he couldn't make out the words over the sound playing in his headphones.

Gage stalked closer, his expression decidedly annoyed. "Can't you hear me?" He shouted the question.

"Yeah, how could I not when you're yelling."

Shaking his head, Gage demanded, "Take off those damn headphones so I can talk to you!"

He simply shook his head. *Whatever Gage wants to talk about, it can't possibly sound better to me than what I'm listening to.*

Gage narrowed his eyes, and after a few moments of searching for the jack, he snatched the headphone cord out of place. "There. Since you wanna be a stubborn ass." He paused, his gaze shifting to the soundboard as the sounds poured into the room. "What are you listening to?" He frowned, tapping his chin with his index finger for a few seconds. "Wait. Isn't this Eden singing?"

He nodded slowly. "I just…needed to hear her voice."

"Wow. You're mighty pitiful right now, bro."

"You're right, and I'm aware of it." He resisted the urge to shush his brother, whose idle chatter was interrupting his listening to the sweet sounds of Eden's melodic crooning.

"This is that Lauryn Hill song." He shifted his weight from one foot to the other. "'The Sweetest Thing.'"

"Yep. It's one of her favorite songs, and she recorded this as a warm-up before she started recording studio demos for Naiya to use."

He gazed off to the side, the way he always did when trying to remember something. "I remember this…it was on that soundtrack to that Black nineties chick flick…what was it? *The Inkwell*? *Jason's Lyric*?"

"Love Jones." He swallowed the lump of pain in his throat. "Don't make me have to revoke your Black card."

Shaking his head, Gage stepped closer to him before stopping and wrinkling his nose. "When's the last time you went home to…you know, shower?"

He shrugged. "Tuesday."

Moving over to the soundboard, Gage shut off the playback. "Nope. That's not going to be acceptable, buddy." He grabbed his brother's hand and pulled him from the chair. "Get up. We're going to your house."

He felt his pulse quicken, the absence of Eden's angelic voice already starting to affect him. Listening to her isolated vocals while picturing her beautiful smile was the only thing that gave him comfort as of late. "I don't want to leave."

"I get that. But if you ever want another shot at someone as classy as Eden, you're gonna have to get off your ass." With one strong tug, Gage moved him toward the door. "Let's go."

"She's not going to talk to me. I tried calling, texting." He felt the pain in his chest, the same pain he felt every time he remembered the look of hurt on her face. "She just ignored me."

"I would, too. What are we, twelve? Grown-ass adults settle their disputes face-to-face." Gage wrinkled his nose again. "You'll see her in person. *After* you bathe, because you funky as hell."

"Stop roasting me, Gage. I'm already in pain."

He dropped his hand. "Whatever. Do you love her or not? And don't even think about lying to me, bruh. Mama already hipped me to the game."

He sighed. "Yes, Gage. I love her." Before she reentered his life, he'd resolved that love wasn't for him. It was simply a youthful feeling, something he'd grown too old and too business-minded to entertain. Now he knew better. Because there was no way he could deny her ownership of his heart and soul.

Gage clapped his hands together. "Sho' you right. Now, man up, get your shit together and go get your woman!"

He didn't put up a fight. He knew his brother was right, though he'd never say it aloud. But how would he convince her to let him back into her heart, when she wouldn't even answer his calls?

What will I have to do to get her to see me?

Whatever it was, he'd have to figure it out. Because the past few days had taught him something, an undeniable truth.

He didn't want to live this life without her in it.

Seventeen

Friday afternoon, Eden and Ainsley sat at the dining room table, enjoying burgers from the Slutty Vegan, Atlanta's premiere vegan burger joint. The silence in the room was broken when Eden's phone started ringing.

"Whew." Eden swiped her mouth with a napkin. "I need a time-out."

Sliding the button on her screen, she answered the call from the 212-area code. "Hello?"

"Hi, I'm looking for Eden Voss?" The female voice on the other line seemed hesitant.

"That's me. What can I do for you?"

"Oh, good. Hi, Ms. Voss. My name is Chanel Titus—but most people call me…"

Eden's eyes widened as she completed her sentence. "Chanel The Titan?"

Chanel giggled. "Yes. Apparently, you're familiar with my work."

"I am. You've worked with some of the biggest names in hip-hop and R & B. Monica. Sevyn. Riri...the list goes on."

"I'm flattered that you follow my career." Chanel cleared her throat. "Listen, the reason I'm contacting you is that I was in the Hamilton House offices here in New York last week for a meeting. While I was there, I overheard a voice singing on a demo reel. I was so taken aback by the talent that I inquired, and as it turns out, the voice I heard was yours."

Eden felt the rush of exhilaration as the heat rose into her cheeks. "Wow. Oh, wow. Thank you so much."

"I looked you up online, and realized I'd already heard some of the songs you've written. But you haven't put out any music of your own. Why is that?"

She clutched the phone, her eyes darting to Ainsley, who could hear the whole conversation.

"Tell her," Ainsley insisted.

So, she gave Chanel the short version of her only attempt at a singing career. "I've just sort of settled into the behind-the-scenes work of songwriting, which I love."

"Well, honey, you can keep writing songs if you like. But you're wasting your vocal talents by not using them." She paused. "Listen, I'll level with you. I'd love to work with you on an album. You've got the kind of voice R & B is missing right now."

"An album?" She blinked several times. "I...just...wow, my own album?"

"If you'd rather start with just a single, to see how things go, I'm open to that." Chanel said something to someone in the background, her speech muffled as if she'd placed her hand over the microphone. "Okay, honey. I've got another meeting. You have my number now, so if you decide to give it a shot, just give me a call."

"Sure thing. Thanks so much." Ending the call, she laid her phone face down on the table.

Ainsley squealed. "Giiirlll! Chanel the Titan wants to work with you!"

She took a deep breath, blowing it out through her lips. "I know. This is wild."

"It gets wilder if you think about it."

She frowned. "What do you mean?"

"In a roundabout way, Blaine helped you get Chanel's attention."

Her frown deepened.

"No, listen. If you hadn't agreed to work with him, what are the odds you'd have recorded that particular demo, which ended up in the Hamilton House office, at that particular time, for Chanel to hear it?"

She felt her face relax. "I guess...if you look at it that way, Blaine played a small part in this."

"No ma'am. Blaine played a big part in this. Give that man his credit." Ainsley went back to devouring her burger.

She leaned back in her chair. "At least something good came of me getting my heart stepped on by Blaine Woodson for the second time in a decade."

"I'm just glad you're not going to turn down the opportunity." Ainsley dabbed the Slutty Sauce from her mouth with a napkin. "And I want you to be open to other opportunities that come your way too, E."

"Like what? I don't have much else going on right now."

"You could. My dating sense is tingling."

"Ugh." She threw up her hands. "The last thing I need in my life right now is a new man."

"You're absolutely right." She stood, stuffing her trash into the paper sack. "Lucky for you, I'm not talking about a new man. I'm talking about Blaine."

"Come on, Ainsley. I told you I'm not going to call him."

"I haven't forgotten what you said. Don't worry. He's going to reach out." She put their trash into the can, then grabbed a sponge to wipe down the table. "And when he does, you're going to give him a chance this time, right?"

She frowned.

"Promise me, Eden. Promise me you'll at least hear him out."

"And if I still think he's full of shit after he's said his piece, then what?" She folded her arms over her chest.

"Then you're free to tell him to kick rocks in flip-flops. I'm not demanding an outcome. I'm just asking you to give the brotha a shot."

"Fine." She wasn't particularly happy about Ainsley's harping, but she knew her cousin. It'd be much easier to say yes now than be badgered about it for days on end. "You get on my last nerve, Ainsley."

"I love you, too, cousin." Blowing her a kiss, Ainsley slipped from the room, leaving her alone at the table.

When Blaine rapped on the door of his father's hobby room Saturday morning, he had no idea what to expect. Knocks on this door often went ignored if his father was busy building or painting one of the hundreds of model military aircraft and vehicles he'd collected over the years, or reading up on military history. Aside from that, Blaine himself hadn't set foot inside the hobby room since his days as a rebellious teen.

Clutching the handles of the large paper shopping bag, he waited a few moments. He could hear his father's movements inside the room. He knocked again, in case his first one had gone unheard.

Caleb snatched the door open this time. He wore an old tee, blue sweatpants and the canvas apron he wore when at work on his hobby. He frowned. "Blaine? What are you doing here, son?"

He took a deep breath. "We need to talk, Dad, and it's a long-overdue conversation."

Caleb's frown deepened. "Not now, Blaine. I'm working on..."

He held up the bag. "Dad, I hate to interrupt you. But I brought something I know you'll want."

His father's gaze flickered to the nondescript brown bag, then back to his son's face. "What could possibly be in there that I'd want?"

"How about two perfect 1/144-scale model kits for the Blue Angels Aerobatic Team aircraft?"

Confusion knit his brow. "Are you serious?"

He shook the bag gently, hearing the pieces inside rustling and rattling around. "Take a look for yourself."

Taking the offered bag from his son's hand, Caleb peered inside. His eyes widened when he saw the contents. He immediately stepped back from the doorway. "Come on in."

Blaine smiled as he entered his father's sacred space for the first time in a decade. The room hadn't changed much in configuration over the years. There was a brown leather love seat and a coffee table to one side. His father's workstation, a huge, custom-built oak table, was littered with paints, brushes and model parts, sectioned off with the four raised dividers built into the tabletop. The table's unique design made it possible for Caleb to work on several models at one time without getting the pieces mixed up.

"Have a seat, Blaine." Caleb sat down on the love seat, already taking the brightly colored, shrink-wrapped boxes out of the bag.

"Thanks." Taking up the seat next to his father, he settled in. He watched quietly as his father inspected the two packages, the spark of interest glowing in his dark eyes.

"Where did you find these?"

"Online. I remember how much you loved Blue Angels memorabilia, and after consulting with Mom, I found out what was missing from your collection." He flexed his fingers. "Took a bit of digging, but I found them. I'd say I

learned a decent amount while searching for the models."
He leaned back. "Why don't you quiz me?"

Caleb chuckled, a rare sound indeed. "All right. What
do you know about the Blue Angels?"

"Cool. The Blue Angels are the United States Navy's
flight demonstration squadron, formed in 1946. That makes
them the world's second-oldest aerobatics team. The squadron had two headquarters, one at Naval Base Pensacola
in Florida, and the other at Naval Base El Centro in Cali-
fornia."

Caleb appeared impressed. "I see you've done some research. Now, what can you tell me about the aircraft you
brought?"

"I've got two models, the Lockheed Hercules C-130,
and the McDonnell-Douglas F4-J Phantom II. The C-130
was developed in the 1950s and has been used ever since
by the US Air Force for tactical transport, parachute drops
of personnel and equipment, and air mission landing. This
particular model has been used to transport the Angels
since 1970."

Tilting his head slightly, Caleb said, "Go on."

Blaine felt the connection growing between them, so
he continued. "As for the Phantom II, it's one of several
models of jets used to provide escort and support to the
squadron during aerobatics demonstrations. This particular model was in use by the Angels from 1969 to 1974—
the Vietnam era."

Caleb blinked several times. His shoulders relaxed, releasing the rigidity that always seemed to reside there, and
he released a slow breath. "Wow, son. I'm…pleasantly surprised."

"It gets better, Dad." He rubbed his hands together, noticing they weren't sweaty the way they usually were when
he was in his father's presence. Talking with him about the
models seemed to have put them both at ease. "I got all the

manufacturer recommended paints as well, and I want to spend today helping you put them together."

Caleb's eyes grew wet. "Really?"

He nodded. "Yes. I figure you can work on the C-130, and I'll do the jet since it's smaller and I don't know what the hell I'm doing."

He laughed, a deep, rumbling sound Blaine hadn't heard in years. "Sounds wonderful. I just so happen to have a couple of slots open on my table that we can use." He put the boxes back in the bag and set it on the floor near his feet.

"Great." He grabbed his father's hand. "Before we get started, though, I want to begin with an apology."

"I'm listening, son." His voice was soft, welcoming, not gruff and irritated.

"I've been so stubborn. I've locked myself away from you and the rest of the family, trying to prove I could do things on my own. For a long time, I relished being the 'black sheep,' thinking that made me daring and independent." He sighed. "But these last few years, even the last few weeks, have shown me the value of relationships with people you love." A vision of Eden's radiant smile passed through his mind, and he cringed at the pain that clenched his chest whenever he thought of her. "I'm ready to try to put this relationship back together, Dad. And I know that begins with me saying I'm sorry."

Caleb gave his hand a squeeze. "I accept your apology, son. But I also admit my part in this. You inherited that stubbornness from me, truth be told." He shook his head, chuckling wryly. "I've been too hard on you. For years, I tried to force you to be someone you're not, just because I thought I knew what was best for you." He looked past Blaine as if seeing something beyond him. "I've been thinking a lot lately about an old friend, someone I lost years ago. He has a son, too. About your age. But the difference is, my friend died." He looked back to Blaine. "He's not here to love and guide his son, to share moments like this with him. Knowing that…makes me so grateful I get the chance to tell you I'm sorry."

Caleb tugged his hand, and Blaine let himself be enveloped by his father's embrace. Several long moments passed with them holding each other, and Blaine smiled. He could see the young boy who lived inside him, who longed for closeness with his dad, smiling as well.

When they parted, Caleb said, "I've got to know…what brought this on?"

Blaine's smile faded. "Actually, it was Eden. She asked why we weren't on good terms and said I should reach out."

Caleb nodded. "Tell her I said thank you."

He shook his head. "I would…but I don't think she'll speak to me." He proceeded to give his father a quick rundown of what had transpired between them.

When he finished, Caleb gave him that stern, fatherly look. "You realize she's right, don't you? It really was your own stubbornness that landed you in this situation."

He sighed. "Yes, Dad. I know she's right, and I'm wrong."

"Well, if I were you, I'd figure out a way to tell her that. A woman like Eden is rare, and second chances with someone like her are probably one in a million." He stood, stretched. "Tell you what. We'll figure something out while we put these models together."

Eighteen

Sitting beneath an umbrella on a grassy lawn at Piedmont Park, Eden watched her nephew running and playing with his friends.

Ainsley sat next to her on the outdoor blanket, grinning as they looked on. "Look at him. You'd never know he was injured, the way he's getting around now. I'm glad we went ahead with that surgery."

She nodded. "Me, too. He's been so happy ever since he started playing baseball." She smiled, watching him turn a cartwheel. "It was expensive but totally worth it." Seeing Cooper so happy melted her heart.

"They've been running like that for a solid hour," Ainsley remarked. "Do you think they've overdosed on sugar?"

Eden snorted. "Girl, please. Of course, they have! We brought seven ten-to twelve-year-olds out here, and fed them a cake, ice cream, cookies and punch." She shook her head as one girl leapfrogged over a boy's back. "We're lucky if they don't start levitating."

Ainsley fell out laughing.

"It's a good thing we brought them to the park. They need the space to run and jump and burn off all that sugar, anyway." Eden giggled.

Cooper ran over to where they sat. He was quite a sight, his blue T-shirt and shorts covered in grass stains, orange frosting and drips of vanilla ice cream. His conical birthday hat sat cocked at an odd angle on his head, just barely clinging on.

"Look at that hat, Coop." She gave her nephew a fist bump. "You're an expert level hat-bender."

He laughed, reaching up to adjust it. Smiling brightly, he said, "Mom, Aunt Eden, thanks a lot. This is my best birthday ever!" He knelt briefly to gift them hugs and kisses, and then he was off again, blazing across the grass to rejoin his friends.

"Is it just me, or did he leave a trail of exhaust behind him?" Eden grinned.

Ainsley shook her head, brushing away at the tears gathering in her eyes. "I can't believe my baby is eleven whole years old. Seems like yesterday he was just learning to walk."

"You can always have another one," she chided, elbowing her playfully.

Rolling her eyes, Ainsley countered, "Not on your life. Cooper keeps me plenty busy. Besides, I'd need a man for that, and I'm fresh out of prospects for the time being."

"Not really," Eden teased. "What about Gage?"

"Whatever. He's my boss."

Eden shrugged. "So what? Are you saying people who work together can't have a romance?"

"Obviously that's not the case. Look what happened between you and Blaine." The moment the words came out, Ainsley clamped her hand over her lips. "I'm sorry, girl. I didn't mean to bring him up."

"It's okay. I know you just want to change the subject from you and Gage."

Ainsley punched her cousin playfully in the shoulder, then returned to her reclining position.

Silence fell between them for a few moments, and Eden returned to watching the kids play. Several were involved in a fierce game of Frisbee, while the others crowded around one of Cooper's gifts, an insect guidebook and collection kit.

As she looked on, she felt a little spark of something deep inside. The part of her that wanted to one day mother a child, whether a smart, thrill-seeking son like Cooper or a little girl with a sharp mind and the fierce determination she'd inherited from her mother. She only wanted one child, whom she'd probably spoil and dote on endlessly. But as the years passed, she'd settled into accepting that maybe a child wasn't in the cards for her. If that were the case, she'd be content to continue playing the role of World's Greatest Aunt for Cooper.

Or at least that's what she told herself.

Blaine's face appeared in her mind. She didn't push the thought away this time, allowing herself the fantasy for a few moments. What if he weren't selfish? What if he stood up for her when she needed him, but wasn't afraid to tell her when she was out of pocket? What if he wanted to build a life with her and be there to help raise that precious child she wanted so badly? But he was loving, an inner voice reminded her. He was caring, and kind, and had more drive to succeed than most. She knew she and this hypothetical child would always be loved and well cared for, because Blaine wouldn't have it any other way.

She dwelt on those thoughts for so long, she started to hear his voice, calling her name.

Then Ainsley's voice joined Blaine's.

Confused, she returned to reality. Turning to Ainsley, she saw her pointing across the field, toward the park entrance.

And when she looked, she saw Blaine, striding in her direction.

He wore a pair of tan jeans, a bright yellow button-down shirt printed with palm trees, and pristine white sneakers. He carried a huge bag emblazoned with multicolored balloons in one hand and had a bouquet of yellow roses and marigolds cradled beneath his opposite arm. With those signature dark sunglasses over his eyes, his locs flowing freely around his shoulders, he was a vision of casually dressed handsomeness.

She swallowed. "What's he doing here? How did he know where I was?"

Ainsley winked. "Oh. Did I forget to tell you I invited him to Cooper's birthday party?" She climbed to her feet.

Standing up herself, Eden did her best to smooth the wrinkles out of her lavender tunic and knock off the blades of grass clinging to her purple leggings. "Ainsley, I'm gonna hide your favorite lace-front for this."

"Don't you dare touch Tanisha!" Ainsley cut her a threatening look. "That wig set me back a pretty penny. The lace is invisible, I tell you. *Completely invisible.*" She gestured toward Blaine, whose long strides were quickly closing the distance. "Look at the size of that bag! Whatever's in there is bound to be a pretty sweet gift for your nephew."

"Whatever." She slid her feet into the jeweled flip-flops she'd worn to the park. "I'm gonna deal with you later, trust and believe." She swallowed again, doing her best to get herself together.

Because in a few more steps, Blaine Woodson would be in her personal space.

As he moved across the grass toward where Eden sat with Ainsley, Blaine ran through what he'd planned to say in his mind.

Eden, you were right. I should have stood up for you.

I'm sorry I didn't make you feel safe and cared for.

If you'll let me make it up to you, I promise it'll be worth it.

He kept a tight grip on the handles of the bag and the flowers, partly because of nerves, and partly to make sure his gifts reached their recipients undamaged. He'd brought something for the birthday boy, of course, but he'd also brought a small gift for his mother.

If it hadn't been for Ainsley inviting me here, I don't know how I would have convinced Eden to see me.

He saw them stand up and could see their mouths moving but still wasn't close enough to hear what they were saying to each other. Piedmont Park was an expansive green space, so getting to them through the gaggles of folks who'd come out to enjoy the mild temperatures and sunny weather of this early September Sunday would take some time.

He could make out the expression on Eden's beautiful face, and it seemed somewhere between surprise and confusion. *I'm guessing Ainsley invited me but didn't tell Eden.*

As he came to the edge of their blanket, he stopped. Smiling, he handed the bag over to Ainsley. "Hey, Ainsley. Thanks for the invite—I put a little something for you in with Cooper's gift."

"Much obliged, Blaine. Thanks for coming."

His gaze slid to Eden. Casually dressed in a two-tone purple outfit, she still looked as beautiful as any runway model to his eyes.

Ainsley giggled. "I'll...just take this over to Cooper. You two go ahead and chat." Still giggling, she walked away with the gift bag.

"Hi, Eden." He didn't move closer, unsure he'd be able to resist the urge to pull her into his arms.

"Hi, Blaine." She blushed slightly, giving him a sidelong glance. "Thanks for bringing Cooper a birthday gift."

"Of course." He shifted his weight from left to right and

back. "I'm afraid I'm not up on what eleven-year-olds are into these days, so I consulted my little cousin Jack. Hopefully, he likes what I got him."

She gave him the smallest smile. "I'm sure he'll love it. I appreciate you doing your research."

He remembered the flowers tucked under his arm and inched just close enough to offer them to her. "Ainsley said these are your favorite flowers. I hope you like them." He genuinely did, since he felt like a fourteen-year-old, cozying up to his crush.

She took the flowers, bringing them to her face for a sniff. "They're beautiful." She gestured to the blanket. "Do you want to…sit down? Chat for a minute?"

"I'll stay as long as you'll let me."

She nodded, then took a graceful seat while balancing the flowers in her hands.

He joined her, leaving a respectable distance between them. He couldn't help remembering that the last time they were on this blanket, she'd been sitting atop his lap, and they'd been kissing passionately. His groin tightened in response to the memory. He knew better than to lead with that, though. "Before I start, I just want to pass on a message from my father. He said to tell you thanks."

Her brow crinkled. "What? Why?"

"Because of your harping…"

She poked him with her index finger. "Watch it, Blaine."

He chuckled. "I meant, because of your *encouragement*, I tried to connect with him. I reached out to him with something he's passionate about and used that to tear down the wall between us."

"Really?"

"Yes. And aside from that, Dad's willing to offer financing for Naiya's album, if I need it. We're on good terms now, and I'm grateful to have his support. I'm glad I took your advice, Eden."

She smiled, soft and lovely. "That's great. But… I can't take credit for that."

"Sure, you can. No one else has ever been able to get through to me when it came to my dad. And trust me, plenty of people have tried." His siblings, his friends, even Trevor, his engineer, had brought it up on several occasions. But no one had been able to move the needle…until Eden. "You're magical, Eden. That's the only explanation I have. I can't tell you how good it feels, after all these years, to be on such good terms with my father."

Her smile broadened. "Wow. That's amazingly sweet of you to say."

"It's true. Every word." He reached out. "Can I…hold your hand for a minute?" He missed the feel of her satin skin against his. And while he didn't expect her to open up to him, he'd take whatever she'd give him.

She nodded.

He enfolded her hand in his own. The words he'd planned to say swirled around in his mind, the imagery as bold as a Hype Williams music video. Yet when he opened his mouth, only four words spilled out. "Eden, I love you."

She gasped. "Blaine, you…"

He squeezed her hand. "Please, let me get this out before I lose my nerve. I'm a fool for not telling you how I felt earlier. And an even bigger ass for not showing you." He looked into the golden-brown orbs of her eyes, seeing the emotion there, silently praying that her feelings matched his own. Yet whatever she decided, he'd accept it. "You were right. Everything you said about me was true. I was being selfish, putting my own desire for success above your feelings, your career. I'm so, so sorry for what I've done. I know I can't go back and change any of it, but I hope you'll accept my sincere apology."

Her mouth hung open.

"And I don't want you to think I'm not going to do something about Naiya's album. I'm not sure what just yet. But we've all worked too hard to let it end like this."

Tears sprang to her eyes, her lips trembling.

He stiffened. "Oh, no. Did I say something wrong? Have I hurt you again?" He'd never forgive himself if he caused her even one more moment of pain. She'd already suffered enough because of him.

She shook her head. "No, you haven't hurt me." She moved closer to him. "You've made me so very happy." She showed him a watery smile before placing a soft kiss on his cheek. "And I applaud your patience. I know I've come across pretty judgmental…rigid…immovable."

He feigned confusion. "What? I hadn't noticed."

She giggled. "Do you have any idea how long I've been waiting for you to come around, you knucklehead?"

He laughed. "Close to a decade, I'm guessing."

"You'd be right." She clamped her soft hands around his face, tilting it until their gazes met. "I'm glad you love me, Blaine Woodson. Because I love you, too."

His heart swelled, warmth flooding his body like he'd taken a shot of brown liquor. Only his beautiful, caring Eden was far more intoxicating than even the finest aged bourbon. "You can't imagine how relieved and grateful I am to hear you say that."

"Why don't you kiss me and show me?" She dragged her fingertip over his lips.

With a groan, he pulled her in and kissed her, long and slow. His arms wrapped around her body, and she leaned in, pressing herself against him. His tongue stroked, hers teased, and before long, he'd forgotten where he was.

It was only a chorus of *"Eeeww!"* coming from several young voices that pulled them apart a few moments later.

"Sorry. I forgot about the young eyes watching." He gave her a sheepish grin.

"Hey! What kind of party you two think this is?" Ainsley

shouted the words at them from a few feet away, in a voice laced with humor.

Shaking her head, Eden put her hands to her face, covering the deep red tinge of her cheeks. "I think we'd better put off the rest of that for later."

"I agree. Because what I plan on doing to you is definitely not G-rated." He winked.

She tossed her curly head back and laughed, and it was the most beautiful sound he'd ever heard.

Nineteen

Eden walked through the halls of Marian Gardens Retirement Home Tuesday morning, her steps measured and slow. Most of the rooms she passed had their doors shut, but she'd occasionally see an elderly woman or man inside their room. Some were asleep or being visited by nurses or other care providers. A few were up sitting in their recliners and made eye contact with her as she walked by. She offered a smile and wave but kept moving. She wasn't exactly comfortable in a place like this, probably due to her limited experience. Still, she'd come here for something important, and she'd already put it off too long. Her time to take care of it might well be running out.

Taking the elevator, then navigating another long hallway, she finally came to the room the nurse at the front desk had sent her to. 4L.

His name was printed on a small plaque hanging on the door, and she silently read it. *Craig Moorhead.*

Drawing a deep breath, she rapped softly on the closed door.

"Who's there?" A deep but quiet voice called from inside.

"It's me, Eden."

A few silent moments ticked by before he called, "It's open."

Turning the knob, she pushed open the door and eased inside the small room. As the pressure-mounted door shut behind her, she hesitated to go very far into the room. She didn't want to encroach on his space; their relationship was strained enough. So, she stood there, waiting to be invited.

He was propped up on a stack of pillows in his bed, watching television. It was *Law & Order: SVU*, his favorite show. He turned his head, meeting her gaze. Raising his hand, he gestured her closer. "Come on over here where I can see you."

She did as he asked.

He observed her for a few moments. "You're looking well."

"Thank you. How are you feeling, Craig?"

"I'm all right, for a young fellow." A dry cough followed his words. "What brings you by?"

"I...just wanted to make sure you were okay and have a little talk with you. That is if you feel up to it."

He nodded, then indicated the upholstered wooden armchair next to his bed. "Sure. Sit on down."

She sat, resting her purse on her lap. "I've been doing a lot of thinking lately."

He chuckled. "Sounds like you."

She smiled in spite of her nerves, knowing this was his way. He always cracked jokes to break the tension, and when it came to the two of them, tension made up a large portion of their relationship. She'd come here today in hopes of changing that. "Anyway, I wanted to let you know that I've...forgiven you."

He frowned. "What you say?"

"I said, I've forgiven you. It took me a long time to... accept the reality of what happened between you and my mother, and how it's affected me." She knew the root of her mistrust for men lay in her childhood when she'd longed for the presence of a father. "I'm just ready to let go of all that negative energy. It's too great a burden."

His frown softening, he said, "I'm glad you came here to say that to me. But... I don't know if I'll ever be able to forgive myself."

She could hear the sadness in her voice. "Talk to me, Craig. Say what's in your heart."

He shifted a bit in bed, angling his body toward her. "I loved your mama. I swear I did. Even though I was fifteen years older than her, I loved her hard. Still do." A tear came to his eye, and he let it fall. "I was married, but the fire between me and Shirley had gone out years before. Jacinda was a ray of sunshine in my life." He smiled, a faraway look in his eyes. "I'd always see her there, working at the desk when I went down to the law library to study. Between the stress of law school and the demands of my wife and son... I needed somebody, you know? And she was there for me. Never meant for...things to turn out the way they did."

She nodded, reaching for his hand. "I know you didn't."

"That day you came here to tell me she was gone..." More tears filled his eyes. "Worse day of my life. I left her behind to try to work on my marriage, but soon as I got sick, Shirley and Craig Jr. just...left me here. Ain't seen or heard from either of 'em in years now." He raised his aged hands, brushing away the tears. "I know... I just know that if Jacinda was still living..."

"She'd be taking care of you." She squeezed his hands. "Mama never had anything bad to say about you, at least not to me. She always said you made the choice you thought was right, and I shouldn't fault you. Still, I held on to that anger for a long time."

"I don't blame you. Every little girl deserves to have her daddy around for her raising."

"That's true. But as I've gotten older, I've come to understand how complicated life and relationships can be. You just weren't there yet."

"I...don't even know how to apologize to you, Eden." He cast his eyes downward, as if ashamed of his choices. "What can I say that's going to make up for what I did?"

"You don't have to say anything." She smiled. "My mama loved you. And I love you, too, in my own odd little way. You did help bring me into this crazy and wonderful world."

He cried full-on then. Between sobs, he said, "You're a special girl. I'm honored to call you my daughter."

She brushed away her own tears. "And I'll be honored to call you Daddy." She stood, hugged his thin shoulders while he held her close. When she sat down again, she said, "I want you to know, I'm going to keep paying for your care, as long as you need it. Don't worry about Shirley and Craig Jr. As long as I'm around, you've got family."

He nodded. "Thank you, Eden. Thank you...for being so kindhearted. You're just like Jacinda... I know she'd be proud."

A vision of her mother's smiling face entered her mind. *I think he's right. Mama would be proud.*

When Blaine got off the plane at LaGuardia Wednesday morning, he felt the buzz of excitement rolling through his body. Dressed in his best dark suit and wingtips, with his hair pulled back in a low ponytail, he was ready to take on the meeting at hand. He pulled his single small suitcase, his only luggage, along behind him as he headed for the baggage claim area to meet his private car service.

The black sedan navigated through the streets of New York, the driver maneuvering through the thick weekday traffic. Arriving in Manhattan at the Hamilton House headquarters, he exited the car and tipped the driver before heading upstairs to the thirtieth floor.

Tucking the suitcase away with the receptionist, he strode into the conference room. Rupert and Marvin were waiting there for him, seated toward the far end of the table.

Both men stood, and the three of them exchanged handshakes and greetings. Finally, with the small talk put aside, they all sat down. Rupert occupied the head of the table, with Marvin to his right and Blaine to his left.

Marvin smiled, lacing his fingers in front of him. "So, we're glad to see you back in New York, but I'm a bit surprised you asked to meet with us in person, Blaine."

"Yes," Rupert added, looking as constipated as ever. "You could have just faxed or mailed the contracts back to us. No need to hand-deliver them, you know."

Blaine smiled. "Oh, yes, gentlemen. I agree. Had I simply been returning contracts, I wouldn't be sitting here today." He rubbed his hands together. "I'll be taking an afternoon flight back to Atlanta, so let's get this meeting under way, shall we?"

"Certainly." Rupert's eyes narrowed slightly as if he wondered what Blaine had planned. Marvin looked similarly confused. Blaine relished their utter ignorance of what he was about to do for a few moments, then stood once again. He wanted to be able to look down on them while he said what he had to say. "When I first got the documents from you, I spent a good amount of time reading them, going over the terms, etcetera. My first impression was that it was a pretty standard change agreement, one that you'd simply altered a bit to fit our particular situation."

Rupert nodded. "That's exactly right. Very astute, Blaine."

He noted the condescension in Rupert's tone, but ignored it. He'd be singing a different tune soon enough. "Anyway, I took the document to Naiya and Eden for discussion and signing. And I've gotta tell you, neither of them was on board."

Marvin frowned. "No? So how did you proceed from there?"

"I didn't. Both of them walked out of the meeting, leaving the documents unsigned on the table."

Rupert scratched his chin. "Oh, I see. So, you've come here to brainstorm with us and work out some ways to get them to change their minds."

"So...how shall we start?" Marvin interjected. "I don't think we should go straight to threats of dropping Naiya from the label—that's a bit harsh. We'll need to use a light touch with them if we want them to agree to the terms."

"I agree. Perhaps a fruit basket or something nice from the corporate gift catalog would soften the tension a bit."

After watching them go back and forth for a while, Blaine could no longer contain his laugh. He laughed, loud and long.

Both men looked at him, their bewilderment obvious.

Marvin said, "Blaine, what's so funny? Have you gone off the deep end?"

He stifled his laughter, sobering up. "No, I haven't. Actually, I've got more clarity now than I've ever had."

"I see. So, you know how to proceed with this situation, then?" Rupert leaned forward in his seat as if anticipating his answer.

"Absolutely." He leaned forward as well, wanting to make sure they heard what he had to say. "I'm going to proceed by telling you that you can feel free to drop Against the Grain from your roster of labels."

Marvin recoiled. "Blaine, surely you don't mean that. Have you really thought this through?"

"Marvin's right. Have you considered how long your label will survive without our backing?" Rupert tugged his lapels. "It's a cruel world out there when you're a little fish in a big pond."

Marvin folded his arms over his chest, nodding in agreement.

Blaine scoffed. "I'm not as small a fish as you two might think. Not anymore."

"You aren't serious." Rupert's expression took on a hard set.

"I'm very serious." Blaine felt his jaw tighten and his resolve grow. "Let me tell you something. I believe in Naiya. I believe in her talent and in her vision. I also believe that Eden has been true to that vision. If following through with the album in its current iteration is a deal-breaker for you, so be it. I'm not going to sit by and let you destroy what we worked so hard on, in the name of some corporate focus-group bullshit."

Rupert's face folded into a grimace. "Blaine! I've never known you to be so unprofessional. I'm shocked, frankly."

"I'd rather be unprofessional than be a doormat. And as far as funding for my 'little label,' don't sweat it, boys. Because effective immediately, Against the Grain is a subsidiary of 404 Sound Recordings. And 404 will be funding her debut album. And just in case it should come up in one of your meetings, 404 Sound Recordings *is not* for sale." He shook his head, a triumphant smile on his face. "Now if you'll excuse me, I've got things to do. But feel free to kiss my 'unprofessional' ass as I leave." With one last look at their flabbergasted faces, he strode out.

By the time he climbed into the black sedan idling at the curb, he could no longer contain his elation. *I'm free!*

Now I can run my label the way I see fit. And he knew exactly who he wanted to be the first to hear the great news.

Taking his phone out of his breast pocket, he dialed a number. "Hello, Naiya? I'm sure you're still upset with me, but I promise, what I'm about to say will make up for it."

After hearing Naiya's happy squeals and agreeing to meet with her at the studio next week to talk marketing strategy, he ended the call and dialed Eden. "Baby, guess what I just did?" He gave her a brief recap of the meeting.

"Wow, Blaine. That was incredibly bold. I'm proud of you."

"How proud?" He didn't bother to hide the teasing in his tone.

She gave as good as she got, as always. "Why don't you get your ass on that plane home, come over to my place and I'll show you."

Cupping his hand over the receiver, he said, "Driver, do you know a quicker way to LaGuardia?"

The driver chuckled. "Sure thing, chief."

Removing his hand from the mic, he said, "My flight lands at two. Why don't you meet me at the airport?"

"I'll be there, honey."

He licked his lips, already anticipating her very special brand of welcome.

I can't wait to get home.

Hours later, they were kissing their way into his bedroom, barely able to keep their hands off each other. Fumbling around for the light switch while reaching over her shoulder, he finally gave up, depending on his other senses to guide them toward his bed while he kissed her.

Pulling back from her sweet lips, he asked, "Is there a reason you chose this dress to pick me up from the airport in?"

She looked down at the fitted black minidress, feigning

innocence. "What, this? I just threw it on so you wouldn't be waiting long."

He chuckled. "You lie so well I almost believe it." He punctuated his words with more kisses as his hands circled the bare skin of her thighs, just below the hem of the dress.

"Mmm." She moaned into his ear. "Why don't you let me congratulate you…my way?" She grasped his arms, turning him so his back was to the bed.

"What do you have in mind?" Moments later, as she stripped him of his clothes, pushed him down to sit on the bed, and knelt before him, her intentions became clear. He growled as her lips closed over his hard shaft, weaving his fingers through her hair. "Shit."

She hummed, the vibration adding to the pleasure of her warm, wet mouth wrapped around him. Her head moved back and forth in time with her impassioned sucking, and he felt his whole body start to tremble. Letting his hands slip down to her shoulders, he gently pushed her away. "If you keep that up I'm gonna…"

"Come?" She teased the tip with her tongue. "What if that's what I want?"

He jerked in response. "No, baby. I want to be inside you when it happens." He helped her up off the floor, drawing her onto his bed. She knelt over him, raising her arms as he snatched off her dress. The red lace bra and thong set she wore beneath only increased the fire in his blood.

"Grab a condom from my nightstand, baby," he instructed softly.

She did as he asked, and to his surprise, rolled the protection down over his shaft.

Unable to wait another moment to be inside her, he nudged her into place. Crooking his finger, he slid her panties to one side, then guided her down onto his dick.

He gritted his teeth against the blinding pleasure as she began to ride, rolling her hips as she held on to his waist.

She moved her hands up, splaying them across his abdomen as she shifted forward, circling her hips like she was working an imaginary hula hoop.

It wasn't long before he heard her moans climbing higher, indicating an oncoming orgasm. He grabbed her waist and thrust up, letting his hips piston to meet hers. She tossed her head back and screamed his name while her body pulsated around him. Moments later, his own orgasm raced through his body, the force of it making him growl and shake.

In the aftermath, they lay sprawled across his comforter. Holding her in his arms felt like second nature, like destiny. He crooked his finger beneath her chin, guiding her face until she looked into his eyes.

"What is it, Blaine?"

"Stay with me, Eden." He was too far gone to worry about whether he sounded weak. He needed her, and there was no way around it. "Forever."

She offered him a soft smile. "I'll think about it."

He chuckled. "C'mon, baby. Don't tease a brotha. Not at a moment like this."

She shook her head. "Don't worry. I'll stay." She snuggled closer to him.

And as he held her body close to his, he felt a sense of peace like nothing he'd ever experienced before.

Epilogue

January

Raising the steaming cup of cocoa to her lips, Eden stood by the large bay window, watching the swirling snow outside. The picturesque image of the fluffy white flakes floating over the peaks of the Loveland Ski Resort provided the perfect backdrop for their honeymoon. She took a long sip, savoring the chocolaty warmth of the beverage and the warmth she felt inside.

Blaine walked up behind her, wearing nothing but a pair of silk boxers. He draped his strong arms around her waist. Feeling the hard lines of his body pressed against her made her shiver, but not from the cold. "Hey, you. What are you thinking about?"

"About how lucky I am. How happy I am to be your wife." She set the cocoa down on the windowsill and turned within the circle of his arms.

"Funny. I was thinking about how glad I am we chose to

marry this way…just the two of us, the justice of the peace and the mountain."

She smiled at the memory of the previous day's mountaintop ceremony. As local Justice Sophia Llewellyn presided, they'd said their vows surrounded by the azure sky, the puffy white clouds and the chilly Colorado winds. He'd worn a charcoal wool suit, and she'd worn a fully lined formal white pantsuit and matching hat, accented with faux fur and Swarovski crystals. Instead of carrying a bouquet, she'd worn a crystal-studded faux-fur muff. "It was a wonderful day."

"A wonderful night, too, if I recall." He brushed his lips over the hollow of her throat.

She blushed, remembering how he'd carried her over the threshold of their cozy little mountainside cabin, slowly undressed her and made passionate love to her until she'd cried tears of joy into his strong shoulder. "You'll get no complaints from me."

He leaned in then and kissed her softly. "I can't believe it took me so many years to get out of my own way and do right by you."

"Me, either." She grinned, touched his cheek. "But better late than never, as they say."

"I love you, Eden Voss Woodson."

With the happy tears gathering in her eyes once again, she whispered, "I love you, too."

He pulled her in for his kiss, and before long, he carried her to the bed again.

And as the moon ascended over the Colorado mountains, her cries of ecstasy rose on the cold night air.

* * * * *

COMING SOON!

We really hope you enjoyed reading this book. If you're looking for more romance, be sure to head to the shops when new books are available on

Thursday 15th October

LET'S TALK

Romance

For exclusive extracts, competitions and special offers, find us online:

Get in touch on 01413 063232

For all the latest titles coming soon, visit
millsandboon.co.uk/nextmonth

MILLS & BOON

THE HEART OF ROMANCE

A ROMANCE FOR EVERY KIND OF READER

MODERN

Prepare to be swept off your feet by sophisticated, sexy and seductive heroes, in some of the world's most glamourous and romantic locations, where power and passion collide.
8 stories per month.

HISTORICAL

Escape with historical heroes from time gone by. Whether your passion is for wicked Regency Rakes, muscled Vikings or rugged Highlanders, awaken the romance of the past.
6 stories per month.

MEDICAL

Set your pulse racing with dedicated, delectable doctors in the high-pressure world of medicine, where emotions run high and passion, comfort and love are the best medicine.
6 stories per month.

True Love

Celebrate true love with tender stories of heartfelt romance, from the rush of falling in love to the joy a new baby can bring, and a focus on the emotional heart of a relationship.
8 stories per month.

Desire

Indulge in secrets and scandal, intense drama and plenty of sizzling hot action with powerful and passionate heroes who have it all: wealth, status, good looks…everything but the right woman.
6 stories per month.

HEROES

Experience all the excitement of a gripping thriller, with an intense romance at its heart. Resourceful, true-to-life women and strong, fearless men face danger and desire - a killer combination!
8 stories per month.

DARE

Sensual love stories featuring smart, sassy heroines you'd want as a best friend, and compelling intense heroes who are worthy of them.
4 stories per month.

To see which titles are coming soon, please visit

millsandboon.co.uk/nextmonth

JOIN US ON SOCIAL MEDIA!

Stay up to date with our latest releases, author
news and gossip, special offers and discounts, and
all the behind-the-scenes action
from Mills & Boon...

 millsandboon

 millsandboonuk

 millsandboon

It might just be true love...

MILLS & BOON
MODERN
Power and Passion

Prepare to be swept off your feet by sophisticated, sexy and seductive heroes, in some of the world's most glamourous and romantic locations, where power and passion collide.

MILLS & BOON

HEROES

At Your Service

Experience all the excitement of a gripping thriller, with an intense romance at its heart. Resourceful, true-to-life women and strong, fearless men face danger and desire - a killer combination!

MILLS & BOON
True Love
Romance from the Heart

Celebrate true love with tender stories of heartfelt romance, from the rush of falling in love to the joy a new baby can bring, and a focus on the emotional heart of a relationship.